a whirlwind of

LOSS

and

RUIN

SAMANTHA HARDY

A Whirlwind of Loss and Ruin

A Loss and Ruin Novel

By Samantha Hardy

ISBN:979-8-9903151-0-5

Copyright © 2024 by Samantha Hardy

Published by SteelyCold Publishing LLC, an imprint

Editor: Kenneth Zink

Cover design team: Mibl Art

To those who dream and those who keep the monsters at bay. The universe is a mysterious place, and we have only scratched the surface.

Prologue

There is no movement in the quiet room that suffocates her thoughts as she scans the space above with her eyes, unable to lift her head. Her body is still, tucked beneath the sheets that grow heavy with every inhale. She can't wake up, as this isn't an unusual event. *Another bad dream*, she thinks while attempting to squeeze her lids shut tightly. The act fails her, and she knows that even though her subconscious is alert, she is only a passenger.

Counting sheep and reciting the alphabet backward on a never-ending loop won't suffice. Prying her eyes open, she focuses on the stars glued to the ceiling that seems to be getting farther away from her. Her breathing is labored and unsteady, with the unsettling feeling that she is not alone.

Something is watching her from a dark corner of the room. Although she is unable to sit up and scan the space to note its presence, she can sense it. An uncomfortable sensation that has the hair on her arms standing, and it's as if her visitor is inhaling the same air as she. Sharing it.

There is no telling how much time has passed since she awoke frozen in this state. The room is pitch black now, and there aren't any sounds of the house settling in. The clock on the wall has stopped its ticking, and cold sweat drips from her body, clinging to her pajamas as if she threw them on after a shower without toweling off.

As she continues to hold her concentration, searching for even the slightest dim glow to let her know the stars are still on her ceiling, the shadows expand and darken until there is nothing. A dark void that she has been running from her entire life. And just when she thinks her nightmare is coming to an end with that black void of nothing that she's forced into, a pair of eyes open above her. The only thing in the room now that glows a yellow. Her body trembles as the beast stares down at her with curiosity, but it remains. Silence so deafening that you could almost hear a small insect crawl across the laminate.

Unsure of how long they have stared at each other, her eyes grow heavy despite the paralyzing fear and dread that wreaks havoc in her body. Willing as much power as she can to keep them open, her strength to do such a simple task begins to fail her as they begin to weigh down like cement.

The beast watches her drift, and before her mind turns off, she catches a sudden tick in its features as its face stretches wide into a smile. The contrast against the dark room and the glow of its eyes is stark with the hint of pointed canines. A notion that tells her they will meet again.

When she finally awakes, she jumps up, scanning the room.

It is morning, and everything is back to normal. The clock on the wall ticks, 7:15 a.m. Her bedroom door opens, and her mother peeks her head in.

"Are you up?" She asks in her cheery voice.

"Yes, Mom," the girl replies, rolling her eyes.

"Good! I made you breakfast. Get ready. I do not want you to be late for the first day back to school!" Her mother chimes before shutting the door.

Thinking about what she had experienced, she assures herself it was just a bad dream despite how real it felt. Making a mental note to forget all about it, she rolls out of bed and begins her routine. It is a new school year and a fresh start, and nothing will interfere with that. A feeling of excitement washes over her. She was ecstatic to see Tara after she'd visited her dad in California for the summer and couldn't wait to hear all about her time there.

Walking over to the corner of the room, she thought she felt the beast in her paralyzed state the night prior; she reaches her arms out, padding the space before her. Shaking her head at the absurdity, she attempts to laugh it off until something catches her eye. Bending down, she hesitantly picks up the sweater that is draped over the chair at her drawing desk and inspects it in the morning light.

The discovery is shocking, and what she notices on her beige sweater sends a chill over her body as her hands tremble.

Her mother returns, breaking her concentration and causing her to jump as she hides the evidence by bundling the fabric in clenched fists. Scowling at the intrusion, her mother raises her hands and points to the clock—a silent demand for her to rush that morning routine. The girl rolls her eyes again, and her mother raises a brow in warning before shutting the door for the final time.

Quickly laying the sweater out on her bed, she runs her hand along the fabric to remove what is attached. Black fur coats her palm in the process, and the girl swallows down the confirmation. Brushing her hands off in the bin under her desk, she balls the sweater and throws it in the laundry basket.

Taking a deep breath, she wipes the tears that escape her eyes and stares at her reflection in the mirror.

"Aella, you will not speak of this to anyone. It never happened." She tells herself. A promise that she will resume the first day back to school like a normal fifteen-year-old girl who has a dark secret that she will be taking to the grave.

Chapter One

Eight years later...

L aying in her bed, the twinkling chime grows louder as the alarm continues its repetitive jingle. Rolling over onto her side, dreading the inevitable, she picks up her phone, forcing as much strength as she can to swipe open the screen. Setting an alarm doesn't do anything, considering the lack of sleep three days prior is prevalent. A few hours here and there midday seem to keep the monsters out, but Aella runs on empty. Disregarding the twenty texts she has yet to open from Tara, she checks the date and time. "Fuck", she breathes with a heavy sigh when she notices the date reads Friday the 13th of October. *How convenient.*

It's ten in the morning, and her body is tight from straining her muscles while she'd tossed and turned throughout the late hours. Staring out her window, the rain falling helps calm her nerves, but never her racing heart. It's *rainy season* in Phoenix, which always seems so magical due to the fact that Arizona gets little rain as it is. Realizing she has a few hours before her shift means she has enough time to mentally prepare herself for the creeps that will come out to play.

Setting her phone down on the nightstand with the charger in place, she slowly begins to drift until a sharp knock startles her, causing a sudden burst of anxiety. Living in a studio apartment on the third floor has its perks, except when the need to hide from the rest of the world becomes impossible.

Unfortunately, Aella knows that knock anywhere.

Getting out of bed is usually lackluster, but she wouldn't want to greet mommy dearest in her underwear. Slipping into her sweats and a wrinkled T-shirt she had thrown on the floor at some point in the previous weeks, she drags her body with her to unlock the door her mother incessantly continues to pound on.

Aella's Mother, Susan, is a lot of things. Life hasn't always been the easiest for her, but she seems to make do with the cards she has been dealt. Always finding solace in her tarot decks and crystals, including the occasional shaman-guided ayahuasca journeys she frequently embarks on.

"Hi, Mom," Aella croaks, attempting to plaster a tired smile, knowing her mother will see through the facade.

"Aella!" Susan gasps, "Have you even slept? Dear lord, you look like hell. Let me make you a cup of hot matcha to perk you up".

The pungent smell of patchouli hits Aella's nostrils, turning her empty stomach. Susan, the bright-eyed, bushy tail woman she appears to be wherever she goes, is wearing a multi-colored maxi dress with berks. Her hair is in a loose braid, seemingly unwashed, and it shows. Susan points out the obvious, often making those around her uncomfortable. Her little to no understanding of boundaries is one of the reasons why Aella didn't want to make her a copy of the key when she moved into her apartment. Still, Susan insisted on it, especially after the *incident*.

"Mom, I'm fine. I was about to make a pot of coffee when you showed up." The lie comes out all too easily, having become quite the expert given the recent events in her life.

"Oh no, that's garbage. I don't mind. I brought some supplies over with me." Barging in through the door, she stops and looks around, clearly judging the state of her apartment. "You need to sage, dear. It feels a bit... stuffy."

Heading straight for where the bed rests against the far wall, Susan stops momentarily as her eyes roam to the nightstand. Cringing briefly, Aella watches her mother notice what is amiss.

"Where is the amethyst I got you? It's supposed to always be next to your bed to keep the negative spirits away!" She exclaims, the hurt laced behind her words making Aella feel guilty. Although the amethyst is beautiful with its jagged edges and deep violet hue that draws you in, it's a bit of an eyesore due to its size.

Turning to the kitchen with an eye roll, Aella begins brewing the pot of coffee, then stops suddenly as she hears her mother sliding open a drawer.

A frustrated huff leaves her nose as the clanking of objects being rummaged through becomes apparent. Too tired to start a fight, she resumes the daunting task. After a few minutes, Susan walks to the counter with a soft smile. Aella's eyes immediately fall to the object her mother is holding, taking everything in her not to spiral out of control. Shame and embarrassment start to override some of the anger, but with the lack of sleep and the invasion of privacy that her mother has deemed unnecessary, handling her pink vibrator like it's nothing more than a toy, Aella snaps.

"What the fuck are you doing, Mom?! That's private and personal! Stop coming over and going through my things!"

"Aella dear, I was just going to charge this for you. I turned it on and noticed that it was dead. Self-love is vital. It's only natural; there is no need to get upset. I'm happy that you're finding bliss on your own." She supplies with compassion, not understanding why Aella would be so bothered by the gesture.

Shaking her head, Aella begins washing a mug for the freshly brewed pot of her only cheap coffee, focusing on anything else. Pouring the hot liquid into the cup, she looks up to face her mother, knowing she means well, consequences be damned.

Being an only child, Aella tries to remind herself that her mother did the best she could in raising her, even if it means there are no boundaries.

Due to her condition, her patience has started to run thin over the years, making it hard for her to maintain control of her emotions, including her mouth. Breaking the silence, Susan clears her throat, swiping away at the crumbs scattered across the counter.

"So... I was thinking, you and I should take a day trip to Sedona this weekend. I think the vortexes there would be cleansing for you, and maybe you can make an appointment with my healer, Magda. She could do a session of reiki. Her hands are extremely powerful. I just know you'll sleep so sound afterward!"

After taking a drink of her coffee, Aella responds abruptly, "I have plans with Tara this weekend, Mom, but let's plan it a different weekend, okay?" Aside from the attempt to sound as gentle as possible not to get her mother's hopes up, it is yet another lie, as she doesn't have definite plans, but that would have to change quickly.

Susan never took no for an answer, especially when her heart was set on something.

"Okay, sweetheart," she responds with disappointment, "I understand, but if you have a change of heart, you know I'm just a phone call away."

Yep, Susan is not taking no for an answer.

"I know, Mom. Thank you. Love you." Aella walks over, gives her a hug, and leads her to the door for overstaying her welcome. Facing her, Susan cups her cheeks and smiles, softening her features with a noticeable tinge of concern.

"I love you too, Aella Rose. Please don't burn the candle at both ends and get some rest. I worry about you. We don't want another *episode,* do we?"

Biting the inside of her lip, Aella forces another smile. Reliving the trauma of what happened to her daily is terrible enough, but having Susan remind her of it is unbearable. The week spent in the hospital, strapped to a bed while being force-fed a cocktail of medications, was enough trauma to last her adult life. She hasn't shared much about her time there, only small cliff notes that have aided her to become the seasoned liar she is now.

Memories leading up to that time in her life are a bit foggy. Therapists have told her the same thing, *"It's a trauma response. The brain blocks things out as a defense."* Because there isn't a cure for sleep paralysis, it is manageable through various sleep medications. Unfortunately for Aella, none of those have ever seemed to work, and instead, they have worsened her symptoms.

She was seventeen when her mother admitted her after the *episode.* It wasn't like her usual episodes, though. There was a shift that happened in her bedroom that night, a shift that caused Susan to fear something, but she never elaborated on that with Aella. The things that come out while she's in that state are unworldly.

Sometimes, Aella swears that she has felt the presence of beings that were more human, and other times, they were something more malevolent. But when she was in that hospital, the paralysis worsened to the point that when she would come to, there would be red marks on her arms as if something was trying to take her. The doctors assumed she was self-harming somehow despite being strapped down.

Giving Susan a tight-lipped smile, she nods and shuts the door.

Trudging back to her bed, Aella curls up under the covers, breathing slowly. Reaching over to the nightstand, she unplugs her phone from its charger.

Sifting through the texts from Tara, she decides to call her instead of composing a message. Like her mother, Tara also doesn't understand boundaries. Hitting the green button, she puts her phone on speaker, listening to the phone ring. Like clockwork, Tara picks up on the second.

"What's up bitch? I texted you a bunch earlier! You better bring something sexy after your shift because we are going out!" She squeals with excitement.

Holding back a sigh, Aella responds. "Tara, I'm so exhausted I didn't sleep again. Can we raincheck tonight? I wanted to make plans this weekend, though..."

"Ell, I have one word for you...*Blanc*. We are on the list, and you are going to get a pep in your step and get your hot ass ready to shake it! You can stay at my place tonight since we will be out late or...early! Anyway, I have to go, babe. I'm getting off on my exit." Before hanging up, Aella agrees to go with her. Maybe a little fun will help with the pity party she's been throwing lately. Tara usually brings her out of the dark cave she tends to retreat to.

When the phone dies, Aella decides not to stay in bed any longer. With just a couple of hours to spare before leaving for work, she walks into the kitchen to pour another cup of coffee. She will need all the caffeine she can get for the long day and night ahead.

Turning on the shower, she waits for the water to heat up. Given that the building is older, the pipes take slightly longer than usual. Looking in the mirror makes her grimace. Aella's hazel eyes are more a shade of green, which usually happens when feelings of sadness or helplessness like she felt now take over. The dark circles under her eyes are a deep shade of purple, and she sighs, noting that layering concealer won't be enough to tone down the color. Her hair is a chaotic mess of tangles and knots from not brushing the strands out for days, and her lips are cracked—a painful reminder to drink more water than coffee throughout the day.

As the mirror starts to steam, she brushes away the destructive self-talk and climbs into the shower, hoping all of her problems will wash away down the drain.

THE BAR IS BUSY, WHICH AELLA KNEW WOULD BE DUE TO her manager making every drink half off for the holiday. With only an hour left of her shift, she was grateful for how fast the rest flew by. Because Tara expects Aella to head straight to her condo so they can get ready together and have a glass of wine before their night out, she is reluctant to approach the table in her section that just gets sat. Huffing through her nose, that reluctance grows when she sees a group of three guys with wicked grins on their smug faces. Feeling nothing but disgust while plastering that forced smile she has practiced effectively over time, she makes her way to their table.

"What can I get you three gentlemen this evening to drink?"

The one sitting to the right, wearing too-tight jeans and a button-up grey shirt, smirks at her. His gaze lingers over her breasts a little too long for comfort. Aella clears her throat, causing his eyes to return to her face again while widening his grin.

"Hmmm, are you on the menu?" He chuckles, struggling to wink. Standing there momentarily longer, Aella waits impatiently when his smile falters and says, "Yeah, I'll take a Coors light with a shot of tequila, sweetheart." Aella struggles with maintaining a neutral face from how he just called her sweetheart, making her stomach turn.

"One Coors light and a shot of tequila. Well, okay?"

"I'll take your top shelf unless you don't mind being on top."

Aella wants to vomit. She hates most men, especially cheese balls like this guy.

"Sir, our top-shelf tequila for the evening is Hornitos. Does that work for you?" She replies as sweet and condescending as she can.

"Yeah, hun, that's fine, and a lime with salt. I do love a little saltiness after a taste of something so spicy." He laughs and fist-bumps one of his buddies with how slick he thinks he is.

Rolling her eyes, she writes down the order.

"And for you two?" Holding back their laughter, they shake their heads, stating they would have the same.

"Great, they will be right up."

"Take your time, please. I hate to see you go but love to watch you leave."

Leaving their table, she could hear them talking about her body. She had always been told how beautiful she was, and she knew she was blessed with curves in the right areas, but all she wanted was for someone to see her as a person for once and not something they could stick their dick into.

Entering their order, Georgia slides in next to her. She is also beautiful to look at with natural strawberry blonde hair down to her ass, which she has half thrown up tonight with a clip allowing the rest to flow naturally. The natural pout to her lips looks sultry with the vibrant shade of red lipstick she has on this evening, and her eyes are such a deep green they almost don't look real. Aella asked her once if she wore colored contacts because they looked haunting. Smiling, Aella hip-bumps her. "Hey gorgeous, I haven't seen you all shift. It has been insane tonight."

"Hey, babe! I know, it's wild. Those guys at that table are checking you out! I've gotten nothing but dirty old men all evening trying to pinch my ass." She complains. Turning her nose up at the thought of older men groping her made Aella hate this city and the cockroaches that infested it even more.

"Do you want to take over my last table with the not old men? I can't say they aren't dirty, though." She laughs, hoping Georgia will relieve her.

"Oh, that's sweet, babe, but I don't want to short you on money!"

"I don't mind! I hoped to leave here early. Tara and I have plans to go out. We are going to Blanc."

Georgia snaps at her wide-eyed with excitement. Aella isn't sure if the table or the fact that she is going to the nightclub has a hold on her.

"Oh. MY. GOSH.! Blanc? As in the *Blanc*?!"

"Uh, yes?" Aella is having a hard time understanding why everyone seems to get so hung up over the club in particular.

"Aella, you have to tell me how it is! I've been trying to go for a year, but they have the longest waiting list ever! How the hell did you manage that?"

Taken aback, Aella didn't realize how long the waitlist is. *How did Tara manage to get us in right away?* Making a mental note to ask her about it.

"I guess we just got lucky." Her response came out a lot flatter than intended.

"Well, I'm sure you'll get lucky! All the men there are Elite. I mean hot, wealthy, well-dressed. You won't have any trouble finding someone worthy." Seeing Georgia's excitement and sensing a pang of jealousy made Aella feel a little guilty for telling her she was going. Still, Georgia happily accepted the table under the condition that Aella tells her all about the club when they work together next. Hugging each other before she clocks off, Aella collects her tips and heads out back to where her car is parked.

THE AIR IS CRISP AND SMELLS OF WET DESERT—ONE OF the few things she doesn't mind about Arizona. The rain just smells different. It is warm and sweet but also inviting, unlike the showers she experienced when she visited Seattle for a yoga retreat last year with her mother.

Inhaling the fresh air, Aella walks to her parked car under a palo verde. Her lime green Kia Soul looks even more adorable, covered in rain droplets, making her feel accomplished that she won't have to wash it.

Opening the door, she notices something sitting on the windshield before sliding inside. Checking her surroundings, she hastily reaches to grab what is waiting for her. A chill skims across her body before shutting the door and locking herself inside of the car, a precaution she takes when alone at night in the city.

Turning on the overhead light, she holds what appears to

be a flower with a card attached to it. Inspecting the flower a little more intently, she notices it isn't just any ordinary flower but an orchid. Orchids aren't necessarily rare in Arizona, but they aren't expected, especially this time of year.

The card attached is no larger than a standard business card, and the sleek black design with gold writing catches her attention.

With one side of the card remaining blank, turning it over, she reads 3:30 *a.m.*. and a date, *October 15th*. A strange feeling sweeps over her then. Clicking the light off, she shoves the key into the ignition, turning the heat on low from the lingering chill. Thinking that someone had to be messing with her, *who would put a card and an orchid on a stranger's windshield like that? Friday the 13th,* it had to be a prank. Laughing it off, she stuffs the card inside the glove compartment and places the flower on the dash. Backing out of the parking spot, she begins driving to Tara's, forgetting about the little black card altogether.

As she arrives at the condominiums, Aella pulls into the vacant guest parking space next to Tara's pearl white Range Rover. Looking in her rearview mirror, she sees her friend running out in the rain to greet her. Rushing to grab her purse and overnight bag, she exits her car and quickly hugs Tara as they run to Tara's condo to escape the pouring rain.

Tara enjoys the finer things in life, and materialistic items are her favorite. She and Aella couldn't be more different in that regard. Tara is a maximalist. Less is never more, in regards to the appearance of her living conditions. Her condo is super chic, adorned with leather sofas and plush pillows, and her coffee table always remains scattered with Vogue and French interior design magazines she subscribes to.

Tara loves all the new trends and hopes to become an interior designer one day and live her dream in New York City.

"We have one hour to look like we just stepped off the red carpet!" Tara exclaims, rushing to grab two wine glasses and a bottle of Pinot, "What are you wearing tonight? I hope you bought a hot dress. Otherwise, you'll have to look through my closet."

Aella wasn't worried about her appearance, as she hasn't been feeling all that confident, given the night terrors that continue to wake her.

"I brought a couple of things, you be the judge," Aella responds, not wanting to fight with her friend over it. Tara tends to control anything and everything she can. Being a perfectionist by nature, Aella just goes with the flow. However, those characteristics didn't bother her because she knows it makes her best friend happy.

Aside from Tara being her best friend, she is the closest thing to a sister Aella would ever have.

"Yes, queen!" Tara snaps her fingers, then tosses her braided hair over her shoulder, handing Aella one of the wine glasses. Drinking more than she should have in that first gulp, the Pinot slides down too quickly, loosening her up while she watches Tara rummage through the overnight bag while the wine does its magic by lessening the tension in her shoulders.

The enjoyment from the wine is short-lived when Tara gasps dramatically at what Aella's choices are. Picking up the articles of clothing between her pointer finger and thumb, Tara scowls at Aella, causing her to cringe internally a bit.

"I'm not judging your taste in style, Ell, but what the fuck? We are going to *Blanc*. There is a dress code! You can't wear a sundress or shorts there."

"Sorry, I didn't know there was a dress code, and you know I'm on a tight budget, Tara," Aella says sheepishly, tamping down the slight embarrassment from her lack of effort.

Huffing out a breath, Tara shakes her head and smiles, with

that excitement creeping back in. "Come on, let's see what I have in my closet!"

Following her up the stairs, a sensation comes over Aella again. It was a familiar feeling, one that makes her feel uneasy. Grabbing the railing to hold her balance, she shakes it off and continues into Tara's bedroom. By the time she reaches the door, Tara had already torn a handful of dresses off their hangers. Pulling out a black satin slip dress from the pile, she hands it over for Aella to try on. The soft material is light and breathable. Coming down to just above the knees, the slit on the left side shows enough thigh to keep to the imagination still. The dress, although simple, screams power.

"Perfection!" Tara grins at her handiwork and hands Aella a brush and hair tie. Checking the time, she quickly tears through the tangles that have been gathered into a ponytail with little effort and throws them into a messy bun. With the Uber only 20 minutes out, Aella applies a slight blush to her cheeks, conceals her dark circles, and opts for a bold berry lip.

Tara, on the other hand, looks like a knockout. The dress she'd ordered is a strapless cobalt blue number; the color always complimented her dark skin tone. Short and straightforward, she accessorizes with long chain earrings and bangles. After tying her braids up and pinning them in place, she turns to face Aella from the mirror, awaiting her response to how she looks.

Tara demands attention and an audience, another vast difference between the two peas aiding the perfect balance of extroverted and introverted personalities.

"Tara, you look stunning!" Aella says in between sipping her wine.

"Thanks, girl, so do you. You look like a snack! I can't wait to see the look on all the hottie's faces at Blanc tonight!"

The compliment makes Aella feel good about herself for the first time in a long while. Glancing at the mirror one final time, she wonders if perhaps she will get lucky and meet someone tonight. There are two things she longed for. One: sleep and plenty of it without the paralysis and monsters that haunt her.

Two: Love. Even though she knew little about the topic or its meaning, she craved it.

Downing the rest of their wine, Tara's phone pings, letting her know their Uber driver is one minute away. Stepping into their heels, the two girls head out the door with their purses and phones. Not knowing what to expect, they climb into the car, having little expectations for the night ahead.

Chapter Two

Blanc is only a fifteen-minute drive, located in the heart of Scottsdale. The club looks massive on the outside. There are no windows, which adds to the illusion that it is private, creating that desirable effect. Surprised by the architecture, it looks modern, with a classic twist.

Coming up to the front of the building, the outside walls are all mirrored, and substantial green plants are arranged along the entryway. The cost alone to keep them alive had to be a fortune here in the desert. Sliding out of the Uber, Aella and Tara thank their driver, who hesitates before leaving. He gives the girls a wary glance, which in turn gives Aella pause.

Something about the look on his face put her intuition on high alert, but before she can say anything, he gives them his number for a ride back home when they are ready.

Walking up the pathway to the entrance, they are greeted by a tall security guard as they approach. Tara states her first and last name along with Aella's, and the security guard reads down the list on his clipboard, asking for identification. Digging out their IDs, the guard looks them over a few times before granting them access.

"Once inside, hand all personal belongings to Sergio. No purses. No cell phones. If caught with either, you will immediately be kicked out and banned from coming back." A subtle wave of anxiety runs over Aella at the thought of not having any of her personal belongings with her, along with the shared moment between the Uber driver. *What if there is an emergency? What if someone drugs either one of us?* The awful thoughts race through her mind, causing her palms to sweat, but she avoids wiping them over her satin dress.

"What about our cards or cash for purchasing beverages?" she blurts out before having time to process the remark. The security guard notices her discomfort, and Tara doesn't help the situation by snapping her neck in Aella's direction.

"Lady, I don't think you need to worry about getting drinks tonight." He says with a knowing smirk as he takes in their appearance like a dog in heat.

Nodding her head, the security guard grants them access to the club.

A hallway from the front entrance and two huge black doors are closed. Standing in front of them must be Sergio because along the walls are lockers with different locks. Handing Sergio their belongings, he gives them a key with a bracelet attached to it for when they finally have their fill from the long night ahead. Smiling at the two friends, he opens the doors to the club, and when they get a first look, they nearly fall over.

The interior is insane. No wonder there aren't any photos of it; you have to see it with your own eyes. The floors are smooth white marble and surprisingly clean, given all the bodies mingled on the dance floor. Huge midcentury-styled light fixtures brighten the room, casting an intimate glow. With the walls painted black, a massive bar stands out against the largest of the divisions, entirely made of glass, with lights inside pointing outward, reflecting off the gold accents. Decanters of liquor line the shelf, and the bartenders create art by mixing cocktails and garnishes. Watching the cocktails be made is a show all in itself.

Heading for the bar, Tara nudges Aella and points to two men sitting at the end, admiring them in an all-too-obvious way. Tara wants to talk to them so they can get their first drink started. Rolling her eyes, Aella obliges.

The men sitting at the bar are handsome, both wearing black suits and patent leather shoes. They are clean-cut and wear the same cologne, Acqua di Giò; *how original*. Asking what they want to drink, Tara humors them by allowing them to pick for the two of them. Aella didn't care what it was as long as she had something in her hand to keep from fidgeting.

Taking in the club's space, she can't get over how much bigger it is on the inside. The bartender hands them their drinks after mixing them. Taking the first sip, Aella diverts from spitting it back into the glass. The cocktail is way too sweet, and the pink color has edible glitter. Another reason you don't have men order your drinks for you is their predictability.

Forcing herself to continue sipping her beverage, she thanked the two men, who introduced themselves as Nathan and Eric. Tara has her eyes set on Nathan, who seems more interested in getting to know Aella out of the two, leaving her unimpressed. Nathan is your average Scottsdale douche that probably lives off of Daddy's money and has some trust fund. Eric and Nathan are regulars here. Aella picked up on that fact since the cocktail servers knew them on a first-name basis.

Staring off into space, she notices a man sitting in a dark corner of the room, causing her heart to skip. She couldn't tell if he was staring back at her, but she could have sworn their eyes locked for a moment. Unable to look away, she can confirm that he is the most attractive man she will ever lay eyes on in her lifetime. From where she stands, he seems devastating as she is tranced, unable to take her eyes off him. A dark-tailored suit that is made for just him is the first thing she notes. The second is that his hair is dark, and Aella has a thing for dark hair, especially this man who appears to be searing her soul with his eyes like a brand. Aella's cheeks warm as Tara taps her shoulder, breaking her hold.

"Ell, Nathan asked you a question.." The frustrated tone in her voice makes Aella see that she is being rude to the men who bought their first round of drinks. However, Aella knows she will understand when she tells her about the man who held her attention later. Drawing the focus back to Nathan and his friend Eric, she couldn't help but notice how much more unattractive they became.

"I'm sorry. I was enjoying the club's beauty. What did you ask?" Her attempt to sound polite causes Tara to purse her lips.

Nathan smiles and shakes his head to assure her it is no problem.

"Are you from the area or visiting out of town?"

"Oh, I'm from the area, Arizona Native, so they say. You?"

"I'm from Boston, moved here for business. You don't seem all that impressed being from here. Why?" Setting her drink down, she shrugs. Maybe she was wrong about the assumption that he lived off of his Daddy's money. He works for Daddy's company, which almost makes it worse.

"I'll tell you why in a moment. If you'll excuse me, I need to use the restroom." Leaving Tara chatting with the two men, Aella wanted to get a closer look at the man swallowed by the dark corner of the club.

But to her dismay, he was gone. Feeling a sense of defeat, she begins to look for the restroom. Just as she is about to walk away, the hairs on her neck rise. Instinct takes hold as she feels someone standing behind her, and a warm feeling low in her stomach forms. Hot breath hits her earlobe, causing her body to lock up and her heart to skitter. Standing there frozen, the need to turn is compelling, with the hope that whoever is standing behind her is the man she is looking for.

"Are you looking for me?" The voice is solid and quiet, causing chills to sweep over her body.

"I-I don't know. Should I be?" She breathes playfully, crossing her fingers mentally that it is the man who was staring back at her a few moments ago.

Glancing over her shoulder, she realizes it is him. Her heart speeds up, feeling the space between them close in, sucking the air from her lungs. He is tall, and from what she can make out from the corner of her eye, he is also built solid. The suit he's wearing looks black from a distance; up close, however, it appears to be more of a deep crimson. The scent of bourbon, spice, and sandalwood kisses her nose. Turning to better look at him, she tilts her head, meeting his eyes. They are the deepest blue she's ever seen. Like the oceans in Greece, you could drown in them. His teeth are perfectly straight and white as he smiles at her invitingly.

This man's beauty is intimidating and scandalous, causing her to fumble in her heels and roll her ankle slightly. The floor begins to come into focus, and in a smooth motion, the man gently grabs her arm before she embarrasses herself due to the clumsy misstep.

She has never been great at walking, let alone in heels, and her body trembles from the close call as she works a swallow.

Feeling her cheeks heat again, she looks into this man's eyes, feeling a comfort she has longed for.

"Thank you for saving my life." She says abruptly, trying to defuse the awkward situation.

"Oh yes, of course. I couldn't let you fall to your death, now could I?" His tone is teasing, and her cheeks start to hurt from how much she is smiling back at him. His smile is contagious, like the common cold. Aella couldn't help but stare at his full, firm lips, curious how they would feel alone.

Holding out his hand, she returns the favor by extending hers for what she thought would be a handshake. His mouth grazes the top of her wrist as he looks up to meet her eyes again.

"Gabriel, nice to meet your acquaintance. You are?"

"What a gentleman," she exasperates, "Aella, my friends call me Ell. Nice to meet you, Gabriel." Her heart is pounding so loud that she wonders if everyone can hear it over the music playing on full blast.

"Beautiful... the name and the woman who claims it." After smiling at one another, he gestures to two velvet seats with a table. Looking around to see if Tara is okay, Aella spots her dancing with Nathan and Eric on the dance floor. Allowing Aella to lead the way over to the corner with two chairs, he signals a server.

"I will have a glass of bourbon straight, and the lady will have?"

"Oh, a glass of pinot is fine, thank you." Knowing she will hate herself tomorrow after mixing different alcohol, it would be worth it with Gabriel accompanying her.

Watching him sip the glass of bourbon should be illegal with how he holds the glass in his hand firm enough to break yet controlled while his eyes never stray from her.

A predator in the best way. Anything this man does should be considered illegal. He seems so confident and sure of his every move, yet still resembles some humility.

His eyes shoot down to her hands, and Aella feels the urge to become embarrassed yet again. She has been picking the skin around her fingernails for so long that she forgets about the habit.

"Sorry, a nervous habit."

"You have nothing to apologize for, especially to me. Why are you nervous?"

"I've never been to this club, and as beautiful as it is, I'm a little peopled out, I guess." Becoming overwhelmed in big social situations never seems to get any easier the older she gets, but he didn't need to know that.

One of his eyebrows rises; thinking to himself for a moment, he responds, "People can be draining. Always wanting something, but never seem to give without receiving."

"That is a good way of putting it, I don't know. I didn't sleep well last night and didn't want to go out initially. My best friend Tara made the reservation. I'm surprised we got in, considering how long the waitlist is. Do you come to Blanc often?" Keeping the rambling in check, she waits for his response, trying not to interrupt him before he can answer.

"I've come a few times but haven't enjoyed it until tonight."

My damn heart again... Aella, pull it together. You just met this man. He is not your forever, even if you think you've known him for a lifetime. He could be a serial killer. She thinks, while still staring at Gabriel sipping from his glass like a model—the sudden urge to get Tara and get out of here before she does something reckless tickles her.

"Well, I am happy to hear that tonight has been refreshing. It was nice to meet you, Gabriel. Thank you for the pinot. I should get Tara and call our Uber." Aella says, breaking the trance again, but especially when she sees a very sloppy Tara on the dance floor. Feeling a sense of happiness for her friend that she's having fun, Aella is even more happy that she met Mr. Sinful.

However, when she glances back over at Tara, she notices

that something is very wrong. Furrowing her brow, Gabriel reaches over, grazing his fingertips slightly to pull her attention back to him.

"Did I say something wrong?"

"No! Not at all! I'm just exhausted and have had a long day. Tara also looks a lot more wasted than I thought she was. I think it's time to get home and put her to bed." She says, trying her best to reassure Gabriel, even though sleep did start calling to her. In Aella's mind, only an idiot would leave so soon after sitting with a man like Gabriel, but something about the encounter is a little too good to be true, no matter how handsome and charismatic he is. It's almost as if she knows him from somewhere but can't place it. Another lifetime even, but it could also be the alcohol.

Standing out of his chair, Gabriel continues to face her, and a longing for her to stay almost takes hold.

Great, he must think I'm a freak.

"Aella, it was a pleasure to meet you. I am delighted you came out tonight. I hope to see you again soon. Please allow me to have my driver take you home; it's no trouble. Ben will make sure you get home safely." He says, pulling out his phone to call the driver. She is stunned that he has his phone on him since the rules are you couldn't have it in the club at all. Noticing her reaction, he grins, placing a finger to his lips as if to say don't tell anyone.

"I appreciate your offer, but I'll just order the Uber when we collect our belongings." Feeling slightly uncomfortable by that gesture, she isn't too keen on Gabriel knowing where Tara lives. Despite his charming and handsome appearance, he is still a stranger she had just met at a club.

"I insist. Like I said, it's no trouble at all. Since it is nearly two in the morning, I am uncomfortable with a couple of beautiful young women waiting alone for a ride in the dark. You can trust that Ben will not give me the address to your residence if you're worried I might stalk you." Taken aback by the joke, Aella grimaces, hoping that she didn't say what she was thinking out loud. Being as exhausted as she is, she could have sworn she only thought those things.

Pondering his offer, she accepts. Walking alongside her to grab Tara, Aella gets the confirmation that something is definitely off, and Gabriel also knows it.

Tara isn't just drunk; she is intoxicated. She can hardly stand, and her eyes are glazed over, which is also a sign that makes Aella's intuition falter. Aella has seen Tara drunk plenty of times, and she had no issues carrying on a conversation like nobody's business. In the state she was in now, she could hardly speak.

Wondering how much her friend really had to drink when she left the bar to chat with Gabriel, Nathan and Eric attempt to keep Tara from leaving. Aella knew then that their intentions were not pure in the least and that one of them had to have slipped her something.

"Leaving so soon? The fun is just starting. We have Tara—"

Aella feels that Gabriel is behind her at that moment because one look from him is all it takes and the two men back off.

"I think it's time for both of the ladies to get home. You two have clearly had enough fun for one night, and I would advise you both to do the same before someone gets...hurt." Gabriel says in a stern, confident tone that causes even Aella to stiffen. The open-ended threat is more than enough for Eric and Nathan to scurry and move through the club out of sight.

Helping Tara exit the club as Aella collects their belongings from Sergio, she wishes him a good night.

When she walks outside, Gabriel is standing before a black Escalade. The driver, who she assumes to be Ben, greets

Gabriel and nods to something Ben says before glancing over to Aella and opening the back door to help Tara in. Returning to the driver's side, Ben hops back in and shuts the door, giving Gabriel and Aella the privacy they didn't need. It isn't like she would kiss this man or take him right here on the Escalade, even though she really wants to.

Within seconds, she feels a large hand gently grace her chin, turning her head to face him. The subtle gesture sends butterflies that fill her stomach.

"I meant what I said about wanting to see you again, Ell. You are..." He sighs, "You are everything I have been searching for." Either she just passed out, or he just said that. *He just met me!*

Gabriel could have any woman he wanted, and Aella didn't know she was all that special. The whole night was a little strange, and her concern for Tara was at the forefront.

"We will have to see if fate works in our favor. I typically turn into a pumpkin after midnight, though. It would appear my fairy godmother went easy on me this time." Surprised by the witty response that came out of her, Aella is impressed by her smooth efforts.

Gabriel laughs, and the sound caresses her skin like smooth velvet. Remembering that her mom had charged her vibrator, she has plans to use it when she returns home.

"Well, with that princess, I bid you a goodnight. Get some rest." He leans down and kisses her forehead tenderly before opening the door.

Sliding in, they stare at each other for a moment longer before he closes the door and walks away. A feeling of sadness sweeps over her as he turns to reenter the club. Aella wanted this night to end, but she didn't want her time with Gabriel to. Would she ever see Gabriel again, or was this a fun, flirtatious endeavor? Watching him enter Club Blanc, Prince Charming is swallowed by the darkness as she sits in the backseat of the car with a drunk and most likely drugged Tara, wishing she had left one of her heels behind so Gabriel could find her.

Giving Ben Tara's Address, he drives as if they were precious cargo in the back seat. Tara moans and groans, looking like she is going to puke, and Aella frantically searches around the car for something she can vomit in. Pulling off on the side of the road as they exit, Ben stands by, watching out for anyone who may cause harm, as Aella rubs Tara's back as she expels whatever other poison aside from the alcohol inhabits her body.

Tara can drink anyone under the table; something is definitely wrong. Once she finishes heaving, Aella helps her up and into the car, thanking Ben for pulling off.

Resting her head on Aella's lap while she strokes her hair, Gabriel moves in, living rent-free in Aella's thoughts and will most likely stay there forever. From the moment they locked eyes inside of Blanc to the moment he saved them both from her worst nightmare, Gabriel was an enigma of everything she hungered for in a man. Danger. She will never be able to shake him, no matter how hard she tries, and something about that terrifies her as much as it excites her.

Chapter Three

Spending most of the following morning mending their hangovers, Tara's is far worse than Aella's, which wasn't surprising considering the state she was in last night and having told her about Gabriel and how he generously had his driver take them home when they awoke. Ben was a man of few words, but she trusted him. Assuring Tara that she didn't get a bad vibe from him and that he was a solid driver. Popping a bottle of champagne in the kitchen, they begin drinking mimosas while making chocolate chip pancakes. Tara allowed Aella to put on her favorite *Smiths* album, singing along in between reminiscing on their night out.

"Hey Tara, I forgot to ask you yesterday, how did you get our names on the list for Blanc?" Remembering that she had meant to ask her since it was such a hard club to access.

"Well, if you ever read the texts I send you.." Her response is dry. Clearly, the mimosa hasn't hit her yet in aiding her hangover.

"I didn't put our names on the list. It was wild! I got a text from Blanc saying our reservation was accepted. Someone must have put our names down a while ago on the list, or we just got lucky."

Stunned by the response, Aella didn't know what to say. She couldn't think of anyone who would put their names down, and that night of all nights when they met Gabriel. What a strange turn of events.

"Huh, that's odd. Whoever it was must have been a friend of yours or someone you know that's been before because I can't think of anyone who would do that." Aella wasn't the most approachable and kept her circle of friends reasonably small, aka Tara.

"Yeah, maybe." Tara isn't in the mood to talk logistics. The pancakes are done and smell divine. Susan would have a cow if she saw how they chose to nourish their bodies after a night of drinking. Spreading butter over the hot pancakes is the best part. Once the syrup is warm from the microwave, Tara hands over the pitcher so Aella can drizzle the hot sugary goodness first. They both agreed early on in their friendship that if they didn't meet a man to marry, they would marry each other and live a platonic, happy life. Everyone deserves an ever-after.

Sitting on the couch with their pancakes and mimosas, Tara puts on a *Sex and the City* rerun. It is their ultimate favorite show, having watched every season together at least 20 times by now. Aella loved doing these things with her. Going out is fun occasionally, but sitting on the couch with a good show on and sipping a drink with her best friend while eating chocolate chip pancakes is utter perfection.

"Oh, I wanted to ask how you slept. I know I got pretty wrecked last night. Thank you for helping me out of my dress and shoes and into bed. I couldn't have done it without you, wifey." Tara's gratitude didn't go unnoticed, considering she was shaken up about potentially being drugged and could have been taken advantage of. Aella would have never allowed that to happen, though. She didn't mention her vomiting on the side of the road either. Some things don't need to be said, and that is one of those things.

"Actually," Aella mumbles with a bite full of pancake, "I slept great! I think I got a solid seven hours of sleep. It was just what I needed."

"Seven hours? That's it? Jesus girl. So, you've gotten what eight total hours the last four days?" Her brows rise, meeting her hairline. Aella hates nothing more than being put on the spot, especially while trying to enjoy chocolate chip pancakes. *There goes the moment of utter perfection.*

"With the naps midday here and there.." Defending herself isn't going to cut it. She knows where Tara is headed with this conversation and doesn't want to have it right now, let alone ever.

Sighing out loud, Tara sets her plate down and shifts criss-cross apple sauce to face her.

"Ell, I care about you. That is not nearly enough sleep for anyone. Maybe you should call Dr. Jacobs and tell her you're having episodes again." Aella could feel her blood start to boil. Tara's eyes soften as she reaches over and places a hand on her knee. Forcing her tears down, Aella can feel her eyes start to well up. Dr. Jacobs was the worst sort. She hasn't shared every detail about the week in the hospital with Tara. Swallowing her pride, Aella looks her in the eye.

"I can't call Dr. Jacobs. She just wants to medicate me, Tara. The medication made things so much worse... Sleep paralysis isn't an uncommon condition; many people suffer from it. I've done extensive research and have to figure out how to manage it."

"I understand, but doing this on your own isn't working. Maybe she can recommend something else that might be of aid?" The hope in Tara's voice makes Aella pity her in a way.

Having told her a lot, she hasn't told her what haunts her at night because she doesn't think Tara would understand. Not even Aella fully understands it. She could never tell anyone about that. Even Tara would think she was having some psychotic break if she knew half the things Aella experienced and experiences still while having sleep paralysis. It isn't the typical can't move your body and panic for a second or two until you force your body to relax and wake up. It's that for Aella, without being able to wake up at all, and what stares at her next to the bed, just smiling. The worst experience she ever had was when one of those things crawled on top of her chest, speaking into her ear some otherworldly language. She can still feel the weight on her chest and the graze of its long, cold, bony fingers across her skin, chilling her to the bone. Trying to forget that nightmare, she swipes at the fallen tears and perks up. Grabbing their empty glasses, Aella saunters off to the kitchen to make them another mimosa.

"I'll call her Monday Tara, scouts honor. Maybe you're right. There has to be something else I can try." *No way in hell am I calling that bitch of a Doctor.*

"Sounds good, girl." The smile is light but sincere. Changing the subject, Aella asks Tara what dating sites she's been using as of late, which pulls her out of the funk she is in. Taking her phone out of her sweatpants pocket, they spend all afternoon swiping right and left on the apps. Messaging different guys, some were complete assholes, and others were quite funny. By the time Aella gets ready to return to her apartment, Tara has three dates lined up for the following week.

Once she throws everything she brought back into the overnight bag, Tara walks with Aella to her car. The weird thing about Phoenix is it can be cloudy and rainy one day, with the following blue skies and sunshine. It's three in the afternoon when Aella leaves to go to the grocery store and clean her apartment.

Tara leans in, hugging her like it will be the last time she sees her, and Aella gets that weird feeling all over again. Melatonin: She is going to take the whole bottle tonight.

"Text me when you get home! Love you."

"I will, love you too!" Aella yells out from her window.

***

SHE CAN'T GET GABRIEL OUT OF HER HEAD WHILE DRIVING on the freeway. Wondering if he has also been thinking about her just as much, her mind takes a different direction. Thoughts about his personal life consume her, from whether he is married with kids to what he does for work. She was becoming obsessed. Saved by the bell, her phone rings, breaking the focus on all things Gabriel.

"Hi, Mom, I'm driving right now. What's up?"

"Hi, sweetheart! I just wanted to check in since I haven't heard from you all weekend," Susan exclaims with a tone of agitation behind her remark.

"Mom, I saw you yesterday, remember? You came to my apartment and *overstepped*."

"What? I missed that last part; you must be in a bad area. Anyway, I wanted to check in with you and see if we were still going to Sedona tomorrow! It will be great, such a fun girls' day." She constantly expects Aella to be available at her every whim.

"I never agreed to go this weekend. I told you Tara and I had plans. I promise we will set a date. This weekend isn't a good time for me." Knowing that her response is going to bite her in the ass, she feels terrible pushing her mom away momentarily. Being all her mother has is a chore, and accommodating her needs at all times can be mentally exhausting.

"Okay dear, we can go next weekend. That will be perfect, actually! I'll book us a room! We can stay the night and spend quality time together."

Shit.

"Sounds good. I love you. Talk to you tomorrow."

"Love you, sweetheart!"

While ending the call, something catches Aella's attention out of the corner of her eye. The orchid. She'd forgotten all about the flower sitting on her windshield. Reaching over with her free hand from the wheel, she picks it up and notices it hasn't wilted since sitting in the car. It still looks freshly cut, with a sheen of sweat. Orchids are her favorite kind of flower, and the one she is holding is all white. Representing purity and innocence, which was not Aella in the slightest. That's probably why she's so drawn to them, and the fact that it hadn't wilted in the car overnight and throughout the day baking in the sun is beyond her.

Once she pulls up to her apartment and unloads the grocery bags, she carefully sets the orchid down on the counter in the kitchen the moment she walks in the door. Not getting much at the store and being on a budget is hard when you're supposedly allergic to everything. Gluten-free this, dairy-free that, Susan is convinced her sleeping habits have to do with food allergies, which Aella humors her by avoiding the couple allergens on the list.

When she's out, however, that's a different story, and she indulges when she can. Attempting to naturally heal Aella with various herbs and chants, she lets her do what she wants, which is more for Susan's benefit than her own. A lot of the herbs have given her the worst case of diarrhea. If cleaning her out is the point, then point proven.

Opting for a frozen gluten-free, dairy-free pizza that costs three times as much as a traditional frozen pizza, she preheats the oven. While waiting for the range to reach its desired temperature, she gently picks up the orchid and places it in a glass of water.

For some unexplained reason, she wants to care for this orchid; there is something special about it.

Too exhausted to clean tonight, she slices the pizza, pours herself a glass of cheap red straight out of the box, and heads for her bed. Opening her laptop to find something to watch, her phone buzzes with a text from Tara. Forgetting to text Tara like she promised she would when the moment got home, she swipes open the screen.

> Tara: Did you forget to let me
> know you're alive?!

Tara's biggest gripe in the world is people keeping their word impeccable. Aella doesn't fault her for that; it's a reasonable expectation. Laughing to herself, Aella begins typing back. Tara knows she's home since they have shared locations with each other. Thanks, Apple!

> Aella: Sorry, I went to the
> store and forgot to text you. I
> am safe and sound snug as a bug.
> It will never happen again.

> Tara: You better stick to that
> statement. Those are large shoes
> to fill, Ell!

Finally, when she gets into bed and picks something to watch on *Netflix*, she inhales the slices of pizza and drinks her glass of cheap box wine.

It's 10:30, and Aella begins to feel her eyes grow heavy. She is slowly slipping into the best sleep she hopes she will ever have.

WAKE UP. WAKE UP. WAKE UP. AELLA IS UNABLE TO MOVE. Her body is entirely frozen, and she can feel her skin start to sweat. Looking around the room with only her eyes, she doesn't see anything out of the ordinary. She knows that she is having an episode. *Breathe Aella, in through the nose, out through the nose.* She tries to gain control over her body to do so, but she fails. Panic takes hold, and her eyes start to sting from the tears that are forming. Listening with intent, she hears a soft thump hitting the floor. Her heart is pounding into her ears as she holds her breath.

Footsteps begin skittering across the floor, but she is paralyzed, unable to move her head to see who her visitor is. In the past, she never heard any unwanted visitors moving about until one was on top of her. This is an entirely new discovery.

A body then jumps onto the dresser in front of the bed. Trying to make out the figure, she notices it is engulfed in black. What she can make out of the silhouette is a long animalistic body, perhaps more feline, but definitely not one you would be enticed to stoke. Sitting tall on the dresser, it doesn't move for what seems like a long stretch of time until it opens its eyes, which glow a deep shade of yellow.

Terrified, Aella is helpless. As the creature smiles down at her, tears take over, and a warm sensation seeps between her thighs.

"Why are you crying, girl?" the thing asks. Its voice is masculine but sounds more human than it appears as it continues to watch Aella with curiosity.

"W—Who are you?" Surprised that she can speak, that's

never happened before either, even though her voice is quiet and shaky.

"Speak up, human." He demands.

Without hesitation, he jumps down. Aella is shaking so badly that her body feels like it's vibrating the entire room, and she is going to pass out. *Wouldn't that be something?* The thought occurs to her, *passing out while already asleep.*

The beast then jumps onto the bed and crawls over her body. Getting a closer look, it appears to be a cat. Not just any cat, though; it is a large slender black cat, smaller than a jaguar but one you wouldn't want to fuck with nonetheless. Appearing malnourished with floppy ears, its eyes are human-like, with a mouth that reminds Aella of the Cheshire Cat in *Alice in Wonderland* but far more sinister.

"Aella." The cat states. Somehow, knowing her name doesn't help her feel better in the current situation. *This is how I die, having a heart attack in my sleep under a fucked up looking cat that can speak.*

The cat then chuckles in an uncomfortable way, and Aella shakes even more under its weight.

"I'm not here to kill you, girl. I much prefer my prey to fight back."

"Who are you, and what do you want?" She demands with trembling limbs, the wet sheets getting colder beneath her.

Silence engulfs the space in the apartment, except for the cat's purring.

"I have been called many names in my life; I have been many things. What I want is neither here nor there, as I do not want, nor do I need or seek."

Unable to swallow, Aella isn't entirely sure that she's even breathing. Watching the cat stretch his back, he begins kneading the blanket, and then something occurs to her.

"I don't understand... How am I able to speak with you? This has never happened before."

"You have the will to speak, yet you do not possess the will to move. You are in control of your mind but lack the strength of your body. Interesting. Try wiggling your big toe." He says as if he is enjoying himself, almost like he would with a tiny mouse. Frustrated by the cat's taunts, Aella wiggles her big toe and gasps. Then, without hesitation, she wiggles all of her toes, moving up her legs and arms. She then pushes all the willpower she has to get out from under the cat and sit up against the headboard, folding her knees into her body.

"Look at that; the girl can move. Nice work."

"What. The. Fuck. Do. You. Want. Cat?"

"Language, Aella, please. We have an appointment scheduled at 3:30 a.m. on October 15th. I apologize for my lack of memory. Dates and times don't exactly exist the same in our realm. "

Confused by the appointment she did not make with anyone, let alone something that came straight out of *Pet Cemetery*, the time and date strike a cord in her memory...

"The business card!" She shouts, not entirely sure why. "But how?"

"Ah yes, the business card. I am simply a messenger, Aella, a personal assistant. We have been watching you for quite some time now—the how isn't important. What is important is that we get acquainted with one another. We will be seeing much more of each other moving forward." He states matter-of-factly and waves his paw. Spreading his body out along the bed, he relaxes and moves his tail in idle circles. Getting way too comfortable, real or not, this cat is no guest.

"Listen, I don't know what you are or what *they* want, but I am not going to allow this shit to go on any further! I need sleep, and I need you to get the fuck out of my apartment. You are not a guest. You are an uninvited Demon." The words came out in a rush and tasted like venom the second they left her mouth. Pressing her lips together, the cat's eyes narrow. He sits up and stalks towards her, his body moving with fluid grace, closing the space between them. Within a few inches, she can feel his whiskers brushing the sides of her cheeks as he inhales the air around her. Trying to stay strong, she wants to run out of the apartment and never look back.

"I can smell your fear, girl. Never call me, or my kind, a Demon ever again. I may not have received a formal invitation to your pitiful excuse of a home. However, you unlocked the door and left it wide open. I am the least of your concerns; there is evil you couldn't imagine. Evil that books old as time wouldn't dare speak of. This is only the beginning of what you will face, and we will spend much more time together. So I advise you to hold that tongue before something other than myself snatches it from your delicate mouth. Are we understood?"

Aella's eyes feel like saucers, and her jaw aches from clenching her teeth so hard. She's frustrated and scared, but above all, she is helpless. Unsure of what door he spoke of, she didn't leave any door open, let alone unlock it—unless this door wasn't one in a physical sense. Knitting her brows together, she nods, unsure if this is real or another night terror.

"I just don't understand any of this. What are you, and why are you here? What door?"

Sitting back on his haunches, the cat takes a deep breath with an air of annoyance, as though explaining the mechanics to her would be too exhausting.

"Are you familiar with what a portal is?" He says, still eyeing her.

"Like as in what? Movies and stuff?"

The cat rolls his eyes at her, shaking his head before continuing.

"We are not sure how you have managed to do it, but somehow, in your subconscious state, you have been able to open portals that have long been locked for reasons far greater than you could comprehend. I am from the realm of Isethas, where we will be going tomorrow. Our goal, Aella, is to understand your ability more and help you stop doing it."

Aella's jaw goes slack, forcing herself to hold back a laugh. *Yep, I have fucking lost my mind.*

"So you're telling me that somehow, I have this magical ability to open portals? Nope. I'm not buying it. This is an episode, a really crazy one, and everything will go back to normal. Also, if I have this ability, then how is it you're here, huh? Clearly, I'm conscious enough to even talk to you if you say that I open them in my subconscious state... wait."

It dawns on her then, and the cat continues, "Yes, your subconscious. Not unconscious. Please, by all means, continue with your internal spiral."

"That's... that's impossible. Right? How is this even possible?" Aella asks, her throat becoming dry.

"That is why I am here. We are going to figure it out because the alternative is far worse. Your ability has grown stronger over the years, and when it happens, it is felt throughout our realm like a ripple. If we can feel that sort of power, every other realm has the ability to feel it as well."

Attempting to wrap her head around what the cat has just informed her, she still thinks that this is just one of her episodes and she will awake as if it never happened. The alternative, however, would be if this is, in fact, real, and what little information she has received from this encounter, then she will be able to check off one of the things she has been longing for:

sleep and no more paralysis. Wishful thinking on her end, but stranger things have happened, like talking to a cat.

"Sure, okay," She says, laced with sarcasm. What else can she really say at this point? She still doesn't believe any of this, and even if it were true, she can't tell anyone. Nobody would believe her.

"Good. Now, I do have to pardon myself. I have another appointment, and since you have taken up far too much of my time with your dramatics, I will see you tomorrow. Same time as our appointment today. Oh, and Aella, I suggest you get all the rest you can. You will need your energy." He says, but before she can ask any more questions, he is gone in the blink of an eye as if he was never there to begin with.

She sits in the same spot until the sun rises, squeezing her knees tight to her chest until she feels nothing.

Chapter Four

E xhaustion would be an understatement. The suggestion from the cat to get some rest was laughable and insulting. The fear that had consumed Aella at three in the morning didn't even touch the fear that consumes her right now. This is real. This isn't some nightmare she had or some episode; sleep paralysis is different. Studies on sleep paralysis are still being done. New research gets published on the disease weekly. Nothing in those pages she'd read had stated anything about people being able to speak to their monsters, let alone move. This is different. If she wanted to hold onto what little sanity was left, she needed to get to the bottom of it quickly. Today is going to be a long-ass day, and coffee is the first order of business.

Not wanting to make a pot of the shitty coffee she has in the cupboard, she treats herself to her favorite coffee shop down the street, which is well-earned after this morning. Grabbing her laptop and keys, she runs out of the apartment and double-checks the locked door just for safe measures. After her encounter, she isn't going to be taking any chances, even though this cat supposedly entered through a portal that she has managed to open. *Take that asshole.*

Happy Grinds makes the best Americano in the city. Whenever Aella wanted a quiet place to read a book or sketch some drawings, this is the place she always comes to. Sitting outside on the patio when the weather wasn't a million degrees was the perfect retreat, and today was her lucky day. Only 75, exceptional weather for researching the predicament she's gotten herself in.

"Good morning; what can I get for you?" The barista asks as Aella approaches the counter. Taking in the vast array of pastries and breakfast sandwiches, she couldn't help but bask in the delicious, rich scent of freshly roasted beans.

"Good morning, may I have an iced Americano with oat milk and a....bacon egg croissant, please? Oh! And a slice of coffee cake?" Happy Grinds has the best coffee cake. Made fresh every morning, the secret to their recipe is cream cheese, which keeps it extra moist. The hint of nutmeg and cinnamon adds color to anyone's taste buds. Today, she is breaking the dairy and gluten-free rule, especially since her mother isn't around to keep watch.

"Coming right up!"

"Thank you. I'll be out on the patio." She says with a smile, handing the barista her debit card. Returning the smile and the debit alongside the iced cold beverage, the barista lets her know it will be a few minutes on the croissant. As she sips from the straw, she starts to feel like a new woman.

THE TABLE AELLA DECIDES TO OCCUPY IS IN THE SHADE, nestled next to tall oleander bushes. Oleanders grow all over the

Phoenix area. The purple and pink flowers are beautiful but highly poisonous if ingested by animals and humans alike. She bounces from the various tabs she has opened on the screen of her laptop, ranging from sleep paralysis reports about different people and their experiences to vetted theories of realms by scientists. She even goes as far as pulling up more spiritual guides on realms by people with a similar faith like her mother. Taking notes on all her reading, Aella feels more hopeful that she can find a common thread here, or at least something that makes a little more sense.

As her eyes start to come out of focus from reading so much on the screen, she realizes that it's her queue to take a break despite still needing to find answers, even after being at the coffee shop for over an hour. Pulling out her phone, she maps the closest library, which is less than a mile up the street, to her pleasant surprise. Shutting her laptop, she collects her things until a man's voice speaks from behind her, causing her to jump.

"I had a feeling we would see each other again soon." The amusement that snakes out of him sends a shiver down her spine. As she turns, her elbow knocks an empty plate off the table, causing it to break.

"Oh my god, Gabriel! How are you?" She says nervously, crouching down to pick up the broken pieces. Beating her to the mess she's made, Gabriel stops her, kneeling to pick them up himself.

"Better now that I'm graced with your presence. What is it you're working on? I noticed you from the window but didn't want to break your concentration. You seemed so determined to complete your task." Seeing Gabriel in the light of the early afternoon makes him look even more attractive. Before the crazy shit that happened earlier with that damn cat, Gabriel was all Aella could think about. His semi-casual attire includes a pair of fitted black jeans that hug him in all the right areas, matched with a fitted black V-neck.

Gabriel is ripped, his muscles flexing under his shirt as he scoops the broken ceramic into his large hands. Either the chaos in the club was overwhelming for her enough not to take notice of his physique, even while wearing a tailored suit, or she was too nervous about their encounter; she's one happy girl now that she gets a full view of him.

Walking over to the garbage, he dumps the pieces, brushes his hands off, and takes the empty seat across from Aella.

"Thank you, you didn't need to do that for me. And I was researching a couple of things for a project I'm working on."

"Do tell?" he says, quirking a dark brow, and he genuinely seems interested in her little *project*.

"It's nothing, just silly. I've never seen you here before. Do you come here often?" Aella responds quickly, attempting to change the subject.

"I've actually never been here before, first time. A colleague recommended it to me. He told me they had the best coffee in the state! I suppose fate has worked in my favor yet again." He says with a wink and a sexy tip of the side of his mouth. Aella's cheeks start to redden as she clears her throat.

"I don't know if it's necessarily the best coffee in the state, but it is delicious. Their coffee cake is to die for if you haven't had a slice yet."

Gabriel chuckles, "I will have to have a slice next time since it's to die for," he drawls humorously while still holding eye contact.

"What do you do for work?" She asks, growing more curious about Mr. Sinful.

"I am in the business of making deals with high-profile contacts; it's kind of boring, honestly. I am far more interested in you. What do you do, Ell?" Her name rolls off his tongue like a warm caress, making her legs feel weak in the best way.

"Right now, I'm just a cocktail server at a local bar down the street. It's not much, but I've been saving to go to art school on the East Coast next year."

"Oh? What kind of art piques your interest?" Gabriel asks as he leans back into the chair, crossing his ankle over one knee, making her feel like the most important person on the patio.

"I love to paint. It's therapeutic for me. I'm not a savant by any means, but I do enjoy it."Aella responds sheepishly and toys with a dead piece of skin off of her bottom lip between her teeth. *Ugh, why do I have to be such a mess?*

"I would love to see some of your work. I bet you're a natural! You have yourself a new collector."

Aella can't help but notice how his response drips with enthusiasm, and then her mind went a different direction, thinking of what else could be dripping. *Knock it off, Aella, you sick perv.*

Smirking at him, she says, "We will have to see about that then, won't we?"

Cocking a brow, his eyes darken. This man couldn't get any more sexier even if he tried.

"That we will. It's going to happen."

They sit for a moment longer as Gabriel takes her face in with his eyes one last time before standing up. Unsurprisingly, he towers over her while sitting down but standing, he's a giant compared to her small size. Extending his hand out, Aella returns the gesture, and when his lips brush the back of her wrist, her heart flutters a little.

"Ell, it was a pleasure running into you this morning. I have somewhere to be in a half-hour; otherwise, I would stay and talk with you the rest of the day. Thank you for the little chat and for allowing me to be of aid again." He says teasingly but endearing all the same.

"Gabriel, it was a pleasure running into you as well. Thank you for saving me yet again. I hope our next encounter will be less dramatic." She replies, pursing her lips together, hoping that he doesn't view her as the hot mess she actually is.

"I wouldn't want you any other way. I prefer to see people as they are, and you are perfect," he says with a warm smile. His phone rings then, interrupting their moment. Saying good-bye, he answers while walking off the patio. Aella can scarcely hear a muffled *"be there in 15"*. Then, just as fast as he'd arrived, Prince Charming was gone without any indication of when they would see each other again.

By the time Aella could go through the bookshelves at the library, it was past 2:00 p.m. Not having a library card, she had to apply for one. Unfortunately, the woman who set her up had to be over 100 years old. Time was valuable, and she acted like time was nothing more than a ticking clock. Starting in the history section, Aella worked her way down to religion and science. Spending most of the after-noon into the later evening reading and typing away on her laptop, her notebook was nearly full of notes until something grabs her attention as she reads an old text on a war between kingdoms.

She should have known about this already from taking history in high school, but she skated by. What grabs her atten-tion, however, is a subchapter about what she interpreted could have been referred to as realms at one point in time. Typing the names of the different realms in the search engine of her laptop, she found nothing other than the realms being translated into kingdoms in the late 1200s.

Glancing at a map of the continents on her laptop, they look nothing like what was pictured in the subchapter. It's odd that the only book where she found any mention of realms was when a massive war broke out against different rulers. Although she hated everything to do with academics in high school, history intrigues her now as an adult. Factual evidence is important to her, especially now, since she needs it to prove to herself more than anyone else that she isn't actually going insane.

After getting lost in her extensive research, a security guard comes by the table she has been diligently working at, littered with books and printed-off paper—all from her doing. He is polite even though he looks concerned and informs her that the library is to close in twenty minutes. Checking the time on her phone, which reads 11:00 p.m., she dismisses the thirty missed calls from her mother and Tara.

> Tara: Why are you ignoring me?
> And why are you at the library?!

Putting the books back on the shelves and collecting the research, Aella begins typing as fast as her fingers will allow, with only a few minutes left before the library closes.

> Aella: Sorry Tara, I've been
> researching something all day. I
> will call you tomorrow!

Thanking the security guard, she leaves the library feeling slightly better than before, embarking on this massive journey of a headache. Not able to find too much of what she was looking for, she has some questions she will ask her visitor for when he returns in a few hours. What she knows about her condition is that she has sleep paralysis. But what she still doesn't understand is how that has anything to do with opening portals to different realms. The subchapter on the war between the kingdoms that were considered to be realms is one thing, but not being able to find anything more about it has her intrigued.

SHOVING LEFTOVER PIZZA INTO HER MOUTH, AELLA BREWS a pot of coffee. There is no way in hell she is going to *rest*. It was midnight, and she still had some things to do before her *appointment*. Changing into a pair of yoga pants, she throws her hair up into the staple messy bun she always opts for and sits at the small bistro table she had found at a local thrift shop. Fully aware, she'd doze off the second she lay on her bed. The need to be wide awake so the cat knows she's not to be messed with helps her maintain some form of power.

Going through all the research she'd compiled, Aella began writing out questions to be answered in a fresh notebook. Drinking the *I don't know how many cups I've had today cup of coffee*; she starts to get shaky from all the caffeine, heightening her nerves. Her visitor will be here in an hour, and the realization makes her feet and palms sweat, causing her stomach to cramp. With way too much coffee and not enough time to relieve herself, she puts on a pair of socks and comfortable Adidas to take her mind off of it.

Sitting at the table again, her patience runs thin as she checks the time every few seconds.

This is torture. Every minute that ticks by seems like an hour, making it feel like time itself is slowing as her anxiety grows with every second that passes. *Pull it together, Ell. There is no way out of this; you need answers.*

3:30, and still nothing. With what little patience she has left, the cat suddenly appears on the bed in the same spot as before. Aella startles and scowls in his direction as he sits, waving his tail in idle circles, completely unbothered.

"Oh, goodie, you're awake and...not well rested." He pouts, sitting tall. With the lights on, the cat is even more terrifying than in the dark. Taking in his size fully, he has to be the size of a small bobcat, with his bones protruding from his fur, making Aella uneasy.

"I'll survive." She drawls, not caring for his opinion. Wondering how he would like it if some fucked up creature disturbed his sleep and scared the piss out of him.

"I assume you have some questions you would like answers to. I'll make you a deal, Aella," he says, sounding the slightest bit amused. The desire to punch this cat in the face eases her cramps just a little.

"Why would I make a deal with you? You're the one that came into my home and violated my space." She snaps back, her temper pushing towards the surface.

"You have questions; I have answers. The time you must have spent compiling all that research had to be draining. Tell me, did you find anything in that little book at the library worth of value?"

Anger digs its way into Aella as she stands out of the chair, balling her hands into fists at her sides.

"Tsk Tsk, Aella, anger will not get you anywhere, let alone answers. How about this: I will answer a question for one of my own. You're curious about our realms, and I am curious about yours. Curiosity killed the cat." He sings, waving his tail around and taunting her. She didn't necessarily want to make a deal with him, but she will have to settle for that. She is curious about the realms and what is true in the world.

"You have yourself a deal," she says, trying to tamp down

some of her anger. As annoyed as she is with the uninvited guest, she will have to settle on an agreement.

"I'll answer your first question. You asked who I was yesterday, and I rudely ignored your request. Apologies. You can call me Cahtel. I much prefer that than being called *Cat*." He says dryly.

"What is Isethas?" She says, growing more curious.

"That is what you are going to find out. I will explain when we arrive. The air will be crisp, so bring a sweater. You will need it." Cahtel states, giving Aella an unnatural-toothed smile. She doesn't think she will ever get used to looking at a cat with human-like features in her lifetime.

"Okay, how will we get there?" She asks, not seeing him enter any door. He just appeared out of thin air.

"This is where the fun begins!" He smiles wide, eyeing her as she walks to the dresser to pull out a hoodie. She doesn't trust Cahtel, even though he could have hurt her if he wanted to, and he didn't. Tracking her steps, he continues to hold that toothy grin.

"Ready." She says, pulling the hoodie over her shoulders, grabbing the notebook, and plugging the charger into her cell. She has a feeling she won't need her phone for where they are headed.

Chapter Five

"Close your eyes, Aella. You need to ground yourself for this to work," Cahtel says calmly, although it is easier said than done. The struggle for her to get her subconscious mind to work in opening a portal is all-consuming. Growing extremely frustrated, she feels his paw touch her hand, and the contact jilts her eyes open.

"I don't know how to ground myself. I can't get my mind to turn off! Why can't you do it? I mean, you entered in her yourself, did you not? I don't know how to open a damn portal! I didn't even know that's what I was doing this whole time." The frustration is making the jitters from all the caffeine intake much worse.

"I never left. I am only able to enter when you create a portal, and after our encounter, I knew you weren't going to heed my advice on sleep so that you could subconsciously open another, so I stayed here and hid in your closet." He says, stretching his neck from side to side like he has a kink.

Confusion takes root for Aella then, still not understanding what he means.

"But I saw you vanish! Like you were here one moment and the next you weren't. Then you just appeared out of thin air!"

"It's called teleporting. Now focus," Cahtel says as if doing something is as common as going for a walk.

Her teeth begin to hurt with how hard she's trying to *focus*, but to no avail; nothing happens.

"You've done this before, you see your closet? Imagine there is no door. And instead of a closet, imagine a...hallway."

"Cahtel, you say that, yet I don't realize I'm doing it. I have sleep paralysis, not some magical power or gift. I need you to be more specific? Like how am I just supposed to imagine a hallway out of thin air?"

"When you have this sleep paralysis, what happens? What do you feel in that moment?" He asks, appearing a lot more patient than Aella is.

"It's fucking terrifying, and I want to wake up. I can't move, until I did with you, let alone speak. This all just seems so ridiculous. Maybe I have lost my mind entirely." Her head falls into her hands as she is ready to give up altogether.

"Clear your mind, Aella. Clear it of everything as if you are about to drift off into rest. Don't think about anything. Focus on your breathing and that alone, and allow your subconscious mind to do the rest. Trust me." Cahtel says, and Aella cocks a brow at him like he's the crazy one.

Laying on her back, she takes a deep breath and shuts her eyes. Focusing on clearing her mind except for imagining that she is an orchid still in the ground, roots growing and expanding, keeping her planted in place. Not even a slight breeze can knock her over. A part of her wants to fall asleep now despite still having the caffeine coursing through her body.

After some time, there is nothing—a black void that encapsulates everything around her in her mind. There is no sound or feeling, just floating in the nothingness. She doesn't know how long she's been floating in the nothingness or if she is even present. She's weightless, asleep but not. Cahtel's voice filters through then, like an echo. Nowhere and everywhere all the same.

"We must be cautious about our intentions for the realm we aim to enter. Think only of Isethas, and Isethas alone."

Without having a visual of what Isethas even looks like, Aella thinks of the name and does as instructed. With her eyes still closed, she envisions a hallway leading to this place. A place that might not even exist, and this could really all just be a dream.

"Open your eyes." He commands gently.

The black void continues to suck her in deeper—a paralyzed state of just being. *Wiggle your big toe, wiggle your big toe.* She repeats to herself, and suddenly, the black void eases as the light filters through her closed lids. Gently opening her eyes against the stark bright light, she rubs at her lids, sitting back up on the bed.

"I told you this wouldn't work—"

She looks at the space before her and sees a silvery glow. Anyone could miss it just by walking past, but Aella knows her apartment, and she has created a portal where her sad excuse of a closet stands.

Standing up, she becomes dizzy, swaying from side to side. Cahtel places his paw on her shoulder to keep her steady.

"Careful. The main reason I insisted on your rest was to prevent fatalities," he says sarcastically.

"How? How did I do this?"

"Well, I'm pretty sure you drifted off. You've been out for almost twenty minutes. This is something we will work with you on, but for now, it will do."

Swallowing down the acid that tries to make its way up, her throat feels dry. Knowing that this is what happens when she falls asleep doesn't ease her nerves. Aella hasn't really had much sleep since she can remember, and seeing this firsthand makes her want to curl into a ball and hide forever.

"Come on, we need to get a move on," Cahtel says, bringing her back a little.

Jumping off the bed, Cahtel prompts Aella to follow through the silvery sheen. As she continues to stand, her hesitation keeps her feet firm, but uncertainty evades her.

With a shaky hand, she grazes the invisible wall, not expecting it to feel like anything. The silver swirls dance across her fingers, an energetic force not even the vortexes in Sedona transmit. It's all-consuming in the sense that it feels unnatural. Taking a deep breath, she forces herself to step through, mentally preparing herself for the unknown of what is on the other side.

The hallway, though dark, is dimly lit by wall sconces. Cahtel is standing a few feet before her, with an air of impatience due to the time she's taken from not wanting to enter.

"I understand this is a lot to wrap your head around, but we must keep moving." He says with no amusement, looking at her like she's a child who doesn't listen the first time she's called.

Folding her arms across her chest, she glares back at him.

"Oh, my apologies, *Cahtel*, but you can't just expect me to run into a swirling wall and not be nervous about my survival."

He makes an audible sound of annoyance, huffing through his nose as if this is just a normal everyday thing. He doesn't say another word and turns to stalk down the hallway, which looks like a waking nightmare.

The sconces flicker with every step she takes, and the air is stagnant. Sweat forms at her temple, even though she's not hot. She stays focused on Cahtel, watching his shoulders rotate in that serpentine way of his, hoping that she's not entering into some sort of purgatory.

Once they get close to the end, she looks behind her and has to squint her eyes to make out the silver sheen to the portal, but it's pitch black. They had to have walked for miles, which only took seconds, even if the impending silence seemed much longer.

Cahtel stops before the end of the hallway, the wall appearing to be a black void of nothing.

"Why does this look different than the one we entered?" She asks as a draft blows over her, the void attempting to suck her in.

"Every portal has an opening and a closing. This is the end. Let's just hope you opened the right one. I will warn you, you may feel a little out of sorts when we get through."

Cahtel walks through the black void then, and Aella contemplates running back towards the way she came. *Well fuck. If I die, at least it will be quick.* She thinks before stepping through.

SHAKING LIKE A LEAF, SHE WALKS FORWARD, AND A BLAST of air hits her while it feels like she's being pulled in different directions. The feeling is so intense she can't even form a scream until she's tugged onto the other side. Rolling over, she begins retching; once she's expelled what little she's had in her stomach, she checks to make sure all of her limbs are still intact, breathing evenly. Cahtel is standing over her, looking down with disgust, but Aella could care less, even if the smell of her bile is grotesque.

After taking a few beats to recover, she stands on shaky legs, trying to find her footing. She glances over to where she came out, and the silvery swirling wall she initially entered through is before her in the open field.

"So when we enter a portal, it looks like this, but when we exit it, I feel like I'm being torn apart?" she says, trying to make sense of it all.

"You will get used to the feeling. Only one other person I know of had the ability to create portals, and that was many years ago, and she was Isethanian. Because you are a mortal, we are unsure of how you possess this gift. Be that as it may, portals can be dangerous, especially if the wrong person can access them. Only the person who opens a portal can close it. We will work on that together."

Stumbling to her feet, she takes in what she can see so far of Isethas and the field they entered. It's stunning. The grass is vibrant green and incredibly soft, dancing in the breeze. Looking up, the sky is the color of indigo with giant stars that twinkle with no moon or sun. Continuing to walk down the hill, Aella struggles to keep up with Cahtel, still dizzy from the transportation. The trees are full of life and color, with crimson and yellow leaves suffocating every branch. Weeping willows that have flowers in full bloom fall like rain. The buildings that occupy the realm are something unworldly. Even the little cottages are impressive, built entirely out of glass with green plants decorating the inside.

The people of this realm wave and smile as they walk through the city. Cafes are in full swing, and laughter and conversations echo all around them. Aella can picture herself living in a place like this, which reminds her of a foreign country.

As they are about to head into what appears to be a garden, a winged figure flies down, startling Aella.

Cahtel rolls his eyes, not at all impressed, and as Aella's eyes focus, she can't help but stare at the beautiful man with wings. They are stunning, covered in grey feathers that grace-fully blanket the ground.

"Aella, Torin. Torin, Aella." Cahtel introduces the two dryly.

"So you're the Aella everyone has been talking about. It's a pleasure to meet you," Torin says, extending his hand. Embarrassed by her delay, she quickly reaches her hand out. Giving her a welcoming smile, Torin takes her hand in his and kisses the top of her wrist. She thought it strange since Gabriel was the only other person who had done something similar.

Torin stands tall with his beautiful golden curls falling around his symmetrical face and sparkling brown eyes. His smile is one that could easily send any woman to their knees. Wearing nothing but pants, his olive skin glistens in the sun with a sheen of sweat.

"It's a pleasure to meet you, Torin. I've never seen a real angel before," Aella says. Then laughter booms from him as he looks at her with those eyes sparkling brighter. Mashing her lips together, she hopes that she hasn't offended him.

"What a compliment! I'll take it, although I am no angel." He says, still humored by the compliment.

"Don't flatter yourself, Torin. Is Michael in?" Cahtel retorts, seemingly growing impatient again. It's apparent that Cahtel isn't a fan of Torin. Maybe it has something to do with the fact that he has wings, and Cahtel can't catch him.

"He's in the greenhouse tending to the orchids," Torin says, enjoying Cahtel's discomfort.

Orchids? How ironic.

"Thank you, Torin, if you will excuse us," Cahtel says condescendingly.

"Don't keep him too long. He needs his beauty rest," Torin says before shooting into the sky.

What Aella can make out of the garden as they wander in is magical. Getting lost in its lush blooms of different flowers would be easy with the roses and tulips of every color that line the stone pathway. A vine archway encompasses the walkway, leading into a field of sunflowers and daisies with vibrant poppies that add warmth and peace. Off to the right, a greenhouse sits larger than her apartment.

Cahtel stops Aella from entering as he proceeds forward. She can see through a small window where a man stands with his back to the entrance. His long dark brown hair is tied in a bun at the nape of his neck; Aella watches him as he waters the orchids, taken aback to see they are all white.

Cahtel is speaking with him when he stops watering the flowers. He turns his head slightly, and she can see part of his profile. He is also beautiful, which was no surprise. With his dark brows and long black lashes that curtain his light blue eyes, they appear to be almost pale. Aella can make out a light dusting of facial hair cropped to his defined jaw, and his high cheekbones add perfect symmetry to his facial structure. His nose is intense and looks almost identical to Gabriel's. From his profile, he looks as though the gods carved him themselves.

When Cahtel comes out, he starts walking away from the garden altogether.

"Where are we going?" Aella asks, a little more demanding than intended.

"Michael doesn't want to see you at this time." He responds.

Anger roots inside her as she turns around to march into that greenhouse herself. She did not go through all of this to be pushed away. Aella needs answers, and she won't stop until she gets them.

"Aella! Stop." Cahtel yells frantically, trying to keep her from going inside that greenhouse.

Ignoring his pleas, she barges in. Michael is still watering his orchids as if nothing was amiss.

Unsure of what to do after that courage she built recedes, she stands there, unable to calm the jitters.

Still unfazed by the intrusion, he doesn't turn to face her.

"I am so sorry, sir. I told Aella not to come in here, but she didn't listen to me. Aella, let's go." Cahtel looks at her with urgency in his eyes.

Now, who's the scaredy cat?

"Leave us, Cahtel," Michael says calmly but also sternly. There is power behind it, and she would be lying if it didn't do something to her. Still annoyed that he hasn't turned around to acknowledge her presence, Cahtel looks back at her with a *you're in trouble now* look on his face as he stalks out.

The silence is making Aella even more pissed off. Still watering those stupid orchids, she begins to feel so small.

"What can I do for you, Aella?" He asks so innocently while engulfed in his chore.

"Excuse me?!" She snaps with frustration. The built-up rage is now fire oozing out of her pores.

Setting down his plant mister, he finally turns to face her, and the anger simmers just a little. Leaning against the counter where his orchids sit in immaculate rows, he crosses his arms over his chest.

His body language remains relaxed, even with his sculpted stature. His white button-up bunches where the sleeves are rolled carelessly, yet the intention is there. With the first three buttons unlatched, showing off his naturally bronzed skin, she can't stop gaping at how his chest maps out every cut and curve of his lean muscles. His linen pants hang loose off his hips. Trailing her gaze lower, she notices he isn't wearing any shoes. The way his eyes take in every part of her body, mirroring what she is doing to him, makes her hot inside. He's not making her uncomfortable like every other man has done when they would stare. She feels like this man is worshiping her, really seeing her, and that is power.

Clearing her throat, she says, "I was informed upon arrival that I was to meet you."

His eyes lock into hers before responding with a blank expression.

"That is correct. However, you are late. Plans changed." His tone is even and unbothered.

"Plans changed?!" She says, cringing at the screech, making her sound more like a child and not the woman she is.

"Yes, that is what I said."

Embarrassment and defeat cloud her emotions, making every last-ditch effort for her not to break down in front of him. Aside from the anxiety she'd felt earlier and the exhaustion, she wanted nothing more than to get out of this greenhouse. Being late wasn't her fault. She'd done the best she could. Balling her hands into fists at her side, she turns to leave.

"Stop." He orders.

"Why? You're busy, and I've done enough to interfere with your *propagating*."

"Because," Michael says, still standing there unmoved and unimpressed.

"Because? *Because* isn't an answer I am willing to accept. Good day, or good night, or whatever." Tears are forming from the anger and frustration. But she would not allow them to consume her or show some man in another realm that weakness.

"Because I demand you. Because I was busy, and you interfered with my propagating." Still, there is no amusement in his tone, which causes Aella's jaw to drop. *The fucking nerve.*

"Then I'm leaving!" She shouts and takes off until a hand grabs her arm to keep her in place. It wasn't aggressive, but enough to stun her.

Michael was so fast that she didn't have time to process the response time.

"Let's go for a little walk, shall we?" He says as he escorts her out of the greenhouse.

THEY WALKED THROUGH THE GARDEN IN COMPLETE silence. Aella didn't know why she felt ashamed. Anyone would lose their ever-loving mind if they were in this position. *I'm twenty-three years old, for fuck's sake.* Although she craved the idea of living a normal life and having fun, making mistakes that every other adult in their twenties made, and not having the worst form of sleep paralysis that causes her to open portals into different realms, knowing that the things that haunt her dreams are real slipping through the cracks, she now wishes she never learned about this curse altogether. *Whatever I did in a past life, I hope my karmic lesson is learned.*

A small stone table with cushioned chairs sits near a stream with a willow swaying back and forth. Taking to the chairs, they sit down and listen to the water moving. It was calming, making her less emotional, but it could just as quickly lull her to sleep.

"How is your orchid holding up?" Michael asks, a slight smirk tugging at the corner of his perfectly shaped full lips.

He left the orchid in my car. How the hell?

"How did you leave— you know what, never mind. I have had enough surprises for one day, or night, or whatever."

Amusement fills the space between them as he arches a brow and side-eyes her.

"I didn't leave it personally, no. Cahtel did. Does it not bring you joy?"

Of course, he did.

Thinking about his response momentarily, she bites the inside of her cheek, too tired to argue anymore.

"Orchids are my favorite flower, so yes, it brings me joy. It doesn't make it any less uncomfortable that a stranger left it on my car with a business card, who is now asking me if it brings me joy."

A moment goes by, and Aella decides to continue.

"I just don't understand any of this. Until yesterday, I thought that I was one of the unlucky ones cursed with sleep paralysis. Then Cahtel barges into my life completely uninvited, might I add, and tells me that I can open portals and there are different realms. Not to mention, he's a talking cat, and there are people with angel wings but aren't actually angels?" Unloading this onto Michael makes her feel lighter. The tension was dwindling, and she could finally accept this strange new reality, maybe.

Sitting in silence some more, Michael's brows knit in understanding.

"Cahtel hasn't always been a cat. Many years ago, he was a guardian like Torin. I think he misses the feeling of flying." Michael says, gentling his tone, noticing a flicker of sadness in Aella's eyes.

"I'm going to tell you a story. Whether you want to believe it as truth or merely folklore is up to you." Awaiting a response, Aella nods.

"There was a time when all the realms were joined as a unit. Each realm had an appointed Watcher to them, a ruler or king and queen. During this time, everyone lived amongst each other in complete harmony. There was no hatred, jealousy, or vengeance because no one knew they could feel any of those things. That is until one day, a mother gave birth to two children, twin boys. They grew up to be best friends, playing together and causing havoc.... Until their father grew very ill.

He was the Watcher of Isethas. One of the brothers was to take over the realm when their father passed. An argument broke out between them. You see, one of the brothers wanted to keep the peace and continue life as it was, while the other wanted full power and control over all realms. The tension caused an uproar amongst the rulers of the realms, as they, too, questioned the same thing. Then, a war came. Everyone sought power after the brother spoke about that being a possibility. Greed and hunger for that kind of power rotted the minds of some of our most gentle Watchers; evil overcame them. When the war ended and an agreement was set into motion, the realms broke apart, each forming their own separate realm. In that agreement, the realms were sealed, granting each Watcher the ability to rule over their own how they saw fit without any interference. The only way to access other realms is through a portal."

Digesting what he said, Aella had questions until the last part of his story where it concerns her. Aella's heart suddenly sinks with that knowledge.

"But, I can open portals... Are there any others like me?" She asks with anxiety, rooting its claws into her chest, hoping that she's not the only one.

"Fortunately, no, how you came into this gift is still a mystery. We have been studying you for years. Cahtel discovered you eight years ago when he was checking the lands. It's when he first noticed the portal."

That's where she'd seen Cahtel before. She was only fifteen and thought it was a nightmare. Having completely forgotten all about that, she asks, "So you're telling me that I am the only one with this condition, and you and whoever else has been *studying* me for the last eight years like some lab rat?" She doesn't feel like her own person. She is a prisoner in her body all because she unintentionally has been opening portals.

"Not quite, but I suppose in a sense, yes. Aella, you are the key that many Watchers will seek. If any of them finds out about this gift, another war will break out, causing all the realms to collapse into each other, including the mortal realm." He warns cautiously.

"So why am I here? How do I stop opening portals unintentionally? I do it in my sleep, for fuck's sake." She says with more urgency in her tone. The sooner she could stop this, the sooner her life would become *normal*. She's willing to give her left breast for a normal life at this point.

"You are here, Aella, so we can help you suppress your gift and prevent it from happening—for now and for eternity."

"But I still don't understand; being here won't prevent it from happening. I have a life and my mother and Tara." For a moment, it seemed her whole world was crumbling down around her.

"You will not remain here indefinitely; our goal is to aid you in honing your ability. You've already tripped the wire in your sleep. I guarantee others know there is a key but haven't found the source yet. Once we have worked on suppressing this part of you to the point where you forget you can do this all together, you should never be able to open another portal ever again."

Aella was fucked. She knew she was cursed, but this was no gift. It was a burden.

"Okay, so by suppressing my gift, I won't be able to open a portal, and my sleep paralysis will finally come to an end?" She asks impulsively, wanting to get the ball rolling.

"Because your subconscious opens portals when you are in REM sleep, and in turn, you have sleep paralysis from it, then yes. I suppose it will fix your condition."

Aella blinks, processing how much easier all this sounded than actually doing it. Michael stands from the stone chair and leads Aella back to the greenhouse without so much as another word.

This is whack.

CAHTEL IS PERCHED IN A TREE NEXT TO THE GREENHOUSE when they arrive, looking up at the sky. Aella wants to ask him about his former life before he became a cat, but it would take some time for that trust to build for them both before she would be comfortable asking something so intimate.

"Enjoy your stroll?" Cahtel says nonchalantly as they get within earshot.

"It was informative," Aella's response is dry. The sooner they can get this under control, the sooner she can get away from Cahtel. This whole time, she spent countless hours researching and trying to cure a disease that couldn't be cured; all the while, it was never a disease. She couldn't help but wonder if her father may have possessed the same condition as her, given she never knew her father; the thought made her curious to find out what she could. Not knowing what he looked like or where he was, she didn't have a name to go off of since she'd taken her mother's surname, Clarke. Susan had told her that he was mentally unstable and had episodes but never clarified what those episodes entailed.

"Cahtel, I am going to send Aella home with a combination of sleep herbs and suppressants. She knows why she's here, and we will do everything we can to help her. Your duty will be to ensure she follows the schedule for when to take the herbs. Training will start in two days," Michael informs.

Jumping out of the tree, Cahtel gracefully lands on all four legs.

"Yes, sir," he responds as they walk inside.

Michael opens a cupboard that has jars and tinctures of various sizes. Pulling out bottles with different dried herbs, he measures them on a scale and combines the concoction into sachets. Once the sachets were filled, he carefully ties them off and places them neatly in a box. Opening an empty glass bottle, he pours liquid from the tinctures, creating an elixir. Once satisfied with the right amount, he seals off the bottle, giving it a little shake. The liquid swirls in the bottle, changing the transparent color to a deep purple. Wrapping the bottle with a cloth, he sets that into the box alongside the sachets, closing the lid.

"Aella, write this down in your notebook." He instructs. Fumbling with the pad, she drops it, then quickly picks it up again. Cahtel sighs, causing Michael to glare in his direction.

"In this box are twelve sachets and a bottle. You must brew one sachet every evening before sleep at the same time and drink it with nothing else thirty minutes prior. This tea will guide you into a resting state. However, you will not go directly into REM. It is enough to rest your mind and body, but you will still feel tired, leaving your conscious mind awake but turning the subconscious part of it off. Please start this tonight. The only time you will not take the herb is when Cahtel returns for you. The bottle is a stimulant. It is incredibly potent, so only one drop under your tongue when Cahtel is with you at 3:30 a.m. mortal time. Twelve sachets for twelve days. After our ten days of training, you will have full control of your gift and lose the ability to open a portal again." Writing down Michael's instructions, Aella was curious about why it had to be 3:30 a.m. every morning, so she asked.

"Are you familiar with what that time in the human realm signifies? It has a different meaning to everyone. Some believe it to be the bewitching hour. 3:30 a.m. is when you're most inept at opening a portal. I know it's not ideal. However, it is the only time that we have noticed it happen." Michael explains, and it makes sense. Even when she would nap occasionally during the day, she didn't have the feeling that something else was there with her.

"Cahtel isn't the only *visitor* I've had. Are others able to do this?" She asks, and Michael's jaw tightens, his brows creasing, causing her to worry.

"What did these visitors look like?"

"Not like Cahtel." She replies jokingly. Closing her eyes, she tries to remember what they looked like.

"They were dark... not the body, they were cloaked. Elongated fingers that were cold, and—"

Michael cuts her off, interrupting her train of thought with an edge to his tone, "Did they have eyes?"

"No, they were empty. Dead." For a moment, she couldn't tell if she had said something wrong. Cahtel and Michael look at each other knowingly, sending chills down her body.

"Aella, what visited you was no guardian from our realm. It sounds like it could have been a succubus, but I am unsure of what realm it came from. It could have come from Diatturus, a realm that once was peaceful, like Isethas, but is now full of evil and death. Cahtel, ask Torin about Damien's whereabouts." Michael orders, with stress taking hold for a split second.

"On it. Aella, I must get you back home first. There is a lot to be done." Cahtel says, nudging her leg.

Knowing that a succubus is what came through that night doesn't make her feel any better, nor does Michael, as he seems unsure of where it originated from.

Even after parting ways, Aella will be back in two days, and the work has barely started. Being near Michael made her feel at peace, or was it Isethas that beckoned her to stay and never return to her shitty life. What she saw so far in this realm made her long for something more than what she had. She wanted to explore and visit where Michael lived along with the rest of the realm. She wondered if he was a boxers or briefs guy, or maybe he didn't wear anything, given his lack of shoes. *Stop thinking inappropriate things, Aella.* She needed to get laid desperately. Michael is intriguing, though, forbidden fruit. Although they have a duty and a mission, she didn't see any harm in fantasizing; anything could happen in the next twelve days.

Chapter Six

C losing the portal took more energy than opening it did. Despite Cahtel assuring Aella that it would become second nature, she had difficulty believing it. Once she had made it through, she did what Cahtel had instructed from when she initially opened it, even though he was on the other side. Grounding herself will take more work, along with turning her conscious mind off without falling asleep.

Wiggle your big toe, wiggle your big toe, wiggle your big toe.

Coming out of the haze, she sits up to look at the wall and notices that the silver glow is gone, except for a tiny sparkle in the upper right corner.

Just to make sure the portal is, in fact, shut, she swipes across it and realizes that it is nothing more than the wall inside of her apartment.

Probably just an after-effect, Aella shrugs, examining the fissure as it appears to be stretching.

Checking the time, she notices that it is the same as when they initially left. For the tea to work, she needed to reset her internal clock. Taking the bottle out of the box with the stimulant, she did as instructed without Cahtel present. *I'm sure it's fine.*

The high she experiences is out of this world. No amount of caffeine or cocaine could give her the energy and euphoria she is feeling. If this stuff were available for purchase, everyone would become addicted. Michael had informed her that the buzzing desire that would come with it would subside after fifteen minutes, heightening every sensation. It is pure ecstasy, and she hates that she is alone in the apartment.

The high wore off after fifteen minutes, and she was surprised that she no longer felt exhausted. She was still slightly fatigued, but nothing like she had been feeling. Becoming dependent on the elixir is why it's advised to use it in moderation. Cahtel had made sure she had everything for the next couple of days before he returned for her, running over the times she would take the tea, which became annoying by the third run-through. He also instructed her to lay salt along the edges of the floorboards. *Susan would love that.*

One of the few rituals that keep evil entities away is that they don't like the smell of salt, Cahtel had told her, because it burns their senses. Aella had asked him about sage, and he informed her that it had medicinal uses and was an excellent herb, but it was more of a nuisance than anything. If a succubus or entity wanted in, they would suffer through the smell, but it doesn't hurt in combination with the salt. Sage does a great job of clearing out negative energy.

Looking at the time once more, 4:30 a.m. Aella decides to make some more coffee, opens the windows to air out the staleness, and lights the bundle of sage Susan had left. Stripping the sheets off of her bed from the accident she had the other night, now is the perfect time than any to clean the apartment.

The last time she deep-cleaned was three months ago, and she would be lying if she admitted that she was not ashamed of how she'd been living in such a mess. Unsure of what clothes are clean or dirty, she scoops them up along with the sheets, stuffs them into a basket, and heads down to the laundry room in the basement.

The laundry room is empty, which is no surprise, given how early in the morning it is. She likes that she has first pick on the washers and dryers. The ability to get all the laundry done in one go excites her.

Placing the sheets, darks, and lights in three separate washers, she hits start and walks back to her apartment. When she gets to the door, however, it is open. Unease quickly rushes over her. She was almost sure she had shut the door behind her when she'd left. Pushing it open slowly, Aella peeks around the corner. The open concept didn't make it easy to go unspotted because it's a studio apartment. With little hiding unless you try to fit in the closet or bathroom, in which case Cahtel made himself at home while he overstayed his welcome.

Stepping in, she walks to the bathroom, turns the light on, and pulls back the shower curtain. Feeling relief that no one is to be found, Aella brushes off the eerie feeling and proceeds to turn on a Bluetooth speaker and connect her phone, opening the music app. Playing her trusty 80's radio station, she starts with the kitchen, washing dishes, and throwing away expired food. By the time she finished scouring her apartment and making the bed, it was only 7:00. Having more energy to burn off from the elixir, she contemplates what to do next.

Twiddling her thumbs, she picks up her phone and dials Tara. Tara always has Tuesdays off, and since Aella isn't scheduled back to work until tomorrow, a girl's day is just what the doctor ordered.

"Hello?" Tara answers, voice scratchy and sleep-riddled.

"Hey, girl! What are you doing?" Aella asks energetically.

"Uh, sleeping, Ell, like a normal person. How long have

you been up, and why do you sound like you snorted some crack?" Tara asks with suspicion, ready to fall back asleep at any moment.

"A few hours, I cleaned my apartment. It smells and looks so fresh! Want to hang out? I need a girl's day!" Pacing around, Aella is afraid to sit down with how wired she is.

"Yeah, let me get up and shower—"

"Great! I'll be over in 30!" Aella cuts her off and hangs up the phone.

Jumping in the shower, she scrubs at her body as fast as possible, avoiding getting her hair wet. Pulling out a pair of jeans and a T-shirt, she throws them on at an unnatural speed while brushing her teeth and throwing her hair up in a knot. Admiring the clean apartment, she walks over to the orchid.

To her surprise, it had grown twice its original size since she put it in a glass of water and hadn't noticed it while she was cleaning. Making a mental list, she adds a pot and fresh soil to it. While she inspects the orchid, she notes the roots that are now expanding around the stem. Shocked that a cut orchid could do such a thing, she is impressed nonetheless.

As Aella parks in the empty spot next to Tara's car, she receives a text from an unknown number. Sliding the screen open, it reads,

```
Unknown: Hey, Ell, it's Gabriel.
I got your number from Georgia
at your job. I hope that's okay.
Some friends of mine and I went
in on Sunday for a couple of
beers and to watch the game. She
asked if I was seeing anyone,
and I told her I had eyes on a
girl I met at Blanc. When I told
her about you, she gave me your
number. Small world!
```

Her heart does that little flutter again. Holding back the urge to text him immediately, she shoves her phone in her purse and jumps out of the car, sprinting to Tara's condo. Busting through the door, Tara is in the middle of making coffee in her kitchen with two mugs and creamer on the counter.

"Tara, guess what! That guy Gabriel from Blanc just texted me! Oh my god, I can't believe he texted me!" Aella shouts, jumping up and down with giddy joy.

Tara tenses from Aella's excitement and snaps, "Ell, what the fuck is up with you? I haven't even had the first sip of my coffee yet!" *Someone woke up on the wrong side of the bed.*

"How did he get your number? You didn't give it to him?" She then says, slightly weirded out.

"No, that's the thing, he never asked for it, and we ran into each other yesterday at *Happy Grinds* and talked for a few minutes, but it never got brought up. Georgia from work gave it to him the other day! Maybe he didn't want to tell me when he saw me because that would have been weird?" Aella explains still not able to contain the excitement, as well as the energy from the stimulant.

"Hmm, don't you think that's a little odd? He didn't ask you for your number at *Blanc* or when you ran into each other at *Happy Grinds* the second time meeting, but he got it from your coworker?" Tara responds with a tinge of judgment and skepticism in her voice. Ruining Aella's high, the urge to snap back at her is short-lived as she mentally agrees that it was odd he didn't, or at least give her a business card with his number on it.

"It is a little strange, but he is so hot and mysterious. Maybe he didn't want to come off too forward. I don't know. Either way, he has it now, and I have his!" Caring less about Tara's opinion right now, she was on cloud nine, and given what she had gone through the past few days, she wasn't going to let anyone ruin her little happy dance, no matter how small it was.

Taking a few sips of coffee and eying Aella warily, she says with skepticism laced in her tone still, "I'm happy for you, Ell. Just be selective and careful. Guys can be assholes, don't give yourself away quickly, make him work for it."

Aella grabs the second mug, nearly dropping it from her shaking hands, and Tara's eyes bug out of her head, judging how much caffeine Aella has already consumed. Then she shakes her head and laughs as Aella grabs the pot, filling the third cup she has been eager to consume since cleaning the apartment.

They spent the morning chatting about life and the first date Tara had gone on that they lined up when Aella had slept over. It was a disaster. She said the guy was a complete douche, and when the check came, his card was declined, so she had to pay for it. It wouldn't have been an issue had he not been a complete jackass, only talking about himself and how much of an outstanding person he was. *Gross*, Aella hates that for Tara. Her encounters with Gabriel didn't feel like that, but it was still early. He at least asked more about her in the small moments they shared than he talked about himself, which reminded Aella to text him back. It had been long enough.

> Aella: Hey stranger, I will have
> to thank Georgia for giving you
> my contact information. Small
> world indeed, how are you?

Hitting send, she sets her phone down on the coffee table, returning her full attention to Tara.

Quirking a brow, Tara asks, "Did you text him back?"

"Yes, yes I did!" Aella beams, grinning from ear to ear. She hadn't felt this excited over a boy, let alone a man, in a long time.

When her phone vibrates, she immediately snatches it off the coffee table, opening his message.

> Gabriel: I've been decent. Work
> has me by the balls right now,
> though. What are you doing this
> evening? I know it's a school
> night, but I wanted to ask you
> to dinner.

"Well, what did he say?!" Tara demands as growing excitement begins to radiate from her, a drastic shift from when Aella first arrived.

"He wants to go to dinner tonight. What should I say? I want to go but don't want to come off too needy!" Feeling anxious and nervous, Aella needs Tara to tell her how to respond; Aella has never been great at this, especially when she is interested in someone, for fear of rejection.

"Ask him where he wants to take you. That way, you know if it's formal or semi-formal. Then, await his response. When he does respond, tell him that you had a prior engagement, but this one time, you would reschedule. Show him that you are a very busy girl and your time is of value." *That is good.* Tara has always been so smooth with her delivery, being a much more seasoned dater than Aella.

Doing what Tara suggested, Aella could tell that Gabriel became even more interested. Letting her know that the restaurant is semi-formal and reservations were made for 7:00. Aella told him she would meet him there, still not entirely comfortable with him knowing where she lives yet. She is also ashamed of her tiny apartment and assumes that he probably lives in a penthouse in Scottsdale.

After agreeing to the date, Aella and Tara went shopping for a new dress since the clothes she owned wouldn't fit the bill, given what she'd brought over to choose from for their outing at Blanc. Aella had difficulty justifying spending over $20 on a T-shirt and shopped primarily at secondhand stores.

They did end up going to the mall and found a sexy red dress at *Nordstrom's*, reminding her of the color Gabriel's suit was when they first met at Blanc. A deep crimson red that could have looked black from a distance, Tara and Aella were elated until she looked at the price tag sticking out the side of the dress.

"Tara, I can't afford this. It's $150..." She says, saddened by the discovery.

"Ell, sometimes you have to spend a little to get a little. This dress is amazing on you! It fits you like a glove. One look at you in this, you'll have him wrapped around your finger." She urges while Aella glances at her reflection in the mirror wearing the dress.

It looks incredible, and she feels confident wearing it. Biting her lip, she stares at herself and dreams a little about Gabriel's reaction. *Fuck it, you only live once*, reminding herself of all that she has coming up in the following weeks; a little fun won't hurt anyone.

Wrapping up their morning and afternoon filled with shopping and eating, Tara and Aella part ways. She has less than two hours to prepare for her date, but she still needs to stop by the local nursery to find the right pot for her orchid. What she loved most about this mom-and-pop shop was how affordable everything is, unlike your large corporate hardware stores. Shopping locally is her favorite, especially when she finds a hidden treasure.

Rushing into her apartment, she runs straight to the closet to hang the dress, airing out the wrinkles. Proceeding to the kitchen, where the orchid alarmingly grew out of the glass, she quickly opens the bag of soil. Taking the ceramic sap green pot she purchased, she begins filling the bottom. Carefully placing the orchid inside, she covers the roots and pours more soil, packing it gently until it is complete. Checking the time, Aella frantically runs to the bathroom to get ready with only forty-five minutes to spare.

She had gotten so lost in the nursery observing every plant and pot that she lost track of time.

Finally ready, she zips the dress up and mists the air with *Yves Saint Laurent, Black Opium,* walking through, letting the perfume blanket her skin in a light dusting. She only ever wears it for special occasions or a date because it is her favorite and because of how expensive the bottle is. Opting for a pair of black strappy wedges, she makes a mental note to keep it semi-formal. Taking one last look in the full-sized mirror, smoothing out the dress and her straightened hair, she grabs her purse, keys, and cell phone and heads for the door.

THE RESTAURANT IS NOWHERE CLOSE TO SEMI-FORMAL...IT is formal. Two cars are ahead of her for valet, so Aella grabs her phone to text Tara quickly.

Aella: TARA… I feel so
underdressed. I should turn
around and tell him I'm sick or
something. This place is beyond
formal! I can't be seen like
this!

Because Tara always has her phone on her, she never sets it too far away. Usually scrolling *Instagram* and *Twitter* any chance she can get.

Tara: I'm sure you'll be fine.
That dress looked amazing! Don't
stress about it! Call me as soon
as your date ends. I want every
detail!

When it's her turn to get out of the car so the valet can take it wherever the parking garage is, Aella gives the attendant her name and asks him how much it will cost. She had no issues parking it somewhere else and walking a few blocks back to the restaurant, but she would be at least twenty minutes late if that were the case.

He smiles and informs her that it was already taken care of. Gabriel either pitied her or was being a gentleman. Either way, she didn't want someone she barely knew paying for her car to be parked.

After she hands the attendant her keys with trepidation, she walks into the steakhouse. The hostess greets her with a friendly smile and asks for the reservation. Once she gives her the name, the hostess stalls slightly, turning her nose up, clearly judging the not-so-formal dress and shoes. Most likely assuming that Aella was an escort, considering every other woman who walked into this restaurant wore *Versace* and heels. Stalling momentarily, she gives a tight-lipped smile and walks Aella to the table where Gabriel is already sitting. A server stands by with a bottle of wine and two long-stemmed glasses. A rush of embarrassment sweeps over Aella due to her tardiness, but Gabriel stands up, thanks the hostess, and kisses the top of her hand, pulling out the seat for her unbothered.

"You look exquisite, absolutely beautiful, Ell." He whispers in her ear before he retakes his seat. Feeling her cheeks redden, she smiles at the compliment.

"Thank you. You look very handsome yourself." She replies shyly, and he does. Tonight, he's in an all-black button-up dress shirt tucked into a pair of black slacks and a belt. His hair is styled, keeping the same textured, unkept look, making Aella wonder what running her fingers through his locks would feel like.

Sensing her desire, Gabriel nods to the server to pour the wine into a glass, letting Aella take the first sip. The wine is a full-bodied red blend. She didn't love blends, but this one is delightful. With her approval, the server pours their glasses and leaves the bottle on the table. Glancing at the menu, Aella's curiosity tugs at her about how much the bottle costs. Searching for it on the menu, her eyes widen, costing more than the dress she just purchased. Noticing her reaction, Gabriel reaches over and grazes his fingers over the menu to pull her attention towards his.

"Order whatever you wish, Ell. The price is no issue." He assures with a gentle smile. The first dates Aella had been on in the past were never this fancy. She typically went for more of the sports bar feel, considering the guys she attracted were dense and cheap. It was a rarity for one of them to fit the tab, resulting in her slapping her card out and gesturing to split the bill. Every blue moon, she would get someone waving it away and telling her next time they can split it. Eating at an expensive restaurant was something she considered to be pretentious and stupid, especially when it came to buttered steak that you could grill yourself at home for a fraction of the price. Trying to find the cheapest thing on the menu, which is bread, she decided the chicken Caesar salad would do. They didn't even give you bread for free, *unbelievable*.

"I'm sorry, I've never been to a nice place like this. I feel underdressed. I thought you said it was semi-formal?" She blurts, unintentionally sounding somewhat frustrated.

Gabriel is intently looking over the menu, taking his time. Shutting it, he sets it down, and his full attention returns to Aella as he folds his hands together before him in a relaxed way.

"It is semi-formal, and you look amazing. Did I do or say something wrong?" He asks, knitting his brows. Her cheeks warm again, knowing that she probably sounded like a brat. Softening her features, she reaches over, touching his hand for assurance.

"Not at all, Gabriel. I'm just not used to being wined and dined. It's nothing on you, and I appreciate you taking me to a nice place and paying for the valet," and she meant it. Aella needed to check herself and her pride. Gabriel was different; he wasn't like any of the men she'd pined over in the past.

"Good, but don't thank me yet. Do you know what you want to order? The lamb is my favorite." He says with a gleam in his eyes, but the thought of ordering Lamb unsettled her. For whatever reason, she felt terrible eating the animal because they are so cute and innocent, which sounds hypocritical considering she is no vegetarian and loved a fat juicy burger after a night of drinking.

"I think I'll do the Chicken Caesar salad."

"You don't want a steak or the lamb? It is delicious here. They cook their meat at a low temperature, keeping it tender and juicy."

The way he said tender and juicy makes her feel tender

and juicy. Maybe she should have let him pick her up. However, she needed to keep to her three-date rule. No sex until after she's had at least three dates, then it's game on!

"I had a late lunch with Tara. The salad actually sounds perfect!" She says, and they both smile, unable to keep their eyes and hands away from each other. When the server comes by to take their order, he brings another bottle of the red blend to the table, making Aella realize she would have to take an Uber home since she was on her second glass already.

When the food arrives at their table, it smells delicious. The salad was surprisingly delicious, which she had hoped for, given that it was triple the price of an ordinary Chicken Caesar salad.

Aella didn't know what to say in the quiet moments between bites of their food. Gabriel made her nervous, and she didn't want to ruin their date by saying anything awkward.

Taking a bite of his lamb, Gabriel smiles and cuts a piece off for Aella to try placing it on her plate.

"One bite, you won't regret it, I promise. How is your salad?" He asks, and then his eyes sparkle when she shoves the piece of lamb into her mouth, chewing it as she savors the taste.

"It's perfect; your lamb is delicious, too."

"So, tell me," Gabriel says, wiping his mouth off with the linen napkin even though he doesn't have so much as a piece of pepper on his face, "what is it you and Tara did today?"

Aella is caught off guard by the question; they didn't do anything too crazy, and she didn't want to bore him with their girly activities.

"We just hung out and had a little bit of a girl's day— nothing crazy, really. What did you do today?" she asks, keeping the conversation flowing.

"I worked at the office for a little bit and messaged a woman I'm interested in getting to know more about; other than that, *nothing crazy,"* Gabriel responds, winking. Aella rolls her eyes and smirks back at him, feeling loose from her two glasses of wine and into her third.

Leaning back into the chair, Gabriel drapes his arm over the backrest and says, "I am curious about what other engagement you had that you rescheduled for me."

Shit. Think Aella, think... where is Tara when I need her?

Sipping from her wine glass, Aella thinks of a believable fib she can tell.

"Oh, that? That was—"

"Nothing crazy?" Gabriel asks teasingly while quirking a brow, and then he laughs, "I like you, Ell; I wanted to take you to dinner even if you didn't have a prior *engagement.*"

Aella's jaw drops open slightly. *Is it that obvious that I don't have a life?*

"Well, thank you. I appreciate you wanting to take me to dinner." She says, trying not to take offense to what Gabriel said.

Gabriel changes the subject, and they continue talking about little things, keeping the main focus on Aella. Asking her about where she was from initially and, about her mother, Susan, down to what her favorite music to listen to is.

After they finished dinner, Aella checks the time on her phone and is stunned at how long they had been talking for. Since scooting their chairs so close, Aella feels loose and relaxed from the wine. Her desire for Gabriel had grown more vital from their date, and the want to take him on this table was heavy. She wondered if he felt the same way since his hand was resting on her upper thigh, sending electrical waves to where she needed to be touched.

Once the tab comes, Gabriel removes his hand from her upper thigh, leaving a cold chill in its wake as he reaches into his jacket to pull out his wallet. Placing his black American

Express card in the check presenter, Aella peers over to see how much the tab is and nearly falls out of her chair when it reads $500, not including tip. Gabriel hands the bill to their server, completely unfazed that he's spending that much on a first date, and Aella almost considers breaking her three-date rule just this once.

"I'm too drunk to drive. I should call an Uber," Aella says as she reaches for her purse.

"Let my driver take you. Your car is safe here tonight. I'll have Ben pick you up tomorrow morning and escort you back to your car." Gabriel insists, and Aella is too drunk to care or argue.

"Thank you for everything, Gabriel. The dinner and wine were, *chef's kiss*, amazing."

Her quirky remark and hand gesture cause Gabriel to chuckle and look at her endearingly.

"Thank you for accompanying me, Ell, shall we?" He says. They both stand up and walk out hand in hand together, and Aella can't help but cock her head slightly over the hostess that snubbed her on the way out, smirking as they exit the restaurant.

Ben is already pulled up, waiting outside the black Escalade, greeting them as he opens the back door. Aella climbs in first as Gabriel follows, and the air between them becomes thick with need. Thirty seconds is all it takes when Aella makes the first bold move before Ben takes the driver's seat. Straddling Gabriel's legs, their lips come together in the most sinful, seductive way. There is nothing gentle about it, dancing their tongues across each other's open mouths.

She couldn't get enough of him if she tried. His hands grab her upper thighs, applying the pressure her body so desperately craves. She can feel his hard length between her thighs, begging to bust through the seam of his slacks. Aella's panties are soaked, and she is ready to take it one step further until Ben clears his throat, reeling them back in. Sliding off Gabriel's lap, she looks down to see his arousal, causing her to bite her bottom lip.

"Where to sir?" Ben asks with composure as if what was happening in the back seat was nothing.

Gabriel looks at Aella with lust and desire in his eyes, staring at her disheveled state. This is far from over.

"My apartment is fine, thank you, Ben," Gabriel replies, slightly out of breath.

Putting the car in drive, Aella was ready to be devoured like she'd watched Gabriel devour his little lamb.

Chapter Seven

Gabriel's apartment is more significant than Aella's childhood home. Walking through the front door, she takes every square inch in awe. The vaulted ceilings open the apartment, making you feel like you can breathe, unlike the stuffy studio she rents. With the white walls, the paintings hanging in a line create a beautiful gallery. The living room appears simple, with only two grey sofas in the center facing a wall entirely made of bookshelves littered with books.

A cement coffee table nestles between the sofas, decorated with candles and plants. The only colors she can see are the paintings and a large textile rug, most likely hand-woven from another country. The floors are all epoxy concrete, reflecting the canister lights embedded in the ceiling.

Following Gabriel around the corner of a wall that separates the living room is the largest kitchen she has ever seen. It looks like something that would make the magazines Tara subscribes to jealous. Stainless steel appliances, white cabinets, and a quartz island sit in the center for prepping, which would aid in every cook's dream.

Gabriel stops beside her unrushed, giving her time to roam every corner with her eyes. After a moment, he smiles and takes her hand, leading her down a hallway. Thinking they would get straight to business, he turns another corner, which leads into a lounge with a bar.

A very classy and sophisticated lounge, with a desk in the space and a couple of leather chairs. Decanters of liquid line the shelves behind the bar, and a fully stocked wine fridge the size of her studio's fridge stands by. Moving behind the bar, Gabriel pulls out a wine glass and a tumbler.

"Would you like a glass of wine? Or something else?" He asks, grabbing a decanter of bourbon off the shelf.

"Wine is perfect, thank you." She responds, seemingly still impressed by his apartment.

"Feel free to pick a bottle out of the fridge. If you don't see anything you like, I have a cellar we can walk through."

A fucking cellar?! How the hell could he have a cellar in a penthouse apartment?

"I'm sure I can find something in the fridge. This apartment is incredible. I had no idea an apartment could be so big."

Gabriel opens a metal ice bucket and adds two cubes to his tumbler, coating them with the bourbon. Swirling the liquid around, Aella allows him to take a sip first before handing him a bottle of Pinot she found. While he uncorks the bottle, she hoists herself onto the bar. Pouring a tasting amount into the glass, he waits for Aella to try it before filling it. Giving her approval, he tops it off and then hands the now full glass back and leans against the back bar with his bourbon in hand, watching her like prey.

Feeling the heat from his gaze, she starts to count every decanter along the wall, impressed that he knew what was inside of each bottle since there were no labels. Sipping her wine, their gazes latch.

Pushing off the bar, Gabriel creeps in, closing the space to where there is only a few inches of separation. Setting his glass down, he places his hands on either side of her hips, leaning on the counter.

"What are you thinking about right now?" He asks, whispering into her ear as he begins kissing the side of her neck. Letting out a soft moan at the feel of his lips, Gabriel growls in approval.

"I'm thinking about your big beautiful...apartment." She responds seductively, even with the nervous flutter, enjoying his pause when big and beautiful leave her lips. Biting her lower lip, he moves his face only a breath space from hers, his blue eyes hungry with sensation and desire.

"If you do that again, Ell, I don't think I'll be able to control myself." He says, moving his hands closer to her hips. Due to Aella's stubbornness, she does precisely that. Grabbing her hips, he pulls her in close with no space between. In a rush, his lips are on hers again. With them both eager and greedy, they suck and nip at each other until they are both swollen. Reaching up, Aella threads her fingers into his hair, tugging gently. Another growl escapes him, kissing her more profoundly with every tug and pull. His large hands move down her thighs, exploring her soft skin, then slowly trailing his fingers under the hem of her dress. Feeling the small piece of fabric that clings to her hips, he stalls momentarily.

"What's wrong?" Aella breathes with her cheeks and chest still flush from the wine and arousal.

"Nothing is wrong, Aella, you are perfect. I want you so badly, but I also want you to know that once I have you, I am never letting you go."

The confession startles her, reeling her back to reality a little. Gabriel seems perfect from what she has gathered this far, but he is still a stranger. She didn't really know what to say, especially when things were getting so hot and heavy for a moment.

"Fuck, I just ruined this moment, didn't I?" He says, hands still firmly planted on the counter, looking away from her. Clearing her throat, she pulls his attention back towards her.

"No, you didn't ruin the moment. I would like to get to know you a little bit better before we do anything too intimate. Three-date rule!" she says awkwardly, attempting to defuse their awkwardness.

"I know we just ate, but are you hungry? I'm thinking a late-night snack is a necessity." He says in a calm voice against the shell of her ear.

"I would love a snack." She responds in the same way he spoke. Anything to spare her this awkward moment is appreciated.

Helping her down from the counter, she tugs on the bottom of her dress to straighten herself out while they walk out to the kitchen. Even though she's sexually frustrated, she can't imagine how Gabriel must feel, given the fact that he now has to live with blue balls. In all fairness, she appreciates the fact that he stopped even in the heat of the moment, and even though she was more than willing to give herself to him completely, he gets brownie points.

Sliding out one of the barstools at the island, she sits down while watching Gabriel as he grabs an apple and a cutting board.

Placing the sliced apples on a plate, he scoops peanut butter onto a spoon and spreads each slice with precision. Licking his fingers, he hands over the plate, leading her to his paintings.

"I want to show you some of my collection while you enjoy your snack. At *Happy Grinds,* you mentioned wanting to attend art school. Maybe this will trigger some inspiration." He says with amusement.

Biting into the apple slice, a moan slips from her throat. It is the most crisp, juicy apple she'd ever eaten, bursting with flavor and color. A small dribble of juice escapes, running down her chin. Gabriel notices and chuckles, scooping the juice that trails down her chin with his finger.

"Sorry," she says sheepishly, enjoying the apple.

"Don't apologize for something like that ever." He responds, "Come, I want to show you my favorite painting."

Trailing after him, she's mindful not to drop any of the slices or dribble juice onto the epoxy. Stopping before the painting, however, she nearly drops the plate entirely. She can't believe she is looking at *Death and Life* by Gustav Klimt. It is one of her favorite paintings by him, not only because of his use of color but the way she perceives it. On the one hand, you have this dynamic of a mother holding her child and the emotionalism of the circle of life. On the other, you have something equivalent to death or the Grim Reaper watching and waiting. It's powerful in that, no matter what, there is always death in life and vice versa.

"Is this the original, or is it a remake?" She asks in disbelief, especially if it was the latter.

Smirking at her question, he says, "I only ever purchase original works of art, or I don't purchase a piece at all. The sentimental value is no longer intact if you purchase a remake."

Before she has time to stop it, her brows shoot up her forehead at that remark. It's unbelievable that the piece she is looking at is the original. Aella understood the statement about original art being more sentimental and valuable. However, not everyone could purchase an original Klimt painting. Even if they could, it would cost hundreds of millions, and even then, having one in your possession would be impossible.

"So you're telling me you purchased *Death and Life* by Klimt?" She says, still in disbelief.

"Not quite. I inherited this painting from an old friend of mine. I have a deal with some European museums that allow them to showcase the painting at certain times throughout the year. It's your lucky night because it will be packaged and shipped back next week." Tears begin to fill her eyes. She is inches away from one of her favorite paintings in the world, and it's the original. Stepping away, she didn't want to breathe on the painting wrong. Photos didn't do this painting the justice it deserves.

She continues to stare at *Death and Life* for twenty minutes before moving down the wall. If she were Gabriel, she would be stressed out about people knowing she had this collection. Each painting he has is priceless. If the wrong person knew, they would become the wealthiest man or woman on the planet.

By the time she's had her fill on every piece of art, Gabriel takes the plate from her hands and heads back to the kitchen. Sleep was starting to call to her then, and when she checks the time on his oven, it was a quarter after two in the morning. That awkward feeling came over her again as she did not want to overstay her welcome or assume she was to stay the night, so she asked Gabriel if she should call an Uber.

"Are you crazy? It's a quarter after two in the morning!" He says dramatically, making it seem as though he's offended by the assumption.

Turning to wash the plate, he says, "Nonsense, you can have my bed, and I'll sleep on the sofa. I have a meeting early in the morning. Ben can give you a lift back to your car whenever you're ready to leave. Unless you would rather have Ben take you now, but be forewarned, he's cranky when he gets woken up at this time."

"No, that's alright. I don't want to disturb him. If you don't mind me staying here, that's very kind of you. I can sleep on the couch," she says, trying not to sound as uncomfortable as she feels, even though she had no issues straddling him in the back of the car while devouring his face.

Waving his hand to dismiss her offer, he grabs a glass and fills it with water for her. Walking the glass over to her, he takes her down the hall to his bedroom.

The room is dimly lit with wall sconces, and there is only a king-size bed in the center with dark grey satin sheets. A minimalist through and through. The bed was big enough for both of them, but she didn't want to push anything. Opening his closet, he pulls down a couple of pillows and a blanket for himself, then grabs a quilt, laying it over the bed.

"In case you get chilly. I normally run pretty warm, so I never need anything other than the sheets."

"Thank you, Gabriel. Thank you for everything this evening. The dinner was amazing, and it was nice to be wined and dined. I just..." Aella pauses, pulling at some dead skin with her teeth, contemplating whether she should say anything else.

"Ell, I like you a lot. I know we don't really know each other, and sex was definitely on the table tonight for me, especially seeing you in that dress, but I want to do things right with you and not rush into anything. Obviously, this is a little different, with you sleeping over, but I don't think it's the worst situation either. Look," he sighs, sitting on the edge of the bed, pulling her closer to him and gently placing his hands on her hips, "I feel like I know you from somewhere. I can't explain it, but it's like I'm drawn to you, and I can't shake it. You may think I'm crazy and never want to see me again after tonight, but I will sleep better knowing that I didn't make you feel like all I wanted from you was sex." The sincerity in his voice makes Aella feel weak in the knees. She has never had a man take her on a date and not expect anything in return, let alone spend what Gabriel did. Hell, even on the lousy dates she went on where they had to split the bill, there was always some sort of expectation that followed.

"I like you a lot, too, Gabriel, and I want to get to know you better. I have some weird shit going on the next couple of weeks, and I won't really be available, but after I get it sorted, I would like to see you again." She says, refraining from over-thinking about her little *condition*. And as weird as this situation might be between her and Gabriel, it was the most normal she'd felt in a long time, and maybe, just maybe, there would be many more *normal* moments like these to come.

Chapter Eight

Wake up. Wake up. Wake up. FUCK... It's happening again. The tea! I didn't drink the damn tea. Im so fucked. What if Gabriel wakes up and comes to check on me?! Fuck, I'm going to have to explain to him that it's sleep paralysis, even though it's not. I can't move! Goddamit, how could I be so stupid? Okay, take back control. What did Cahtel tell you to do... Wiggle your big toe, Aella. Wiggle your big fucking toe.

Wiggling her toes, Aella remembers to ground herself. After a moment, she emerges from the episode, sitting up to let her eyes adjust to his bedroom. Getting out of bed, she walks around the bedroom, making sure there isn't an unexpected portal. Proceeding down the hallway towards the living room, she keeps her footing light not to wake Gabriel up. Just making sure he is still there and asleep, but to her dismay, he isn't on the couch. Thinking he probably went to use the bathroom, she turns to head back to his bedroom and jumps when he is before her, rubbing at his eye with one hand.

"Are you alright?" He asks with a yawn.

"Ye—yes, sorry, I thought I heard something." She

responds, not knowing what else to say. "Where were you?" she asks, trying to get her heart to slow down and realizing how she sounded accusatory without meaning to.

"I went to the kitchen to grab a glass of water. You okay? Here, take a drink." He says, searching her face in the dark.

"I must have walked right past you. That's probably what woke me." Attempting to deflect from completely fucking up and putting Gabriel at risk. Thankfully Cahtel's instructions were helpful in this situation, but how would she explain her fuck up to him? *Lie. Just lie, lie your way out of it.*

"Ell, are you sure you're alright? It's dark, but you look a little pale."

"Yes, I'm fine, no worries. Goodnight, Gabriel, or I guess good morning." She says lightly. It has to be after three at this point.

"I have to be up in a couple of hours. If you need anything from now until then, don't hesitate. I'll leave you a key. Go get some sleep," he says, walking back over to the couch.

Taking that as her queue to return to his room, Aella nods in agreement even though she feels guilty for not taking the tea. Anything could have come through while she was having an episode. What would Gabriel think of her then? Just more ammo for her to get focused so that she has a chance of getting a *normal* life and the man of her dreams.

Aella awakes at 10 a.m. to a note on the pillow next to her that reads:

Aella,

You were sleeping so peacefully I didn't want to wake you this morning when I left for the office. There is coffee in the kitchen. Please make yourself at home and don't rush to leave. Feel free

*to use the shower as well if you would like. I
will be gone most of the day, so I apologize if
you don't hear from me until later. I left a business card with Ben's cell phone number, and he is
expecting you to call, so don't be bashful. I had
an amazing time with you last night and into the
morning. You are a vision.*

-Gabriel

Reading through his note a couple more times makes her the happiest girl in the world. Needing to get home and call Tara, she wasted no extra time. Dialing the number on the card, she let Ben know she was ready to return to her car. After making the bed, she grabs her belongings and locks the door on the way out. She knew that she would have a zillion missed calls and texts from Tara and her mom, but the one that stood out the most was from Georgia.

A weird inkling tingles, and she hopes Georgia is okay. It wasn't like her to call, but maybe she called to let her know that she gave her number to Gabriel, which Aella will thank her for today when she sees her at their shift. Thanking Ben for taking her to her car, she dials Tara's number, spilling all of her dirty laundry from her night with Gabriel, not leaving out a single detail.

Once she returned to her apartment, she couldn't wait to strip out of the little dress she wore on her date and shower. Standing in the shower for almost an hour, letting the steam and heat loosen everything up, she begins to dread going back to work. The only thing that excites her about today is seeing Georgia. Wrapping the towel around her hair, she slides into her bathrobe before turning to the kitchen to make some coffee and jumps at the sight of her orchid.

The orchid had reached the ceiling from sitting on the countertop, having grown three times as much since she left. Walking over to inspect it, she notices it isn't just the one orchid, but there are new blossoms of baby orchids. Picking up the pot, careful not to bruise the plant, she places it on the floor by the only window in the apartment.

The amount of growth since potting the orchid is bazaar and extremely unheard of. Assuming that since the orchid came from Isethas, she would have to find out more about the growth where time allowed.

"Look at you growing big and tall. I'm so impressed, little big orchid." She says to it with praise before brewing the pot of coffee.

While the coffee is brewing, she returns to the bathroom to prepare for another long night of work and travel back to Isethas. She keeps thinking about her date with Gabriel and spending the night with him. At one point, she even thought about how it would be possible to balance her two realities without interference, knowing that it probably wouldn't be wise. When Aella had a crush on someone and started even casually talking to men in the past, it rolled over all of her priorities, even if it didn't work out. This is different, and it makes her nervous because it is the kind of longing that would make her do crazy things.

Maybe we should have just fucked. She thinks, then scowls at the thought. Gabriel made his intentions known; he could have taken advantage if he really wanted to, but he was a complete gentleman.

After Aella finishes her cup of coffee, she says bye to her orchid and heads out for her shift.

The bar is slow, which isn't surprising for a Wednesday.

The manager of the establishment where she works always advertises new specials for the week, hoping that business will pick up during slow days. Unfortunately, not everyone seems enticed by some of the random food items he boasts about. Today's special is a sloppy Joe with chips and any alcoholic beverage for a whopping $18.99! *More like a yuck bomb*, not including the tip. Georgia and Aella always worked together on Wednesdays, but Georgia wasn't there when she clocked in for her shift. Assuming that she most likely took the day off, Aella would text her after work to see if she was okay. With only two tables in her section, even though the bar is slow, their manager hated it if he saw that the servers were standing around. Taking up an empty chair at a table with a bin of silverware and napkins, Aella joins her coworker, Adam. He's a simple guy, typically polite and never gossiped, the get-in and get-your-work-done type.

"Hey Adam, how's your shift been?" She asks, trying to make small talk while they roll the silverware together.

"Hey Aella, oh, you know it's work. Another Wednesday." He replies casually.

"I'm surprised to see Georgia isn't here. I wanted to thank her for helping me with something the other day," she says, pushing gently, hoping that he knows why she took the day off.

"Oh, you didn't hear? I guess she texted Dan asking for some time off. He was pretty irritated since it was such short notice, but she hasn't taken time off since she started working here. I guess he couldn't deny her the days." *Huh, that's interesting. I wonder what she took time off for.* Now, Aella really hoped that she was doing okay. That was so unlike her. Georgia loved working and making money.

"Did she say why she wanted to take time off and how long?" She asks, thinking she could use *Nancy Drew's* expertise on the situation.

"No, not that I know of. She just said she needed some personal time and kept it pretty vague. I told Dan I would cover the shifts we weren't scheduled together. I could use the extra cash." Adam didn't seem worried about Georgia—every man for themselves.

They continued to roll silverware until the bin was empty, placing their tightly rolled bundles back in. The task is enjoyable, even though the work required to do something so mindless is short-lived.

Adam signals her, letting her know she has a new table. Standing up, she ties her apron around her waist and grabs a notepad and pen. Walking over to the table, a man sitting down is hiding behind a menu.

"What can I get started on for you, sir?" Aella asks in the fake polite voice she's practiced hard on over the years.

Pulling down the menu, her cheeks instantly warm.

"Hm, the special sounds delicious, but I think I will just do a bourbon on the rocks for now," Gabriel says, clearly joking about the special, giving her a toothy grin. Rolling her eyes, she places a hand on her hip before writing down his order.

"Will that be all, sir?" She asks in a teasing yet seductive way while batting her eyelashes.

He's intrigued by the game she's playing. Aella doesn't mind a little role-play, and she thinks this could be fun.

"Yes, that will be all for now...Aella. What a pretty name. Do you know what it means?" Gabriel asks as he reads her name tag.

Surprised by the question, Susan had told her that Aella was a name from Greek mythology, and that's about all. She probably should have looked into its meaning, but she didn't care much about it until now.

"Oh, do tell me, Mr...."

"Please, call me Gabriel. Aella was an Amazon warrior in

Greek mythology. The name signifies whirlwind or tempest. Your name holds power. You should be proud. Not everyone can wear it." Learning about the meaning behind her name makes her feel special. She also feels a little ashamed for not looking into it, but she had other things on her plate, like not sleeping and wanting to just feel normal for once. Even though she struggles with her mother on a regular basis, she has her cool moments, and she wonders if she'd known its history or had just liked how it sounded for a daughter.

"Well, I guess the name is fitting then. One bourbon is coming right up. Happy hour doesn't start for another thirty minutes, but I'll make this one exception, thanks to your history lesson." As she's about to go place his order in, she turns around and says, "I also want to thank you again for last night and the wonderful note you left me this morning." Then she scurries off, giving herself some time to come back from admitting to herself how much the note really meant without seeming like she was already falling for this guy. Even with her back turned to him, she can feel his gaze burning into her, which is oddly comforting.

Returning with his drink, she sets it down, and he happily accepts it.

"Are you sure I can't get you anything to eat? The food here isn't all that great, but I can point you toward the safest option on the menu." She says, cringing at the menu as he looks it over. Everything is frozen and tossed in grease. She won't touch the food here, which says a lot because Aella has never had a problem eating anything when she's hungry enough.

"No, that's okay. I just wanted to see you. Also, I know you said you're busy the next few weeks, but I was hoping we could do something later if you aren't sick of me yet?" He says, and her damn heart. She wants to so badly; hell, she would spend every night of the week with him if she could, but it would have to wait.

"I am definitely not sick of you, and I would love nothing more than to get together with you again, but I have to help my mom with something, which unfortunately starts this evening." *Pathetic excuse, but better than saying, "I can't because I have sleep paralysis that causes me to open portals into different realms due to my subconscious mind being awake, and Cahtel, who is a talking cat from a realm called Isethas, came to me and brought me to their Watcher who told me that if we don't suppress my gift, then other Watchers will find out and they will use me as key to take control and cause the realms to collapse into each other which in return would be bad for everyone." Yeah, much better than the alternative.*

He doesn't say anything to her excuse; he just smiles and nods, sipping from his glass.

"No worries, it was a long shot. Let me know if I can help with anything; I don't know what your mom needs help with and if it's personal, but you have my number." He says, and Aella can't help but notice the disappointment, so she takes the opportunity to change the subject while acting like she is taking his order.

If Dan checks the cameras and sees that she's flirting with Gabriel or making conversation, he would say something like, *"I'm not paying you to sleep with our customers, Aella. Do that on your own time"*. Dan could be a real asshole.

"So I guess Georgia took some time off. I wanted to express my gratitude to her for giving you my contact info. She texted our manager after her shift the same night you and your friends came in, telling him she needed personal time off. Did she seem okay when she served you guys? I guess you didn't know her, but if something seemed off, maybe you might have been able to pick up on it."

After taking another sip of his bourbon, he folds his hands on the table. Looking into Aella's eyes, she notices something shift slightly at the mention of Georgia that she can't pinpoint. An uncomfortable heaviness sweeps over her, causing her to bite the inside of her cheek. The suspense is killing her.

"People take personal time off, Ell. I'm sure there's nothing to worry about," he says, void of emotion. Unsure of what she did to agitate him, she's only curious if he picked up on something from Georgia, considering he talked to her and she gave him Aella's number.

"O—okay, yeah, you're right. I just have a weird feeling that something happened to her and want to ensure she's okay."

Gabriel breathes out through his nose and snaps, "She's fine. She's an adult. I'm sure everything is okay."

Aella doesn't like that or how he spoke to her. There's no reason for him to get short with her, especially over her asking him about Georgia. Did one of his friends do something? A range of questions starts filtering into her mind then, but she holds her ground. No man, not even someone like Gabriel, will talk to her in that way. It's not what you say; it's how you say it, and she has enough on her plate at the moment.

"I don't really appreciate being talked to like that, Gabriel. All I was asking is if you picked up on anything with her, or maybe one of your buddies has something to do with it?" The last part came out too fast for her to catch, and when it left her mouth, Gabriel looked as though she physically slapped him.

Leaning to the side, he pulls out his wallet, sifting through cash, and throws it on the table, leaving just enough to cover his drink without a tip. Stepping out of his chair, he downs the rest of his bourbon, placing his glass over the bills.

"Thank you for the drink." He says bluntly and walks away.

What the fuck was that? Aella is shocked as tears threaten to burn the back of her eyes. Picking up the empty glass, she counts the crinkled-up cash that are all in ones. Where was the gentleman she met at Blanc, the kind man who wined and dined her? Did she imagine this, or was he actually pissed off that she may have accused one of his friends of doing something? Sadness, replaced by anger, takes hold. She didn't deserve that. *Fuck him.* His demeanor changed the moment she mentioned Georgia, and she wasn't going to forget about that or the way he just treated her like some cheap whore throwing crinkled-up ones on the table without so much as a tip.

The remainder of her shift dragged out too long, and she still wasn't over what had happened between her and Gabriel. Clocking off, she pulls her phone out of her bag to see if he'd texted to apologize for his behavior. To her dismay, there was nothing from him. If that's how he wanted to act, she was glad his true colors had shown before things went further. She didn't regret her time with him entirely because she enjoyed his company and the slight distraction. She would be lying to herself if she thought she wasn't disappointed in the man he portrayed himself to be, especially after that little stunt.

Coming home made her happy for once, making her appreciate her small space for the first time. Her apartment isn't much, but it's hers. She worked hard for it all on her own. Money can buy many things, like a big fancy penthouse and expensive artwork, but what it can't buy you is love.

Greeting the orchid as she walks by, she mists her petals, caring for her like she watched Michael tend to his. That was love at its purest, caring for something alive and growing. People underestimated plants. Tara is a prime example; she has killed countless by neglecting them. They aren't for everyone. Patience is key, and Aella lacks much of it.

Washing her face for bed, she throws a pair of leggings on

and a hoodie, deciding to be already dressed for when she would have to wake in a few hours. Because Michael had told her not to drink the tea this particular evening so that Cahtel would be able to come through the portal, she gets anxious about not being able to fall asleep. Remembering that she bought melatonin at the grocery store the other day, she popped a couple and swallowed them dry. He didn't say anything regarding melatonin, but then again, it never occurred to her to ask. Setting the alarm for 3:35, she turns out the lights and jumps into bed, closing her eyes so that she can drift off into rest.

PUNCTUAL AS EVER, CAHTEL ARRIVES ON TIME, WAKING Aella up before her alarm has the chance to go off. Groggy from the melatonin, she takes her time rolling out from under the covers, clearing the fog, and flips on the bedside lamp instead of the overhead light as she slips into her shoes. Looking up to give Cahtel a wave, he doesn't seem to acknowledge her but is fixated on something else.

Turning his nose up, Cahtel begins sniffing around the apartment without greeting Aella, which she thinks is rude since she was trying to be polite.

"Uh, hello to you too. Why do you keep sniffing around? Does something smell bad to you?" she asks, her voice still thick with sleep. Searching every corner of the apartment, approaching where Aella still sits on the edge of her bed, Cahtel sniffs her, then jumps back, hacking.

"Has anyone been in the apartment?" He asks. Whatever he's smelling isn't pleasant. Lifting her underarms, she sniffs herself to make sure she'd remembered deodorant.

"No? I don't understand, what stinks?"

"I'm not quite sure. The scent is familiar, but I can't place it... It reeks of death." Was his response. *How rude.*

"Well, I don't smell anything. I would be the first to know if something was decaying in my apartment." The assumption offended her, especially since she cleaned her apartment from top to bottom. She was proud of the work she put into it. *Fuck you, Cahtel.*

"Not that kind of death, Aella. It's the kind you can't see. Mortals don't have the nose for that kind of scent... Did you take the tea as instructed?"

Biting the inside of her cheek, she didn't want to lie to him, but she also didn't know how to answer the question truthfully.

"Yes?... Okay, I fucked up Tuesday night and forgot to take it, but I wasn't even home Tuesday night, so whatever you smell is probably coming from you." She blurts out defensively. There is no way she could have let something in that reeked of death. She wasn't even home.

"Aella... you had rigorous instructions. Where did you stay on Tuesday evening? Michael is going to become rigid." Seeing Cahtel unnerved makes her anxious. She didn't do anything wrong. She can still have a life and doesn't think she needs to explain herself to anyone. Justifying her minor fuck up, she's gone her whole existence without the knowledge of this condition she possesses. One night of not taking the tea isn't going to do too much damage, she hopes.

"I stayed with a friend, Cahtel. Everything will be fine. I'm sure Michael will understand!" she says, trying to reason with him, but the look in his eyes tells her otherwise.

"Right, well, we need to get going. Do you remember how to open the portal?" With no time to waste, Cahtel wants to get right to it, which intensifies her anxiety. He knew something was amiss by the smell he picked up on. What makes it worse is that it wasn't just in the apartment but on Aella.

"Yes, I remember. Let's do this," she replies, pulling her big girl pants up. But when she looks at the wall, the portal is still there from when Cahtel entered. He must have just noticed this as well from being so involved in his investigation because he, too, is stunned that it's still standing, given that Aella is fully conscious now.

"I don't understand. How is the portal still there?" She says breaking the silence.

"Honestly, I'm not quite sure myself. Did you take anything?"

"I popped a couple of melatonin before I went to sleep, but I was... What? What did I do wrong now, Cahtel?"

Shaking his head, he closes his eyes, taking deep breaths.

"Aella, again, you were given instructions, in which you did not follow them. The melatonin obviously is keeping your subconscious in control."

Throwing up her hands, she scoffs at him.

"Well, how was I supposed to know? Michael didn't say anything about melatonin; in fact, he didn't specify that I couldn't take anything else aside from when I take the tea, how I take the tea, and the stimulant. So add that to the list of Aella's Fuck Up's, yeah?"

Staring at her after her little outburst, he sighs, breaking eye contact.

"Is there anything else you would like to tell me before we head in?" His tone dripped with that disgruntled, cold void as if she was nothing more than a bratty child.

"Yeah, I have a headache. Care if I pop an ibuprofen or five?"

Scowling at her, he shakes his head again and prompts her to follow through the portal. This is going to be a long night, and Aella's not sure if she has the strength to deal with any more shit. *Better not mention the silver crack that remained.*

Chapter Nine

The landing is much more graceful than the first time they had arrived. Cahtel informed her that they would be going to Michael's home, causing Aella to feel jitters at the thought, almost forgetting for a moment how annoyed with Cahtel she is. She's excited to see where Michael lives and what his home looks like. As they stroll through the city, everyone stops and gives a friendly wave as they pass by. She could get used to how nice and welcoming the people here seem. At least, she thinks they're people since she has yet to ask Cahtel for clarification. Any further questions for him would have to wait, especially since he hasn't really asked her anything like they'd agreed upon.

Walking through the garden, Aella stays somewhat behind Cahtel. The tension between them is making their trek take longer than it seems. Between her huffing and puff-ing, Cahtel glances behind occasionally, equally annoyed. After having had enough, he stops mid-walk, causing Aella to trip over her footing so she doesn't walk right into him like a wall.

"What is it now, Aella?" Cahtel asks in a way that tells her she's grating on his nerves.

Crossing her arms across her chest, she steps around him and glares in his direction.

"And why do you assume there's something else wrong with me, Cahtel?"

Rolling his eyes, he deadpans her in disbelief.

"I've known you for a short amount of time; your brain is always thinking of things. It has to be draining with all of the thoughts that course through that head of yours. Come out with it."

Her lips flatten in a straight line, and her eyes narrow while he sits on his haunches and waits for her to speak.

"I have a question." She says, knowing that it could go one of two ways.

"That doesn't surprise me. Go on," Cahtel's tone, though flat, is giving her his full attention. Aella takes this moment as an opportunity to get to know him somewhat personally, hoping it may alleviate some of the tension between them. They aren't off to the best start, and even though they would be dealing with each other more frequently, getting to know him a little bit better is essential in whatever relationship this is.

The field of poppies is dense but soothing. Butterflies flutter, adding more color to the fields, while bees collect pollen for their Queen. Clearing her throat, she relaxes her arms.

"Michael told me you haven't always been a cat. He said you were a guardian like Torin. May I ask what happened?"

A flicker of pain is noticeable in Cahtel's eyes, and Aella immediately regrets asking. She hit a sore spot, one that Cahtel has been coddling for a long time. The flicker of pain, however, is short-lived as anger mixes in, clouding his features. Every muscle in her body tenses as she waits for the blow. *That's what my curious nature gets me.*

"How dare you ask of my former life, girl? That is no concern of you." He spits, and her cheeks become hot with embarrassment for overstepping. *Too soon, Aella, too soon.*

"I—I'm sorry, I didn't mean to offend you. I just wanted to break the ice a little. I mean, you know a lot about me, and I hardly know you at all." She supplies with sincerity and means it, and it appears as though Cahtel has to take a few deep breaths before continuing to Michael's home.

Grunting, he rolls his shoulders back and begins walking without so much as another word. Aella is becoming increasingly accustomed to the silent treatment, and perhaps that isn't the worst thing. She's not here to make friends, after all.

After some time had passed, he side-eyes Aella, still facing the direction they are headed. Softening his features, he senses her obvious discomfort, and Cahtel breaks the silence, this time with a sigh.

"Some things should be forgotten in life, Aella. I've been alive for centuries. I've seen things that I can't describe, done things I am ashamed of. My condition is something I have had to live with, and the person who I suspect did this is one I try to forget about. Though I understand your curiosity, I try not to mourn what my life once was. There is no point in doing so, especially since I will never get that life back. I apologize for snapping. You meant no harm. That was a poor reaction on my part." His confession shatters something inside of Aella. Unable to face him because if she did, she would burst into tears with how heartbroken he must be. She wasn't the best at comforting people, so instead, she shakes her head in understanding, changing the subject.

"You haven't asked me any questions about the mortal realm yet, and I'm surprised that the only time you ventured out was to put the orchid on my car. Also, I still can't get over the fact that you stayed in my closet the entire day after you came to visit me. What did you even do that whole time?" She was still weirded out by the fact that he was in there without her knowledge. *Creep*

Cahtel clears his throat, then says, "Unfortunately, I have found comfort in the small space. There have been long stretches where I have had to stay in there, especially when you refused to sleep, which has made my visits less frequent. As far as putting the orchid on your car, I teleported. I am a little wary of the mortals in your realm, especially the one that comes over from time to time smelling of different herbs."

Aella thinks about who he is speaking of and laughs when she realizes he is referring to her mother.

"Yes, my mother has that effect on most, but she is harmless."

"She has a chaotic sense of self, but then again, you carry some of that as well." *Ouch*

Then he says, "What is that box you carry around that lights up, and you can hear others speak?"

"A cell phone? Do you not have cell phones in Isethas?"

"Ah, a cell phone like a communicator device?" he asks, and Aella only nods, hoping she doesn't have to explain the logistics of a cell phone. "We have other ways of communication, primarily teleporting and leaving letters. Otherwise, we communicate directly."

That makes sense. She isn't in the mortal realm, and even though things in Isethas appear to be more modern, it is still a foreign place.

"Sometimes I wish we didn't have cell phones. They can be addicting but are also convenient when you need to reach someone." Aella says, then continues, "So, going back to what you said about being in my closet sometimes longer than you were the other day, is that because I subconsciously closed the portal?"

Cahtel nods, responding less broody, "There are times when you open a portal, and it remains open for a period of time. Other times, you wake, and it closes before I have a chance to get back. It has happened more frequently in the last six years."

The time frame checks out, especially since six years ago was when she had been hospitalized. Ever since, she has fought the urge to sleep, fearful of another bad episode.

When they approach Michael's home, she almost forgets about the tension between her and Cahtel. Talking about cell phones and how many times Cahtel has hidden under her nose was oddly comforting. Even though the looks of him still creep her out a little bit, he is harmless.

Michael's home isn't any ordinary home; it's a fucking palace. The modern architecture is impressive, creating an illusion from a distance that it looks like an angular box. Giant trees and lush green plants decorate the front, vines ebbing and flowing up the walls. Sculptures of what appear to be warriors stand around a fountain in the center of the walkway, carved entirely out of marble. They look so realistic, holding their swords high. The detail of their armor alone is cut and carved with precision.

The entry steps to the palace are also marble. Climbing them, two large, beautiful black doors welcome any visitor, adding contrast to the white and grey. Brass knockers hang, and the doors open before she can use them. Cahtel heads inside, exchanging pleasantries with a woman who looks like a goddess. Cahtel introduces Aella to her, and if she didn't know any better, she would have thought she was Michael's better half.

She is absolutely beautiful. Long, wavy golden hair cascades down her shoulders, and her flawless porcelain skin looks delicate enough to crack. Piercing blue eyes that could break your heart and soft lips with a natural pink pout.

Ashlyn isn't wearing anything that resembles being a housekeeper, so Aella puts that theory to rest as she adorns a loose-flowing gown that hangs off her body in an ethereal way. The light green color brightens her already piercing, large blue eyes. Shoeless like Michael had been when Aella first met him, her toes are painted yellow, and a silver anklet is wrapped around the base.

Aella begins to question whether anyone wore shoes in this realm. She didn't pay too close attention while she and Cahtel walked through the city, so she will stick this question in her back pocket for now.

"Pleasure to meet you, Aella," Ashlyn says in a delicate voice, holding out her hand gracefully. Returning the gesture, she takes Aella's hand in both of hers, pulling her into an embrace smelling of chamomile and vanilla.

"It's a Pleasure to meet you, too, Ashlyn." Aella couldn't recall the last time someone hugged her with such warmth. It wasn't a quick hug, either. This hug was genuine. It was a hug your grandmother would give you, cradling you to their body.

"We are going to work together during your visits, Aella. I can't wait to get to know more about you." Her voice is like rain on a warm summer day.

"I look forward to it." Smiling back at her, she squeezes Aella's hand gently and glides out the front door down the steps.

From what Aella can see, the foyer is open, with floors made of white marble that sparkles beneath the natural light. A prominent modern light fixture of iron hangs from the ceiling, matching the iron staircase leading to the second floor. Tilting her head back, she sees that the roof is entirely made of glass, creating the illusion there is no ceiling at all, and hanging planters of every size accompany the fixture.

Grabbing her attention, Cahtel guides her down a hallway to a glass door. Prompting her to slide it open, they enter a space similar to the lounge in Gabriel's apartment, except it is much more extensive and bright. The ceiling is the same as when she entered the palace: a glass skylight with iron beams stabilizing it. A chaise sits next to cat palms the same size as her, with two green velvet chairs occupying the space across. It looks like an indoor greenhouse with all the plants and over-flowing succulents. A custom-made bar with brass accents takes up a corner, with decanters of liquid and mismatched glasses—Cahtel motions for her to sit in one of the chairs. Aside from a water feature singing songs, it is quiet in the space.

Michael walks in wearing black dress pants and a black dress shirt tucked in, sleeves rolled, and buttons buttoned, except for the first three, exposing his gorgeous chest. His hair is down, layers falling around his face in an unmade bed of a man sort of way. His eyes lock on Aella before turning and heading for the bar.

Eyeing him, she looks down to see that he is again barefoot. Placing a glass on the bar, he drops two ice cubes and swirls what looks like bourbon into the glass. Swallowing too loud for comfort, it is almost like she is staring at Gabriel's twin.

Pinching her brows together, Aella is slightly offended he didn't offer her anything to drink. It's only polite to offer your guest a beverage.

Rounding the bar, he leans back onto the chaise, draping his arm over the back with his glass in hand. Something about the way he relaxed into the chaise, holding his bourbon, is painfully sexy. She starts to get hot and also uncomfortable with the way he is staring at her with stoicism, though his eyes remain kind and gentle.

"Are you going to offer me a drink?" She asks suddenly, not able to contain her discomfort. Seeing how beautiful Ashlyn is, Aella thinks she looks like a troll in comparison.

"No, alcohol will only impair your ability to train. You're not here to indulge in pleasantries, Aella. You're here for business. Although, what I can smell from you, you have already indulged in certain *unpleasantries*." Taking a sip of his drink, she bites her tongue at how rude he is being.

What unpleasantries? I didn't do shit.

"What you are *smelling*, Michael, is agitation. If we are to train, then let's get down to it." She seethes, balling her hands into fists, nearly coming out of the chair. Just when she thought things were going to go a bit more smoothly, Michael's demeanor proves otherwise.

"We have a problem, Aella. You see, the smell coming off of you is one I am acquainted with all too well. You didn't do as instructed, which will now cost us time. Time that you, my dear, don't have."

The fucking tea. Did Cahtel tattle to Michael? That's impossible, considering he was with her this whole time... She must have tripped another wire when she had the episode at Gabriel's.

"What smell? Cahtel said the same thing." She says, sniffing herself once more.

Dread fills her. This is going to get messy, especially since she has been denied a drink.

MICHAEL CONTINUES TO SIP FROM HIS GLASS WHILE Cahtel stands by. The tension in the room is so heavy a knife wouldn't be able to cut through it.

Gritting her teeth, Aella opens her mouth to speak, "I don't understand what the problem is exactly. Explain it to me."

Leaning forward, he places his elbows on his knees, still holding the glass, and downs the rest in one fluid gulp. Another moment passes before he elaborates on the massive issue they are facing.

Directing his attention away from Aella, he focuses on Cahtel and says, "Torin has informed me that Damien hasn't been seen in Diatturus for some time except for a brief moment yesterday."

"That is concerning, sir. Did Torin mention who he got this information from?"

"A Messenger from the Illusion Plane. How accurate that is is to be determined. The Messenger said his whereabouts are unknown."

"Who is Damien?" Aella asks with frustration, inserting herself again into the one-on-one conversation the two are having. They'd mentioned that name the last time she was here but didn't go into detail.

"Damien is the Watcher over the realm Diatturus, the one that wants to obtain control, breaking the barrier of all the realms. And you, Aella, smell of Diatturus, which means you opened up a portal to that realm."

Aella's heart stops beating. This was worse than bad. She was fucked, they all were fucked, but then she remembered that she'd taken control like Cahtel had shown her the first time he visited.

"Wait, when I started having an episode, I controlled it. I couldn't have opened a portal, or at least long enough for anything to slip through... This Damien guy, what does he look like?"

There's no way it's who she thinks it is... Gabriel may have proven to be a dick wad, but that doesn't mean it could be him. Replaying her encounters with him, from the tender kisses on the top of her hand to the paintings he showed her. Then, when she had a *small* episode in his apartment and how he suddenly became unhinged when she brought up Georgia. Georgia... *oh fuck.*

"He looks like me, Aella. He is my twin brother."

The moment those words leave Michael's mouth, the world stops moving around her. She is going to be sick. Standing up from the chair, her legs give out, and Michael runs to her side to help her back down, urging Cahtel to get Torin for help.

"Aella, I need you to breathe slowly in through the nose, out through the nose," Michael coaxes in a calming way.

"Michael, I fucked up. I don't think I only opened a portal to Diatturus. I think... Fuck." The last part comes out nearly inaudible, while shame and regret lace the words she can barely force through trembling lips.

Torin runs into the room, picking up on the panic, but she can't bear to look at any of them. How will they view her when she explains what happened? Would her actions repulse Michael? She wants to run and hide in a cave.

"What do you mean, Aella? I don't understand," Michael says, crouching before her so they are at eye level. She spirals, disgusted with herself.

"It all makes sense now. I wasn't special. I was desperate, and I walked right into his trap," taking another deep breath, she continues, "The night I found the business card and orchid on my car, my best friend Tara told me we got into a club called Blanc. I met a man there named Gabriel. I didn't put it together until now... He had to have known about me already. Getting into that club is nearly impossible. He must have done something to push our names to the top of the list."

Michael, Cahtel, and Torin listen intently, urging her to continue.

"After Cahtel visited me for the first time, I couldn't sleep for obvious reasons, no offense. I went to a local coffee shop to research and ran into Gabriel again, thinking it was all some big coincidence. Then, the following day after my first trip to Isethas, I got a text message from him stating he got my number from a friend I work with, and he asked me to dinner..."

She didn't want to continue, hoping everyone got the hint. But after a few minutes, she knew she wouldn't get out of this one.

"The dinner went better than I imagined, and I went home with him. He was kind and charming, actually a complete gentleman, and let me stay at his apartment. I didn't drink the tea that night and had one of my episodes."

Michael looks at Aella, confused about what an episode means.

"My sleep paralysis—I refer to it as an episode. Anyway, I managed to pull myself out, but if Gabriel is actually Damien, then I was right there with him. I just don't understand how I opened a portal to Diatturus. I usually open one here, in Isethas, and I'm still trying to understand why."

Cahtel cuts in then, "You most likely opened a portal to Diatturus because you were in Damien's presence since he is technically the Watcher of that realm. How he has been in the mortal realm for so long is a mystery. Why you continue to open a portal into Isethas most likely has something to do with a familiarity because you have done it before, and your subconscious mind recognizes it without meaning to."

Deafening silence closes over the space. Michael walks over to where he had his glass and throws it against the wall, shattering it. His back is to Aella, and in a smooth motion, he pulls his hair back and ties it in a knot at the nape of his neck.

Fear digs its nasty claws into her as she smashes her lips together. It keeps everything inside from crumbling like a piece of paper you wrote mistakes all over.

Turning back to face her, his eyes glow an unnatural shade of white. Cahtel slowly moves closer to Aella's side in preparation.

"Are you so desperate for touch that you would sleep with any man who showed you a sliver of interest?" Venom spews from his mouth, and his eyes continue to glow, "Do you know what your actions have cost? How could you be so stupid, mortal."

"Who I choose to sleep with is my business, Michael! And for the record, we didn't sleep together, although I wish I had, especially now! Do you think I asked for this? Do you think I enjoy any of *this*? I am a living, breathing human with emotions, needs, and wants. My actions have cost nothing, especially since I have lived with this my whole life. My whole life, Michael. I apologize that I'm not cold and heartless like YOU." Hurt and helplessness invade her. All she ever wanted was for someone to see and want her all the same. She didn't ask for this. Aella is placed with an impossible task and a curse that she can't talk to anyone about. If she did, they would check her into a nut house.

Michael inches in closer to her, his features void of any emotion. He is terrifyingly beautiful, his pale blue eyes getting some of the color back and his sharp cheekbones accentuating his dark brows. Even with the anger that churns beneath the surface like a hurricane, ready to take out everything in its wake.

Leaning down, he brushes his lips across the shell of her ear, keeping his tone even.

"Aella, you're right about one thing. You did fuck up, good luck."

He storms out of the room, leaving Aella frozen and unable to move. Aella realizes she has been holding her breath because when she finally inhales, fire laces her lungs, and a sob breaks free, shattering into a million pieces like the glass Michael threw at the wall.

Chapter Ten

Pumping her legs as fast and hard as possible, Aella runs towards where she'd opened the portal. No matter how hard she tries not to allow the opinions of others to affect her, for some reason, the look on Michael's face and hateful words wreck her. *Who is he to judge?* She thinks as the air dries her tears while she continues running.

Michael is still a man. He has needs and wants, but she doesn't understand why it hurts as badly as it did to see his anger and disgust toward her; even though she never actually slept with Gabriel (Damien), it still wasn't any of Michael's concern.

Nearly halfway to her destination, Torin swoops down and picks her up, flying them away from her target. Twisting in his grasp, she screams, making it difficult for him to hold her.

"Put me down!"

"Aella, I suggest you stop moving like a toddler. If I drop you, it's not only going to hurt, but it's also going to do some serious damage that we can't afford right now." He grunts with her struggles. That realization helps her relax in his hold.

Wrapping her arms around him, she didn't want to fall to her death necessarily but also didn't care if she did die at this point. She supposes the plus side of falling to her death would be her last moment: being held by a strong man with a chiseled body won't be so terrible.

Cahtel was waiting, perched on a large rock as they reached solid ground on top of a mountain. *Point proven, Cahtel, point fucking proven.* Marching toward him with her hands flexing at either side, he stares down at her from the top of a boulder.

"And where, Aella, were you running away to?"

Scoffing, the anger returned. Her blood is boiling so hot she could explode at any moment.

"Home, Cahtel, I was going home. Did you forget about everything that happened back there?! You had to have *Torin* take me against my will?!" Her voice cracked, and the urge to throw something at him gave some relief as she thought about how good it would feel.

"What happened back there wasn't ideal, and it could have gone much better. Michael doesn't know how to handle his emotions properly. Ashlyn has been working with him on that. Be that as it may, he wasn't entirely wrong with what he said. He shouldn't have faulted you for feeling for someone or exchanging... what's the word I'm looking for? Ah, yes, intimacies. Damien, who you know to be Gabriel, is very dangerous. You couldn't have known he wasn't who he claimed to be. In this unforgivable circumstance, the lesson to be learned is to do as instructed, which you did not. I am also at fault. I should have visited sooner, and Michael should have told you all the truth. He harbors regret for what happened to his brother and the war his greediness caused, but what's done is done. We still have work to do."

Throwing her hands in the air, Aella shouts, "But I didn't

sleep with him! Ugh, whatever. It doesn't matter. None of this actually really matters. I want to go home."

Jumping down from the boulder, Cahtel strides towards Aella and Torin.

Torin then takes the opportunity to add in his two cents.

"Cahtel is right, Aella. The work is far from over. Damien may be two steps ahead, but he hasn't won yet. We have to pull together and win this war before it begins."

"You keep saying that he's this horrible person, and I am not too fond of him myself at the moment, but he was great, all things considered. Also, how do you expect that we all work together? Cahtel and I equally grate on each other's nerves; Michael finds me repulsive for assuming that I slept with his brother, in which case I didn't, and if time is so precious, then why did you all wait until now to tell me about my *condition*? Why not come sooner so that we could have done something and I could be enjoying the rest of my twenties? Now you put this pressure on me and give me a list of rules? Fuck it. Maybe the world and the realms should come to an end. Save us all from this chaos. And if you didn't know this little fun *fact* about me yet, Cahtel, since you found it so comforting stalking around in my closet for who knows how long on your little jaunts through *my* portal, I hate nothing more than being told what I can and cannot do." Aella's outburst on top of the mountain caused even the birds to go silent, and the only sound to be heard was the crashing of waves down below. Torin tucks his hands in the pockets of his pants, looking at something on the ground that wasn't actually there but seems interested in it regardless.

Cahtel waits a few seconds in case Aella has anything else she wants to get off of her chest. Her gaze is fixed on the horizon, and her features soften in a form of defeat. She's tired, and not just from getting so many sleepless nights. A part of her

Samantha Hardy

doesn't care if everything ends around her aside from the love she has for her mother and Tara; at the end of the day, Aella is selfish and wants a little peace.

"Don't worry about Michael." Cahtel says, muting her thoughts, "Michael may be many things, but he doesn't carry hatred in his heart, especially for you. He's angry that his brother took advantage of you at your most vulnerable, but he does not hate you, let alone find you repulsive."

Snorting at Cahtel's attempt to lighten the air and give her some relief with Michael, she shakes her head, rubbing her face with her hands.

"I honestly don't care about his opinion of me Cahtel, and Gabriel didn't take advantage of me. If anything, I feel as though I took advantage of him, which is really fucked because he took me to a really nice dinner." She sighs, thinking about how that is something she should work on through therapy, amongst other things.

Sticking to my three-date rule from now on, actually, make that a twelve-date rule, given I ever date again.

"Cahtel and I will speak with Michael once he calms down. In the meantime, you and Ashlyn will start working on meditating and grounding yourself. This will help you maintain control of your conscious and subconscious mind even though you're ready to throw in the towel." Torin says, gently cupping her shoulder, the contact causing her to flinch.

Cahtel notices and clears his throat, realizing that he and Aella have more in common than not.

"Walk with me a moment. I want to show you something."

Following him, they head toward the edge of the mountain. Cahtel gestures for her to take a seat. Dangling her legs off the ledge, she sees an incredible view. Peering out, an ocean takes up the horizon, stretching farther than the eye can see, swirling an indigo purple that reflects the sky. It's truly breathtaking.

124

"This is my favorite spot in all of Isethas. I come here when I need to clear my head or just simply be," he says, pausing as they sit and watch the waves dance below them.

"Look, Aella, I know how unfair this must be for you and how terrifying it is, but whether you want to believe me or not, we do want to help you. We also don't want another war, let alone all of the realms, including your own, to diminish. You are right, though; we should have acted sooner. Michael wanted to be sure the time was right, and he also battles with his own traumas from what happened before."

Aella remains quiet, listening to Cahtel in the calm state of just sitting and being. It was a nice distraction, focusing solely on him instead of all of the filing cabinets in her brain that never fully close.

"Michael told you I was a guardian like Torin, which is true. Before the war of the realms, Michael, Damien, and I were inseparable. We would practice dueling each other with our swords. Friendly competition had a way of strengthening our friendships. Nothing could get between us, not even a beautiful woman." He says with a chuckle that makes Aella glance at him as he reminisces on how good life was between them.

"Damien and Michael had issues like most siblings would, healthy rivals, but loved each other nonetheless without question. Their parents were incredibly kind and generous, remaining madly in love until their father's passing. The pain from losing such a fearless man broke something in them both. You never truly get over the loss of a loved one. You see, we don't age the way the people do in your realm, nor do we get ill with diseases or cancer. Eros, their father, lived 7,200 years and would have continued living had a rare plague not have attacked a ship he and his men were sailing on. Many have theories on how this plague came to be. Some believe a sea serpent cursed Eros and his men for sailing into uncharted territories. The plague was not contagious, however, and countless healers aided Eros along with his men while the illness quickly took their lives. Unable to find a cure, the healers made them comfortable. Damien wanted to go out and find the source. Fighting Michael on it, he snuck away, sailing the sea alone. When he returned, he came back empty-handed, and unfortunately, Eros had already passed without being able to say goodbye.

Michael was so torn up over the death that it was on me to tell Damien myself. That's when I saw the change. He came back cold and dark, something sinister. I don't think he could forgive himself for leaving, feeling as though he failed his father. That kind of guilt is hard to get over."

A warm breeze blows past them, moving loose strands of hair away from Aella's face, causing a chill spreading goosebumps. Gazing out at sea, Cahtel continues with his story,

"The war between the realms soon after was brutal. Every war is, but this one was the most devastating. Some of the most kind and generous Watchers become consumed with greed and hatred, wanting the same thing as Damien. He corrupted and rotted their minds, coercing them into the darkness that swallowed him up. It was misery, a plague far worse than the one that took Eros and his men. Thousands died from every realm, fighting for power and control. Brothers and sisters alike slaughtering their own, the seas and fields that were once serene and colorful were stained red. Once the war came to an end, the Watchers that remained agreed upon a contract. They would have control over their realm, and becoming a ruler was the only way we could satisfy those wanting power, closing the portals into each realm for good. Defeated, Damien's hatred grew, cursing anyone who tried to get in his way. I tried to reason with him, but he wouldn't hear me out, so in return, he stripped me of my guardianship and turned me into the beast I am today."

Heartbreak took on a new meaning, learning what happened to Cahtel and everyone involved. Aella couldn't imagine what that must have been like. It was hard enough for her to process listening to it. The loss of a father, then to lose your brother and best friend to something other than death, was unbearable. Although she never knew her father or who he is now, it would be like losing her mother and Tara all at once.

"I am so sorry, Cahtel. That is terrible." She says to him, not knowing what to say or how to respond. What people know in the world is so tiny compared to the bigger picture.

"Aella, I didn't tell you this so you could pity me. I told you so you know what is at stake. There is a natural order to things in your realm and every other. Interfering with that natural order can cause more than a war. It would be a disaster collapsing every realm into each other until nothing is left. People clutch onto their faith tightly like pearls around their necks, needing reassurance for what happens when their soul leaves their body. Not even I have the answer to that. If I did, there would be no natural order to things."

Imagining the realms collapsing into each other makes her feel slightly nauseous, as it most likely wouldn't be a painless or quick ending despite her self-loathing earlier and how she didn't care; that was just her being dramatic. Setting aside her pride, Aella decides to work with them on saving the realms even though she is the center focus on that due to her portal opening condition. But, at the end of the day, it isn't all about her. It's about everyone and everything. There is no time to be petty or selfish. They have to get to work. Standing up, Aella brushes her dusty hands off onto her jeans. Looking at Cahtel, she smiles at him softly and says, "Well, what are we waiting on? We have realms to save and shit to do."

Laughing at her, he nods, and for a second, he looks more human than animal. Until now, Aella loathed him, but her appreciation grew after opening up to her and letting her in, even if it was just the smallest amount. Cahtel is no longer the uninvited guest; he is somebody. Somebody who wants what's best for his realm and all of the realms combined.

WHEN THEY RETURN TO THE PALACE, ASHLYN IS WAITING for them in the foyer by the front door. Her beauty and grace are painful. Peering behind her, Aella's stomach lurches as Michael emerges from the second floor. Moving down the iron spiral staircase with fluid precision, another trait Aella lacked, given her history of missing a step or three, is confidence. As he approaches, Ashlyn moves to the side, giving him room. His gaze never leaves Aella's as her cheeks start to flush and her underarms begin to perspire.

"Aella, I apologize for my behavior earlier and how I spoke to you. You did not deserve that. I can promise you that will never happen again."

His apology was sincere. If it ever did, shame would take some time to go away, but she mentally accepts. Pursing her lips together, she thinks carefully about her response. She could counter his apology to ease some of that shame, but that would help nothing.

"Thank you. It's okay. I take responsibility for not doing as instructed. I apologize as well," she says, considering she didn't fully follow instructions.

"You have nothing to apologize for, Aella. You're human. You couldn't have known. My brother is persuasive, always has been, and is very good at finding a way to get what he wants. None of this is your fault. You were right earlier. You didn't ask for any of this. You will have a normal life soon, Aella. That is another promise I am willing to make."

A normal life... The one thing she ever wanted was *normal*, and soon, she would have it even if there was nothing normal about it right now. Creasing her brows together, she is trying to picture what a normal life would look like and how that would pan out, knowing that there are other realms and magical beings. Would she ever be able to see Cahtel again after a couple of weeks of learning how to suppress her gift? What would sleep feel like with a normal life and not having sleep paralysis? Her mind is riddled with questions that she will soon have answers to.

Normal.

Chapter Eleven

Ashlyn led Aella down a stone pathway around the palace into a small building. No larger than a shed, it appeared to be similar to most of the architecture she had noticed when walking through Isethas. Made entirely from glass with lush green plants, the iron French doors are wide open, airing the space out. The only furniture in the room is plush Moroccan floor pillows with soft tassels lazily draping onto the cement floor. A shrine of incense and bundles of sage sits in the center, along with a sculpture of someone she doesn't recognize.

Walking over to the shrine, Ashlyn begins lighting a sage bundle, clearing the area, and letting it burn out on its own on a ceramic plate. Pulling out three different incense, she lights those also and places them strategically so that the smoke creates a triangle as they burn.

"Please, take a seat, Aella." Ashlyn gestures to a pillow across from hers.

Sitting on the pillow, Aella crosses her legs, adjusting her body to get comfortable.

While waiting for further instructions, Ashlyn sits on her

pillow, reaching for a set of crystal singing bowls. Susan would just fall in love with Ashlyn, and thinking about her mother makes Aella miss her. When Aella returns to the apartment, she makes a mental note to call her and check in.

Gliding the mallet around the outer edge of the center bowl, Ashlyn's eyes drift shut, prompting Aella to do the same. Listening to the music she's creating, Aella feels herself drift off into a relaxed, dreamy state. In a soft voice, Ashlyn speaks, hand never leaving the mallet or the bowl.

"I want you to clear your mind. We will be going into a meditative state. Don't think about anything, past, future, or present."

That will be difficult since her brain tends to have several of those filing cabinets open all at once. *You got this, Aella, close those cabinets.* After a few minutes of trying to force them shut, those cabinets remain open. Peeking one of her eyes open at Ashlyn, she has a feeling that this isn't going to work.

"Relax, Aella, close your eyes," Ashlyn says, still circling the bowl with her mallet.

"I can't. I'm trying, but I can't. You know, when Cahtel had me do this, I was lying down. Should I lay down?" Aella's response is rushed. She's nervous around Ashlyn and can't relax. Her skin feels itchy, and her muscles are strained with how hard she is forcing herself to close those damn filing cabinets.

Stopping mid-circle, Ashlyn stands up, picking through some oils. Taking a cloth out of a steaming bowl of water, she dabs a concoction onto the fabric and urges her to lay back. Folding the warm towel, she places it over Aella's eyes, and the aroma of eucalyptus and lavender settles into her nostrils. Breathing in the oils, Aella hums as her body begins to relax.

"Remember, this is a mental exercise to gain some form of

control over your subconscious mind. Gaining control over your ability will help you with suppressing it."

Ashlyn must have retaken her seat because the bowls are singing songs once more. Aella's struggle to turn her mind off was still there, but with every inhale of the essential oils and following the rhythm of the singing bowls with her ears, the chaos in her mind slowly quieted. She pictured herself as an orchid, much like she did with Cahtel, roots growing and planting herself deep within the soil. The image of her as a beautiful, resilient orchid slowly comes in and out of focus until nothing but that black void is sucking and pulling her in different directions. Yet, her body is weightless, floating and falling all at once.

The rhythm that forms from the singing bowls sounds as though they are moving away from her until she hears nothing. A still quiet, like floating in space, going nowhere and everywhere simultaneously. Completely alone and at peace.

When Ashlyn speaks again, her voice echoes into Aella's quiet mind, bouncing off of the walls in the black void she is weightless in.

"You're in deep meditation. You are safe; nothing can harm you here," Ashlyn says softly, but even with her soft voice, it carries through the void for millenniums.

"You're doing so good, Aella. Now, I want you to imagine a portal before you. What does it look like? How does it feel? Remember, you are safe."

Aella looks at the black space before her, not seeing anything. With her mind empty and body still, the black void stretches on forever without a sliver of light.

What does it look like? How does it feel?

She repeats the same questions until, far off into the black void, a speck of silver sparkles, looking like a star in the night sky, moving its way closer at a rapid speed. Suddenly, the star grows and stretches long until it's within reach, and the star is no longer but a wall made of silvery shimmering swirls. The energy that radiates off it dances across her skin. It's part of her, and yet it is its own entity.

The silver shimmering swirls move and breathe, beckoning her to enter, pulling her closer with its blinding light like a flame attracting a moth. She can feel her heart race, an impulse to walk through to see what exactly is on the other side that wants to suck her in.

A voice comes through the wall, not of hers or Ashlyn's, one she hasn't heard before.

"Aella, come through to the other side." It beckons, sounding neither man nor woman.

"W—who's there?" Aella asks, staring at the portal and becoming hypnotized by its dance.

Ashlyn responds soothingly, not to break her meditative state, "Aella, what are you hearing? It's just me and you, remember you're safe."

"Aella...We have been waiting for you." That voice comes again, causing her breathing to quicken as she begins to panic.

"Who are you? What do you want?"

"You know who we are." It answers, sounding closer. In an instant, a hand reaches through the portal with bony fingers stretching out towards her. Falling backward in her meditative state, she squeezes her eyes shut tight.

Wiggle your big toe. Wiggle your big toe.

Cracking her eyes, the portal is no longer there, and a mirror takes its place with her reflection staring back at herself.

What the fuck?

Aella and her reflection stare at each other for a moment until the reflection of herself smiles in a sinister way.

Aella screams, and the mirror shatters fragments floating in space in time, feeling like she's falling back into her body.

A bell chimes and Ashlyn is before Aella's face, bracing her shoulders. Coming out of meditation, she feels nauseous. Pulling the rag off from over her eyes, Ashlyn hands her a glass of water.

"What happened?"

"I'm not sure. I saw the portal, and something was on the other side. It reached through and tried to grab me." Aella says, taking a drink of water, not wanting to close her eyes, fearing she would be pulled back in with whatever, or whoever that thing was.

Glancing over at Ashlyn, her eyes widen, and her face visibly begins to pale.

"What?"

Ashlyn is obviously struggling with the attempt to remain calm as she says, "Aella, could you see what it was?"

Although Aella appreciates the effort not to freak her out more than she is already, it isn't working.

"No, I could hear it, and whatever it was, wanted me to come through, but I couldn't see who was there. The voice was also unrecognizable."

Once the nausea subsides, Aella stands up, getting to her feet.

"We need to tell Michael now. I don't think Damien is the only thing we need to worry about."

Barging into the lounge, Michael is sitting on the chaise with a glass of bourbon, speaking with Torin and Cahtel. Stopping mid-conversation, they turn to face Ashlyn and Aella in their frantic state, causing Michael to stiffen, noting the shift in their demeanor.

"Michael, we have another issue..."Ashlyn begins.

"What happened?" he says, furrowing his brows. This is the first genuine expression Aella has seen besides the slight quirks of his lips the first time she arrived.

Pushing forward, Aella moves to the front of the bar so they can face her head-on.

"Ashlyn guided me into a meditative state, and I completed my first lesson, well, kind of. Everything went smoothly until someone, or something else, was there on the other side of the portal. I didn't recognize the voice; then it reached through, trying to grab me." Chills run up her body as she relives what just happened.

Michael's eyes widen, and Torin and Cahtel shift in their seats.

"Did you see what it was?"

"No, just the bony fingers. It wasn't something of this world. I mean, like mine or yours..." Aella trails off, her body feeling cold and drained from the experience.

Silence engulfs the room as Michael stands from the chaise and walks to the bar's other side. Grabbing two wine glasses and a bottle of Pinot, he uncorks the bottle with a loud pop and pours the wine into the glasses. Handing the first glass to Ashlyn, he gives Aella the other. Apparently, the no-drinking rule doesn't apply to her anymore. Savoring the taste, she realizes it is her favorite bottle.

"How did you manage to come out of it?" Michael asks as he comes over to sit back down.

Taking another big drink of the wine, Aella wipes a little dribble of liquid that escapes down her chin, "I wiggled my big toe."

A flicker of pride dances across Cahtel's features at her response, but Michael appears more confused.

"I'm sorry?" He asks, creasing his brows, trying to understand what that means.

"When Cahtel visited me during one of my episodes, he told me to wiggle my big toe. It works and honestly brings me back consciously."

Torin fails at his attempt to smother a laugh, then gives Michael an apologetic look.

"I'm sorry. This is probably not the most appropriate time to find humor in any of this, but it looks like Cahtel is useful after all," Torin says, and both Michael and Cahtel glare at him.

"Oh, piss off Torin. It's a wonder you even remember to do a simple task such as bathing." Cahtel snaps, and Michael defuses the bickering by holding his hand up.

"Now is not the time to throw jabs at anyone; cut it out, both of you. Aella, you mentioned when you were last here that Cahtel wasn't your only visitor, and I wrongly assumed that it may have been a succubus from Diatturus. After doing some research, and with the knowledge that my brother has been in the mortal realm until you opened the portal inside of his home, I'm afraid that whatever that was then, and whatever it was in your meditative state, is more or less the same entity. An entity from a realm that has long been sealed, even before my time, and forgotten about. A realm that needs to stay that way. So, moving forward, I feel that you should stay here in Isethas for the time being until we get a better handle on your condition. Should you need to go back into the mortal realm, Cahtel will accompany you."

Aella's jaw drops slightly, and she shakes her head, "Wait, I can't, like, stay here... I have a job and an apartment. My mom and Tara, if I just leave without any reason, they will become suspicious. Also, Cahtel doesn't need to come with me. He has spent enough time in my closet." She says, looking over at Cahtel like he's an annoying babysitter.

"Then I suggest you both go back so that you can contact them and inform them that your communication will be minimal. We have much to do, and as you are aware, time is different here. The moment the portal is closed, time in your realm will resume normally. Ashlyn will make up your room for you."

Aella doesn't like this; she wants to balance her life still. Staying in Isethas for two weeks isn't at all what she had in mind. The longest she'd gone without seeing Tara was when Tara had visited her dad during the summers, and the time away from each other felt like a limb was being torn off.

Downing the wine in two large gulps, she looks at Cahtel and motions for him to lead the way back to the portal.

"Oh, and Aella, pack only the necessities. Whatever else you need, we will take care of it for you," Michael says, but she was already out the door before she could respond.

Once they leave the palace, Cahtel places his paw on Aella's arm.

"What are you doing?" Aella asks, weirded out by the fact that he is touching her.

"We are going to teleport to the portal; it will be much faster." He says, smirking at her.

"Why didn't we do this from the beginning, Cahtel?" Aella grits her teeth with annoyance. *Well, that would have been useful earlier on, asshole.*

"Because you hadn't earned it yet and because you earned it now by wiggling your big toe," Cahtel snickers.

Rolling her eyes, Cahtel chuckles and then straightens his body.

"Brace yourself. You might feel a little nauseous with the transport, but it is something you will get used to." He informs. *Yeah, like everything else in my life.*

Just as quickly as the thought occurs to her, they are in front of the portal, with her surroundings coming into focus. He wasn't wrong in the assumption that she would feel nauseous as she pushes forward with her hands on her knees and begins retching.

After she expels what little she has in her stomach, she says, "shit, you weren't wrong. That's worse than being stuck inside of Graviton."

Cahtel doesn't understand what she means, and she waves it off, not having the energy to explain it.

Thankfully, the portal is still there, but the edges aren't the same translucent silvery swirls. The edges are completely black now, emitting a smoke-like substance. Something about it is off, and Cahtel walks up to inspect it, noting the same.

"Why does the portal look like it's starting to grow some alien disease?" Aella asks, and Cahtel sighs under his breath.

"I'm not sure. I think it's been open too long. Come on, let's get what you need and get back," he says, jumping inside.

AN EERINESS OVERWHELMS THE APARTMENT AS THEY enter. It could be because of the weird, inky substance surrounding the portal that was never there before, but what jars Aella is when she looks at the time on her phone. Pulling back the curtains, the sun is out.

"Cahtel... I thought time stopped here when a portal was open?"

Crickets.

"Cahtel?"

He stalks over to the window and stares out unmoving.

Not wanting to prolong their stay, Aella hastily grabs a backpack and starts opening drawers for some articles of clothing, shoving them into her bag. Cahtel proceeds to stare out the window where the orchid had continued to grow, nearly breaking the pot she had purchased.

"Did you plant this?" He asks while he sniffs at the damp soil.

"Yeah, it started growing after you left it on my car. Cahtel, something about this doesn't feel right. Why are you deflecting?"

Rolling his eyes, he turns to keep examining the plant. Cahtel's disregard for the portal looking the way it does on the side in Isethas and the time change in the mortal realm have Aella's nerves on high alert.

"Impressive, not many know how to care for orchids properly."

Her cheeks warm at the praise. She takes her planting skills very seriously, and having someone recognize such talent is nice. *Focus, Aella.*

Shoving the necessary toiletries into the bag, Aella shuts the bathroom lights off and grabs her cell phone from the bedside table, checking to see if she has received any messages. Her heart skips a beat when she spots the one from Gabriel, *Damien.*

> Gabriel: I apologize for my rude behavior yesterday. I had a long day at work. I want to make it up to you. Dinner tonight?

Showing Cahtel the message, he clenches his teeth as he reads the text.

"Don't respond. He will grow suspicious."

Aella scoffs, "I can't not respond, he will grow suspicious if I completely ignore him. I also need to find a place to hide my phone while I'm away where my mother can't find it. Knowing her, she will come by making sure I'm where I tell her I'm going to be... where do I tell her I'm going to be?" *Fuck. Didn't think that one through now did you Aella?*

Cahtel shrugs, not being of any help. Sitting on her bed, she thinks for a minute, trying to come up with some elaborate story that her mother will buy. There is no way she will stay in Isethas the whole time. She has to come back, but Cahtel didn't need to know that yet.

How are you staying so calm? She thinks, looking at Cahtel in his unbothered state.

> Aella: Hey, Mom, I'm going to be
> MIA for a few days. Don't worry,
> I'm fine. I am going to a
> meditation retreat to help me
> with my sleeping.

That's good, Aella,

> I will call you as soon as I get
> back, and we can plan that
> Sedona trip! Love you.

Tara will be much harder to convince, especially since she knows Aella like the back of her hand. It will have to be something believable and completely off the wall at the same time. Thinking back to their last conversation and how much she and Gabriel clicked on their date, she has it.

> Aella: Hey babe! You won't
> believe this, but Gabriel is
> surprising me with a trip to the
> East Coast to check out some art
> museums and art programs! I know
> it's crazy and super last
> minute, but you always tell me
> to be more spontaneous, so I'm
> flying by the seat of my pants
> on this one. I won't really be
> available since I will be with
> Gabriel, but I will call you as
> soon as I can and give you all
> the dirty deets. Love you!

TARA WILL BE PISSED THAT AELLA WON'T KEEP HER UP TO date with all the juicy details on a trip that she's not even going on, but she will be excited to hear from her when she does. Aella will have to develop a fabricated story for when that happens.

Turning off her cell, she decides the best place for it to be is with her, even if she can't use it in Isethas. Throwing it in her bag, she takes one last look around the apartment, checking the window and making sure it's locked, along with the front door.

Cahtel seems as though he's transfixed, looking around her apartment.

"It's not much, but it's still home." Aella feels the need to justify the size, remembering the jab Cahtel threw at her; *what did he say exactly? Oh, right, pitiful excuse of a home.*

"I like it, it's cozy." He says, and a flicker of remorse clouds his eyes momentarily, "If you are finished, we should be on our way. Time is of the essence." He says then, flicking his gaze towards the portal inside her room.

"Right, I think I have everything I need. Oh! The orchid can't forget her."

Picking up the orchid from the base of the pot, which it will soon outgrow, she walks over to where Cahtel is standing on his haunches.

"She? It's a she?" He asks jokingly, and Aella stands her ground.

"Yes, it is a she. Problem?" Aella scoffs back jokingly, and Cahtel shakes his head.

After they walk back through the portal to Isethas, Aella sets her belongings down and stares at the black tendrils that continue to expand over the portal.

"Cahtel, I'm no expert on portals or anything, but I don't think that's normal, right?"

"No Aella, it is not normal," he lets out a breath, "let's get it closed, you remember how I taught you?"

Shaking her head hesitantly, she lays down on the grass, closing her eyes. Clearing her mind is going to be a bit more of a challenge, especially with what happened in the meditation room and now with the portal looking like it's growing some disease. Cahtel clears his throat, causing her to open her eyes.

"This is the only way I know how. Just shush, let me concentrate, and then you can teach me how to do it standing, okay?"

He doesn't say anything, allowing her to quieten her mind and ground herself. Going through all the steps, forcing those filing cabinets shut, she focuses on closing the portal, remembering to wiggle her big toe. The problem is, when she does those things, there's pushback. Something she didn't experience with Cahtel the first time or even in her meditative state. And when she opens her eyes, the portal remains.

"I can't close it. I don't know why, but it feels like an actual wall."

Cahtel's eyes widen, "That's impossible, you opened it initially so you can close it. Try again; we need to get this portal closed."

Aella shuts her eyes again, trying to remain calm. It's not like this whole portal opening and closing thing is something she has mastered yet. Trying not to think about anything other than the black void and closing the portal, her efforts on attempting to do so cause a searing pain that shoots through her skull, feeling like her brain is going to explode. Sitting up, she clutches at her head. Cahtel is by her side then, looking at her with a mix of concern and fear.

"Aella, what is it?"

"I— I'm not sure. My head feels like it's on fire. I can't close the portal, Cahtel."

"If what you're experiencing is what I think it is, then this is bad... This is really bad, Aella."

Cahtel begins to pace around, and the pain starts to ease gradually. Even though she feels as though she just got hit by a truck or, at the very least, is dealing with the worst hangover of her life.

"What do you mean?" Aella asks, even with the pain becoming more of a dull headache.

"There is a possibility that when you opened this portal, you also broke the seal, which means the portal will remain open indefinitely."

Fuck.

Chapter Twelve

Cahtel left Aella in the field with the portal by transporting himself back to the palace to get Michael and Torin. Sitting in the grass, she stares at the mess of a portal she had created—a mirrored image of herself, damaged and broken.

"Why Aella? Why do you have to fuck everything up?" She says aloud to herself, worry and defeat consuming her. The portal being left open wasn't entirely her fault, though. So much has happened in the last seventy-two-plus hours that it feels like a whirlwind. Frustrated and alone, all she wants in this moment is her best friend.

Tara would know the right thing to say to help ease her stress. She is her rock and yes-man, even when things don't go how they should.

One of her fondest memories is when she got fired from a job she had because she didn't sleep the night before and took a nap in the morning but overslept through her alarm. She immediately called Tara when it happened, and Tara insisted she come over to drink wine and forget about it. It was a shitty place to work, anyway.

"Fuck them! You don't want to work at a place like that anyway. They don't deserve you or your talents." Tara had said, always being Aella's cheerleader. The job was just another restaurant, but she appreciated Tara's enthusiasm, especially when it came to making her feel less embarrassed about getting fired. Without a college degree and not even a trade or skill, Aella's options for work were limited. Which is why she wants to get into an art program; even if she becomes a starving artist out of it, she will die happy.

A thought occurs to her then with the portal being left open. The only way anyone on the other side would know about it would be her mother since she has a key. Otherwise, it would be as if it didn't exist. *That's not terrible. Not great, but not terrible.* It's as if Tara was there with her, her soul sister helping her make light of the situation.

Cahtel appears then, along with Michael and Torin, breaking her from her spiraling thoughts. Michael walks over to the portal in silence, stopping before it with his hands on his hips, concentrating on where those black tendrils had continued to grow and expand. They looked more and more like tentacles, the way they wrapped and twined, moving as if they had a heartbeat of their own.

"Torin, we need to set up a perimeter a mile down, and a sign of sorts so no one comes this way. I don't want anyone in Isethas to know about this. Cahtel, you and Torin will take turns checking on it. No one will be permitted to come this way until we figure out how to close it." Michael orders wearing stress and irritation like a second skin.

Aella swallows and starts picking at the loose skin around her thumbnail. The sound of her picking is loud enough that Michael glances over at her, narrowing his eyes on the tick.

Aella ignores it and says, "Cahtel mentioned that I may have broken the seal with this portal. If that's the case, then what will that mean or look like?"

"We are getting this damn portal closed if my life depends on it," Michael shouts, and Aella flinches at the direct blow that she knows was intended for her. Looking away from her, Michael rubs the back of his neck, looking off into the distance of his realm.

"The portals were sealed for a reason. I have worked so hard rebuilding Isethas after the destruction of the war. I cannot afford to have my people live in fear of another war or the possibility of having their lives stripped from them." His voice softens, and Aella feels not only the remorse he carries from what happened before but also his own fear should something like that happen again.

"On the plus side, the portal is opened in my apartment, so no one will know about it unless, of course, my mom decides to pop in. Unless I get my locks changed, which is something I've been meaning to do." Aella says, hopeful that it will lessen some of the stress. Getting her locks changed wouldn't be the worst idea anyway. It would provide an extra level of privacy for when she returns and has a normal life. *Normal.*

"Actually, Aella, that's not a bad idea. Tomorrow morning, you and Cahtel will return together but don't take too long. We have training to do and need to be diligent about it moving forward," Michael says, and Aella feels a slight sense of relief.

EVERYONE IS TIRED FROM THE DAY THEY HAD. TORIN LEFT an hour after they got to the palace with Cahtel to work on the perimeter and ensure no one was nearby. Michael headed to what she assumed to be the kitchen, and Ashlyn showed Aella the room she will be staying in on the second floor. When they enter, the first thing she notices is the bed. Larger than a California king with an abundance of fluffy pillows and a thick white down comforter, leaving the bed would easily be a struggle. She knew the second her head hit the pillow, she would crash.

Turning the lights on to the bathroom, Aella follows Ashlyn in. The shower is an open concept with a floor drain and a brass rain shower. Black tiled floors cover the floor in a herringbone pattern, leading to an infinity tub that beckons you to walk into. Shelves of lush plants decorate the space, and two soft towels sit folded neatly on a stool with a basket of citrus and lavender-scented soaps and lotions. The vanity stretches long, covering an entire wall with his and her sinks on either side. The modern round mirrors hang down over each sink with warmly lit wall sconces, giving a romantic glow. Glancing into one of the mirrors, Aella watches Ashlyn walk to a door, opening it to showcase a massive walk-in closet. Velvet hangers dangle off brass bars, inviting anyone to overstay their welcome.

After she receives a tour of her bathroom, they reenter the bedroom. Then, without hesitation, Ashlyn pulls back thick blackout curtains, exposing two French doors. Opening them, they stride onto a balcony lit with string lights and a cute little table with two chairs. Plants and succulents fill the balcony, and the view is spectacular—a full view of Isethas just from taking a few steps out of the bedroom. The air is chilled, smelling of fall from the light breeze that caresses the fields of flowers below.

"Is everything to your liking?"

Unable to contain her laughter, only an idiot would complain about staying in such luxury.

"This is incredible, Ashlyn. Thank you."

Smiling, Ashlyn returns inside and closes the doors to the balcony, drawing the curtains.

"We should head back down before you turn in for the night. Michael had the cook prepare soup and bread for everyone, and there are some things we need to go over."

Her stomach growls at the mention of food. Then curiosity strikes because time isn't necessarily a thing here; she wonders how they recognize dawn and dusk.

"How do you know when it becomes nightfall?" Aella asks before they leave to meet with the rest of the group.

"Hmmm, that is a good question. Unlike your realm, we do not recognize time in the same way. However, we still have seasons and moments of rest. The sky remains indigo during daylight, but... here, let me show you." She walks back to the curtains, opening them slightly.

"The sky deepens and darkens into a black, though the stars remain, shining a vivid white. The sky is beginning to deepen, so if we recognize time like you, it would be evening. After the sky rotates, it will lighten to the indigo you are accustomed to by now, which is why we have blackout curtains in case we need more rest." Ashlyn explains before drawing the curtains shut.

That will take some getting used to.

"What happens if I accidentally oversleep?" *Or sleep the whole time I'm here.*

"Sleep is of the most importance, Aella. If you sleep all day and night, then that is what your body needs. You have no need to worry about that. Rest is necessary with learning how to suppress your condition."

Giving Ashlyn a gentle smile for answering her questions, Aella has plenty of days to ask more, and she didn't want to add to the exhaustion because they were all tired and stressed.

Leaving the bedroom, they walk down the spiral staircase

that would soon be the actual cause of Aella's death, or so she thinks. With shaky legs, she makes it to the end of the last step. Ashlyn waited patiently for her, hiding a smirk with her spindly fingers.

"I don't have the best experience with staircases. Add that to the list of things for me to work on." Aella blurts, containing her embarrassment.

"That's quite alright, Aella," Ashlyn replies with gentle humor.

The dining room is smaller than she imagined. She thought it would be huge like everything else in this palace. The rustic table sits six; Michael, Cahtel, and Torin are huddled in close, conversing about the perimeter that's been set up and a notice that will go out to the residents first thing in the morning informing them that there is a toxin in that area, and no-one is allowed to go near until it is dealt with. Although the formal conversation isn't dinner table talk, Aella notices they all have glasses of red wine.

Ashlyn leans into her ear then, picking up on the curious state.

"Michael prefers meals shared with close friends to be more of a gathering and informal. He likes to keep the family tradition." She whispers, and Aella's heart warms with the sentiment. She wasn't accustomed to having family gatherings like this, even on holidays, since it had always just been her and her mom. Dinner in front of the TV was as informal as it got, but this? This was more of a *special* occasion, not a typical Tuesday night, and certainly not with everything that was happening.

"It's about time. I was wondering if you two ran off together," Torin says, smirking. Cahtel rolls his eyes, carefully licking out of the wine glass, not finding humor in the joke. Now, Aella has to hold back a laugh. Watching a cat lick wine out of a glass is hilarious and enduring.

"Please, join us. The cook will be out shortly. He made yellow squash soup from the garden and rustic baked bread." Michael announces as Aella takes a seat across from him, sitting down awkwardly. He leans over, picking up a glass while looking Aella in the eye as he pours the wine. Handing it to her, their fingers graze with a featherlike touch.

Taking a sip from the glass, the liquid seduction sails down her throat like sweet velvet.

Michael takes another sip from his before speaking again, eyes lit with a glimmer of curiosity.

"An aged Cab, heavy-bodied, with notes of woodsy sweet vanilla and spiced black cherry." His subtle reference to woodsy and sweet doesn't go unnoticed. The warmth from the wine and his smooth words aid in making Aella's cheeks flush.

"So, the perimeter has been set up?" Aella asks, reeling herself back a little with the more pressing matter.

"Yes. Tomorrow morning, we will deliver letters to all of the residents telling them that a leak from the underground pipes has caused a toxic substance to seep through the soil in that area. They will be prohibited from passing the perimeter, and a sign will also be placed there."

Though not a complete lie, technically, there is a leak of some sort that appears toxic, given that Aella put it there. She is the pipe that broke.

"And what if Cahtel was right? What if the portal remains open indefinitely?"

Michael tenses at the question, tightening his hand around the wine glass hard enough to break. Aella presses her lips together, regretting asking the question for the second time, even if it is essential to consider.

"It will not remain open, and we will get it closed, so there is no need to worry about something that isn't going to happen," he says through slightly gritted teeth. Everyone takes a drink from their wine glasses to ease the tension that now occupies the space. Thankfully, the cook enters the gathering room through the doors leading to the kitchen, *a mercy*.

Pushing a cart with clay bowls of soup, plates, and a wrapped basket of bread that smells divine, Aella's mouth begins to salivate at the different spices that permeate the room.

Placing a plate out in front of each taken seat, he carefully sets the piping-hot bowls on top. A seamlessly folded linen cloth is then placed to the right as the cook lays down a gold-plated soup spoon to accompany it. Once everyone has their bowls, he sets the steaming basket of bread in the center of the table. For a casual dinner, Aella thought the layout was pretty formal.

Tasting the soup makes Aella's taste buds dance with delight, the flavors mingling in her mouth, complementing the wine's notes—yellow squash at the forefront and a bite of cayenne pepper. Soaking a slice of bread in the creamy substance fills her empty stomach without leaving her too full or heavy.

After their meal, the cook collects the empty bowls and plates and returns to the kitchen. By then, another bottle of wine has joined the table. Aella was on her third glass, relaxing back into her chair, enjoying the numbing sensation from the buzz of the wine.

"So, Aella, I am curious about something," Michael starts, now that everyone has had some food, "Prey, tell what you told your mother and your friend... ah yes, Tara, is it?"

Obviously, Michael is also feeling relaxed from the wine and full from his meal since the tension seems to have eased from his features regarding the open portal.

"I told them that I was going away for a meditation retreat

on the East Coast and would be looking into art programs while there." She says nonchalantly. It was not a complete lie, but she wasn't going to bring up the small fact about telling Tara she was going with Gabriel. Two completely different stories combined into one. She is in no mood to elaborate any further, riding her buzz.

Michael quirks his brow at the mention of art programs. His body language straightens to solely focus on Aella, and interest peaks in his tone.

"I didn't realize you enjoyed the arts."

Sipping wine, she nods her head, setting the glass back down. "I paint a little and have always wanted to learn different processes. Art history intrigues me. Some of my favorite paintings are from the Renaissance era. How the old masters created such beautiful oil paintings blows my mind," she gushes. The truth is she admires art history and tends to become overzealous when learning about the different artists of those periods.

It's evident that Michael is becoming more intrigued by Aella's fondness for art, and for the first time, she questions how old he actually is. He probably met some of the old masters himself.

"Well then, we will have to find time while you're here in between your training. I have some original pieces of art in my library along with books on art history, if you're feeling up to it."

That didn't surprise her, considering that Gabriel has originals himself. Klimt himself most likely gifted him *Death and Life* at some point in his life.

"I would love that, Michael." She says, and she really would. A little inspiration never hurt anyone, and it would most likely give her the push to proceed with her dream for when she has a normal life. *Normal.*

"Wonderful, now onto more pressing matters... Damien knows of you and your gift. You are safe here in Isethas. He cannot enter without a portal, and since he doesn't know where you live, that won't be an issue. However, I worry about the safety of your mother and friend Tara you speak so much about. Has my brother met either?"

Biting the inside of her lip, a wave of anxiety settles, not mixing too well with the wine.

"The night at Blanc, Gabriel... Damien, helped us into his driver's car. Tara got intoxicated, but we think she may have been drugged, so Damien escorted us out and made sure we got back to her condo safely. He didn't come with us, though, and I didn't tell him where she lived. I also met him at the restaurant when we had our date, even though he offered to pick me up."

Michael tenses again for a flicker of a moment, then shakes the feeling off and relaxes back into his chair.

"That was very wise. However, I'm concerned his driver may not be reliable with confidential information such as Tara's address. I'm assuming that Damien maintains the facade of being a wealthy businessman and hired a driver to do just that, but we can't be so sure."

Aella has an epiphany, "I have Tara's location on my phone; ah, wait, never mind, I can't use it here." *Tara, you brilliant bitch.*

Michael snaps his fingers, "While you and Cahtel go back through the portal tomorrow, check in with her then." He pauses to take another sip of his wine before continuing, "Ashlyn will continue training with you, strengthening your will to keep anything out while you are in your meditative state. As I said, you are safe here, so should another occurrence happen, whatever entered before cannot harm you. I think first and foremost, controlling on how to close the portal will be of importance. It will take some work, but I am confident you will succeed before our deadline. Torin will also train with you on physical combat should another war happen.."

"I'm sorry. Did you say physical combat?" Aella knew she could not physically train. She always thought she was nothing more than dead weight, especially with her unskilled coordination on stairs.

"Yes, that is what I said, Aella. We can't be too careful. Suppressing your gift is only part of the issue, and it won't be long before the other Watchers learn of your ability. Damien has a big mouth."

"I don't think you understand. I can't even stomach the thought of using pepper spray, let alone be able to wield a sword or punch someone."

Laughter breaks out across the table, and she feels stupid for not being in on the joke that is apparently her.

"Aella dear, we may be old, but we aren't *that* old. We no longer use swords. Although they are fun, we have an arsenal of guns and modern-day weapons. It will be much more brutal if another war comes, but we are prepared nonetheless." Torin says between chuckles.

Shooting a gun sounded more terrifying than spraying someone in the face with pepper spray. Aella abhorred guns, especially since it was a common accessory in Arizona. Men walking around with a pistol strapped to their hip always disgusted her. *"Look at me. I'm a power-hungry douche with a small penis, but look at how big my gun is." I think I'll pass on that.*

"Actually, I want to learn how to wield a sword."

The laughter subsides then, and the table becomes silent. Michael taps his finger on the glass stem, momentarily contemplating her request, and the corners of his mouth tip up. He leans back into his chair while draping an arm over the backrest.

"Interesting. How about this, you learn how to use a gun properly, don't want you shooting an eye out, and then we will revisit this sword-wielding. Although, for someone who gracefully deescalates down a flight of stairs, watching you wield a sword will be most entertaining." He teases. Rolling her eyes, she wanted to reach across the table and... She wants to jump on him. *There is something wrong with me.* The wine has entirely gone to her head, coaxing her into making bad decisions. What she needs is to go up to her room and sleep. Pushing out of her chair, she stands up, retiring to do just that.

"Aella, before you go to bed, we must make the tea. You have the right idea; it's getting late. We have a busy day tomorrow. Let's all get some rest. Here, come with me." With that, everyone gets up from their chairs. Cahtel gives her a friendly nod while Ashlyn gives a tired smile. Being the last to leave, Torin tracks Ashlyn down the hall, glancing at Michael with mischief.

"Keep it down, Torin. Some of us don't want to hear you two all hours of the night."

Oh, Torin and Ashlyn are lovers? For some reason, Aella feels relieved even though she has no real reason to.

Saluting Michael, Torin runs after Ashlyn, and a seductive giggle echoes down the hall, cut off by a soft thud of the door being shut.

Leading Aella into the kitchen, it is just as open and beautiful as the rest of the palace. Everything is neutral, aside from a green tiled backsplash along a wall behind where the stove and black quartz countertop are. Clicking on the burner, Michael places a kettle of water to boil, then grabs a ceramic mug from the top cabinet above. Realizing she had forgotten the tea sachets he made for her, Michael pulls down a box of sachets and places one in the mug. Waiting for the water to boil, she sits on a bar stool at an island in the center of the kitchen.

His back is to her, and he is stretching his neck side to side. Untucking his shirt, he pulls it over his head and sets it on the counter. Aella's mouth falls open at the sight. His back, like the little glimpses of his chest, is completely chiseled in cut muscle.

There are a couple of jagged scars, and she becomes curious about how he got them. Taking the tie out of his hair, his tendrils fall over his shoulders, and the wine coursing through her makes her want to lick up the salty sweat that gleams off his back.

Michael is definitely the better-looking twin, or at least he appears to be at this moment. Aella also desperately needed to get laid.

The sound of the kettle whining breaks the trance she is in, pulling her back to reality. Michael pours the hot water into the mug over the sachet, letting it steep for some time since it hasn't yet been a full thirty minutes. Turning to Aella, he places the mug down on the island.

The front side of his body is every girl's wet dream, even if he still has his slacks on. Folding his arms across his chest, it's evident that he is getting enjoyment from her gawking. Pursing her lips together, she reverts her eyes back to the mug.

"Thanks." She says, not giving him any more satisfaction from how her body and mind are clearly betraying her.

Michael smirks, "You're welcome. Usually, I charge for being eye fucked, but since you're a guest in my home, I'll let it slide."

Aella's jaw drops at the vulgar remark, and her cheeks instantly warm with embarrassment for doing precisely that.

"Don't flatter yourself, Michael. How did you get those scars along your back?" She says, changing the subject.

Straightening his back, he clears his throat and swallows, then sticks his hands in his pockets, reverting his attention to an invisible crumb on the countertop. Because Aella doesn't have a good read on him yet, she starts to worry that she may have offended him with the silence that now takes up the space. Her hands fall to her lap as she mindlessly picks at the skin around her thumbnail.

"During the war of the realms." He says, cringing at the noise that comes from her picking.

Aella nods, moving her hands away from each other so that she can consciously stop the habit, "Did it hurt?" *No shit it hurt Aella. What kind of question is that?*

"That kind of pain is temporary. The one who did it stays with me forever. The scars are a constant reminder of whom I entrusted and cared for only to be betrayed by in the end." He says, eyes getting lost in a faraway place. Aella didn't push any further, even if she wanted to know more. She could tell that it was a sore topic and one that still haunts him.

"The tea is cooled down enough to drink," he says abruptly, blinking away the memory.

Turning her nose up at the smell, she knew it would taste just as terrible. Pinching her nose, she tosses it down, trying not to gag. Wiping her mouth with the back of her hand, she hands him the mug, wishing she could chase down the taste with something else.

"I meant what I said earlier. I would love to show you the library and paintings. It's one of my favorite rooms."

Her eyes begin to grow heavy. Stepping off the stool, she looks at him before carrying her tired body up the torrential staircase.

"Okay. Thank you, Michael, for everything. Your home is lovely."

He nods, turning to wash the cup, and she takes that as her queue to leave before saying something else she would regret. He then stops her by grabbing her arm so she can face him.

"If you need anything while you're here, just ask. If I am not around, Torin or Ashlyn will be of assistance."

Searching his beautiful pale blue eyes with hers, she wants to say how sorry she is for burdening them, but she just nods instead. He lets go of her forearm, grazing his fingers down her wrist, leaving a cold chill in its wake.

Going up the stairs to the room she will be staying in, her body and mind feel exhausted and light. The stress is still there, and even though the tea will send her into rest while putting a bandaid on her subconscious, there is an inkling of fear that it won't work.

Too tired to use the bathtub, she opts for the shower. Turning the knob allowing the water to heat to her liking, the water pressure is going to feel amazing on her tight muscles.

Once she is out of her grimy clothes, she slides them across the floor, eager to wash the day off. Lathering shampoo between her palms, an eucalyptus and tea tree aroma opens her senses.

Scrubbing her scalp clean, a fresh loofa beckons her to pick it up. "Don't mind if I do," she says to herself as she washes her body with the loofa and lemon-scented soap. Rinsing the suds off her body, her mind is numb, and for the first time, those filing cabinets are closed without forcing them to do so.

After the shower from heaven, she dries off with the soft white bath towels left for her. Rummaging in her backpack, she realizes that she has forgotten her pajamas. Having always slept in the nude, it doesn't surprise her that she forgot a pair. *Really,*

Aella? Throwing on a clean pair of underwear and a T-shirt, she pulls back the covers to her new bed and fires on her cell.

Unsurprisingly, there aren't any cell towers, so instead, she looks through photos of her and Tara, bringing her slight joy. *Normal.* That damn word again that seems to filter through her head. Powering off her cell, she sets it face down in the top drawer of the bedside table. Tucking herself in, sleep starts overtaking her, and she drifts soundly, listening to the soft turning of the blades attached to the ceiling fan above. Allowing her new bed to swallow her up and thinks of nothing.

Wiggle your big toe.

Chapter Thirteen

A gentle knock pulls Aella out of rest. Squinting her eyes open, a radiant Ashlyn peeks her head in.

"Good Morning," Ashlyn says softly, clearly not hungover.

"Good morning," Aella's response is hoarse with sleep. "How long have I slept for?" Sitting up, a throbbing migraine starts to form.

"Ten hours! You needed the rest. I brought you some coffee and breakfast!" Ashlyn is in a chipper mood. Most likely having nothing to do with Torin staying over. Walking into the room, she sets a silver tray with an assortment of fruits and freshly baked muffins on a small coffee table across from a sofa in the far corner.

"Ten hours?!" She gapes, shoving the covers off of her, her movements jerky due to the migraine. "You don't happen to have any Tylenol, do you?" She then asks, rubbing at her temples, hoping to stop the migraine before it takes her out for the whole day. Aella and Cahtel still have to go back to her apartment and change the locks, not to mention the training she will be tasked with today.

Smiling, Ashlyn approaches the side of the bed with grace, handing her the cup of coffee she brought in. Reaching inside the front pocket of the pair of cream-colored linen pants, she pulls out a bottle of pills.

"Take two, and your headache will go away completely."

Letting out a breath of relief, Aella happily takes the bottle. Leaning on an elbow, she tosses two pills back and swallows them with a sip of the most delicious coffee she's ever tasted.

Ashlyn gives Aella a moment to adjust her eyes before pulling the blackout curtains open. She then opens the doors to allow fresh air to breeze through. Having forgotten that she was only wearing a T-shirt and underwear, Aella rolls out of bed, giving Ashlyn an apologetic look.

"Oh, Aella, I'm surprised you're wearing anything to bed. I sleep in the nude. Clothes are far too restricting." Feeling less self-conscious, Aella walks over to the beautiful platter of fruit that Ashlyn kindly brought in, popping a piece of melon into her mouth.

"I'll have to grab some more things from my apartment since I was in such a rush. I didn't bring too much with me. Cahtel has probably been waiting on me; I should get dressed and head down there." Aella says, stretching her back. Even though she slept, she still feels like she got hit by a truck, much like she did when she tried to close the portal, which is weird.

Waving her hand, Ashlyn says, "Bring whatever you wish, but should you need anything else, we have you covered while you're here. Michael will pay for it. And not to worry about Cahtel. He and Torin are still out informing the residents about the... spill. Please, take a seat. I want to talk with you about something."

Aella sits down on the couch with her coffee in hand, giving Ashlyn her undivided attention. Her migraine has turned into a dull headache at this point from taking whatever the pills were, and with the caffeine, she knew it would become more manageable once she gets moving. She can't help but stare at Ashlyn, mentally comparing herself to her. She looked beautiful no matter what she wore. You could put her in a potato sack, and even then, it wouldn't detract from her radiance.

Her hair is pulled back in a perfect bun, the big handmade turquoise and silver earrings hang from her ears, and a tight, form-fitting white tank is tucked into those loose-fitted linen pants.

With only the bare minimum on her face, she doesn't need makeup because she is so beautiful. Her full, perfectly arched brows compliment her big blue eyes, a single coat of mascara opens them up, and her lips have a sheen of gloss. Aella wondered if she ever had a day where she looked like a slob. You couldn't hate Ashlyn even if you wanted to. She is just as beautiful on the inside as she is out.

Sitting next to Aella on the sofa, she leans over to pick out a couple of grapes and berries. Watching her eat is graceful, like everything else she does, compared to how Aella tends to shovel food into her mouth when no one is looking. Sipping on her coffee, Aella's mind wanders into space, opening all those filing cabinets again.

"What are you thinking?"

"Everything," an awkward laugh escapes. "It's like I have these filing cabinets that decide to open and overwhelm me with everything. Sometimes, it starts small, like I need to do my laundry and what I'm going to have for dinner, to how I am going to save the world and the realms, and if my mom is going to give me space when I get back to my normal life." *Normal.*

After her rant, Ashlyn nods in understanding, "I can imagine how overwhelming this all must be for you." She says, then pinches her brows together, "What is your relationship like with your mother?"

The question catches Aella off guard, considering her relationship with her mother has always been somewhat difficult. Ashlyn picks up on Aella's sudden discomfort and reaches her hand over, gently placing it on her shoulder.

"I'm sorry, Aella, did I overstep?"

"No, not at all, just thinking again. She means well, which is the issue. When I have these *episodes*, they get really dark sometimes, and now that I know a little bit more about what it means, it makes sense. The doctors I would see diagnosed me with sleep paralysis. One night, it got out of hand, and I had what they described as a psychotic break. I tried explaining to them and my mother what happened, and they recommended I be hospitalized for a bit. I had to sign myself in, where they treated me with a cocktail of medications, which in turn made my condition worse. After that, I stopped going to the doctor and told my mother that I was *cured*."

Ashlyn's tone softens, and she looks at Aella with understanding. "That sounds awful. Humans can be so... simple-minded, can't they?"

"I suppose you have a point there... After some time, my mother noticed the bags forming under my eyes again due to lack of sleep and tried every naturopathic thing you could think of, from herbs to crystals to specialized *healers*. None of it worked, but it made her feel good to help me, like it was her purpose, which makes sense since I'm her only daughter."

Perhaps Susan thought Aella was the issue, which didn't make her feel any better. Picking at the skin around her fingernails, she thought about that more. Being positive wasn't her best attribute, whereas Susan never had a bad day. *"Life is what you make it, honey."* She would tell her, *"Put out what you want to receive."* A typical quote you would find on a *Pinterest* board for positive thinking and self-help bull shit.

"That must have been hard, not knowing what this gift was that haunted you. You haven't mentioned a father figure in your life. Do you know about yours?"

Gift. This was no gift, or is it? At least Aella hasn't thought about her condition as such.

"No, unfortunately, I don't. My mother never shared anything with me about who my father is other than they briefly dated, and she got pregnant with me, and that was that. I don't know his name or what he looks like, let alone where he is. He could even be dead. Why do you ask?"

Ashlyn turns her whole body to face Aella then, and the suspense makes Aella's nerves tense with anticipation.

"I only ask because I have a theory. One I have been thinking about since Michael told me about you and then when I met you in person for the first time. I couldn't get over the striking resemblance. Michael didn't want me to say anything to you yet unless we were positive, but I feel it is best to know at least, especially if you had an idea of who your father could be." She says, then swallows before continuing, "Before the war, you could go through portals to different realms, but depending on the portal, it could take time. Depending on what realm it was you wanted to get to, sometimes you would have to travel by either boat, horse, or even foot, that is until Elissa. Like you, she could manifest a portal to wherever she wanted and enter that realm within minutes. Some referred to her as *the Wanderer* due to her gift. She had a husband and a son named Christopher, but because both Elissa and her husband fought and died in the war, Christopher was all that remained in his family's lineage. As far as we know, he did not inherit Elissa's gift, which has me curious about something... After the war, Christopher asked to live in the mortal before the portals were sealed. I guess he felt like he never really fit in here in Isethas and wanted to start anew. Aella, Christopher could be your father, which means you are Elissa's granddaughter. If my theory is correct, you are only half mortal, which could change everything."

Clutching the mug of coffee to her chest while she processes Ashlyn's theory, she wants to find out if Christopher really is her father. If he was, and Elissa was her grandmother, then why did he leave and want nothing to do with her?

Swallowing another sip of coffee to moisten her dry throat before responding, the number of questions swarming her mind bombards her, making it hard to speak.

"Do you know where Christopher is?" Aella croaks out.

A few seconds goes by before Ashlyn responds.

"Unfortunately, I do not. Your mother, however, may know where he is." she sighs, finding the right words to continue on, "When I met you for the first time, it was like I was staring at a spitting image of Elissa. It was almost overwhelming. You and she have the same eye color along with the same point to your nose. She was so beautiful and stubborn, much like you," Ashlyn giggles, "I am sorry that I didn't tell you about my theory sooner, but if there is any way we can access Christopher, then it might help us understand your gift a little bit better."

Aella feels a slew of emotions at once, with heartbreak at the forefront. She has been lied to her whole life, especially by the one person who was supposed to be in her corner. Christopher could be her father, and he is alive—at least, she hopes he is. Determination and anxiety cause her palms to sweat and her stomach to turn.

"I can't believe she lied to me. She told me my father wanted nothing to do with me... How could she do that?"

Aella wants to scream at her mother, along with telling her

what a terrible excuse of a parent she was for lying to her about her father her whole life. She had no right. Anger rears its ugly head, leaving an acidic taste in her mouth.

"I am unsure why your mother would have lied to you. Perhaps she thought it was the right thing to do at that moment. I am also unsure of what Christopher may have told your mother, but maybe she thought she was protecting you... perhaps she knew more about your gift than she led on. The guilt she must carry is heavy; remember that when you speak with her, for she is the only person who knows where he may be. I need to meet with Michael and Torin. I will leave you to get ready. We have a lot scheduled. Eat as much as you like."

Giving her thigh a gentle pat, Ashlyn stands up from the sofa with a sympathetic smile, leaving Aella with more thoughts to add to the file cabinets in her brain. She continued to sit in that spot, frozen with anger and sadness, until forcing herself up and finally heading into the bathroom to shower and prepare for the day. She now has the name of a man who could potentially be her father, and all at once, nerves mixed with excitement replace some of the anger.

Would we even look like each other? Are our mannerisms similar? Does he look aged like Susan? All of these questions could soon be answered the moment she met him for the first time.

LESS THAN AN HOUR LATER, A KNOCK ON THE DOOR sounds. Aella is still in the bathroom when she shouts, "Come in! I'm just finishing up!"

The door opens, and footsteps round the corner.

"Sorry, just a few more minutes, Cahtel, I'm almost ready— Michael!"

His name flies out of her mouth with a gasp. Dressed in his usual button-up shirt, he donned a black satin number with the sleeves rolled and the first few buttons open, exposing his chest, tucked into a pair of fitted and tailored black slacks. His hair is down except for half, pulled back into a bun, and his facial hair is cropped with precision to his face. Leaning against the entryway to the bathroom with his arms crossed as his eyes bore into her.

"You have a hot date?" He says with a teasing tone.

"Do I look too overdressed? I can change. I didn't bring that much with me..."

"No! You look... beautiful."

Her cheeks warm at the compliment. She decided to wear the only dress she had brought, a simple black cotton and shin-length dress with straps. It's casual enough, and she can always dress it up or down, one of her favorite dresses to throw on in a hurry back home. She pulled her hair back into a loose ponytail, leaving enough flyaways to frame her round face. Her makeup is subtle, with a slight flick of eyeliner accentuating her already cat-like eyes. Sticking two small gold hoop earrings into her lobes, Michael walks behind her in the mirror to help with the clasp belonging to the dainty chain of her necklace.

"Thank you," She breathes from the soft touch of his big hands. "I thought Cahtel was coming to get me. We have to get a move on."

"He and Torin just returned from making their rounds. It's still early enough, and I wanted to see how you slept." An all-knowing look shadows his features, which doesn't seem to ease Aella's nerves.

"I slept pretty good, all things considered. I had a headache when I woke up, though. Is it from the tea?"

Leaning away from him, she watches his reflection in the

mirror and then turns to face him, knitting her brows with concern.

"You shouldn't have gotten a headache from the tea, but it may have a different effect on you than it would on Isethanians," he says as he turns to leave the room.

Following him out, she hopes that the headache won't become more of an issue, especially if she has to continue drinking it.

Everyone is waiting in the lounge, chatting as Aella and Michael enter. Cahtel and Torin are in the middle of arguing about something, and Ashlyn is leaning against the bar, rolling her eyes at the two of them.

"Aella, you look exquisite!" She exclaims, a smile tugging at her lips.

"Thank you, Ash!" Aella responds with enthusiasm. Even though she would be going back through the portal, she wanted to try a little not to look like a slob.

"Why don't I have a nickname yet, Aella? We knew each other first, after all." Cahtel cuts in, scoffing.

Rolling her eyes at him, she says, "Because the only thing I can think of to call you would be *Vanilla Ice*, in which case you haven't solved any of my problems yet." *Or Cat*, and the last time she called him that, he was offended.

Torin cracks up at her retort, making Cahtel even more aggravated.

"Alright, alright," Michael interrupts the banter, "we have a busy day ahead of us and a lot to go over."

Michael spends the next half hour filling them in on the schedule for the upcoming days. Mornings would be spent with Ashlyn in the meditation room, afternoons Aella would train with Torin on hand-to-hand combat and how to handle a firearm as well as shooting one with target practice. Cahtel is in charge of the history of Isethas and the different realms, as well as who their rulers are. He would be educating Aella on their weaknesses should they see another war, who they were before, and what kind of alliance they could have with them. After he was finished, they dismissed themselves.

Cahtel and Aella are heading out to teleport towards the portal when Michael stops her briefly.

"Ashlyn told me about your conversation earlier. I want you to know that there is no pressure to find Christopher unless you want to. It could, however, help us in understanding your condition."

Condition. Gift. Episodes.

"I know, thank you. I would like to find him if possible or at least find a way to contact him... We have quite the schedule, but it might help us understand something we could have missed."

Softening his features, he reaches up, tucking a strand of hair behind her ear from the light breeze, the act causing her to stiffen slightly. Michael retracts his fingers, noticing, then nods his head in agreement.

"Should you have no way of getting in touch with him, I am confident that more sessions with Ashlyn will give us a better grasp," he says, and after a moment, he gives her a gentle smile and returns inside the palace.

Cahtel looks at Aella, silently asking if she's ready for the teleport. Breathing in through her nose, she closes her eyes, and before she has time to exhale, they are in the field where the portal still stands.

"You could have at least waited until I let out a breath, Cahtel!" She snaps, bracing her hands on her knees as the realm spins around her.

"Who's *Vanilla Ice?*"

"What? Oh, right. He was a hip-hop singer in the '90s, kind of a one-hit wonder, doesn't matter." She says, standing up, and when her eyes can focus, dread takes over as she stares at the portal.

The entire portal is black without a trace of the silvery swirls, unlike the black void she had entered on her way into Isethas. It looks like tar with those strange tentacles ebbing and flowing.

"Cahtel?" She says, unable to form a sentence, hoping he will give her some assurance about walking through it. But he, too, has no words.

"This isn't normal, right?" Aella asks with hesitation.

He shakes his head, staring at the wall of black death. "No Aella, that is not normal. If we don't make it, at least we go together." He says, and Aella wants to retch all over again.

And this, Aella, this is how you die.

AFTER ABOUT FIVE MINUTES OF CAHTEL AND AELLA contemplating whether or not they should risk it for the biscuit, they pull it together and walk through the portal's opening. It feels exactly like you would suspect, like treading through water. Once they got through the opening, the black tentacles had grown down the manifested hallway, taking over the walls like an infestation of overgrown vines.

They move slowly, too scared to make a sound, fearing that if they so much as breathe wrong on one of the tentacles, it would wrap around them, making them a part of whatever has inhabited the portal.

Unable to bear the silence and the only sound of the squelching her shoes make across the hallway's floor from the sticky substance those tentacles had oozed, Aella keeps her voice down to a mere whisper.

"Have you seen anything like this before? I can't imagine

this is how the portals looked when they were all open before the war."

Cahtel huffs as he shakes his paws out, flinging the substance with every step, and Aella wrinkles her nose up, thankful she at least has a pair of shoes on despite how heavy they feel.

"No, I honestly don't know what this is, but I don't like it."

A shiver cascades over her body, and even though it seems as if they are both walking through uncharted territory together, she would be lying if she said she wasn't a bit relieved in that they are experiencing something new together.

As they creep closer to the end of the portal, that relief grows stronger with the last couple of feet ahead of her. Aella lets Cahtel take the lead, considering he didn't have shoes on; it was the least she could do despite trudging back through all over again. Cahtel bows sarcastically, thanking her for being so kind, and after a few seconds, she, too, enters the black void.

Her apartment looks the exact same as she left it in that those black tentacles haven't cut through to this side yet. What she wasn't expecting, however, was her mother. Susan is sitting at the table with a manilla envelope before her.

Aella jumps with shock and that same anger she harbored from earlier, along with the fact that her mother had indeed stopped by to ensure she was where she said she would to be.

"Hello, Aella." Her mother says in a soft, quiet tone, eyes widening at the presence of Cahtel. If Aella didn't know any better, she thought her mother was on the verge of having a heart attack. And there lies the issue: the portal, the cat, and her mother, all in the same space.

"Please, sit. We need to talk." Susan says clearing her voice, while she attempts to keep her hands from trembling and fails miserably.

"Oh, we need to talk, alright. You lied to me my whole life!

My whole goddamned life, Mom. Why?!" Aella shouts, tears burning in the back of her eyes.

"Oh honey, everything I did was to protect you. Please sit, I will explain—"

"Protect me?!" Aella's voice is shrill, "Protect me from what exactly, *Susan*? Take a look around you. Do you know what this is? Do you know who this is next to me? Those *episodes* I had my whole life, where you talked me into hospitalization and force-fed your herbs and crystal bullshit down my throat, yeah, those didn't work, mother. None of it ever did, and now you want to talk?!"

Aella is shaking so badly with anger that it appears as though the walls of her apartment are doing the same. Cahtel places his sticky paw on her shoulder, easing the storm that begins to fester inside of her. Once she takes a deep breath, she looks at her mother again with anger and disgust. Susan's appearance had dulled to a sheet of white with her hands cupping her mouth.

"Aella," Cahtel says softly, "Either there was a mini earthquake, or you just caused one."

Chapter Fourteen

I*mpossible*. Arizona deosn't have earthquakes, and Aella wasn't some powerful being. The headache from earlier begins to form along her temples, and without saying so much as another word to her mother or Cahtel, she stalks off to the kitchen to get some pain relief and grabs a bottle of water from the fridge. Placing her palms on the countertop, she hangs her head down for a moment, thinking about how much more fucked her situation has gotten now that her mother is in the picture.

Walking to the table, she pulls out a chair and sits across from her mother, the anger still simmering under the surface.

"You want to talk? Fine. Answer me one question and do it honestly. Is Christopher my father?" Aella asks in an even tone, crossing her arms over her chest. Susan diverts her attention from her, briefly looking up at the ceiling, holding back tears of her own.

"Yes," she finally says, pushing the envelope towards her. "Everything you need to know about who your father is and where he lives is in this envelope. It isn't much, and he may have moved, but the last I checked, he was still on the East Coast, Pennsylvania. He goes by Chris Davidson."

Aella stares at the envelope, hesitant to flip it open. Her father is not only in the U.S., but he is in the place that she desperately wants to be once she has a normal life. *Normal.*

"I met your father when I was eighteen, Aella. I was so young and wanted to live a life full of adventure. My best friend invited me to go with her to a festival in Vermont," Susan stalls, chuckling as she thinks back to that memory, "My mother didn't want me to go; she was afraid that I would get swept up into some sort of commune, but I needed to do it. There was so much music, dancing, laughter, and psychedelics of every kind. Anything you could imagine, really. It was just Jan and I; we were like *Thelma and Luis*, kind of like you and Tara are. There was a group of guys camping at the festival; Christopher was one of them, and boy, he had trouble written all over him. I was completely and madly in love the moment I laid eyes on him. We had this sort of deep connection, two halves to a whole. After I met him, I never came back, at least not until I found out I was pregnant with you."

Aella listens, not understanding what went wrong and why her mother left the supposed love of her life, and so Susan continues, "Life with your father was so chaotic, and in the beginning, it's what really captivated me. He sometimes would have these *episodes* of his own, not like what you have dealt with with having sleep paralysis, but these angry fits that would scare the shit out of me sometimes. Then, he would come home smelling of alcohol and other women. Being so young and naive then, I gave him multiple chances. One night, while we were asleep, something unworldly happened, and a portal, much like the one that is in your apartment now, was open. I didn't know what it was at the time because what really freaked me out was the woman who was inside of our bedroom. Christopher then

174

told me about different realms and how he isn't from the mortal realm. He told me about how the portals were sealed, and that shouldn't have happened. I thought he was just crazy. Shortly after, I found out I was pregnant with you, and I left. The strange phenomena didn't happen again, that is, until you were born. You hardly slept as a baby, fighting me and screaming. I was lucky if I got an hour of sleep myself during that stage of your life, and you never wanted me to put you down. There was something you were afraid of even then. It wasn't until you got older that I noticed your *episodes*. I should have told you sooner, and I should have done something, but I tried Aella. In all of my efforts, I tried. It may not have been enough, but whatever this is, you are strong and always have been my little rose. I am sorry."

Susan finishes with tears streaming down her face, grief and sadness clouding her hazel eyes. Aella wipes her own tears, hot streams that threaten to keep falling no matter how hard she tries to prevent them.

"Thank you for telling me. I'm still angry and confused by all of this, but it's a start." Aella says, staring back down at the manilla envelope.

"I wouldn't expect anything less from you. Stubborn should have been your middle name." Susan smiles and then looks over to Cahtel, "Who is your friend?" She asks, and Aella remembers there's a talking cat from another realm in her apartment.

"This is Cahtel. He is from Isethas, the same realm as my..." Aella trails off, unsure if she should give Christopher the title she is considering.

"That's okay, dear, you can say it. He is your father."

Clearing her throat, Aella says, "Anyway, yeah, he came during one of my *episodes*. I guess my condition is a lot more invasive, and we have to get a handle on it before something else major happens. Also, why do you seem so calm about a talking cat and a portal that looks like it's straight out of the gates of hell?"

Susan laughs and says, "Honey, I've done enough ayahuasca in my lifetime to see the strange and unusual. This is a cakewalk. Listen, all of this is a part of your journey. I always knew you were special, and your condition is one that I had hoped could be mended through natural and traditional practices. Should you find your father, just know whatever the outcome is; I love you and did what I thought was best at the time. My only regret in doing so was keeping your father a secret and not telling you until now."

"How did you know? I mean, how did you know to come here when you did?"

Susan smirks cocking her brow, "Despite how you feel about me right now and what you think, I am still your mother. I know when you're lying to me. My Aella would never willingly go to a meditation retreat. So I came by yesterday and saw the portal; that's when I knew it was time to give you the truth about your father. I honestly wasn't expecting you to come back when you did and was going to leave the envelope here, but my intuition told me to stay no matter how long it took."

Sliding out of the chair, Susan leans forward, cupping Aella's cheek.

"You are brave, Aella Rose. I will leave you and Cahtel to it. Should you need anything, remember I am just a phone call away."

A strange feeling washes over Aella at that moment, and without a second thought, she stands up, wraps her arms around her mother, and mumbles in the embrace, "You could come back with us. I mean, I'm not so sure you staying here right now is the best until we manage my condition," Aella says, an inkling of unease settling in.

"Don't worry about me. Besides, I am heading to Myrtle Beach for a while to visit with Jan. It's time I do something adventurous."

Aella isn't sure if it was her mother's calm attitude about everything or the fact that she was going on a vacation when the world and the realms could collapse that gave her such pause; either way, this was typical Susan. Shaking her head, Aella pulls back from her mother.

"Of course, you plan a trip when shit hits the fan." Aella sighs, "Just be careful, Mom. I don't have cell service in Isethas, but I will be back again to check in on you."

Heading for the door, Susan turns and gives Aella one more once-over. "Give 'em hell," she says, and Aella raises her brows in surprise. Winking at her, Susan then says, "What? I'm on vacation time now. Besides, you're an adult; you got this! I'll send photos of my trip, which reminds me I have to pack! Love ya!"

"Wait, when are you leaving, and when will you be back?" Aella asks with a little more force than intended.

"Tomorrow morning, and I will be gone for a week. I will be fine, Aella. You have other things to worry about right now."

That's the understatement of the year.

"Oh, I almost forgot. Here," Susan reaches into her pocket, pulling out the key to Aella's apartment. Handing it over to Aella, she takes it, unsure of what to say.

"I have no use for this anymore. Sometimes, I forget that you are an adult and not my little girl any longer. You will always be my daughter, and as hard as it is for me to accept you are grown and are fully capable of doing things for you, it's time I let go."

Tears threaten to well up once again as Aella clutches the only copy her mother bribed her into making for her. It is so small and silly, but a symbolic reference to having even the tiniest sliver of freedom back and a boundary that is now set has the strongest impact on her—a new beginning for when her life would become normal.

Normal.

Shutting the door behind her mother, Aella turns to see Cahtel staring out the window, watching cars as they pass by.

"Well, I guess we don't need to change the locks any longer." She sighs, walking back over to the small table where the manilla envelope sits unopened.

Cahtel continues to stand there in silence as he looks out the window.

"Cahtel?" She says, and he finally turns to face her.

"It's interesting. I have spotted the same vehicle driving by a number of times but with a different person inside. Life here seems so... routine."

"Coming from where you come from, I would think so too. However, nothing is routine about a portal being open and my mother giving me every last shred of information she has on my father."

Cahtel stalks over, eyeing the envelope himself, then looks over to meet Aella's gaze.

"You going to open it?" He asks, sounding more curious than Aella is feeling.

Aella shoots him a look of *no shit,* but she is hesitant. Because inside that envelope wasn't just a man, who was her father. She had gone her whole life thinking he never existed, and despite needing to contact him to get as much information as they could get, Aella would be lying if she didn't fear even the slightest bit of rejection. Picking the skin around her thumbnail, Cahtel lifts his paw, placing it on her hand to stop her.

"What is it?" He asks, "What are you afraid of?"

"What if..." Aella sighs, shaking her head, "What if he

doesn't want anything to do with me or this? I mean, he left Isethas for a reason and a new life; he could have a whole new family. Then we are back to square one, and I'm back to feeling..."

"Feeling what?" Cahtel asks sincerely without any tinge of the usual sarcasm. Taking a deep breath, she has to force out the word. A word she has grown accustomed to from her own projection and discomfort of being in her own skin.

"Unwanted."

Unwanted, a single word that she never said aloud to anyone, including Tara. *Unwanted*, because that is how she has viewed herself due to her condition and never feeling worthy enough to have a typical relationship. *Unwanted*, because she believed with every fiber of her being that her own father didn't want her then, even though he didn't know she existed.

"Well, that's just silly, " Cahtel scoffs, rolling his eyes, then waves his paw towards the envelope. "Open the envelope, Aella; it's not like opening a portal, and if all else fails, you can close it and forget all about it," he says, and he has a point. It wasn't like opening a portal, but that didn't make it any less terrifying.

Mustering up a little courage, Aella snatches the envelope and flips it open. Her hands tremble when a photograph is the first thing she sees. A very young Susan is in it, laughing at the camera, looking the happiest Aella has ever seen her with dark brown hair all the way past her waist and her arms wrapped around a man who must be Christopher. Aella's breath catches as she looks at the photo closely; the resemblance between her and her father is striking. His hair is shoulder-length, and his skin is the same olive tone as hers. They have the same almond shape to their eyes, though his are a honey brown.

The bridge of their nose is identical aside from the slight upward point she has, and their high cheekbones are placed in the exact same spot, although his are slightly fuller. Their mouths are exact, however, from the divot of their cupid's bow down to the fullness of their lower lip. There is no doubt that Christopher is her father.

Wiping a single tear, Aella sets the photograph down on the table where Cahtel looks at it. There are a couple of old bills in the envelope that have an address on them and a torn sheet of paper with a phone number. Holding the piece of paper with the phone number on it, Aella walks over to the bed, where she had tossed her cell phone before she snapped at her mother. Waiting for her phone to turn on, she looks at Cahtel nervously.

"What do I say?"

"The truth. Tell him who you are. The rest will follow." He says, still looking down at the photo.

Nodding her head, she directs her attention back to her phone, and a smile stretches across her face when she sees three text messages from Tara. Disregarding them, she would read them once she called her father.

Breathe, Aella, breathe. It's only a phone call.

Typing the numbers on the screen, her finger stalls over the green button as her heart rate accelerates.

It's now or never.

Counting to three, she finally hits dial. Holding the phone up to her ear, she listens to it ring. After the fifth ring, a woman answers the phone.

"Hello?" The woman says with a crying baby in the background.

"H—hi, um, is Christopher there?" Aella asks nervously, hoping that she called the wrong number.

"Just a minute, Chris! Someone is on the phone for you!" She yells, and Aella's heart falls to her stomach.

"This is Chris," He says, walking out of the room where the

baby crying is nothing but a muffled sound in the background. "Hello?"

"Uh yes, hi Chris, my name is Aella. Aella Clarke? You used to date a woman named Susan Clarke?"

"Oh my god, Susan? I haven't heard that name in ages, it seems like. What can I do for you—"

Reality must have hit him at that moment because he was utterly silent.

"Are you still there?" Aella asks, her voice sounding more like a whisper.

Clearing his throat, he says, "She was pregnant, wasn't she, and that's why she left? You're my daughter, aren't you?"

Aella holds back tears, and she hears the woman yell, "*Chris, who is it?*".

"Can I call you back? I need to figure out how to tell my wife." He says, quieting his voice.

"Look, I know this just came out of left field, but there's a situation..." Aella says, thinking about how to tell him.

"If this is about money you think I owe you—"

"I don't want your money," Aella blurts, his assumption hitting her like a blow to the gut. "I'll make this short; I have the same ability as your mother did, except mine isn't quite controlled. Basically, I opened a portal into Isethas, and now it's open. I don't know—"

"Where are you now? I'll catch the next flight out," he says, cutting her off.

"Phoenix, Arizona."

The sound of keys tapping on a keyboard breakthrough then.

"I will be there at 8:00 am tomorrow."

"Okay, I will pick you up. Look for a green Kia Soul."

Christopher doesn't respond, and Aella is met with the phone going dead.

"So? How did it go?" Cahtel asks warily.

"He's getting on the next flight out and will be here in the morning." She says, staring at the dark screen.

"Well, we have one of two choices for the time being, I suppose. Either we go back through the portal so that you can get to training, or we kill time here, and you show me around the city. I also don't want to get my paws sticky any more times than I need to." He says, holding up one paw and waving it around with a grimace.

"Won't Michael be mad if we don't come back? I mean, he is expecting us, probably is already pissed that we aren't back yet."

"Ugh, you're right. I suppose it's best we get back and let Michael know about Christopher's arrival."

Nodding her head, she remembers about the time thing in Isethas and creases her brow.

"How will we know when to come back through since time is such a mystery in Isethas?"

"You have a point... I guess we will have to take our chances and stay here! Bummer." He drawls the last part, clearly not excited about the former.

"Cahtel, as much as I don't want to go back through the portal of hell, we have to tell Michael and the others."

Blowing out a breath, Cahtel stretches his back and walks over to where Aella is still sitting on the edge of her bed.

"Alright, let's get on with it then."

As Aella is about to power her cell phone off, she opens up her messages so she can read what Tara has sent.

> Tara: Is everything okay?
>
> Ell, I'm worried. Gabriel contacted me, call me!

```
Wtf, dude? Now I'm seriously
worried I'm coming over.
```

Realization sinks when she checks the time and date the texts were sent. Checking her location, the little red dot is nowhere to be found, and when she dials her number, it goes straight to voicemail.

Tara was gone.

Chapter Fifteen

Pacing around her apartment, Aella drags her fingers across her scalp, tugging on strands that loosen in her ponytail as she tries to focus on breathing instead of doing something impulsive like going to Damien's apartment.

"If Damien has her, there is nothing we can do at the moment, and we need to tell Michael, Aella."

"You don't understand! She is my best friend, I need to—"

"No," Cahtel cuts her off, "You are not going to do anything. Damien is dangerous, and this is exactly what he wants."

"What do you mean it's what he wants?" she blurts frantically, listing every awful thing that could have happened to Tara and how he got her contact information.

"He wants you to spiral and come right to him; he won't kill Tara yet."

Aella stops pacing and deadpans Cahtel. *Not helping Cahtel!*

Letting out a sigh, Cahtel motions towards the portal.

"Let's just get back to Isethas. Michael will know what to do."

Aella doesn't want to leave now. She wants to go look for Tara, but Cahtel has a point. Even if she did show up at Damien's apartment and demand that he give Tara to her, then what? She had no idea of what he was capable of, let alone if that's where Tara was being held hostage.

For all she knew, along with Damien being portrayed as this monster, he could be working with human traffickers in the mortal realm, and Tara could be a victim of that now.

Or, perhaps Georgia is with Tara, and they are in this together—a slight relief but still not unsettling.

"Okay, fine. You're right; we need to alert the others, but I will not allow any more time to go on without finding her. If I have to come back through alone and tear down his front door Cahtel, then I will"

Cahtel only gives her an expressionless look as a response because they both know she wouldn't, and just as they are about to head back to Isethas, her phone buzzes with an incoming call.

Looking down at the screen, her blood runs cold. Cahtel shakes his head in warning not to answer, but Aella slides the screen open anyway, putting it on speakerphone.

"Tsk Tsk, you know you really should have texted me back, *Ell.*" Damien taunts.

Sweat forms at her temple as she swallows. *Stay calm, stay calm.*

"What's wrong? Cat got your tongue? You really got yourself into quite the predicament here. Tell me, how is my brother these days?" He chuckles, with amusement lacing his tone.

Nausea and resentment swirl within her. Gritting her teeth, she wants to kill him, but he is untouchable at the moment.

"Where is she?" She seethes, not wanting to play any more games.

"Who? Which one? I should be thanking you, really; while you stayed over, you managed to open a portal back to Diatturus, and to my luck, that portal remains."

Fuck. Cahtel looks down, shaking his head at the new knowledge. Aella could have sworn that the portal was shut.

"What do you want, *Damien?*"

Aella is then met with silence.

"Let's get one thing straight, *Aella.* My name is Gabriel. You will refer to me as such."

"You're a monster."

Cahtel's eyes widen at her calling him a monster without a second thought, and regret from doing so begins to form. If she thought he would give her any indication of where Tara was, that spark of hope quickly died out.

"I may be a monster in your eyes based on what little facts and assumptions you have concluded. However, some of the most ruthless monsters walk in a falsified light. If I were you, I would sleep with one eye open from now on. Otherwise, you may never wake up. Or, perhaps that's exactly what you want... you fear many things, and death, it seems, is not one of them."

"What did you do with Georgia and Tara?" She demands, completely over this phone call and his little game.

"They are safe for now. Oh, and by the way, your mother makes the most excellent cup of hot matcha."

Aella's breath catches. Her mother was just here; how did she not mention anything to her about Damien? Something wasn't right, and she knew that her mother was way too calm for comfort while she was in the apartment.

"If you touch one hair on either of their heads, I will find you and rip you apart."

Damien chuckles again, his amusement bordering on the

line between dark and sinister as if Aella's promise to do just that brings him sick satisfaction.

"What. Do. You. Want." She says again, but with more force, cutting the bullshit.

"Patience, Aella," he purrs, "Don't be so eager. Although the slight demand to your tone is very arousing, and I do miss the sweet smell of desire that consumed you, that ship seems to have sailed for now. I am curious, though... Has my brother made you come yet? Or has he restrained from touching what doesn't belong to him? He's always been the more jealous one out of the two of us. Sloppy seconds are his favorite. Oh... right, we never did seal the deal. Shame."

His words are like daggers tearing into her chest. She was right to call him a monster. Damien is cruel and unrelenting. However, she would not let him have the upper hand, no matter how hurt and insulted she was. Aella would not show this man any weakness. He wants to play games? *Bring it on.*

It is she who laughs on the other end of the phone then, and as much as Cahtel being there in the room listening to everything that had been said so far between them, she straightens her spine, taking on a more menacing tone of her own.

"Oh, *Gabriel*," she taunts, "There is a lot you don't know about me. You think you have me all figured out, don't you? Well, you listen here, *sweetheart.* You haven't even scratched the surface. This is far from over, and when I get Tara and Georgia back safely, you're going to wish you never had the pleasure of meeting me in the first place."

"Time is a ticking clock, Aella. Eventually, there will be no metronome."

That is the last thing he says before hanging up, leaving Aella completely frustrated and angry all over again. Throwing her phone, it meets the wall with a loud thud, causing the screen to crack.

"Fuck!" She yells, and Cahtel continues to stare at her with those wide eyes. If he was human, she knew his skin would have taken on a pale sheen by now.

"You left the portal open to Diatturus. Do you know what this means?"

Balling her hands into fists at her sides, Aella grunts audibly before taking a deep breath.

"Cahtel, look at the wall in front of you. Obviously, I know what this means. We are fucked, anything else you would like to add?"

"Yes, in fact, I—"

Cutting him off before he has a chance to continue, Aella holds a hand up, squeezing her eyes shut as the headache from earlier seeks permission to return.

"You know what, on second thought, save it. Let's just go back and tell Michael how royally fucked we are. Not to mention, Christopher will be arriving in less than twenty-four hours, and I will need to pick him up from the airport."

Cahtel keeps his mouth shut, narrowing his eyes on her. Aella crosses her arms over her chest, gawking back at him.

"What?!"

"I warned you not to answer that call."

"Technically, you didn't say anything, so you are just as much to blame here as I am. Are you just going to sit there judging me, or can we go back through to Isethas in silence?" She asks with impatience, getting the better half of her. Her nerves are shot from coming back to her apartment, and Aella isn't looking forward to having to explain to Michael what has happened since the time they left.

Rolling his eyes, Cahtel jumps off the bed, turning his nose up at the opening of the portal.

"Ladies first." He huffs, and Aella just shakes her head as she enters the black void.

By the time they get through the hallway of sticky black tar, Torin is on the other side of the portal with his hands on his hips.

"What the fuck took you guys so long? Michael is having a bitch fit. And why do you both look as if you walked through a sewer? Scratch that. Why do you both smell like you walked through a sewer? What the fuck." Torin hacks, backing up a couple of feet as he covers his nose.

Cahtel shakes his paws out and says, "Two things, actually make that four. The portal seems to be having a mind of its own, hence the smell and sticky substance. Aella's mother was there waiting for her with information on Christopher. He will be arriving at eight in the morning tomorrow, and Aella will have to pick him up and bring him here. Lastly, Damien contacted her. Apparently, Aella left the portal open to Diatturus, so make that five."

Clearing her throat, Aella glares at Cahtel, then looks at Torin.

"And he has Tara along with Georgia, so make that six."

Torin nods his head, slowly processing the short rundown of everything.

"O—kay... so this is bad. Oh fuck, this is really bad! Aella! You left a portal open to Diatturus?!"

Throwing her hands up, Aella starts walking, wanting to get away from both of them.

"Out of everything, the portal is what you're most concerned about? How about the fact that Damien has my best friend and coworker? That's a problem! Or the fact that after twenty-three years, my mother finds it in herself to finally tell me the truth about my father, and at the most convenient time? Honestly, it doesn't surprise me that the portal is open to Diatturus, given the portal to Isethas from my apartment is open, and not only is it open, but it also smells like ass and has tentacles growing all over oozing shit. So yeah, Torin, this is all really fucking bad, okay?!" Aella yells, stress and anxiety blanketing over her nerves like a ticking time bomb that hasn't yet exploded, threatening to leave confetti made of nothing but chaos and ruin.

"As much as I would love to walk it off, Aella, I think it is best we teleport to the house," Cahtel interjects, keeping pace behind her. "Torin will meet us there."

Scoffing over her shoulder at him, she says, "Correction, it's a palace. Let's call it what—"

Bent over her knees, Aella starts retching from the teleporting and the stench that is all over her legs from the portal.

"You really need to give me a warning when you do that." She says, wiping her mouth with the back of her hand.

"Or, you just learn to get used to it."

Michael comes running down the steps of the palace with a look of agitation before Cahtel and Aella can even make the ascent.

"When you said you were going to get the locks changed to your home, I didn't think it would cost you all damn day!" He shouts, approaching them, then quickly covers the lower half of his face with his hand.

"It's from the portal," Aella says, wincing at the smell herself, wanting nothing more than a shower.

"Michael, you might want to sit down for this," Cahtel warns, and Michael stays firm.

"Just get on with it; I don't want either of you sitting on anything inside of the palace with that stuff all over your bodies."

Torin lands then, walking over to where Aella and Cahtel

are standing, quickening his pace so he can hear everything for the second time.

Aella huffs out, taking the floor to catch Michael up to speed. "So, like we told Torin, there are a few things that have happened since we went back to change the locks initially. Obviously, the portal has gone rogue, and Cahtel said this isn't normal. I don't know what happened or how, but it appears it is its own beast. My mother was there in my apartment when we showed up; she knows about the portal, so there is no need to change the locks at this point. She gave me Christopher's contact information. He will be arriving tomorrow morning at eight, and I will need to get him from the airport and bring him back here. Lastly, Damien called me... He has Tara and my coworker, but apparently, I left the portal open to Diatturus."

Michael pales, and Aella prepares for the next blow.

"You left a portal open to Diatturus?" Michael reiterates in a calm tone that makes Aella want to crawl out of her skin.

Looking down at the ground, she nods her head, bracing herself for what might come next.

"Do you have any idea what this means, Aella? Do you—"

"She didn't mean to sir." Cahtel cuts him off. Aella glances over at him, appreciation flaring that he would stand up to Michael over this, even if it were technically her fault for not drinking the tea as instructed. Had she done that, the portal being open to Diatturus would have been prevented. Had she not gone on that date with Damien in general or entertained the idea of him, Tara would probably be safe right now. Aella feels responsible for both, and no amount of lectures from Michael would make her feel any worse than she already does.

"Perhaps she didn't mean to open a portal to Diatturus, but she did, and now it remains open for the foreseeable future."

A moment of silence stretches on, and before Aella can say

anything else, Michael heads back inside the palace with his hands cupped behind his back.

"You two should go get cleaned up, and we will continue to discuss Christopher's arrival. Meet me in the lounge when you are finished." He says over his shoulder, and with that, Aella lets out a breath she has been holding.

"Thanks." She murmurs to Cahtel for interjecting.

"It was the truth. You didn't intend to open that portal, nor did you mean to leave it open."

She nods, and they both walk up the steps without another word as they part ways to get cleaned up.

WHEN AELLA ENTERS THE LOUNGE AFTER SHOWERING AND changing into a pair of leggings and a pull-over crewneck sweat-shirt, Cahtel catches Ashlyn up on what happened back at the apartment. Torin stands at her side while Michael is behind the bar pulling down five glasses.

Dropping two cubes into each glass, he picks out of a silver bucket with tongues and pours a generous amount of amber liquid coating the ice. Rounding the bar with two glasses, he hands Ashlyn one, who is still engulfed in the conversation, and then gives Aella hers, avoiding eye contact.

Taking a drink, the bitter liquid runs down her throat, warming her up and slowly loosens some of the tension. Notes of oak and pecan with a hint of vanilla, a delicious bourbon that probably costs more than she would ever pay.

"Oh my goodness, Aella, hearing from Damien had to have been unnerving. I am so sorry about your friend Tara. We will find her." Ashlyn says, causing Aella to worry for her friend all over again.

"Thank you. Yeah, it was not something I enjoyed, and we will find her."

Ashlyn's eyes soften, and she nods her head, sipping on her bourbon. The phone call from Damien was the closure she needed. One thing she couldn't help repeating in her head, though, was something he said: *"Some of the most ruthless monsters walk in a falsified light."* It very well could have been a rhetorical statement, but what if there was something more to it than a warning? It's not like he has anything to gain by telling her that. Pulling her from her thoughts, Michael sits on the chaise and begins to speak.

"So, Christopher will be arriving tomorrow morning. I feel it is best that Cahtel escorts you back and you stay there this evening. You will have to drink the tea in your realm so that you don't *accidentally* open another portal. I'm assuming that you still have the sachets?"

Aella nods her head, swallowing another bite of the bourbon.

"Good. I will have Cahtel make sure of it, and you both will retrieve Christopher when he arrives."

Cahtel grunts, clearly not wanting to have anything to do with going through that portal again.

"Why can't you have Torin or Ashlyn go with her? I mean, they technically could pass as humans, aside from Torin's obnoxious wings. No offense."

Rolling his eyes, Torin smirks, "Don't be jealous, Cahtel; even when you had wings, mine were surely larger."

Cahtel scoffs at his remark, and Michael rubs at his temple.

"Cahtel, you will go back with her. This is not a suggestion but an order. When you three return, we will begin our training like we were supposed to earlier. There will be no more interferences with that, especially knowing that the portal to Diatturus is open."

"Surely there will be a welcome home dinner for Christopher? It has been ages since we've seen him." Ashlyn says, with a strange sense of longing. Aella couldn't help but notice that Torin winced before downing the rest of his glass.

"Actually, Ashlyn, that sounds lovely if you don't mind, Michael. I'm sure we can afford a dinner in the mix; I mean, we have to eat." Aella says, hope flaring for something a little normal in this not-so-normal situation. *Normal.*

"I will have the cook plan a meal, but we will stay on task. Christopher is more than welcome to stay here, even though he still has his family home in the city. Let him know the option is there."

Downing the rest of her drink, Aella sets it on the bartop, looking to Cahtel, who is stretched out on the chair. After some time, he sighs and straightens up.

"Fine, let's get on with this." He says, stepping down.

Michael stands and walks over to Aella, placing a hand on her shoulder gently, making her tense and uncomfortable with the contact. The concern in his eyes are equally unsettling, and she doesn't know if it was because of Damien's phone call or the fact that she would be meeting her father in person for the first time. Either way, both make her uncomfortable, especially if it is about her father.

She is no expert in handling her emotions, even if she has dealt with her issues her whole life. Sometimes she didn't have the best approach, but she has made it twenty-three years with the shit life has thrown at her.

"Why are you looking at me like some pathetic puppy? I'm fine."

Michael removes his hand from her shoulder and steps away then, focusing his attention on Cahtel, avoiding how Aella just snipped at him.

"Right, see to it, she drinks the tea. We will see you three once you get Christopher."

Nodding his head, Aella and Cahtel head out of the palace, just to end up in a sticky, nasty mess all over again.

"Told ya we should have just stayed," she whispers, teasing Cahtel. And just to prove he has the one up, he teleports them to the portal without warning.

Chapter Sixteen

When Aella and Cahtel reenter the apartment, they are both exhausted and smell terrible all over again. Checking the time on the oven, it's after ten. They had only been gone for what seemed like a couple of hours, but the time between here and Isethas was different.

Aella lets Cahtel know that she is going to shower for the second time, but before she heads into the bathroom to do such a monotonous task, she turns the kettle on the stove with water for the tea.

Plugging the charger into her now damaged cell phone, she's relieved to see that it still has the ability to charge. The wet sound of Cahtel licking the sticky substance from his paws in the corner of the kitchen turns her stomach.

"Is that what you have to do every time?" Aella screeches, covering her ears. Cahtel just ignores her as he continues his bathing.

"Whatever, I'm showering. Be out in a few." She says, grabbing a pair of clean sweats and a T-shirt to throw on in the bathroom after she's bathed. Shutting the door behind her, she turns on the water to let it warm up and stares herself in the mirror. Given how tired she is, she's surprised that the dark circles under her eyes have lessened since the last time she really took notice of them. Inspecting her skin, she's also surprised to see no new blemishes, especially with the amount of stress she's been under.

When the water is warm enough, but not as warm as the showers she's had in Isethas, she gets in and does a quick scrub. It's lackluster in comparison, and the first order of business for when she has a normal life will be to get a new place with an amazing shower. *Normal.*

Once she's clean and dry, she throws on her clothes and walks out of the bathroom, detangling her hair with a comb. Cahtel is sprawled out on her bed with his paws under his chin.

"You don't think you're sleeping on my bed with me, do you?" She says, yanking on a couple of tangles.

"Where else do you suppose I sleep, Aella? On the floor? I'm not an animal." He says, yawning, "Besides, there is plenty of room for us both, and I am technically a guest."

Rolling her eyes, she pads off to the kitchen when the kettle starts to whine. Rummaging around her cupboard, she pulls out the box of sachets and places one in a mug, topping it off with hot water and allowing it to steep for a few minutes.

Walking over to her side of the bed, she sets the mug down on her nightstand and waves her hand at Cahtel to move over. Grunting, he adjusts himself to where he's facing her.

"So, what does one do at a sleepover?" he asks, and the question catches her off guard a little.

"I guess this is kind of like a sleepover, huh? Well, when Tara and I have sleepovers, we typically watch our favorite movies together or our favorite show." Thinking about Tara again makes her heart hurt, and the urge to do something impulsive about it now that she is back in her apartment tugs at her.

"What kind of movie or show?" he asks, reeling her back in.

"We like to watch rom-coms together, or *Sex and the City*. I suppose you don't have that sort of thing in Isethas, do you?"

"Well, we do have sex and a city, you know…"

Slapping a hand over her face, she refrains from giggling.

"No, Cahtel, I meant like Television. You don't have Television over there since you don't have cell phones?"

"Ah, I see; no, I suppose we don't."

Sliding her laptop from under the nightstand, she sets it out on the bed before them opening the screen. His eyes widen, and he reaches his paw out to touch the picture on the background that was most likely taken of a vinyard in Florence, Italy.

"This, Cahtel, is a laptop. You can search anything you want on it, although there are some rules as to what you should and shouldn't look up." *Like where to hide a body, aka Damien.*

"We have tomes in Isethas with information, but this looks much faster!"

Aella laughs. His excitement is innocent and endearing all the same. Clicking on one of her entertainment apps, she searches *Sex and the City* and pushes play on her favorite episode setting the laptop to where it's between her and Cahtel but far enough away so they can both enjoy it. Jumping off the bed, she hastily flips the lights off and pulls the covers back before she can get comfortable fluffing and propping the pillows up behind her.

Grabbing the mug of tea, she leans back and pretends it's not as horrible as it tastes while she sips on it. Cahtel and Aella watch in silence, with her occasionally glancing over at Cahtel, who is completely invested in *Carrie* and *Big's* story.

By the end of the episode, Aella's eyes grow heavy now that

she has finished the tea. Placing the mug back down on the nightstand, she sets the alarm on her phone so they wake up early enough to get Christopher from the airport, and when she glances back over at Cahtel, a single tear falls down his face.

"Are you crying?" She asks, shocked to see an emotion other than his irritable brooding.

"No, I am not." He sniffs, turning away from her.

Shutting the laptop, she slides it back under the nightstand.

"You totally are! I won't tell anyone; it will be our little secret." She laughs, laying back down as she adjusts the pillows and pulls the covers up over her body.

"Why do they fight it?"

"Hmm?" Aella mumbles, starting to drift off further, "What do you mean?"

"The girl, *Carrie*, and the man. Why do they fight their love for each other?"

"It's just a show, Cahtel, but I don't know. It's complicated, forbidden love and all that."

"Well, that's just silly." He scoffs, still seemingly invested in their story.

"Go to sleep, Cahtel; we have a busy day tomorrow. We can talk more about *Carrie* and *Big* then." Aella mumbles. A smile stretches over her face with Cahtel's presence as he, too, adjusts on the bed, curling up next to her.

THE ALARM GOES OFF AT SEVEN, AND CAHTEL GRUMBLES still curled up tight next to Aella. Reaching over, she slides the screen off and stretches, getting out of bed. She slept really well, even with Cahtel next to her, his body giving her comfort despite the fact that he scared the shit out of her initially.

Perhaps she will adopt a domesticated cat for when she has a normal life.

Normal.

"That sound was obnoxious." He says with his eyes still closed, sleep clinging to his voice.

"Yeah, it's an alarm. They aren't supposed to be pleasant."

Going into the bathroom, she does her typical morning routine of brushing her teeth and splashing cold water on her face after she relieves herself. By the time she's finished, Cahtel is sitting up fully awake.

Rummaging through drawers, she finds a clean, comfortable pair of joggers and a T-shirt to change into.

"I'm assuming you would like to use the bathroom before going as well?" She says, not entirely sure how a large cat like himself, who was once a guardian like Torin, relieves himself.

Clearing his throat awkwardly, he nods his head and jumps down from the bed. The whole situation is a bit awkward, which is silly since they'd just shared a bed.

"Do you mind closing the door behind me?" He asks, and Aella quickly shuts the door with a loud thud that makes her flinch.

I wonder if you can train a cat to use the toilet. The idea makes her chuckle to herself quietly, something she would look into when adopting one.

While Cahtel is using the bathroom, Aella takes the opportunity to get changed and slips on a pair of sneakers she didn't care about since they would become a sticky mess. *What is taking him so long?* Then she remembers that she will need to open the door for him again.

"Cahtel, are you finished in there?" She shouts and flinches again.

"Yes, I have been finished for a while." He says dryly.

Opening the door for him, she gives him an apologetic look smothering a laugh.

"What? It is normal to have to relieve yourself, Aella."

Her attempt to smother a laugh fails her, and she has to look away from him to control herself.

"I'm sorry, I was just picturing what it would be like to teach a domesticated cat how to use a toilet instead of a litter box."

Cahtel doesn't find it amusing or funny, which makes her laugh even harder.

"If you are finished, we should get going." He says, turning away from her.

"Right, okay," she says, catching her breath, "Should you even come with me? I mean, I don't know how people would perceive a cat like you…"

The comment causes his back to stiffen, and Aella feels bad for not catching herself before the words fell from her mouth. She knew it had hurt his feelings, but the truth is he wasn't just any ordinary cat at first glance, and she didn't want anyone to notice him and end up having an aneurysm.

"I'm sorry, that came out wrong."

Cahtel glances over his shoulder at her with sadness in his eyes. She definitely hit a sore spot, no matter how much of a point she had made.

"You're probably right. It would be different with the sun out; I can't move with the shadows."

His voice is somber, and Aella realizes that he has longed to see what the city of Phoenix has to offer. Snapping her fingers, she walks back over to her nightstand and pulls out her laptop again.

"Traffic around this time is going to be hellacious anyway, and I know how much you enjoyed the episode we watched last night!"

Pulling up the entire first season of *Sex and the City*, she hovers over the first episode so he can start from the beginning, even though she had skipped through to the second season.

"By the time I get back, you will probably have watched all of the first episode, if not the second. I promise you won't be missing much from staying here other than angry drivers on the freeway."

Cahtel perks up, then jumps back on the bed. Pressing play, she walks over to grab her keys and leaves without saying anything else because Cahtel is enthralled in the show, which makes her happy.

TRAFFIC BEING HELLACIOUS IS AN UNDERSTATEMENT. IT'S a complete shit show, with cars bumper-to-bumper dead stop.

"Come on! What the hell is happening?!" She grunts through gritted teeth. The time is now fifteen past eight, and Christopher is probably wondering where his ride is. She's been stuck on the offramp to get to the airport for twenty minutes now.

Her phone rings, and she answers using her *carplay* without looking to see who it is.

"Hello?" Aella answers impatiently.

"Hey, Aella, it's Chris. Just wanted to let you know that I am off the plane and waiting outside of terminal D. What kind of car did you say you have?"

"A green Kia Soul. I am stuck in traffic, but it looks like it is starting to let up now. I should be there in fifteen minutes."

"Okay, sounds good. I will wait for you here. I'm wearing a black T-shirt and jeans." He says, sounding nervous. *Helpful.*

Aella's reply is abrupt now that cars are moving at a normal speed, and she says, "Okay, I'll be there soon." Then hangs up.

Hearing Christopher sound as nervous as he did on the phone makes her feel a little better about how nervous she is now becoming as she approaches the onramp to the airport. The traffic jam was due to a light outage, and police officers had to conduct the traffic flow while it was being worked on.

I hate this city.

Driving the loop to terminal D, she creeps up as slowly as possible, looking around at every man who is dressed in a black T-shirt until she spots a man flagging her down. Pulling over to the curb, she puts her car in park and steps out.

"Oh my, you look so much like Susan!" Christopher exclaims as she opens the back door so he can toss his overnight bag inside.

Seeing him in the flesh is so bazaar, especially since he looks as though he hasn't aged a day since the photo of him and her mom was taken.

She chuckles awkwardly, not knowing what to do other than get back in the car so she doesn't end up getting a ticket for holding up the line.

"We have to get back on the road, so I don't get yelled at for staying parked here. We can talk more on the ride."

Christopher nods, then slides into the passenger seat and buckles up. Exhaling a breath, he looks over at Aella, but she remains focused on the windshield as she puts the car in drive.

"So, you're my daughter." He says, breaking the too short minute of silence. "I can't believe it!"

"Yeah, pretty weird. Sorry I called out of nowhere like that, my mom just told me about you and gave me your contact information. I honestly wasn't expecting you to have answered, or I guess your wife to." *Fuck Aella, why did you have to bring up the wife?*

He looks out the window and clears his throat, "Cindy is

great. We have a son, his name is Jaxson, eight months old. Look... I didn't tell her about you yet, but I—"

"That's okay; I didn't expect you to, honestly. Again this whole situation is pretty weird and quite frankly fucked. It's good you didn't tell her about me." Aella says, deflecting her feelings as she focuses on driving. Christopher has a whole other life, one that is normal. *Normal.*

"Aella," he sighs, "I want you to know that I fell madly in love with your mother. It didn't surprise me that she left if I'm being honest. I was a different man then, and I made a lot of mistakes. Mistakes that I never want to make again."

Christopher confessing all of this to her is making her uncomfortable, but she lets him continue talking. There are two sides to every story, and even if this is the only time she sees her father, she will take what she can from the experience.

"Anyway, I had no idea that she was pregnant with you. If I had known, I would have made it a point to be in your life. Your mother left one morning when I went to the market to get items to make breakfast, a typical Sunday, you know? When I returned, all of her personal belongings were gone, and she left a note saying she needed time and space from me. I assumed she went back to stay with her mother, even though she kept that part of her life private from me, and because cell phones weren't around then, I had to sit and wait. The days of waiting turned into months, which turned into years, and I moved on with my life."

Aella swallows, thinking about what that would feel like. He probably felt like she did most of the time, unwanted and alone.

"How did you and Cindy meet?" she asks, changing the topic. For some reason, she doesn't want to hear about how her mother wronged him; even if she doesn't agree with it, she knows that her mother did what she thought was best at the time.

"Cindy and I actually met at an AA meeting, believe it or not. I have been sober for twenty-three years now!"

Glancing over at him, he looks like he could pass for twenty three aside from a few small wrinkles around his eyes that make him look slightly older.

"Does she know about you? I mean, like being from another realm where you don't typically age?"

His smile falters with the question. "No. I haven't thought that far ahead yet."

Aella only nods then, and they pull onto the street where her apartment building is. The irony with his current situation is he will most likely be forced to leave when the time comes, abandoning his son and wife. Because she will age and grow old, eventually whither away while Christopher remains the same.

Pulling into her carport, they get out, and Christopher grabs his overnight bag while they walk inside the building.

"Oh, one more thing, Cahtel is here with me."

Christopher stops in his tracks and raises his brows. "Man, I haven't seen him in ages. What a reunion indeed."

When they get inside the apartment, Cahtel is still on the bed watching the show and looks as if he hasn't moved a muscle since she left.

"Honey, I'm home!" Aella chimes, dropping her keys off on the counter.

"Shh! *Samantha* is telling *Carrie* the goods right now!" He whisper yells, and Aella rolls her eyes, chuckling. Walking over to the laptop, she closes the screen, and Cahtel hisses at her.

"Hey! That was rude."

"We have *business*, remember?"

Samantha Hardy

Cahtel scoffs and rolls over, "Fine. Christopher, you look well."

"And you look... the same! How are you, old friend?" He asks, walking over to embrace him. Cahtel tenses and swats him away.

"I was great until Aella ruined the show."

"And what show was it you were watching?" He asks, raising a brow with mischief

"Se—"

Cutting Cahtel off, Aella says, "Okay, that's enough; we need to get back to Isethas. Christopher, you have everything you need?"

"Yep! Everything in this here bag!"

"Great, now the portal is a bit of a mess, so just a heads up. I hope you brought an extra pair of shoes, they're going to get... sticky."

Cahtel turns his nose up, not wanting to go back through for hopefully the last time.

"What do you mean *sticky?*"

"You'll see." She says, then feels her phone vibrate in her pocket.

Swiping on the cracked screen, her mother just sent a selfie wearing a large floppy hat and a pair of sunglasses with the caption that says: *Made it! Margaritas on the beach, here I come!*

Aella sends a heart and a *Have fun, Love you,* before powering off her phone and shoving it back into her pocket.

"Are we ready?"

Christopher nods, and Cahtel lets out a huff.

"If we must."

Chapter Seventeen

"Well, you weren't kidding. That portal is a disaster. What the hell?" Christopher says, and hell is right. The only thing that has changed from the time they came through it yesterday to now is that the black tentacles have completely covered every square inch of the walls. Aella had to turn her phone on so that she could use the flashlight feature and they could see where they were walking.

"It's gotten worse. I would be curious to know what the portal to Diatturus looks like." Cahtel says, flinging the dark, sticky substance off his paws.

"Did you say Diatturus?" Christopher pales while looking directly at Aella.

"Yeah... that's a thing I did, too."

"So Damien is back?"

"It appears he went to the mortal realm like you and hasn't returned to Diatturus until Aella opened the portal in his home."

Christopher does not seem to like that, and the look he gives Aella is one that makes her feel like a small child who is about to get a lecture. She doesn't need any more backlash for what she did, and certainly not from a man she just met, even if he is her father.

"Christopher, you still teleport, yes?" Cahtel asks, breaking the awkward tension that Aella will thank him for later.

Glancing over at Cahtel finally, he creases his brow, shaking his head.

"I haven't since I left after the war. I can certainly try, but I am afraid I may have lost the ability to do so."

Cahtel sighs and then says, "That might take too much time, and walking will also add time. I'll teleport to the palace and see if Torin or Michael can come back with me."

Aella looks at Cahtel with a sense of urgency, wanting him to take her with him. Now that Christopher knows the portal is open to Diatturus, she really doesn't want to explain the reason to him. She knows he has made his own assumptions by now. But without another word, Cahtel is gone, and Aella is stuck in the field with her father.

Staring down at her shoes, which now have grass clinging to the edges, she thinks about what to say until Cahtel comes back with Michael or Torin. The silence is awkward, even more so than the few moments on the drive back to her apartment, but at least she had something to focus on, like driving. *Say something.*

"I know that I have no right to tell you who you should and shouldn't sleep with, but—"

"Woah!" She can feel her cheeks heating up from embarrassment, then says, "You are correct, but I didn't sleep with him, not that it is any of your business. Why does everyone automatically assume that I did? Adults are more than capable of having a sleepover without any motives. Cahtel slept over, do you think we did something?"

Christopher chuckles and shakes his head, "Oh, Aella, you

remind me so much of Susan. Not that it's any of my business, but did you?"

Her jaw slackens, and the urge to throw up comes over her. "Gross, no, I did not. Cahtel is my friend, or at least I think we are at this point. Besides, he's technically a talking cat. Not my type."

Christopher shrugs, "So tell me, how did Damien charm someone like you?"

Thinking for a moment on how to respond she says, "He seemed genuine and was a complete gentleman until recently. I didn't even know about this condition until recently; it's not like I did any of this on purpose. I just thought it was sleep paralysis, and now everything is a complete mess. He has my best friend and coworker, or at least knows where they are, and I feel completely helpless in that I should be out there looking for them even though I don't know where to start."

Pursing his lips together, Christopher rubs at his jaw, "Interesting. Sleep paralysis, you say?"

"Yeah, what is it you're thinking?"

Christopher creases his brow again, going into some thought or memory.

"My mother, when she was alive, could manifest portals. She explained it to me as if there was a switch in her brain that she could turn on and off. Whenever she created a portal, she would ground herself and turn her subconscious on while turning the conscious part off. She said it was like being present but not at the same time, like—"

Aella cuts him off, "Floating or wading through water?"

"Exactly!"

She had felt that same thing with Cahtel and the time she'd meditated with Ashlyn.

"So, how was she able to close the portal? Did they ever look like what we just walked through?"

"That I am not entirely sure of, and no, they didn't. Unfortunately, my mother kept many secrets. Her gift to open portals was one that many knew of, but how she came into that gift is even a mystery to this day."

Gift.

Cahtel and Torin appear soon after. A wide smile stretches across Christopher's face as he approaches Torin with his arms outstretched.

"Torin, look at you! You've been keeping up with training, it seems." He chuckles, giving him a hug and clasping the back of his head.

"You don't look like you've been keeping up with training since I last saw you. What gives?" Torin says, picking him up like he weighs nothing but a bag of sand.

Throwing his head back with a roaring laugh, Christopher says, "Hey now, don't judge the Dadbod. It's a thing."

Cahtel interrupts their banter, taking on a more serious tone, "Right, well, we need to get back. Aella, Ashlyn is waiting for you in the meditation room I will take you to her. Torin will fly Christopher back to the palace so that he can get caught up on everything. Once you are done with Ashlyn, you will begin training with Torin."

Aella's stomach growls, realizing that she hasn't had anything to eat since breakfast the day before. Torin raises a brow at the loud rumble her belly makes, "When was the last time you ate?"

Biting the skin off her lower lip, she says, "Yesterday morning when Ashlyn came into the room."

Shaking his head, he puts his hands on his hips.

"Aella, you need to eat something before we train; otherwise, your body will burn out. I'll have the cook prepare you a smoothie with protein-packed nutrients before we begin."

Nodding her head, she decides not to argue. She's hungry,

and by the looks of Torin, she can tell that training is going to take it out of her.

"Okay, Cahtel ready—"

I'm going to kill him.

Due to not having anything in her stomach, she only hacks from the teleport.

"Seriously?! Warning Cahtel, warning."

He snickers and saunters off without so much as a rebuttal.

Entering the meditation room, Ashlyn has her back to the door, muddling various herbs with a mortar and pestle at a station in the corner of the room.

"Ah, Aella, please take a seat," she says in her calm, serene voice.

Sitting down on the same floor pillow she occupied the last time she was in the meditation room, Aella did as requested, waiting for Ashlyn to begin.

"Okay," Ashlyn says, walking towards Aella with the mortar, "We are going to try something a little bit different today!" Her tone causes Aella to grow wary of how overly confident she seems.

"Okay... Should I be worried?" Aella asks, trying her best not to crease her brows together.

"No! Uh, well... never mind, no, you should not be! Everything will go perfectly fine. I will prepare you, I have only done this two other times, and the first time didn't go so well, but the second was a success!" *I was wrong, this is actually how I die.*

Setting the mortar down, Ashlyn pulls out a black blindfold, ushering Aella to close her eyes. Wrapping the fabric around Aella's head, she could feel the fabric tighten, but it was not enough to cut off any circulation should it be tied to a different part of her body.

"It will be similar to last time. I chose the blindfold so you don't lie down like you did when I laid the towel over your eyes.

It seems that taking away one of your five senses helped guide you into the meditative state and allowed you to shut your conscious mind off. Vulnerability appears to be the string, we just have to figure out which end of that string to cut so that you gain that control."

Sitting with her legs crossed and the blindfold on, Aella listens as Ashlyn strikes a match, lighting the herbs she had muddled and placing the mortar directly in front of her. The smell is atrocious. Even with the blindfold on, Aella's eyes begin to water from the smoke that drifts up through her nostrils.

"Solanum americanum, commonly referred to as black nightshade. It is an extremely toxic plant if ingested. Dried and muddled with white sage and lavender, however, eases you into a soothing relaxation, although it can cause hallucinations."

"Hallucinations?" Aella asks more calm than intended. The herbs coaxing her body into a relaxed state.

"Yes, but not to worry about that. I measured the right amount. After the first time I did this, I realized that too much of the Solanum americanum was used, and I came up with the perfect balance on the second attempt."

"What happened the first time?" The question comes out with more of a mumble, and any fear Aella had after entering the meditation room fell away.

Ashlyn didn't respond. But after a moment, she begins circling the mallet around the crystal singing bowls, guiding Aella further.

"Quiet your mind. Close those cabinets and ground yourself. Allow your subconscious to take over; you are a passenger now." Ashlyn says, soft and quiet. Quieting her mind comes easy, the mixture of the herbs proving to be a useful tool in this scenario.

Envisioning that she is like her orchid, delicate and pure yet strong and resilient, planted firmly in the ground. However, something is different as she pictures herself as the orchid, in that she is, in fact, one with the orchid and not entirely the orchid at all.

The singing bowls drift away like the first time, but instead of the black void she had been accustomed to being sucked through, she was in the same field the portal has been opened into Isethas.

Looking around for the portal in her meditative state, there is none. No silvery swirling translucent mass or the inky black tentacle growths that look as though they would outgrow their capsule. Just Aella in the field with her orchid.

Everything around her is still. There is no slight breeze or any sound of birds chirping nearby. Everything looks as though it's frozen in time, with the orchid firmly planted in the dirt below.

Then comes a voice, and this one is recognizable from another lifetime.

"Aella, how you have grown." The voice says, feminine and pure.

Aella looks around again, finding the source of the voice or perhaps even a portal that it could have echoed from, but there is nothing.

The voice chuckles, and when Aella looks at the orchid again, it moves slightly.

"Is that you little big orchid?" she asks in disbelief but remembers that she is in her meditative state and will take this over what happened the last time.

"Yes."

"Who are you? How is this possible?"

"Anything is possible when you put your mind to it, dear." The orchid says, sounding wise as if it has lived a life outside of the bulbs it is now sprouting.

"In a former life, I was called Elissa."

Aella's breath catches, "Elissa? As in the Elissa who manifested portals?"

"Yes, the one and only."

"You're my... grandmother," Aella says in a whisper as tears prick the back of her eyes.

"That would also be correct. You carry the same gift as I once did; you, my child, are very powerful."

Aella scoffs involuntarily, "It doesn't feel like a gift. I can't control it. How did you manage to manifest a portal and close it the way you did?"

The orchid stays quiet for a moment, swaying as if it is contemplating its response.

"Acceptance."

Knitting her brows together, Aella is unsure what she means by that.

"Acceptance for what you are and what you are capable of is only the beginning. There are, of course, outside forces that can alter or change the course of action."

"Like in physics?"

"In a way. For every action has a reaction; what comes up must come down."

Becoming more confused, Aella is trying to fit the pieces together in Ellisa's puzzle.

"I still don't understand what you mean?"

"For you and me, a portal can be opened by shutting off our conscious mind while leaving our subconscious awake, or, for lack of better terms, your subconscious is the driver while your conscious is the passenger—like flipping a switch."

"Well, if that is the case, then why are there portals that are still open and look like they have an infectious disease growing on them?" Aella states with more agitation than intended.

"A portal is a mirrored image of yourself, dear. You have

been fighting this gift your whole life, unable to accept it. For every action has a reaction."

Throwing her hands up, Aella says, "So I just have to accept this gift, and the portals will magically disappear? It's that simple?"

Elissa chuckles, and the orchid dances, matching the vibrations.

"For you, it is not that simple. You see, acceptance isn't just admitting to everyone else that you have. It goes deeper on a personal level. You have to believe it yourself, and that takes work. Work that only you can do and figure out. No one else can show you or lead the way."

"I don't understand! I don't know how..."

Elissa goes quiet once more, and the orchid stills. Aella stares at the orchid, waiting for a response, but when nothing comes, she thinks she is left alone all over again without any significant answer.

"You will. You have already started the process. Give Christopher my love for me."

"Wait, you can't leave now. I need you; I can't do this on my own... can you just send me a sign or something? Like a signal that tells me I'm on the right track?"

"I never left, Aella. I may be gone in the physical sense, but I have always been with you, watching over you." Elissa says as her voice grows farther away until Aella feels that her presence is finally gone, and it is just her and her orchid in the field.

Closing her eyes, Aella focuses on releasing herself from her meditation state while pulling herself back into the room with Ashlyn. When she opens her eyes, she is still greeted by the field instead of the black fabric of the blindfold.

"Shit," she sighs, looking at the orchid. Shaking her head, she thinks about what Elissa had told her.

Acceptance, gift, physics.

Frustration creeps in, slithering its way like it always does, ready to strike any moment the longer she fixates.

This has to be a hallucination, right? Aella redirects her thoughts, justifying what had just occurred. Ashlyn told her that hallucinations could happen, especially using black nightshade, so perhaps this is exactly that.

Turning from the orchid, Aella looks at the same open space where the portal would be standing. An idea strikes, and because she is technically in that meditative state where her subconscious mind is the driver, she decides to try and create a portal. *This should be interesting.*

Closing her eyes, she focuses on her breathing, which is the only thing to be heard on the open field and works on grounding herself standing. Instead of envisioning the orchid, she envisions herself as a tree with thick, deep roots winding down to the deepest parts of the earth.

She then pictures a portal, a translucent wall with silvery swirls. When she opens her eyes, the portal she just manifested in her subconscious mind is before her, ebbing and flowing.

Breathing out her nose, her hands begin to tingle with a clammy unease. The portal looks like it should, or at least that is how she had imagined it to look, but that could easily change.

Acceptance. Nodding her head, she looks at the portal as if it were a mirrored reflection of herself. Closing her eyes once more, she shakes out her limbs and thinks about what it means to accept her condition. *No, gift. Accept my gift.*

Cracking an eye open, the portal turns into a physical mirror. She opens both eyes and then approaches the mirror with caution while she stares at her reflection, staring back at her. Behind her, she could see the orchid and the green field through the mirror, and as she gets closer, she taps the glass with her finger.

Taking a step back, she clears her throat, "I, Aella Rose Clarke, accept my gift."

Repeating the same thing three times, she begins to feel stupid as the mirror remains mocking her. Frowning at her reflection, she starts to turn from the mirror until she notices her reflection also remains standing still.

Fear starts to take over her, and the frown she is wearing turns upward into a smile, but Aella isn't the one who is smiling but her reflection.

"What do you want from me?!" she shouts, but the smile her reflection wears doesn't falter.

Aella begins to walk backward from her mirrored reflection, and the mirror matches every step she takes back by moving forward.

She's trapped, with the mirror only inches away from swallowing her.

Searching the ground for a rock to smash the mirror, Aella is out of luck.

"Tick tock, tick tock, you're running out of time." Her reflection taunts, or at least she thinks it is her reflection even though its lips don't move.

"What do you want?!" Aella demands again, her body shaking violently. *This is just a hallucination.*

Her reflection says nothing, only smiling at her while trailing her with its eyes that go from hazel to an all-black void. Seeing the transition causes Aella to jump back, tripping over herself to where she is on the ground.

Her reflection then crouches down, contorting its body into an animalistic form, crawling out of the mirror, looking like something you saw in a horror film.

"Tick tock, tick tock Aella..." It says again, sounding less like herself and more demonic. It crawls slowly like a snake, and Aella scrambles to get her footing. Tears stream down her

cheeks from fear and desperation to get out of this place, with her reflection threatening to drag her through the mirror.

"Help! Help me! Please! Ashlyn!" Aella screams, pleading for some escape, but nothing comes.

When she finally gets up, her reflection's hand nearly grasps onto her ankle, and when it looks up at her, those eyes are a deep black void, and its smile is full of razor-sharp teeth that ooze the same sticky substance as the portal she had opened.

Panicked and afraid, Aella is helpless and on the verge of giving up until she thinks of her grandmother again. Of course, this is a reflection of herself; the ugly negative thoughts she has allowed to consume her and that she has buried so far down are a projection of herself now.

Instinct takes over, and Aella decides to fight instead of fleeing. Kicking out her foot, the bottom of her shoe smacks her reflection in the face. Falling backward on its haunches, it hisses and crawls back toward the mirror.

"I accept my gift. I am in control! I accept my gift. I am in control!" Aella yells, following after the reflection. Her reflection pulls its body back into the mirror, and when Aella looks at herself, her true self, she repeats it, with more power and control.

"I am done with this shit. Time *is* up bitch." She says, and pushes the mirror down, shattering it into tiny pieces.

Smoke rises up from the rubble, floating up toward the sky, forming a cloud. The cloud breaks apart, and silver droplets fall, landing in a circle around where Aella stands. The circle then glows a bright, blinding white that causes her to clench her eyes shut. When the light dies down, Aella opens her eyes and is greeted with the black fabric of the blindfold.

Pulling the blindfold off, Ashlyn is before her with wide eyes.

"Aella, are you okay? I tried everything to pull you from your meditation. I could feel your panic, and you're drenched in sweat!" Ashlyn says franticly, placing a cold, wet rag on her forehead. Standing up, Aella feels dizzy but is relieved to be in the meditation room.

"Yeah, I'm fine. Elissa—"

Aella stops mid-sentence when she sees Michael standing in the doorway with his arms crossed. His jaw is tight, and his brows are furrowed.

"I grabbed Michael when I couldn't pull you out. Oh, Aella, I was so worried. I am so sorry." Ashlyn says with guilt lacing her tone. Aella then realizes that the apology is directed more toward Michael.

"Wait, did you not tell him that you were going to use black nightshade on me?" Aella asks in a low voice. Michael relaxes his arms, straightening his back.

"No. She did not. This could have been very bad, and it could have killed you." He says, and Ashlyn flinches, looking down at the floor.

"Well, I'm not dead, and it actually worked. Or at least I think it did."

Ashlyn lifts her head to look at Aella with a flicker of hope, and Michael moves into the room.

"What do you mean it worked?"

Knitting her brows together, Aella swallows, her throat feeling dry, wishing she had a glass of water to chug after that journey.

"Elissa spoke to me. I thought I was hallucinating because Ashlyn told me that could be a side effect. I was in the field where the portal is now, but there wasnt a portal at all except for the orchid. She told me how I can control my... gift. It is going to take some work, but I think I understand a little bit more as to why I haven't been able to close the portals. I think I can find a way to manifest them like she did and close them all the same."

Michael raises a brow in disbelief, "What did she tell you? How can you control it?"

Aella takes a second before answering and nods to herself, believing the word as if it were a feeling before it leaves her mouth.

"Acceptance."

Chapter Eighteen

Michael informed Aella that training with Torin would wait until tomorrow. After she had given him and Ashlyn the full rundown on her meditative journey and how she fought off her reflection, Michael felt that training would exhaust her even more.

Aella wasn't going to complain about it either; even in her meditative state, she felt winded from kicking her reflection in the face and pushing over the mirror. They had returned to the lounge to find Torin and Cahtel, and when they entered, Aella was a little disappointed that Christopher wasn't amongst them.

"Where is Christopher?" She says, hoping he didn't end up leaving altogether.

Michael rounds the bar, pulling out three glasses, and she notices that Torin and Cahtel already have one. Cocktail hour is evidently a thing here.

"Torin took him back to his townhome in the city. He decided to stay there instead, said he didn't want to impose." Michael says, filling the glasses with two ice cubes in each.

Torin scoffs, rolling his eyes, "Yeah, except he is imposing by having me be his chauffeur."

Cahtel snickers, finding amusement in Torin's obligation, says, "About time you get tasked with something useful."

Coming back around the bar, Michael hands Aella and Ashlyn a glass, then reaches across the bar to grab his own before sitting down at his usual spot. Aella decided to remain standing since she was unsure how long she had been sitting in the meditation room and felt like her legs needed circulation.

"So, how was your meditation Aella?" Cahtel asks, licking out of his glass.

Michael cuts in, draping his arm over the back of the chaise, and says, "Elissa spoke to her."

Cahtel coughs, choking on the bourbon, and snaps his head up toward Aella.

"She visited you? What did she say? How?"

Aella takes a moment to enjoy a couple of sips from her glass before going into it again. It wasn't that she didn't want to talk about Elissa speaking with her; it was that she knew she would have to repeat the story for a third time with Christopher and was tired of it.

"She didn't say a lot, but what she said was a lot, if that makes sense?"

Cahtel cocks his head, looking confused, and she lets out a breath, "Basically, she told me that I have to find acceptance, and every action has a reaction and some other things. To sum it all up, I have to do the inner work."

Cahtel deadpans her, not appreciating her tone, and she doesn't blame him. Aella was tired and a little on edge, and even though she had conquered something awful, she just wanted to soak in a tub and eat a good meal.

"Right, Torin will pick up Christopher for dinner. We have another busy day ahead of us tomorrow, and we still need to discuss some things with Christopher present. I would prefer not to do it over dinner, but I am afraid we must, even though we are celebrating his...homecoming." Michael says, tilting his glass while contemplating whether he should have a refill, "You may all be excused except for Aella. I would like a moment to speak with you privately if that is alright?"

Aella only nods as nervous jitters cascade over her body, mixing with the warmth from the bourbon that summersaults in her belly. Being alone with Michael made her nervous in general, and she can't quite place why.

Once the room clears out to where the only people left are Michael and Aella, he stands gracefully, walking over to the French doors, closing them shut, and drawing the curtains for added privacy. Finishing off her glass, Michael takes it from her, returning to the bar for a refill on both glasses.

Raising an eyebrow, Aella watches him in silence, unsure of what he would need to speak to her about in private. She told him everything that happened while in her meditative state, and a small part of her is concerned she might receive some sort of lecture with how tense his body language is.

Handing her glass back to her, Michael returns to his seat and gestures for her to sit in the chair across from him. Obliging him, she sits down with an awkward thump, causing the bourbon to splash a little out of the glass onto the green velvet of the chair.

"Sorry," she says with a grimace, attempting to wipe up the spilled liquor with the sweaty palm of her hand. Her cheeks warm with embarrassment, and when she looks up at Michael, his eyes soften.

"There's no need to apologize; accidents happen. How are you feeling?" he asks, relaxing back on the chaise and focusing entirely on Aella.

She swallows another sip of the bourbon before responding, "Aside from being tired and hungry, I think I feel alright."

Michael cocks a brow and then shakes his head, and Aella continues, "I mean, this whole situation isn't your normal, right? I can't stop thinking about Tara and hope she's okay, I want to go fin—"

Michael cuts her off, "Damien is a monster, but he isn't a murderer, not like that anyway. He is using Tara as leverage; if anything, Damien is portraying to her that he is the good guy and probably has her somewhere on a... vacation, so to speak. He wants to bait you."

Pinching her brows together, Aella realizes she has been doing that more and more lately and will have to add Botox to the list for when she has a normal life.

Normal.

"Why would he want to bait me? I opened the portal to Diautturus."

"He wants you to open all of the portals so that he can finish what had started when the first war of the realms took place. He wants to take full power and rule over all."

Digesting his theory, Aella takes a much bigger sip of her bourbon this time.

"So Damien has Tara and my coworker Georgia, most likely on a vacation somewhere with the intent of baiting me to give him what he wants so that I can get my friends back?" Aella asks, trying to understand Damien's process.

"Yes. You have what he wants, and he has what you want." Michael states as if he knows exactly what Damien is doing.

"Then how will I get my friends back unharmed? The whole point on me controlling my...gift is so I can avoid opening portals, but if he has my friends..."

"Which is why we play into his game; we bait him back. You see, he knows that you can open portals and that you have been to Isethas. What he doesn't know is that you are working on controlling this condition to suppress it. Once you have accomplished this, we make an agreement with him so he thinks he gets what he wants in the end. You will trap him in Diatturus, closing the portal so that he may never return to the mortal realm."

A realization hits Aella like a ton of bricks then, "You want me to trap him in Diatturus? Why?"

Michael lets out a sigh, rubbing his temples, "Damien chose his fate long ago. Diatturus is where he belongs, and now that I know he has been in the mortal realm all this time, he has had his fun and will be returning where he belongs."

Aella can't believe that Michael is going to make her wait to get to her friends and play into Damien's game, but what other choice does she really have?

"Look, I know this isn't exactly what you want to do, especially with everything else you have been through up until now. This is the only thing I ask of you; it's torturous enough to know he..." Michael trails off, holding back what he so desperately wants to confess to her, and swallows the rest of his bourbon in one gulp, hissing through his teeth.

"He what?" She asks, concern blooming that turns her stomach with the liquor.

Michael looks at her with a desperate need that then eases some of the concern but sets her blood on fire for some sort of touch.

"It's torturous enough to know that he touched you and could have had you for his own selfish desires, Aella. Being near you is intoxicating. From the moment I met you, I wanted you. There is this gravitational pull I have never felt with anyone else before you. When you told me that you were with my brother, I was consumed by anger and jealousy, even though I had no right to be. I knew then that you weren't just some mortal girl with a condition that could open portals. You are forbidden fruit, a drug that if I were even to try once, I would become an addict. I can't stop thinking about you, and when you are within reach, like right now, I want to consume you like a starved wolf, hungry for what your soft pink lips would taste like between mine."

Aella's eyes widen to the size of saucers from Michael's confession, leaving her speechless and equally hungry with that same need. In this moment, all she could think about was how she must be in her *Carrie* era because *Big* is literally sitting in front of her, being completely honest, pouring his guts out in the most animalistic way someone could. Except, Michael is more than that; he is an absolute God.

"What are you thinking?" He asks, with a slightly panicked expression from spilling his secrets.

Aella was thinking about everything and nothing at the same time. She wanted Michael to do whatever he wanted to at that moment. Her thighs are on fire, dripping with arousal, and she wondered if he can sense it. Shifting towards the end of her chair, Michael growls low with caution, causing her heart rate to kick up in tempo and her chest to flush from the bourbon and the desperation for him.

"Kiss me." She breathes, and in a quick motion, Michael kneels before her like she is a queen, grabbing the back of her head with a fierce control that makes her knees go weak.

His lips are on her then, all-consuming, sucking, and greedy, tasting like bourbon and sweet mint. Pulling him closer, she wants him to make her forget about everything. She wants to forget about opening portals, Damien having her friends, the monsters she created, and the real monsters hiding in the shadows when no one is looking. Aella needed this moment, no matter how long or short-lived. She needed to get lost in lust and desire and feel something other than the guilt and sorrow that is a constant in her day-to-day life.

Trailing her hands down the front of his body, she maps out every muscle from his chest down to his stomach. When she reaches the waistband to his pants, she can feel his hard length pushing through the fabric. Her fingers move to the button of his pants, the need to feel him inside of her overriding everything else until his hands grab her wrists, stopping the agonizing exploration.

Michael pulls back from her, equally pained by the abrupt stop that is his own doing.

"Aella..." he sighs, standing up before her, "We can't; I'm sorry."

Confused and ashamed, Aella sits back in the chair from his rejection. Embarrassment creeps back in, and she feels stupid for assuming the confession, followed by the hot makeout session, was an open invitation. Seeing the hurt in her eyes, Michael crouches before her again so they are at eye level. Sliding the fly away from her face, he tucks the strands behind her ear.

"Please don't think for one second that I don't want you. What I said is true, and I would love nothing more than to take you right here in this moment. Until we know what Damien's next move is and how we will suppress your condition, we cannot afford any distractions."

"I know," Aella says in a quiet tone with the hope that Michael is suffering a bad case of blue balls to help ease her embarrassment. A knock sounds then, pulling Michael back to his feet and his attention from Aella.

"You may enter." He shouts, and Ashlyn opens the door, entering the space. A flicker of shock dances across her features briefly, and she straightens her back, forcing a smile.

"Looks like your conversation went well," she says, avoiding eye contact. "Christopher is walking the grounds with Torin."

"Wonderful. Let them know we will meet in the dining hall within the hour."

Ashlyn nods and looks at Aella with a *you're going to tell me everything later* look, then winks and hurries out.

Aella stands to excuse herself when Michael reaches down and gently touches her hand.

"One more thing, I got you something earlier for the occasion." Rounding the bar, Michael leans down and places a silver box with a black bow tied around it on the countertop. Aella hesitates, and when Michael motions for her to open the box, her hands shake a little as they hover over the bow.

Carefully pulling on the tie to loosen the bow, she lifts the lid, and inside lays the most magnificent shade of green silk. Gently lifting the piece out of the box by its straps, the dress appears to be form-fitting but elegant.

"I hope you like green; it's my favorite color," Michael says, sounding nervous.

"I love it, Michael. It's beautiful."

Michael beams with a smile that reaches his eyes, deepening the light blue of his irises joyfully.

"Ah, almost forgot," he snaps his fingers, "Ashlyn brought a pair of shoes for you to wear as well." Leaning back down, he sets a pair of finely strapped nude sandals with a small heel, the tags still on them. "I have never been good with shoes. Dresses, however, I have a taste for."

"Thank you," she says, holding back a tear.

"I will await your return whenever you are ready."

Aella wipes her eyes with the back of her hand and carefully lays the dress back in the box, closing the lid, and places the sandals on top.

Without another word, Aella turns towards the door, stopping momentarily to look over her shoulder, and gives Michael a warm smile.

AFTER TAKING A HALF HOUR TO RINSE OFF AND FRESHEN up, Aella decides to leave her hair long, brushing out the kinks. Inspecting the dress to ensure there aren't any undesirable wrinkles that need to be aired out, she slips it on, careful not to snag at the silk.

Once satisfied with her appearance, she heads out the door with the pair of shoes Ashlyn lent her. When she reenters the lounge, Michael is in the same spot he said he would be.

His hair is now half pulled back into a bun, and a tailored all-black suit replaces his earlier attire with a freshly cut white orchid in the front pocket of his jacket. Michael looked handsome typically, but seeing him dressed like this now makes Aella's desire for him more potent.

"You look magnificent, Aella." He says, admiring her in the green silk dress he got for her. Aella's heart warms, and butterflies form in her stomach at the compliment.

Taking her hand, he guides her to a corner of the lounge she hadn't really noticed before. A giant floor-length mirror is leaned against the wall with intricate gold design work around it.

A tremor of anxiety pulls at her, bringing her back to her reflection in her meditative state. Swallowing down the uncomfortable notion, she stares at herself in the green dress that compliments her hazel eyes.

Aella doesn't just look beautiful as she stares at her reflection; she feels beautiful, which doesn't happen too often. With Michael standing behind her, bracing her shoulders, they could easily pass as a king and queen ready to protect their kingdom.

"That, that look right there; I want to see more of it," Michael says, looking at her in the mirror.

Crinkling her nose, she turns her head, raising a brow, "What look?"

"The look of happiness."

Aella did feel happy in this moment; she felt at peace even.

Leading her out of the lounge, Michael takes her hand in his as they walk down the hallway, entering what could only be considered the dining hall based on its massive size.

A long Mahogany table is in the center that stretches down the entire length of the room with an abundance of chairs that Aella nearly loses count of. Ashlyn approaches them as they walk in, wearing a long sapphire gown that flows like water trailing behind her. Her hair is also down in loose waves, looking like a real-life mermaid. Embracing Aella in a tight hug, Ashlyn pulls back, admiring her in the green dress.

"Aella, you look like a queen! Nice choice, Michael." She says in that kind, genuine tone. Aella's mind returns to the thoughts of how people back home would assume her to be condescending, but Ashlyn could never. Ashlyn didn't have one mean bone in her body. *Tara would hate her.*

"And you look like a literal mermaid!" Aella says, returning the compliment. Ashlyn's smile drops instantly, and her eyes widen. Aella then looks over to Michael, who is smothering a laugh, and her brows furrow with concern and confusion about why her compliment would offend Ashlyn.

"Mermaids aren't what you think they are, Aella." Michael begins to explain, "They are nasty foul creatures that lure anyone they can into uncharted waters, causing them to drown and be eaten. The mermaids you know of in your realm are magical and beautiful. Pretty ironic, turning a monster into something beautiful and harmless."

Aella is stunned to learn that detail about mermaids and

looks to Ashlyn with an apologetic grimace, "I had no idea that mermaids were real and also terrible. I am so sorry, Ash! You don't look like a mermaid; you look like a goddess," trying to rectify her stupidity.

Ashlyn smiles and softens her eyes, "Thank you, Aella, that is quite alright. I wish mermaids were the beautiful creatures you know of, but unfortunately, what Michael said is true. They're nasty." She grimaces at the thought of one of them slithering across the floor.

Walking down the length of the table, Torin is standing with his back facing the entrance, chatting with Cahtel and Christopher. When they get within earshot, Torin turns to face Aella fully. He looks dapper, wearing a tailored light grey suit that matches some of the greys in his feathers.

Christopher is also dressed for the occasion, wearing a light brown suit that has a gold chain attached to what appears to be a pocket watch. A folded cream-colored lapel stands out of the front pocket of his suit, and his hair is slicked back on the sides with loose layers that relax on the top, reminding her of the *Gatsby* era.

"Ah, Aella. You look exquisite." Christopher says while cupping one of her hands in his.

"Thank you, you clean up nice." Aella smiles back at him.

Cahtel clears his throat, "Yes, Aella, you look lovely."

All of the compliments she had received felt like too much, but she enjoyed them nonetheless.

Finding their seats, Aella takes the seat to Christopher's right while Michael sits a quarter of the way down at the head of the table. Aella couldn't believe how many people this table seats and wondered if it had ever been full.

Once everyone is fully seated, the cook comes out with a bottle of Pinot. Coming around the table, he begins pouring the glasses until he gets to Christopher's seat. Aella notes the hesitation, and Christopher declines to have his glass filled.

The cook then announces the first course will be a light dinner salad before turning on his heels with a straight back and head held high, returning to the kitchen. When the doors swing open, Aella makes out several people clanking dishes together and laughter that filters in; a harmonious effort to create a perfect meal.

Michael taps on his glass to gather everyone's attention, raising his for a toast, "To friends, new and old, I want to thank you for coming together and making it a special union for Aella and her father, Christopher. May we enjoy this meal together and many more gatherings to come. May we cherish each other's company, for eternal life is never guaranteed. May we laugh and reminisce about those that cannot be here in the flesh, but those that are in spirit."

An echo of cheers around the table sounds, and Michael looks at Aella with a light smile and winks as he leans over while Torin whispers something into his ear.

Christopher leans in toward Aella then, speaking low enough to where she can hear him, but the rest of the table can't. "We didn't really get a lot of time to talk as much earlier. What have you been up to the last twenty-three years?"

An awkward laugh escapes him, which causes Aella to tense as she reaches for her glass of wine.

"Well... not a whole lot, I guess. You saw my studio apartment, and I was working at a sports bar downtown recently. My best friend Tara and I do most everything together..." Aella misses Tara desperately and hopes that she's doing okay, or, at the very least, hopes she is on a vacation of some kind, as Michael had insinuated. "We have been best friends since middle school. She is more like a sister than anything."

Taking a bite of his salad, Christopher wipes his mouth

with the linen cloth. "Any plans for college or a career?"

The small talk and questions he was asking were laughable given the situation they are both in, but she shrugs taking a bite out of her own salad.

"I did, or still do? I want to go to art school on the East Coast. If you have any suggestions, maybe you can point me in the right direction for that."

Normal.

"Oh, how awesome! Yeah, for sure. Maybe we could get to know each other more when this is all over. And listen, it's not that I want to keep you a secret from Cindy. I plan on telling her something, but I just need to figure—"

Aella shakes her head as she cuts him off, "Don't worry about it."

The truth is, Aella doesn't really care about Cindy knowing who she is. It wouldn't make sense given her age, and she already knows that Christopher will just abandon her and their son when things get suspicious. *Should have thought about that when you went into the mortal realm.*

Clearing his throat, Christopher says, "There is a fantastic art program in Pennsylvania not too far from where I live now. If you're comfortable with it, I can work something out with Cindy, and you could stay at our place until you get situated."

Nope. Fuck, no.

"Yeah. Maybe. Let's get through this shitstorm first, and then we can reconvene." Aella says, forcing a smile. Christopher notices, and if she doesn't know any better, it looks as though he is white-knuckling it at the table while staring at her wine glass.

Aside from the awkward tension and conversation between Aella and her father, dinner was delicious, per usual, since the food here in Isethas is always delicious. If all else fails, at least Aella will never grow hungry during her stay.

Chapter Nineteen

W hen dinner was over, they all migrated to the lounge
for one last nightcap. Aella was feeling tipsy at this
point from the bourbon earlier and the glasses of pinot, so she
declined to have a nightcap. Before seeing Christopher out
with Torin, he had told her that he would be staying at his
family home so long as they needed him and didn't get a return
flight from Phoenix as of yet.

Some business trip.

She learned more about Christopher and his former life
here, hearing about her grandmother and what a typical day
was like before the war. Aella decided to keep Elissa's visit to
herself from him for now. She also learned that Michael is
much older than Christopher, which would be problematic in
the mortal realm, but the age didn't seem to bother her.

Walking Christopher out with Torin, she starts to fidget
with her fingers as they walk down the steps together.

"Thank you for coming. I know it was probably difficult to
leave Cindy and Jaxson. Hopefully, we won't be taking too
much more of your time, and we can get you back through the

portal and back home." Aella says, refraining from letting her emotions get the best of her.

Christopher leans in for a hug, then, "Oh, Aella, I look forward to whatever time we have here and learning more about you."

Leaning back, he holds her hands, searching her features, and says, "You know, you have a lot of Susan in you, but the more I look at you, you look so much like your Grandmother. You are a delight; Susan raised you well. I have a daughter!" He laughs in disbelief again, and Aella finds herself chuckling alongside him. Torin steps around, impatient to get Christopher back so that he could spend some one-on-one time with Ashlyn.

"Tell Ashlyn to wait up for me, would you?" Torin says with that mischievous look in his eyes.

Aella rolls her eyes at Torin, telling him she makes no promises and heads back into the palace. She could hear Michael, Cahtel, and Ashlyn laughing in the lounge as she got closer and contemplated whether she should just retire to her bedroom.

Leaning against the doorframe, she watches them momentarily, enjoying their joy until Michael notices her standing there. His gaze, soft and warm, reclining on his chaise with a glass of bourbon. A ritualistic comfort.

The amount they can drink without showing any signs of being drunk is impressive. Aella kicks off the door frame and enters the space entirely before saying to Ashlyn with a humorous edge, "Torin asked me to tell you to wait up for him, but I told him it would cost him."

Cocking a brow, Ashlyn crosses her arms across her chest, "Did he now? I guess I better make him work for it, then. Okay, I am going to turn in for the evening. Aella, I am beyond thrilled to have Christopher back for a short time and to help us. I will see you in the morning for another session." She smiles and sprints across the room, embracing Aella for another hug.

"I can't thank you enough for giving me insight on him; I guess it worked out," Aella says, still unsure of how she feels about meeting her father under these circumstances. Ashlyn holds on tighter, and her body shakes beneath her. Pulling back, Ashlyn's cheeks are damp from tears streaming down her face.

"Now I'm crying, dammit! You are most welcome. Christopher and I have been friends for centuries; he is a good man." Considering his age, Christopher is old as dirt, even if he doesn't act like it.

Walking over to the chair she and Michael had been making out in earlier, Cahtel is occupying it, and Aella has difficulty looking at him. Smashing her lips together as she thought about the event, her cheeks redden.

"Is something wrong, Aella?" Cahtel drawls, unamused. Michael had to have picked up on where her thoughts were because he, too, smothers a laugh while attempting to take another sip of his bourbon.

"What am I missing here? Please, enlighten me." Cahtel snaps. He has been extra moody lately. It probably has to do with being unable to binge all of *Sex and the City*.

Defusing the situation, Aella reaches over and rubs between Cahtel's ears, "Thank you also, Cahtel. If it weren't for you scaring the daylight out of me when you did, I would have never known the truth about my...gift or my father, hell I wouldn't have known about any of this, for that matter."

Cahtel purrs, nudging her hand to continue scratching. "More like scaring the piss out of you. You should have seen it, Michael, I...Ow!" He hisses from Aella, tugging on his fur to shut him up.

"Cahtel, anyone would be frightened if a talking cat came into their room while asleep. Don't be rude." Michael interjects, but Aella knows that Cahtel is only joking, and she doesn't love that Michael has taken it that far.

Michael then says, "I think I am also ready to turn in. We have yet another busy day tomorrow. Aella, you and Torin will begin combat training, so make sure you eat enough protein in the morning."

Aella yawns and gives Cahtel one last good scratch between his ears before heading to her room.

SLIPPING OUT OF HER DRESS, SHE HANGS IT UP IN THE closet and realizes it is the only piece of clothing she had cared to hang; everything else is still in her bags. Throwing on a T-shirt she had worn the night before, she washes her face and brushes her teeth, relieved to be getting into the soft, warm bed that beckons her.

The door cracks open as she crawls into the bed, "I brought you the tea. May I enter?" Michael asks through the small opening. His demeanor had changed a little during dinner. When she returned to the lounge after seeing Christopher out, Michael had become a little more closed off, as if an invisible wall had been thrown up, guarding any emotion he may have felt towards her earlier.

"Y—yes, come in." Aella's response is quiet and dry, yet also void of emotion. She was actually looking forward to drinking the tea so that her mind would go silent.

Pulling the covers up over her bare legs, he walks in, and the wall and distance he put between them has become impenetrable. Handing her the warm mug, she downs the liquid, not minding the bitter taste like before. Giving him back the mug, she doesn't speak a word and instead switches the light off on the bedside table like Michael had flipped a switch within himself and rolls onto her side with her back facing him.

The immature and childish behavior on her part may be extreme, but the confusion and lack of communication on his part justified her actions, so she thinks.

Michael lets out a sigh and sits on the edge of the bed. Aella isn't in the mood to have any sort of conversation, especially now that she drank the tea and just wants to sleep. Susan once said: *"Sometimes the best way of saying something and proving a point is to say nothing."* Out of all of Susan's quotes, Aella loved that one the most and kept it in her back pocket.

"Aella..." Michael says softly, yet the anguish is there, which causes her to tense. This is not how she wanted him to speak to her after the amazing moment shared in the lounge, or the dress he got her, or the dinner. *Nope.*

She cuts him off, not allowing him to continue and ruin any joy she accepted earlier. "Michael, don't, it's fine. What happened between us won't ever happen again, I get it. No distractions, remember? Thank you for the tea. I am going to sleep now." The words rolled off of her tongue just as cold and distant as he, mirroring his shift in body language and, really, everything. Her words were a switch, an impenetrable wall, despite her chest feeling tight and her ego bruised. She hated how men could make you feel one way and then take it back as if whatever happened between the two of you was nothing more than something physical.

Even though Michael and Damien are different, they are still men at the end of the day, regardless of how many more years of experience they may have. *At least I didn't sleep with either one of them.* The thought doesn't lessen the blow because even if she didn't give herself entirely to them, intimacy is still intimacy.

Michael doesn't move from the edge of the bed, and Aella finally turns her head over her shoulder to see his face, but he is staring at the wall before him.

"We just have to stay the course, Aella. Now that we plan to trap Damien in Diatturus, distractions will just... they will get the better of us both."

Turning to look at her, that concern he hides so well is stark against his features in the evening light that streams through the curtains' cracks. Shifting her body so she can face him fully, he begins stroking her hair tenderly.

"Trapping Damien is your plan, though, Michael; I agreed to it, but don't put all of that on me, please."

His fingers are still, and Aella knits her brows, waiting for either a verbal or physical slap. Dropping his hand, he looks at the wall, "He has to stay there, Aella. It will put an end to all of this once and for all. Don't think for one second that my feelings for you have changed. You are all I think about from the moment I wake, to when my head rests upon my pillow. Be that as it may, you will suppress your gift, and any threat to cause another war along with the realms being destroyed will come to an end, and so will any chance of you and I. You will have a normal life, as you should. I don't think... I can bear to lose you once I have you, and that terrifies me."

And there it is, the reality. Because the truth is, no matter how awful it is, Aella will suppress her gift for the greater good, even if it means never seeing Cahtel again or Ashlyn. She will never come back to Isethas and see Torin or Michael. Aella will have what she has always wanted, a normal life, and that comes with sacrifice.

Shaking his head, he looks over to her, his eyes dark with need. "Not being able to have you will be torture, but having you and losing you will be worse than death for me. Do you understand?"

A shuddering breath slips past her lips. It seems so unfair to have two people wanting each other and not being able to act on it because of consequences. It was as if Michael was the candy and Aella was the baby, being denied it even though it was waved in front of her face. Swallowing thickly, she closes her eyes and nods. "I understand. No distractions and no heartache. Got it."

"Get some sleep, Aella. I will have Ashlyn wake you in the morning; we are going to begin training earlier. Goodnight." Leaning down, he brushes his lips across her forehead before standing up. Leaving the room, he closes the door with a soft click behind him, and Aella stares at the ceiling, imagining that the glow and dark sticky stars are there from her childhood.

The tea kicks in, pulling her to sleep until there are no more imaginary stars on the ceiling, and her thoughts stop running circles in her mind, allowing the black void to suck her in.

ASHLYN WALKS INTO HER ROOM SOMETIME THE following morning, opening the curtains. Pulling the covers up over her head, Aella longs for at least ten more minutes of rest. "Wakey wakey Aella! Rise and Shine!" Ashlyn says as she rounds to the side of the bed where Aella is huddled underneath the covers. Grunting her response, Aella's stubborn body refuses to budge.

Ashlyn then tugs the covers off, making her shiver and even more grumpy than she is already.

"What the hell? Can't I just get thirty more minutes, please?" Aella whines and Ashlyn gives her an exaggerated pout as she walks over to the coffee table, looking as fresh as ever and put together. *Bitch.*

Picking up the recognizable bottle of liquid, Ashlyn returns to Aella's side handing it to her with the colors swirling and changing in the morning light. Unscrewing the lid, she carefully squeezes the dropper, placing one drop under her tongue, then hands the bottle back.

Given that it had been a few days since she'd had the elixer, her body felt as if it had a resurrection within seconds, causing her to jump out of bed in a rush. Forgetting about how euphoric and energized just one drop could do, she stretches and moves, enjoying every sensation.

"The cook is making us a protein-infused breakfast; Michael, Torin, and Cahtel are already waiting for us in the gathering room. Be ready in fifteen!" Apparently, there will be no coffee on the sofa or chit-chat this morning. *Strait to business.*

"Okay, any suggestions on what I should wear?" Not that she still has a lot to choose from.

"Something comfortable and something you can move freely in."

Wasting no more time, Aella runs into the bathroom, throws her hair into a messy bun, and splashes cool water on her face. While brushing her teeth, she looks in the closet, rummaging through her overnight bag, finding her trusty pair of leggings, a tank top, a pair of already worn socks, and her only other pair of tennis shoes that aren't covered in sticky tar. She stops for a second with her toothbrush hanging out of her mouth and her arms full of clothes to admire the green dress she wore the night before, then gets dressed.

Entering the gathering room, the smell of bacon and eggs overpowers the space, making her mouth salivate. Sitting down next to Cahtel, Ashlyn and Michael were reviewing the itinerary for today's events, and Aella suddenly felt invisible since no one acknowledged her walking in. It was silly to feel that way, but a kind hello or good morning even would have been nice, especially since Ashlyn woke her up the way she did.

"Good morning, Aella. Sleep well?" Cahtel asks, licking coffee out of his mug. It never bothered her before, but listening to him lick and slurp his coffee was like nails on a chalkboard, given how grumpy she was.

"Like a babe," she grumbles, "Tou?"

"I slept rather sound. Coffee?" He nods toward the French press sitting in the center of the table next to a pitcher of cream and a jar of sugar.

"Please, thanks." She says, and Cahtel just stares at her, waiting for her to grab the French press and additional fixings since his paws are useless.

Pouring coffee into her mug with a small amount of cream, Cahtel nudges her to top his off and smiles. Rolling her eyes, she pours a little more into his half-full mug and returns the French press and cream with an audible click, hoping that would gain everyone else's attention.

"They've been going over today's itinerary for a while," Cahtel informs quietly while Aella takes a sip from her mug, "You will meditate in the field today instead of the meditation room. Ashlyn is overly confident that you will be able to manifest a portal and close it. Then, you will train with Torin. Afterward, you and I will meet in the library and review the realms' history. Dinner, bed, repeat." He finishes through his teeth, seemingly annoyed by the repetition.

Shifting in her chair, irritation starts to become more evident. She didn't appreciate being left out of the conversation that had everything to do with her, and frankly, she found it quite rude.

Standing out of her chair abruptly, the legs of the chair screech across the marble floors, the sound making her flinch but gaining the attention she wanted the moment she entered the room. Cahtel stays seated, unmoved by her irritation; in fact, he looks amused, as if he's enjoying what is about to transpire. *Ass.*

Everyone's eyes are on her then, and Ashlyn stops speaking mid-sentence. Michael leans back from being so close to Ashlyn in his chair, which also grates on Aella's nerves as she tamps down a small tinge of jealousy.

Michael folds his hands on the tabletop, waiting for Aella to say something from her disruption.

Clearing her throat, she takes a deep breath, "Now that I have your attention, care to inform me about the itinerary?" Irritation laced every word, and she began to feel stupid for getting so worked up over something that was so small now that the stimulant and coffee were mingling with each other in her system.

Ashlyn shifts in her seat, pursing her lips together, and Michael's jaw flexes, unimpressed by her poor attitude, but she is frustrated with many things, including him. Torin attempts to smother a laugh, enjoying the scene alongside Cahtel, which is no surprise. Torin is the type who relishes in conflict and tension a little too much.

"Sit down, please," Michael says through gritted teeth, matching the dark cloud Aella brought in with her.

Sitting back down in the chair, she is in no position to get comfortable. Keeping a straight back, she rests her hands on the table, proving that she is the one who means business now.

Punctual as ever, the cook enters the gathering room then laying their plates full of eggs, bacon, sweet potato hash, and toast on the table before each of them. Although the food smells delicious, she no longer has an appetite, and as a child would, she pushes the plate forward, proving a point. *Why do you have to be such a little brat?*

Michael glares at her from across the table. The subtle

243

moment was immature and rude since the cook took pride in his work, and when Aella looks up at him, she regrets pushing that plate away when a look of hurt clouds the cook's features.

"Miss Aella, is the food not up to your liking?" the cook asks sincerely, adding fuel to her guilt for doing it while he is standing there.

"No, it's... I'm sorry. It's perfect." She says, pulling the plate back and attempting to smile sheepishly even though her cheeks are now the same color as the strawberry jam.

The cook nods and exits the gathering room through the doors. Aella realizes too late that she should have waited to do something like that after he left the room altogether, but she's impulsive with her tongue and actions.

Those things need work and, most likely, extensive therapy. *Add that to the list.*

"You need to eat. Training with Torin will be intense and exhausting." Michael says, sternly still through gritted teeth. Aella has no plans on touching a single bite of her food, her behavior has taken the driver's seat now and she is too stubborn to give in no matter how hungry she is.

She also wanted to point out to Michael that he is not in charge of her. Cahtel, on the other hand, is indulging himself, scarfing down his food like nothing's amiss. Ashlyn continues to sit silently, taking a small bite of her eggs, while Torin tears through a piece of bacon, moaning with every chew, taunting Aella.

Yeah, he enjoys this shit way too much.

"Fine, suit yourself," Michael says impassively, taking a bite of egg and hash, then wiping his mouth with a napkin before turning his attention to Cahtel, ignoring Aella entirely. "Cahtel, you know the itinerary. After breakfast, Aella will go to the fields and work on grounding herself there without being completely in her meditative state. Training will begin with

Torin, and you will review history." He then glances back over at Aella and says, "Part of the reason why she needs to eat is to feed what little muscle is there and build up her strength. The weak don't survive on the battlefield. We cannot have dead weight aiding us."

Aella is really starting to dislike this man. *Fuck him, and fuck this.*

"Because training with Torin will take up most of the day, it is important that we eat early and get an appropriate amount of rest. This means there will be no more nightcaps or cocktails while Aella trains moving forward. Now, Aella, is that inclusive enough for you? Or would you like to write everything down in your little notebook?" He says, still angered by her behavior and attitude. She understands how serious this all is and doesn't take it lightly, but Michael going from hot to cold in a matter of hours was confusing as hell and also unsettling.

She should have never entertained the idea that there could be something more between them. She was kidding herself from the beginning, especially since she got swept up with his brother and helped create a mess that she never wanted any part of.

Stick to the task and have a normal life. Swallowing her pride, Aella picks up a piece of bacon, forcing herself to eat what she can now that her stomach hurts from guilt and embarrassment.

"Yep. Sounds good." Her response is cold and emotionless as she looks down at her plate. Moving forward, avoiding Michael as much as she can will make this process much more tolerable.

"Eat what you can; we are burning daylight." Michael is becoming more and more of her least favorite person.

Ashlyn took Aella to the field of flowers outside of the palace. She told Aella that being in nature is not only the best way to practice grounding, but being out in the open can feel less suffocating. Ashlyn was confident that Aella was getting close to controlling her gift, and should things go south, there would be no walls to come down.

The foul mood Aella was in still lingers, and she isn't sure she can brush it off. Having said no more than two words to Ashlyn when they left the palace, her negative energy affected her deeply.

"Aella, I need you to be able to focus. Why are you so upset?"

Something inside of her is brewing, there is pressure like a damn threatening to burst, but Aella holds it in and waves Ashlyn off.

"I'm fine. Let's just do this."

Ashlyn hesitates for a moment, then steps back from Aella, centering herself.

"Okay, let's work on grounding while standing. It might help if you take your shoes off so you can feel the ground beneath you."

Kicking off her shoes and socks, Aella stands, fixing her posture so she isn't slouching and mirrors Ashlyn.

"Great, now close your eyes and breathe. In through the nose, out through the nose. Deep inhale, hold, exhale, hold. We will do this three times."

Doing as instructed, Aella inhales and exhales.

"Good Aella. Close your eyes, and really feel the ground beneath you. Imagine yourself as a tree or your orchid. Inhale, hold, exhale, hold. Quiet your mind, and reach for your subconscious. Give her permission to take the wheel."

Going through the steps, Aella envisions she is one with her orchid and gives her subconscious permission to take the wheel. *Acceptance.*

I accept my gift. I am in control. I accept my gift. I am in control.

With her feet firmly planted in the grass, Aella feels grounded and light but still awake, handing over the keys to her subconscious, and envisions a portal. She can see it with her eyes closed, the translucent wall with silvery swirls ebbing and flowing.

"Open your eyes, Aella." Ashlyn coaxes gently with disbelief.

Opening her eyes, the portal she manifested was before her. One that she opened while her subconscious was awake and her conscious was taking the passenger seat.

"Holy shit." She breathes, looking at the magnificence of it. It was exactly how she pictured it in her mind, much like the others she had seen before the black tentacles had taken over the one that currently remains open into Isethas from her apartment."Where does it lead to?"

"Where did you see it leading to?" Ashlyn asks warily, but Aella doesn't know. Her last thought was about Tara, so perhaps it is wherever she is. Aella wants to go through it to see if there is a chance that it's where Tara is, but Ashlyn steps in front of her.

"We need to close it now. Opening the portal is just the first step. I want you to ground yourself again and do everything you did with opening it, but the opposite. I'm unsure what that looks like; it may be more of a feeling than just closing it like a door."

Aella nods, despite the longing she feels to walk through the portal, and begins to go through the steps of grounding herself. In her subconscious mind, she doesn't need to manifest the portal since it is already there.

The energy flowing out of the portal is so intense it feels like electricity that pulls you to come near it, like a warm fire on a cold winter day. Alone in the field of flowers with the portal, Aella welcomes it instead of fearing it as she has so frequently in the past. Accepting this part of her, utilizing her gift as a tool.

The portal breathes and moves, matching her breath and vibrations.

I accept my gift. I am in control.

Holding out a hand, she squeezes her fingers tight into a ball and uses that force to close the portal.

Opening her eyes, Ashlyn's jaw is slack, and when Aella looks over to where the portal had stood in the open field, it was no longer.

"You did it, Aella. You opened and closed a portal. How?..." Ashlyn's voice trails off as she walks to where the portal had been with caution in case her eyes were deceiving her.

"A feeling of acceptance," Aella says, then without any warning, that damn breaks. Every emotion, every half-healed wound that she inflicted on herself, reopened, and a scream so primal escapes her.

The same electrical current that the portal emitted is coursing through her veins. Tears so hot and heavy blur her vision until all she saw was nothing. Collapsing onto the grass, she sucks in as much air as her lungs can take through trembling lips. Every inhale feels like thick smoke, the agonizing pain and hurt becoming too much. She digs her fingers into the soil, grabbing onto the grass, needing something, anything to hold onto.

Ashlyn stands there frozen, eyes wide and skin visibly paler. A dark cloud engulfs the sky, a black void that has no beginning or end, with lightning snaking through the dark mass as Aella unleashes the caged animal that has been trapped inside of her her whole life.

A storm, so devastating, packed full of pain and loss. A loss of a life she grieved every day since she could remember. The loss of a father she never knew existed until now. The loss of many sleepless nights, the loss of love she never got to experience, but most of all, the loss of the many lies she told herself and the secrets kept from her by the one person she entrusted, her mother.

Now that Aella has begun to accept her gift and the process of accepting herself, the dark cloud that blankets the sky breaks as droplets fall down, purging everything.

A long moment passes once the cold droplets turn into nothing more than a harrowing mist. Aella unlatches her fingers from the soil and wet grass, getting back to her feet. When she looks over to Ashlyn, she realizes that they are both completely soaked from the rain that expelled from the angry storm, threatening to strike down anyone who dared to pass.

Aella stands shivering from the emotional fatigue, and Ashlyn shivers from both fear and her wet clothes.

"What was that?" Aella asks, trying to make sense of the storm that matched her emotions like a balanced crescendo.

"I am pretty sure you just did that." Ashlyn manages to get out through chattering teeth, unmoving and frightened by the amount of power Aella truly has buried deep within her.

Glancing up at the sky, the dark cloud dissipates, and Aella feels much lighter.

Fuck.

Chapter Twenty

Ashlyn continues to stand in that same spot, holding her arms tight against her chest, shivering, not wanting to come close to Aella after what had occurred. The look she has on her face is one that Aella is all too familiar with. The same look she often saw in the mirror, a look of fear.

"Ash, I... I don't know how I did that," Aella says, equally stunned and confused. She had never done anything like that before, and now that she has a better grasp on her gift, processing this is overwhelming.

"Are you sure that I caused that storm? I mean, that's like superhero-type shit, right? Elissa couldn't do that, could she?" Aella frantically asks again, hoping for some explanation for the strange phenomena.

"I—Im not sure Aella. That would be something Christopher would be able to answer. This is bigger than what I am capable of helping you with."

Aella's jaw drops open at her response. "I'm sorry, that storm is bigger than what you're capable of helping me with?! Bigger than helping me do something like, I don't know, opening and closing a portal?" Frustration eases its way in all over again, and Aella has to reel it back down in case she somehow manifests a tornado.

"You know what I think? I think that the storm makes more sense to me than the whole portal-opening *gift* I was born into. In fact, I think that Michael doesn't even know the first thing when it comes to *helping* me with my *condition,* and he is making up rules as he goes because of his own self-involved fears that I want no part of. You want to know why I was upset earlier, Ashlyn? Where do I start?... Let's see; I am a half-bred human who, by the way, just recently found out that the other half of me is Isethanian, thanks to you. My father has a whole other life with a child that I also don't want any part of, and I actually liked *Damien* when I met him to be Gabriel, but now he is the enemy and has my friends held somewhere. Now, you are looking at me like I am a monster because of a storm that I created somehow. I can't talk to my best friend. You and Cahtel are the closest thing I have to a friend right now. Im broken. Just a broken fucked up, half-bred human with nothing but some stupid gift I never wanted, and now I can create fucking storms?!" Aella unloads every thought she had prior to the event and what she is now thinking. Because, the truth is, creating a portal with the control she finally has access to was a lot to acknowledge, but projecting a physical storm from the nonphysical one within her takes on a whole new perspective.

Ashlyn drops her arms as she walks up to her finally with an embrace, holding her with care while she brushes her wet strands with her fingers.

"I am so sorry Aella. You have every right to be upset. The pressure you are under right now must be suffocating; I can't imagine how you must truly feel. The storm gave some perspective on that." She says, inserting some light humor, "Listen, I will do everything I can to help understand this other side

251

of your gift. I am sure Michael is aware that something occurred and is probably losing his mind over it. I will speak with him."

Pulling away from her, Aella wipes a few more tears that had fallen from her eyes and says, "My whole life, all I have wanted was... normal. This is far from normal, Ashlyn, all of it. The whole portal-opening gift thing sucks, but I guess, in a way, it's kind of cool? That I can accept since we are working towards controlling it; the manifestations of storms, on the other hand, is not something I really want to figure out..."

Ashlyn creases her brows in understanding; it isn't something she wants to figure out, either. What Aella didn't know about having a secondary gift yet is she could also be used as a weapon. More so than the ability to open portals, and that little-known fact could change everything.

"For now, we will have to keep this under wraps between you, me, and Michael. I will speak with him in private, and we will conduct a plan to let Christopher know. Torin and Cahtel don't need to know about this right now, okay?"

Aella nods her agreement. The less to know about this, the better, even if she didn't want Michael to have something else to hold over her head.

Picking up on where her thoughts were trailing, Ashlyn lets out a breath, "Michael can be... complicated, but he has a big heart. I'm not sure what will come of this new knowledge, and even though we are on borrowed time, patience is key. Michael cares for his people and the realms, and I also know that he cares for you deeply, which is why he has been on edge. It will all work out in the end."

Breathing in through her nose, Aella appreciates Ashlyn's calm after the storm despite how unsettling this new discovery is. She doesn't consider any of this a win, even though she has successfully managed to tap into her primary gift.

Torin swoops down onto the field at that moment, landing in front of them.

"What the hell was that?! Michael is on his way. Are you both alright?" Torin says, on edge and deeply concerned.

Wringing some of the rainwater out of her lilac dress, Ashlyn approaches Torin, easing some of his concern.

"Yes, we are both fine. It must have been a weird thunderstorm. The seasons are changing. But Aella tapped into her gift, opening and closing a portal! We are getting closer, Torin." She says redirecting one problem to the other in a celebratory way.

He creases his brows in shock at the news. "Ashlyn, we have never had a thunderstorm like that in Isethas for all of the years I have been alive."

Flicking her wrist in the air, Ashlyn says, "Stranger things have happened, love; mother nature is a fickle. Aella, on the other hand, did well today; Michael should be very pleased."

Torin's jaw flexes, and it is evident that he is suspicious of how unbothered Aella and Ashlyn both seem, given that they are drenched from the rain.

"Well, I will let you two get to your training and let Michael know it was nothing more than a thunderstorm." Ashlyn pats Torin on the shoulder, turning from him.

"That sounds great in theory, Ashlyn, except—"

"Except what?" Michael demands, appearing behind Torin equally unnerved.

Ashlyn's cheeks warm at the tension laced in his tone that matches his features; she swallows and says, "Ah, I was just about to catch you before you came all the way down here. It was just a small storm, nothing to worry about. Come, let's talk while Aella and Torin begin their training. You will be very pleased to know that—"

Torin interrupts Ashlyn, shaking his head, "That was not just any storm, Michael. You didn't see it fully; it was... bad.

Our people are going to start asking questions, questions that they will need answers to. The biggest one concerning the toxic spill you had Cahtel and I inform them of and how that is getting handled along with the storm that came out of nowhere."

Aella felt the pressure then and didn't want to lie to Michael or Torin about it, especially now. Torin was right; the storm that occurred wasn't normal, even in the world that she was so accustomed to. "It was me," Aella blurts, and she didn't have to look at them to feel their burning gazes on her, "I did that. I don't know how, but I did. It happened shortly after I opened and closed a portal right where Torin is standing now. After, I just felt overwhelmed, and it was like something had broken inside of me. It's hard to explain..."

Ashlyn steps around Michael suddenly, softening her tone, "I was going to tell you in private. Christopher may be able to give us additional—"

"We don't have time for this, Ashlyn!" Michael snaps, and the abrasive tone makes Aella flinch as regret snakes in for breaking the news out in the field.

Torin shifts on his feet, placing a tender hand on Ashlyn's shoulder, "She's right, Michael. If anyone knows about additional powers linked to her gift, it's Christopher."

Michael's irises turn from pale blue to nearly white as he flexes his jaw, ready to snap all over again. But before he can say anything, Torin continues, "We don't have a choice, man. If we don't get a handle on this, then who knows what other chaos will ensue."

Michael remains tense, even though the color has started to return to his irises. Flexing his hands at either side, Aella could see he was stressed, and she was the source. The one to cause all of it, Aella viewed herself more as a burden than an asset.

"Fine. Get to training. After, you will retrieve Christopher.

There will be no more interference." Michael says, and Torin nods in compliance, "Aella, get your emotions in check, or this will cost us everything." He seethes in her direction without so much as a glance, and in a blink, he vanishes, teleporting back to the palace.

Ashlyn left not long after Michael did, assuring Aella the best she could that he would cool down. At this point, Aella didn't give a shit. She and Michael didn't even need to be friends at this point; they had an agreement, and she had bigger things to focus on now, like not inflicting a natural disaster.

Torin stretches out in the grass next to Aella, showing her some basic moves to help loosen her muscles and tension. Her damp clothes are nearly dry now, which she is thankful for since the feeling of wet fabric pulling against her skin isn't one that she enjoys.

After stretching out for a little bit in silence, Torin glances over at Aella, "Don't take what Michael said personally. He's a broody fuck." He says, breathing out as he stretches his right bicep, and Aella starts laughing.

"That's one way of putting it," she smirks, trying to reach down her outstretched legs, only making it halfway down to her toes. "I'm over it, honestly. He can be as pissed off as he wants with me, and he has a right to be, especially over breakfast. Besides, he's right; the sooner I can get a handle on my emotions, the better."

Standing up for Torin's next instruction, she brushes her hands off on her leggings, smearing the damp soil.

Torin softens his features and looks up to the sky. "You know, I have known Michael for a very long time," he starts, and Aella has to refrain from rolling her eyes. They all have.

"His biggest fault in life is that he cares too much, if you should even consider that a fault. Michael has many demons that haunt him from... before, his brother being the biggest monster of them all. Just try to be understanding and forgiving if you can."

Torin then looks at Aella, his eyes more golden than brown in the late afternoon. She nods and clears her throat from the slightly uncomfortable honesty, "So, you gonna show me how to kick some ass or what?"

Torin throws back his head in a roaring laugh, taking in her petite frame, and shakes his head.

"It is going to take some work, but when we have a couple of sessions under your belt, I won't be shocked when you can take me to the ground. First, let's practice your stance. Part your feet hip-width apart like this," Torin moves his feet confident with his posture and how his footing is firmly planted.

Aella does as instructed, blowing a few flyaways from her face through her mouth, waiting for further instruction.

"Good. Now, I want you to practice using only your core to move your upper body. This will help you in case of dodging a fist or ducking. Watch me carefully and use your core."

Aella cocks a brow, and without any warning, Torin kicks his foot out, barely touching her as she falls back.

"What the fuck?!" Aella gasps, and Torin holds his hand out to help her up.

"You aren't paying attention to your enemy or using your core. Try again."

Sweat starts to form at her temple as she gets into the same stance. Torin could have knocked the wind out of her, but his movements were controlled and precise.

Switching it up, he uses his left foot, and Aella squats down, avoiding a kick to the face. Her thighs are on fire from not using those muscles, and her knees buckle.

"Nice job, but you still aren't engaging your core. It will help you with not popping a knee out of its socket." Torin teases. Aella stands, hoping she didn't do just that or pull anything vital in her legs.

They hadn't been training all that long, and she started to feel physically exhausted, wishing she would have eaten her protein-packed breakfast from earlier. Bending over, she braces her hands on her knees, trying to catch her breath.

"Can I have a minute?" She pants, desperate for a sip of water.

Torin shakes his head and crosses his arms over his chest, "Do you think your enemy would grant you such luxury? In battle or defense, you don't have a minute, Aella. You don't even have a split second to react. This is training, and we haven't even scratched the surface. Get back into position."

By the time they finished their first training session, Aella wasnt sure she could walk. Her legs were swollen, and her abs were on fire from all the ducking and squatting; even her back-side was numb from the impact it received from falling.

She took a few minor hits to her right arm and chest that will most definitely bruise, but after falling, standing, ducking, and squatting a hundred times, Aella became a pro and quick on her reaction time.

They had to have been doing just that for a couple of hours when Torin informs her that today's training is over. She is desperate for a hot bath and food from how hungry and sore she feels, and she knows that the following day, she would need a wheelchair to get out of bed, but they still had work to do, and the day was far from over.

Flying Aella back to the palace because there was no way she could walk there, Torin told Aella to drink plenty of elec-trolytes before taking off to get Christopher.

When she entered the front doors, the steps leading up to

the palace left her winded, and her legs threatened to give out on her at any moment.

Cahtel is pacing in the foyer, and the air seems dense. Michael is nowhere in sight, which is a relief, but when Cahtel stops pacing, the look he gives Aella sends guilt clawing at the back of her throat, and suddenly escaping doesn't sound so terrible.

"Michael informed me of what happened earlier in the fields. Has that ever happened before?" He asks, perturbed.

Of course, he did. Not in the mood to argue, she says, matching his cold demeanor, "No. This would be the first occurrence."

Cahtel scoffs, "Lies."

"Excuse me? Why would I lie about something like that? You know what, forget it. I'm going to shower before Christopher gets here. You and Torin weren't even supposed to know about this, by the way, but I had to open my big mouth like I always do." She says, frustrated, moving towards the staircase with each step sending currents of pain up her body.

Cahtel deadpans her and says, "In your apartment when your mother showed up. The whole apartment shook like an earthquake."

Fuck. Point proven. Aella had forgotten about that incident and thought it was just a weird fluke.

"So? What's your point, Cahtel? Why do I feel like everything I do is under a microscope with you people?"

Disregarding her response, Cahtel continues, "What caused you to get so upset that you summoned a storm of that size? Aella, this could have been bad for everyone here in Isethas. It's not just about you, girl. There are lives involved, and you could have destroyed multiple had you continued." He lectures, making the guilt so much worse. Focusing on her breath, Aella thinks about what she could possibly say to justify how it wasn't her fault, but she couldn't because it was.

Ashlyn storms down the hall, leaving the lounge, having heard what Cahtel just said to her.

Standing next to Aella, she glares at him and snaps, "Enough! Between you and Michael, I don't blame her for reacting the way she did. You are doing the opposite of helping her with your lecture. What is done is done, Cahtel. Christopher will be here soon, and we need answers."

Aella saw a strength in Ashlyn that she hadn't witnessed before, a warrior. The kind and generous Ashlyn has a fire in her.

Cahtel stands his ground, snarling back at her, but Ashlyn doesn't cower. The guilt inside of Aella is still heavy, chipping away at the little courage she mustered in the field from training with Torin. *More like a beating.*

To think that she is the cause of this tension and resentment that had reared its ugly head since she came to Isethas was unbearable. *Control your emotions,* she reminds herself, even though the urge to break down all over again bubbles.

"Library," Cahtel says through clenched teeth, and Aella sighs, wanting more than anything to just go up to her room and hide in the giant walk-in closet.

Turning on his paws, he walks down a dark hallway that she hasn't been through yet as they follow.

THE DOORS ARE OPEN, AND THE LIBRARY IS IMPRESSIVE. Thousands of books lined the floor-to-ceiling shelves along the rounded walls. The structure of the room is built like a dome, with natural light filtering through the ceiling.

With the space open, the only things sitting in the center

are sofas and chairs. The space is inviting and comforting, the opposite of how she feels.

Inside the library, Aella notices a small opening to a hallway out of the corner of her eye that stands out with stark white walls and what appears to be paintings hung and lit by sconces. Remembering that Michael had mentioned something akin to a gallery in his library, she assumes that is it and also off the table of ever seeing now.

Ashlyn motions for her to sit down on one of the sofas to rest her sore body while she and Cahtel rummage around for books that could give them any insight before Torin returns with Christopher. Because Cahtel can't carry anything, Ashlyn did all the heavy lifting.

Returning with a stack of books ranging from various dates and languages, Ashlyn sits on the other side of the sofa, setting the books down in the center so they can go through them all.

The books are not only old but also delicate. Carefully opening one of them, Aella grimaces at the crack of the spine. The language is one she does not recognize, wholly hand-written in symbols with rust-colored ink; it is a beautiful work of art.

Ashlyn realizes that Aella can't read any of the words on the pages and smiles at her as she reaches for the tome.

"My, this is an ancient manuscript," she says, carefully turning the pages. "It is a book on old magic." Her eyes light up as she reads a passage and continues, "Before the war, magic was used quite regularly. Those who created magic were referred to as healers or Wiccans."

"Like a witch?" Aella asks with curiosity sparking. The only history she paid close attention to in school was the Salem Witch Trials, and she imagined what it would have been like to have been alive during that time and be portrayed as such.

"Not quite. The witches you know of today were made to

be evil using dark magic, and some of that isn't too far off. The war corrupted many minds, causing some of the healers and Wiccans to turn dark. History is a powerful tool; it can make you knowledgeable and see things for what they truly are, but it can also ruin you if you are not careful. Mortals live in a... bubble. If every mortal read every book from every realm and learned the true meaning of everything, it would be disastrous. That is why the thousands of books you see in this library are books that cannot be rewritten." Ashlyn explains, and Aella digests every bit of it, putting perspective into more of what she thought she knew already.

"What is the book titled?" Aella asks, staring down at the tome in Ashlyn's lap.

"*Diablerie Memento Goety.* It means remembrance of black magic and the spirits evoked." Ashlyn responds, scrolling through the text, "This is interesting..."

Aella scoots closer, looking down at the page even though she can't read the text.

Ashlyn then reads the text aloud, "It says here that manifestations can occur while using a spell alongside a combination of herbs. Manifestations may include, but are not only subject to, specific items, objects, and materialistic possessions."

That would clear things up if she had manifested a physical object. The only problem is she projected how she felt inside, which turned into a nasty storm.

Aella thinks for a moment and remembers the tea, "What are the herbs referenced? The tea Michael has me drink for rest every evening before bed has a mixture of herbs. Could any of those interfere?"

"It's not likely. The herbs mentioned are ones we haven't had access to since before the war. They were destroyed and banned for recreation. I'm honestly surprised that Michael has this tome in his library; you could manifest a portal with this spell."

Aella didn't love that response, but given that the herbs were no longer available, the likelihood of someone manifesting a portal with the spell was slim. They were grasping at straws, trying to figure out what may have sparked the secondary gift, and until Christopher arrived, they didn't have a clear answer.

Cahtel lifts his head up from a book that Ashlyn had opened for him after reading a passage. "Before the war, only a few were born with gifts, Elissa being one of them. Those with gifts carried one of the five elements: Earth, water, fire, air, and space. We know that Elissa's ability to manifest portals was like walking through a black hole in space, and Aella mentioned something about the feeling of both falling and floating at the same time when she would subconsciously create a portal in her sleep. What I don't understand is how you could have a secondary since those born with a gift only carry one of the five elements."

Furrowing her brow, Aella asks, "Who were the other three that carried the other elements?"

"If I remember correctly, there was Zander who carried fire. He was Mia's second of Cleopparim, nasty little shit. He scorched many homes and buildings, setting fields ablaze, but died in the war. Then there was Siranda; she was the Watcher of the realm Ilarene. She carried the earth element and could grow anything from a mere weed to the tallest tree and vine at the snap of a finger. Unfortunately, she, too, perished, and so did her realm, leaving it a wasteland. The other two, I am not sure." Cahtel says, thinking back to a time.

"So whoever carried the air and water element is a mystery?" Aella says, and Cahtel nods as he continues reading through the tome.

Torin enters the library a moment later with Christopher,

and Aella realizes that something is very wrong with the state they are both in. Torin looks enraged, and Christopher looks like he'd had an all-night bender.

His hair is disheveled, and he is wearing the same brown suit as the night before with his shirt untucked, and the smell of booze wafts into the space. *There goes that twenty-three-year chip.*

Christopher stumbles in, and Torin reaches to prop him up with frustration. Ashlyn stands from the sofa, approaches them, and ushers Torin into the hall so that they can speak privately.

Leaving Christopher to stand on his own, he sways, ready to fall over, and Aella jumps up, running over to help escort her intoxicated father to one of the cushioned chairs, not understanding why he would do this, especially now when they needed his help the most. It was selfish and ultimately disappointing.

Once seated, Christopher slurs. "M—my d—aughter oorrr," through hiccups.

"What the fuck..." Aella whispers. *This is bad*; Michael is going to lose his shit. They needed to sober him up before discussing how she could have a secondary gift before Michael saw the state Christopher was in.

Torin and Ashlyn reenter the library, and Ashlyn appears to be a little solemn.

Not caring about the look on Ashlyn's face, Aella says with urgency, "We need to get him water and something to eat now!"

"It's too late. I found him at the tavern. He has been there since I took him back to his home last night." Torin says with agitation. She could only imagine the shitstorm he dealt with while retrieving him.

Christopher's eyes are glossed over, and drool begins to trickle down the side of his mouth. Without too much thought,

Aella has a feeling that he is going to be sick and finds a small metal trash bin, shoving it under his chin on his lap. After a few seconds, he begins heaving, stinking up the space with acidic liquor.

"Will somebody explain to me why my library reeks of a tavern?" Michael's voice booms through the library as he enters the doorway. Torin approaches him then, attempting to guide him back out into the hall.

His valiant attempt to de-escalate the situation fails before it gets out of hand, and Michael storms in with rage.

"I want him out, NOW! Torin, take him back. I don't care where you leave him. Take him to the tavern for all I care; I want him out of my sight. And YOU..." he points at Aella. "You are coming with me."

Remaining crouched in front of Christopher, who is now incoherent, she stays unmoving. She understands why Michael is angry; she's angry and frustrated as well, but she wasn't going to leave Christopher until she knew he was sober enough not to choke on his own vomit.

"Now, Aella Rose." Michael enforces, and her jaw drops. She never once mentioned her middle name because she hates it. The only person who calls her that is her mother. Feeling her anger and rage make their way to the surface, Ashlyn runs over to her side, gently placing her hands around her face.

Ashlyn picked up on the energetic shift and attempted to calm her before she took the palace down. "Aella, I need you to reel in your emotions, okay? Your father is going to be safe. Torin will make sure he gets home. Please do your best right now. Christopher is having a bad moment, and it will pass." She spoke softly with a frantic edge, snapping Aella out of another outburst, but it was too late.

Books start flying off of the shelves. Ducking for cover, Cahtel and Torin move toward the door, and Ashlyn's eyes widen in horror. The books that flew off hovered around Aella, Ashlyn, and Christopher, creating an enclosure. Even Christopher, who is still very drunk, sits in disbelief. Michael stares at Aella, his eyes returning to their natural shade of pale blue from white despite his tense stature in the doorway.

"Good Gods, you have not only my mother's gift but also my father's," Christopher breathes, setting the bin full of vomit on the floor.

With a loud crash, all the books that created an enclosure fall around them in a perfect circle.

Chapter Twenty-One

After the incident, Michael took some time to cool down and left the library. Christopher had started sobering up a little after drinking some water and eating a sandwich, all thanks to Cahtel asking the cook to bring both to the library.

Aella, Ashlyn, and Torin spent a couple of hours putting the books that had fallen from the outburst on the shelves. Aella counted at least a few hundred, and thankfully, none were damaged during the *incident*.

Once finished, Aella joins Christopher on the sofa, where he had moved after eating. Ashlyn occupies one of the chairs before them while Torin stands directly behind her, rubbing her shoulders with such care.

Now that Christopher has some wits about him, embarrassment radiates from him. Aella sympathized because she knew that feeling far too well. It's like an old friend that comes to visit often and overstays their welcome.

"I'm sorry about my behavior. I guess I let my ego get the best of me and thought I could just have one drink." Christopher says sheepishly, remorse and regret for his choices now clouding his features.

"It's alright, I get it. This is a lot; don't beat yourself up." Aella responds, not wanting this to turn into some vulnerable therapy session.

People are flawed and make mistakes. She is seasoned at both of those things, but it is not her responsibility to fix others' mistakes. This is what Aella considers to be a harsh life lesson that only Christopher can learn from.

Torin scoffs and rolls his eyes, "Oh, don't play innocent, Christopher. Everyone knows you are a drunk and always have been. Don't lie to her or yourself about it. It's not very becoming."

Christopher shoots daggers with his eyes at Torin from his remark and says, "I will have you know that I have twenty-three years of sobriety under my belt, *Torin*. That's old news."

"Had. You had twenty-three years under your belt. Tomorrow will be day one." Aella says, raising a brow, and Christopher's smirk falters from the truth of that statement.

Christopher's body tenses, and he becomes defensive from both of their hurtful truths, "Well, I would be lying if I said I didn't like to *indulge*. Who cares anyway? I have a daughter, and that's what is important now." He justifies, nodding his head in an attempt to hold it high.

"You also have a wife and a son. A wife whom you met in Alcoholics Anonymous, right?" Aella says, proving a point that the revelation of having a daughter means nothing, especially when his choices and actions will affect the family he has now.

Christopher looks down at his hands in his lap, pained by her words, and she decides to change the subject, "When the books fell from the shelves and hovered around us, you said I had the same gift as your father. What was his gift exactly?"

Snapping his head up, Christopher creases his brows, "I didn't say that."

Aella, Ashlyn, and Torin look at each other with confusion because he definitely did.

"But you did. You said that I have the same gift as your mother and father." Aella presses, and realization sets in that he wasn't supposed to say anything about his father possessing a gift in general.

Hanging his head back, Christopher runs his hands down his face before explaining and confessing a family secret that had been left in a box, locked, and buried in a place where no one could find it.

"With Elissa's gift, everyone knew about it. It was a part of her, and she didn't keep it hidden; she was proud of the gift she was born into. My father, on the other hand, felt ashamed of his gift and kept it a secret. The only person who knew of what he possessed was my mother until I was of the age they could trust me with his secret and take it to the grave." Christopher swallows, reaching for the glass of water, taking a drink to moisten his dry throat, and continues, "I never saw him use his gift for many years, and to be completely honest, I thought it was a fabrication until we got word of the war that was to come. He snapped. The shock of it all was too much for him to process, making him fearful and emotionally inept to handle such news. Our home almost came down around us, but my mother helped calm him from the storm within him. You see, the gift he possessed very well could have changed the war's outcome entirely, but because my father was too prideful, he fought just like everyone else on the battlefield and died with dignity, just like he wanted. He could create any natural disaster known to man with manifestation, much like my mother could manifest a portal. What he willed, he could create, but just as moods can be overpowering, so could the storms. He could destroy realms if he desired and move objects with his mind like the wind carries a leaf, which would have helped many alongside the warriors he fought with had he used his gifts. My father carried not one but two elements: water and air. My father was a good man, both of my parents were good Isethanians. I think the reason why I never got blessed with such a gift is because I am not as good as they were. But you, Aella, you are good. You are blessed with not one but all three of their gifts, and that is a miracle."

Holy shit. Both of Aella's grandparents were powerful. However, Aella is a weapon, and that alone is terrifying.

"Impossible," Cahtel says, shaking his head in disbelief.

"Prey tell, what is it you find impossible about this?" Christopher responds, the hangover setting in.

Cahtel huffs, trying to call out Christopher's bluff even though he told the truth, "Those born with the elemental gift were subject to one. Your father could not have had two. I don't believe it. You must have been misunderstood."

Christopher laughs with mockery towards Cahtel, "I have no reason to lie to any of you about my father. Had I remained sober, none of you would have known that he, too, had a gift, but the cat's out of the bag now, isn't it? Which, I suppose, is a good thing considering Aella is the most powerful being to have ever walked the realms; she is right up there with the Gods."

Everyone grows silent, and Michael pushes off of the doorway to enter the library. No one realized that he had been standing there listening to the truth about Christopher's father.

Michael appears to be somber, from the reality that the war very well could have ended just as quickly as it had started.

"Why didn't you tell me then? We could have done something..." Michael's voice trails off, and the hurt from what could have been different is prominent.

"It wasn't my place to, Michael. I made a promise to my

parents. Casualties would have still been inevitable. Both of my parents died fighting for their people; I had to watch them take their last breath while you—"

Michael cuts him off, snapping with fury, "Don't you dare blame me for any of that. You do not know the horrors I witnessed, the lives I watched perish, the memories and images that haunt my every waking moment. You lost your parents, and I lost so much more, Christopher."

Christopher stiffens on the sofa, and Aella cuts in, getting back to the real problem at hand, which is the news about all three of her gifts now. "What do we do about the three elements that I inherited from my fucked up genetics?" Her attempt to sprinkle in some dark humor was not the right timing. Then she says, "Our whole goal was to suppress my primary gift of opening portals; how do I prevent my secondary and tertiary gifts from surfacing moving forward?"

With a sigh, Christopher shakes his head, "You cannot. It is not possible. Only you can will it, and because you are coming to the acknowledgment of your gifts, it may take years for you to understand them and how they work, let alone control them fully."

"We do not have years, Christopher. Another war is on the rise if Aella does not control them now! Should the other Watchers learn that she is the key to open portals, we will all be doomed." Michael states with urgency. Christopher stares at him for a moment, void of any emotion other than disdain.

"Well, if I were you, I would focus more on preparations for another war than party tricks. Gifts like Aella's don't just disappear, nor do they become *suppressed*. I was under the impression that you would help her control her primary gift in that she could will a portal like my mother, not try to force her from using what she was born with by creating shame around it."

Oh damn. Aella hadn't thought about it that way, and in a

sense, Christopher was right. There has always been shame associated with what she had considered to be *episodes*, or how Michael still refers to her gift as her *Condition*.

"Oh, and one more thing, Michael," Christopher says again, clearing the bite of acid that still lingers in his throat from vomiting, "If I find out that you so much as speak to my daughter the way that you did in front of me before her gift took over and caused the books to create an enclosure, I will personally end your life with my bare hands."

Aella's brows reach her hairline from the threat, and Christopher turns to wink at her while he stands from the sofa.

"Torin, if you would be so kind as to escort me back to my home, that would be much appreciated. Aella, I will see you soon; although my stay here in Isethas is starting to come to an end, I will need to get back to Cindy and our son."

Aella nods in understanding. There isn't much more Christopher can do to help them with the new discovery of her gifts. This is on her; it always has been.

Christopher walks out of the library with shaky legs, most likely caused by alcohol poisoning, with Torin behind him. Sleep would do Christopher some good after a bender like the one he embarked on.

Michael continued sitting in his chair, staring at Aella like he was about to say something. After some time, he stands instead and storms out of the library, leaving Aella to sit alone with her thoughts and a reality that is harder to swallow than the one she didn't want to accept prior.

Normal.

Ashlyn doesn't leave her chair, though, and the company of having her there gives Aella a slight reprieve. The tables have turned now, and Aella would have to learn how to control and manage her gifts like a third arm that will permanently be attached to her body. *Acceptance.*

Ashlyn breaks her spiraling thoughts then and says, "Hey, want to sneak a bottle of wine and snacks? We can talk in your room for a bit. A small break and moment to breathe after all of this won't hurt anything."

That is precisely what Aella needed after a day like today. Even if Michael had put a rule on drinking, Aella doesn't give a shit. *Fuck it.*

"Say no more. That sounds perfect," Aella says, relieved, as they both get up from where they are sitting. Aella is also glad to leave the library and have a semi-normal moment with a girl she considers to be a friend even though she isn't Tara.

INDULGING THEMSELVES IN A CHILLED BOTTLE OF PINOT on the bed while snacking on a charcuterie board covered in cheeses, cold meats, and fruits, Aella didn't realize how much she needed this, even if it would be temporary.

Hanging out with Ashlyn is the closest thing she has had to a girl's night since Tara, and even that feels like a lifetime has passed.

Aella told Ashlyn all about the many horrible dating stories and hookups and how men could be from where she is from. Ashlyn laughed and cringed at every single one, and reciprocated by spilling her own experiences. Even though they came from two different worlds, the men seemed to be the same.

Aella fell in love as Ashlyn shared the story about her and Torin. His arrogant demeanor was more of an act because, behind closed doors, he was a sweet romantic writing Ashlyn poetry and putting her pleasure before his own.

Ashlyn made Aella promise not to tell anyone that secret, and she swore on her mother's life she would take it to the grave with her.

They continued to drink and eat, laugh and talk for a while, unaware of the hours that passed them by. That was until a knock sounded at the door.

Aella and Ashlyn cover their mouths so as not to make a sound, the wine making it challenging to contain their laughter.

A part of Aella hoped it was Cahtel and not Michael, but that hope quickly fades when Michael speaks through the door.

"Aella, may I come in? I made you the tea." He says, and she had forgotten all about having to drink that garbage.

"Uh, just a sec!" Aella shouts, looking wide-eyed at Ashlyn, mouthing, *"What do we do?!"* Ashlyn shrugs, failing to maintain her composer mouthing back, "I don't *know!"*

Aella breathes out a sigh, sobering herself up a little, then calls back to Michael, "You can just leave it by the door. I will grab it in a minute!"

He seems to have hesitated on the other side of the door and says, "Can we talk, please?" Michael sounded sincere and also a little intrigued by what could possibly be happening on the other side of the door.

"Fuck!" Aella mouths to Ashlyn, whose face is now the same color as a tomato, from how hard she is holding back her laughter. She finally explodes into a fit of giggling and snorts through her nose, blowing their cover.

Jumping off the bed, Aella runs to the door, cracking it open so that Michael can't see inside fully. Cocking one of his dark brows, he smirks slightly, taking in the state she's in.

Aella's cheeks warm when she notices his damp hair. Her eyes betray her, roaming down the front of his body, taking in every muscle all the way to the pair of grey, low-hanging sweats that should be prohibited.

"Y—yes?" she says, clearing her throat, standing her ground while keeping the door taut.

"You have company?" Michael asks, sliding in some humor.

Attempting to close the door slightly more, Aella says, "Nope. Just me, myself, and—"

Ashlyn brushes past Aella, opening the door as she runs down the hallway, shouting, "Night, Michael, see you tomorrow!"

Michael chuckles with the steaming mug of tea and nods towards the room. Stepping aside for him to enter, Aella quickly turns her back as she attempts to clean up the evidence of the now empty bottle of wine and glasses, which is an absolute failure.

Quirking a brow at Aella with her arms full, Michael says, "You two drank an entire bottle of Pinot?"

After throwing the empty bottle into the small trash bin, she puts the glasses down on the coffee table and places her hands on her hips. "A bottle is technically three glasses, Michael. And yes, we did."

Setting the mug down on the coffee table next to the empty glasses of wine, Michael folds his arms across his chest. Shaking his head with a tsk, a sparkle in his eyes shines.

"Well, it looks like I will be hanging around for at least forty-five minutes. Remember, nothing to drink thirty minutes prior."

Aella wasn't expecting that to be his response; she was waiting for a lecture on drinking wine, especially after he set a rule and boundary.

Scoffing at him, she rolls her eyes and proceeds to tidy up the bed, brushing crumbs away that had fallen onto the comforter, and picks up the charcuterie board to set on the coffee table as well.

Once she is satisfied with her quick sweep, she crosses her arms, standing before him.

"So, what's up?" She says, still waiting for him to yell at her.

Michael motions to the sofa with his hand, "May I sit?"

Aella scoffs, "You don't need to ask permission. It's your room."

"Fair enough." Sitting on the sofa, he leans back, crossing his ankle over one knee. "I wanted to speak with you about the events from today. It wasnt my finest moment."

Yeah, except you have been having a lot of those lately.

"Kind of like when I told you about Damnien?" Aella blurts, unable to take it back as she presses her lips together.

"Yes, aside from that, I want you to know that it will never happen again. I am sorry, Aella, for my reactions. I have been selfish in wanting to protect my realm and my people. You don't deserve to be talked to or treated like that. The pressure and stress from all of this have made me bitter and angry. I hardly even recognize myself..." Michael scrubs his face with his hands while letting out a sigh. Joining him on the sofa, she sits on the other side, crossing her legs while facing him.

"Look, a lot has happened in the days I have been here. I can understand why you would be stressed, but I had no idea I could do what I did. All this time, I thought I was just a person who had an abnormal case of sleep paralysis. You think you're under pressure? The entire outcome of keeping people from different realms alive rests on my shoulders, and I barely understand my gifts, let alone the meaning of all of this. We are doing the best we can. I guess things don't always go as planned, even in a different realm." Aella opens up, communicating how she feels as well. A small moment of silence stretches between them. There is no tension or anger, just two people sitting, having a very real and almost normal conversation.

Michael shifts to turn his body towards Aella more fully as understanding dances within his eyes. "You're right. I can't imagine what you must truly be feeling. Being pulled from your life, family, and friends in an unfamiliar place is a lot in general. I never really thought about how unfair all of this must be. You are brave, Aella. Your strength does not go unnoticed, and it's inspiring. A part of me envies you for that. It took me many years after my father's death and the war to find a sliver of the bravery that you hold. Don't ever lose that, even if another war comes of this. Don't lose it."

Viewing herself as brave or, at the very least, strong was unfamiliar. She always thought herself to be more of a coward and avoided confrontation like the plague because, in a way, she couldn't be bothered by it. Aella, at the time, was too self-involved with her own self-loathing.

"Do you think many people will die when there is another war?" Aella asks, thinking about a battle that will most likely come sooner than planned.

"Death is inescapable, especially in war. If I could prevent that from happening, I would, but when the time comes to take your last breath, it is all part of the natural order of things."

Michael's honest view of war and death was poetically justified, despite Aella not wanting to think about having to see someone she loved or cared for die in general. Everyone dies eventually, but if something were to happen to any of her new friends, she would be devastated.

"Do you fear death?" Michael asks with curiosity, causing her to brush the previous thought away.

"I think I used to, but no. I think I fear life more."

Tilting his head to the side, his eyes search her features.

"What is it about life that you fear more than death?" he asks with more curiosity. To him, Aella is like an enigma, and he wants to crack open her mind and know every thought that she has.

"Life is painful. I think, eventually, it becomes nothing more than a distant memory. At least in death, you feel no more pain or suffering." Aella states, biting off a piece of dry skin that is snagging from her bottom lip.

"Pain is inevitable; however, suffering is a choice. Don't choose to suffer in this life, Aella, for there is beauty in pain. If you didn't feel pain and heartbreak, life would be meaningless."

Even Michael's perspective on pain and life gives her some comfort. It was a reminder of the painting she loves so much by Klimt, *Death and Life,* but in a real sense because art is created by experience and raw emotion.

Leaning over to pick up the tea, Michael tested the sides of the mug to check the temperature.

"It's not nearly as warm, but it will get the job done." He says, handing it over to her.

Downing the cooled tea, the taste is never pleasant, but drinking it cold makes it hard to endure. Swallowing a gag, Aella wipes her mouth with the back of her hand and sets the empty mug back on the coffee table.

Before leaving, Michael gives her a soft smile, "I want you to enjoy the rest of your stay here despite our recent rocky moments. Training should and will resume as planned, and now that things have changed with our course of action, we will have to work a little harder in aiding you to grasp your... gifts better." Clearing his throat, this was the first time he acknowledged her abilities as gifts instead of a condition. "I would also like to take you into the city tomorrow once training is done so you can pick out some new clothes if you would like?"

Aella hesitantly nods her head. She did need a few things since her clothes were dirty and worn out by now, and going back to her apartment was definitely out of the question until she took Christopher back.

"I hope we can put aside my previous behavior once more and become friends in the least," he says, prematurely flinching in case Aella declines the olive branch.

It wasnt much, but it was progress. Aella will take what she can get for now.

"I would like that very much, Michael."

A glimmer of relief washes over him as he collects the empty glasses and the board of leftover cheeses and turns for the door.

"I can take that down in the morning; don't worry about it," Aella blurts, a little embarrassed by the crusty cheese that has now accumulated from sitting out.

"It's my pleasure; get some rest. Breakfast will be early again, and so will training. After, I will treat you to the city." Michael responds, shutting the door on his way out with a soft click.

Peace filled the room after Michael and Aella talked, which was a nice change to their tense day. She enjoyed her girl time with Ashlyn and the uncontrollable laughter that helped her forget, even if it was a brief moment, about all of her gifts that she would have to accept. They weren't going anywhere, nor could she get rid of them.

Her gifts are her, and she is her gifts, an extension of herself, like a vital organ that should never be removed.

Having a decent conversation with Michael and communicating ended the night on a sweet note. Aella still finds him very attractive, as anyone with eyes would, even though the dynamic of their relationship has shifted.

Aella's focus and priorities are now centrally focused on honing her gifts and combat training with Torin.

Tomorrow is going to be another tiresome day, but Aella doesn't dread what tomorrow will bring, as she had earlier.

Acceptance.

Chapter Twenty-Two

G etting an early start, Aella made her bed and showered.
Throwing on a pair of jeans and a light sweatshirt, she
makes her way to the door and opens it, listening intently for
anyone who may be up. The halls remain quiet as she proceeds
down the hall with light footsteps.

Tiptoeing past Michael's door, she realizes it is cracked
open. Gently pushing on the door, Aella peeks inside, squinting
into the dark space, and notes that Michael is still asleep on his
chest. The sheet barely hanging off his hips, contouring the
curves of his backside.

There is no doubt that Michael is intimidatingly beautiful,
and watching him sleep is no different. *Okay, Aella, you
fucking creep.*

Returning the door to its original craked-open state, Aella
continues down the hall towards the spiral staircase. Right as
she is about to take the first step, Cahtel startles her by creeping
out from the shadows, almost aiding in the death that she actually feared.

"What are you doing up so early?" He asks with

amusement.

Clutching at her chest, Aella grabs onto the railing to keep her from stumbling backward. "Jesus, you scared the shit out of me. Keep it down; everyone is still asleep!" She whisper screams at him. After taking a second to compose herself, she steps forward away from the steps leading to her impending doom and quiets her voice further.

"I'm going to the kitchen to make some coffee. Would you like to join me?"

Cahtel shakes his head, waving her off, "Any other time I would, but I am on my way out to check on the portal and the barrier surrounding it and the city." He informs, and Aella's eyes light up. Noting the curiosity on her face, he objects before she can convince him to let her tag along. "No. You are to stay here."

Pouting her bottom lip, she is about to protest even though she has training and will be going into the city with Michael later in the day. Rolling her eyes, she continues her journey down the staircase toward the kitchen with Cahtel trailing her behind.

"I will be back soon. Please stay out of trouble." Cahtel teases, leaving through the front doors. Aella misses spending one-on-one time with Cahtel, and even though he has been around, there has been so much that has happened since returning with Christopher it was as if she hadn't really seen Cahtel at all.

The kitchen is empty and spotless when she enters, and she will have to be careful not to make any messes with brewing her coffee. As she opens the cupboards, searching for a mug and the coffee beans, a voice startles her from behind causing her face to heat. Snapping her body around to see who is up so early, the cook stands at the entrance.

"Is there something I can help you find Miss Aella?" The

cook asks, friendly while maintaining his professional demeanor. He is dressed in his usual attire of checkered pants and a white chef's coat.

"Oh, uh, I was just trying to make a cup of coffee." She says shyly, unsure if she is even permitted to be in this section of the palace since it is the cook's domain and Michael isn't with her.

The cook smiles and approaches the cabinets, "Please, allow me. I was just about to get the beans ground and coffee going. The others should be up soon."

The cook is pleasant and kind, but Aella picks up on slight irritation that he is attempting to tamp down.

"I'm sorry. I didn't want to bother you. You know, I never got your name... I've been here for a few days now, and everyone just refers to you as the cook."

Fumbling under the island, he pulls out an electric grinder, then proceeds to the other side of the kitchen, collecting a canvas bag full of beans.

"Louis, although cook is just fine. Do you prefer cream and sugar in your coffee, or take it straight?" Louis asks before he presses the button on the grinder.

"Cream is perfect. Thank you, Louis." Aella says with sincerity, and a slight smile tugs at the corner of his mouth from her calling him by his real name.

Once the beans are ground to the perfect consistency, Louis places the grounds inside of the French press.

"Your cooking is amazing, by the way. I wanted to tell you that sooner but didn't get the chance." The compliment flies out of Aella's mouth quickly, hoping she could amend her rude behavior from breakfast yesterday. She also feared that he would be inclined to poison her food or, at the very least, spit in her eggs, and she wouldn't blame him for it.

Quirking a brow, Louis huffs while pouring the coffee into a mug for her and adds a little creamer, then hands her the cup.

"Nourishing our bodies with food the land gifts us fills me with gratitude, along with the ability to serve those I care about." His response is stoic, and Aella takes a sip from her coffee, thinking of what to say next.

"I am really sorry for pushing the plate of food away yesterday. That wasnt my finest moment, and I feel terrible about that."

Louis nods, accepting her apology, "I have worked for Michael's family for a very long time. You pushing your plate away isn't the first time it has happened; don't let it eat at you. I will start preparing breakfast. Anything you don't like?"

Aella smiles and shakes her head, "Nope. I'm a dumpster! I'll practically eat anything you put in front of me as long as it isn't dog, cat, or human."

Louis chuckles and nods, getting to work, and Aella takes that as her queue to head back up to her room until breakfast is ready.

Peering past Michael's room, she notices he is no longer asleep in his bed and is actually walking into his bathroom completely nude. A fluttering sensation brushes inside the lower part of her stomach as she tiptoes steadily toward the door to her room, careful not to slosh the hot contents.

Once through the door, she closes it behind her with a soft click, taking advantage of the balcony for the first time.

Sitting in one of the chairs, Aella drinks her coffee, watching the sky richen in color. It is calm and peaceful out on the balcony at this time, and she thinks about how this would be every artist's dream—a perfect area to set up an easel and canvases just to paint and be in solitude.

She pictures herself spending hours alone out here, creating in this atmosphere.

Getting lost in the daydream, Michael walks out and sits next to her.

"Beautiful, isn't it?" He says in an equally calm manner.

"Yes, it really is. I was thinking about creating art out here, obviously, if the situation was different." She says, looking up at the fading stars in the sky.

A peaceful moment passes by while they listen to the birds chirping.

"What type of art are you thinking you would create?" Michael asks with interest.

"I would love to paint on canvas. As far as a piece, I'm not entirely sure. I suppose it would call to me." Glancing in his direction, Michael looks to be lost in thought.

"I spoke with Louis this morning. He insisted on making my coffee." Aella says, changing the subject from a daydream that would never come to fruition.

"Oh? First name basis now, I see, and how is Louis this morning?" Michael asks, eyes sparking with the corner of his mouth tipping upward into a smirk.

"He seems to be fine. He's hard to read, but I think I made him feel important by asking his name."

"Louis has been with my family for a very long time. He's like an uncle to me. He and my father were really close. They would stay up late some nights playing around with different recipes in the kitchen, drinking and laughing. My mother found great joy in their bond." Michael beams, reminiscing on the happy memory. The more stories Aella hears about former life in Isethas, the more the realm becomes very dear to her. Keeping good memories of those you love alive is important, especially to Aella.

"What happened to your mother?" Aella asks, hoping the question isn't too intrusive.

Furrowing his brow, Michael peers out into the view of his estate, "After the death of my father, she was heartbroken. They loved each other so deeply. I have never witnessed a love like theirs, which is why I have never married another. Unless I was lucky enough to have found a love like theirs, I promised myself I would never agree to marriage, which is also terrifying because I witnessed what the loss of such a love did to the other person. My mother locked herself away for weeks, refusing food or drink. The healers became fearful that she would wither away. By the time she left her room for fresh air, she was unrecognizable, sick with malnourishment and a broken heart. Life without her lover was a life she no longer wanted. She walked out into the sea that my father came back from with the plague and was never seen again."

Instinct causes Aella to reach for him while reliving the traumatic experience. The thought of being so in love with someone to the point of losing them, resulting in losing yourself, was incomprehensible. That reality was more terrifying than falling in love, to begin with.

"That's awful, Michael; I am so sorry. You have quite the story. All of you do." Aella's voice shakes with the reminder to reel in her emotions.

Michael's features soften then, and he grabs her hand, looking her in the eye with intensity.

"When I told you that life is painful but suffering is a choice, I meant every word of it, Aella. I have lived a very long time and have experienced pain in the physical and emotional sense. With all that pain, I made myself feel and grow from it like I grow my orchids. They were my mother's favorite flower. Whenever I feel that pain creep in, I go to the greenhouse where the orchids grow, and it reminds me of how beautiful life truly is."

Tears that aren't entirely sad escape Aella's eyes and spill down her cheeks as she smiles.

Reaching up, Michael tenderly wipes tears that have fallen from Aella and says, "My mother would have liked you. You remind me of her at times. She was caring and kind but also strong-willed. She had no issues speaking her mind and putting my father in his place when needed."

The comparison makes Aella feel lighter, and she would have liked to have met his mother all the same.

Michael then stands out of the chair and stretches, breathing in the crisp air. "Louis should have breakfast ready any moment now. I will meet you and the others in the gathering room. After your training, I will personally be your tour guide of the city; it is quite the experience."

Aella could hardly wait. Her excitement of seeing the city proper and the culture where her ancestors roamed at one time was something she hadn't realized she wanted until now. Today is going to be the start of many more good days; Aella believes that deeply within her bones.

BREAKFAST WAS MORE THAN FILLING, AND AELLA DIDN'T waste a single crumb from her plate needing the fuel for when she and Torin would begin their sparring. Steak and eggs with a side of hashbrowns and fresh-cut fruit add a perfectly balanced meal with plenty of protein and carbs.

There wasn't much chit-chat in the gathering room, and with Cahtel still out checking on the portal and the city, everyone ate their food and began their tasks for the morning. Ashlyn and Aella broke off, going back to the field of flowers for Aella to practice opening and closing portals before she trained with Torin.

The nerves and hesitation that consumed Aella from attempting to do so before had somehow withered away, and instead, she felt a boost of confidence.

Ashlyn had picked up on the shift, but she was still wary.

"Okay, Aella, just like yesterday, let's practice your grounding technique."

Aella nods impatiently. Despite grounding being the most critical first step to connecting with her primary gift, all she could think about was going to the city with Michael.

"Remember to clear your mind of anything that interferes with your connection," Ashlyn says, noting Aella's anticipation.

"Yeah, I know." Aella snaps involuntarily, but Ashlyn doesn't seem to take offense.

Ashlyn had been quiet at breakfast, but so was everyone else at the table. She wasn't in the normal light, happy-go-lucky mood that she typically displays.

Perhaps Ashlyn and Torin got into a tiff after she left Aella's room last night.

"Last night was fun. I mean, it was nice to laugh and drink wine with you," Aella says in an attempt to get Ashlyn to tell her what is on her mind.

Ashlyn's gaze is off to a faraway place, and then she shifts her eyes over to Aella, "Hmm? Oh, yes, it was. Anyway, let's begin."

Aella can't help but push at this point. This isn't like Ashlyn. "Are you okay?" Aella asks with concern.

"Oh, I'm fine. I'm just a little out of it today, probably from the wine. Don't worry about me. We need to begin so we don't overlap with your and Torin's training." Ashlyn points to her wrist as if she's wearing a watch. Aella's not buying her excuse, though, especially since she had seen Ashlyn drink way more than just a couple of glasses of wine and still wake the next morning right as rain without the slightest hint of a hangover.

It was evident that whatever was bothering Ashlyn, she didn't want to talk about it, and Aella would respect that for now, even though a part of her wanted to be the friend that Ashlyn had been to her since she'd been staying here.

"Okay. Clear my mind and ground myself." Aella says, then gets into position by firmly planting her feet and closing her eyes. Shutting those filing cabinets with a mental slam takes less effort this time, as she envisions herself as one with the orchid by allowing her subconscious to take the wheel.

When picturing a portal, it's as if she can actually project it from the palm of her hand. Electrical currents flow from her fingertips, creating a translucent wall with those silvery swirls that dance and mingle, pushing energy from the portal that radiates off of her.

A push and pull and a give and take, like negative and opposite forces colliding and moving away from each other in a synchromatic rhythm.

Aella opens her eyes, and the portal is exact.

Acceptance.

In this case, she pictured the portal leading to where her mother is with her friend Jan. Selfishly, she wanted to walk through much like when she thought of where Tara and Georgia may be, but knowing that her mother was safe enjoying a vacation that hopefully wouldn't end on a horrific note, Aella just smiles.

Looking over to where Ashlyn stands, a slight scowl crosses her face. Was it a small crack in her perfect facade? Or perhaps a tinge of jealousy that Aella has basically mastered her primary gift and is a lot more powerful than any of them gave her credit for? Or, perhaps, it is nothing, and Ashlyn is really hungover from the wine.

Shaking off the thoughts of what a change in facial expression could mean, Aella closes her eyes again, grounding herself to close the portal the same way she opened it.

I accept my gift. I am in control.

Staring at the portal in her subconscious, she closes her hand the way she did the day before, collapsing it like a small box, sealing it shut. The energy from the portal snakes down with those electrical currents and slithers up her hand back into her body.

When she opens her eyes, the portal is gone, with not even a sliver of silver in its wake.

Aella laughs out in relief and also a moment of pride in herself. She opened and closed a portal in a fraction of the time she did yesterday. A massive accomplishment from when all of this initially started, leaving her fearless and brave.

"Well, it looks like you have a handle on opening and closing a portal. Tomorrow, we will begin working towards you not using that gift when you are back in your real home." Ashlyn says, almost condescending.

Ouch.

"Christopher said that suppressing my gifts was impossible; they are apart—"

Ashlyn cuts Aella off, "I know what Christopher said, and that is not what I am getting at. You need to control them so you don't feel inclined to use them." She finishes giving Aella a tight-lipped smile.

What the fuck is her deal today?

Ashlyn has never spoken to Aella like this. Perhaps she started her cycle. That would explain why she's being such a bitch. Aella isn't going to argue with her or hold it over her head, though, especially since she had been way moodier and snappy in recent events.

At least Ashlyn can't manifest a storm based on her emotions like Aella can.

"Torin should be here any moment; I'll leave you to stretch out before he arrives. Good work." Ashlyn says, turning on her heel with her hands behind her back, fidgeting her fingers, leaving Aella alone in the field of flowers.

Torin arrives not long after Ashlyn has left, and Aella

continues stretching out, thinking about Ashlyn's demeanor and sour mood.

Unlike Ashlyn, Torin is in a chipper mood, pleased to see that Aella got an early start to warming up instead of sitting around.

Giving her a thumbs up, Aella rolls her eyes at him and chuckles. Torin gets on the ground next to her and then does the same.

"Hey, are you and Ashlyn okay?" Aella asks, and the question seems to catch him off guard.

"Yeah! At least, I think we are. Why did she tell you something?" Torin says, creasing his brow with worry.

Aella shakes her head, chewing on the inside of her cheek, "No, she didn't. She was in a mood, and I thought maybe you two had a tiff or something. It's probably nothing; everyone has their moments. Don't say anything to her, please. I'm sure she's fine."

Torin shrugs, reaching down the length of his body to touch his toes. Aella can't help but gape at watching all of his muscles ripple with the effort, and he notices, smirking.

"You can look all you want, Aella dear, but no touching." He teases, and Aella feels her cheeks redden, "Ashlyn is probably on her time of the month; I wouldn't worry about it, but if she caught you drooling over me the way you are now, she would most likely be out for blood."

Pushing his shoulder playfully, Torin dramatically falls over and clutches at his arm like she did damage. "Oww, I'm wounded."

"You'll survive," Aella says, getting to her feet, "All right, big guy, show me what you got."

Torin laughs and jumps up to his feet in a smooth motion, "How are you feeling today? Are you sore?"

Sore is an understatement, but rule number one of any

strength training, or in this case, defensive training, you have to keep moving to push the lactic acid out of your muscles.

"Fuck yes, I'm sore! But I am also ready for more. Maybe I'm sick in the head." Aella says, laughing at herself, and Torin smiles with excitement that reaches his eyes.

"Atta girl! That's what I like to hear. Okay, let's run through your stance again, practicing your squatting and ducking. Then, we move onto movement, allowing your core to carry you, like a dance but in the face of death."

Aella nods, but she needs more. "When will you teach me how to use a blade or how to shoot a gun?"

Torin looks at her with surprise, his brows reaching his hairline. "Aella, I'm in shock. I thought you didn't want to learn how to use a gun initially?"

Shrugging her shoulders, she sighs, "I guess I had a change of heart. Why? You scared I might win in a gunfight with you?"

Folding his arms across his chest, Torin smirks, "Don't tempt me with a good time now. It is important to utilize your body as a tool and a weapon first before getting to the good stuff. Everything I show you leading up to a physical weapon is just the groundwork; it's the foundation and the framework of a home before you can put the drywall up. Once you have mastered the art of moving your body without a second thought, allowing your core to guide you, anything additional is just an added appliance to your arsenal."

Patience, Aella reminds herself. She would be getting to the good stuff, but Torin was right; he knows what he's doing, and if Aella could have even a small fraction of the cut muscle and strength that he does, she would be one happy girl.

"Okay, what are you waiting—"

Without warning, Torin kicks out, and Aella squats down, missing a foot to her face, then pops back up. Kicking out again with his left foot, this time instead of his right toward her shins, she jumps, landing on the balls of her feet, the impact rico-cheting up her legs.

Then, Torin kicks his foot out toward her chest, and she leans back at an almost unnatural angle, missing the blow but secretly needing an adjustment from the crack she feels.

"Nice work. I think you're ready for the next step," Torin says, unbothered and clearly not out of breath like Aella.

She pants and holds up her finger, straightening her back as she twists and moves to loosen it up from the back bend. Sweat pours down her forehead, and she swipes at it with the back of the sleeve of her sweatshirt.

Taking her sweatshirt off, Aella is relieved that she threw a tank top on underneath instead of just a sports bra.

"Get back into your stance. I am going to charge at you, and I want you to watch where I am aiming my attack and sidestep out of the way."

Aella does as instructed, but Torin is too fast, almost knocking into her.

"If I had a sword, you would be dead." He says, and Aella scoffs.

"I thought swords weren't used anymore?"

"They aren't a usual form of weaponry, but they still exist."

"You're too fast; I barely had time to register your move-ment." Aella scowls, rubbing at her arm.

"And that is why you must be aware. Much like ducking and moving out of the way from a blow, should your enemy charge at you with a weapon or even a kick or punch, you must know before they have the chance to which way they are going in for the attack." Torin juts his hand out then, and Aella moves out of the way. "Good."

Fuck. She didn't consider the unnatural speed beings from other realms possessed, and as the thought occurs to her, Torin moves again, striking out his attack.

After an early afternoon of training with Torin, Aella's core and upper body are on fire. She felt like she was going to throw up; it was like cardio on steroids from all the spinning and running, dodging and squatting, jumping and sidestepping. All of it was exhausting.

She knew that her feet would probably smell horrific from the dirty socks and sweat, and she wanted a shower before going to the city with Michael because she reeked like a teenage boy.

Patting Aella on the shoulder, Torin praises her for her hard work and informs her that tomorrow, they will get into throwing a punch.

Michael appears before them in the field after teleporting and steps back a foot, most likely due to the smell radiating off of their bodies.

"I take it training went well?" Michael asks, eyeing them both, then continues, "Ashlyn informed me that you did excellent on controlling your primary gift. Good work."

Aella beams with praise even though her legs feel like noodles, and she wants to lie in the grass and not move for days.

"Thank you. It was actually pretty easy compared to what Torin just put me through." She says, still catching her breath with her hands on her hips.

"Right; well, if you would like to go back to the palace and get cleaned up, I will take you into the city," Michael says. Aella considers the cleaning up part a nonnegotiable rather than a suggestion, which she doesn't mind because a shower is definitely in order.

Aella smiles and nods, but when she holds out her hand for Michael to teleport her back, Torin steps in and picks her up, winking at her before shooting to the sky.

Chapter Twenty-Three

The city was bustling with the people of Isethas when Michael and Aella arrived. Everyone had that same welcoming smile on their faces she had noticed prior and waved at both of them as they passed by. Some children playing in the streets ran up to Michael, giving him hugs and praise. Noticing the lack of shoes is prevalent, so Aella decides to ask Michael why most chose to remain barefoot.

"Grounding is a practice that we use daily here. It's a way we feel connected to our realm. Doing so shoeless allows you to find a deeper connection within yourself," Michael says as they continue to walk the cobblestone street.

Quieting her voice so that passersby don't hear what she says next, Aella also looks around to make sure no one is within earshot. "Since I have been grounding myself before I open and close a portal, I haven't been barefoot except the other day in the field with Ashlyn."

Michael nods, understanding her confusion, "You don't need to be barefoot to ground yourself. Grounding, much like meditating, is however you are most comfortable with." He says, and Aella gets lost in all that the city has to offer.

The storefront buildings are uniquely built and painted a different color. The doors to the buildings resemble a work of art and craftsmanship, decorated with ornate knockers, knobs, and handles that could easily hide secrets behind them. With the cobblestoned streets and sidewalks, the heart of the city reminded her of a foreign country photographed in a travel magazine. *San Miguel De Allende* is the closest comparison that comes to mind, a beautiful city in the heart of Mexico oozing with art and architecture. A rare gem she had only ever dreamed of visiting one day.

Michael directs her into a small cafe that fills the room with the aroma of freshly baked croissants and roasted beans. The owner notices the two of them walking in and appears over-joyed to see Michael, beaming from ear to ear as they approach the glass case stuffed full of pastries.

"Michael! It's so good to see you; what a treat!" The woman exclaims, rounding the counter to embrace him with a warm hug.

"Marisol, you look well. How are things?" He asks, matching her warm energy.

"Wonderful, never been better! Aside from the children growing up too fast, I can't complain," Marisol says with a wink. "And who is our guest?"

"Hi, I'm Aella! You have a beautiful cafe. Your pastries look absolutely divine." Aella says, and Marisol's cheeks flush a light pink, her smile growing wide, reaching her warm eyes.

"Pleasure to meet you, Aella, and thank you. See anything you like?"

"They all look delicious. What do you recommend?" Aella asks, unable to keep her mouth from watering at all the different textures and colors before her in the glass case.

Moving next to Aella, Marisol looks inside the case for a moment. With her apron covered in flour, it is no question that she thoroughly enjoys her work.

"The chocolate croissant seems to be everyone's favorite, but mine is the orange sunrise," Marisol says, clasping her hands together in front of her.

"Then I will have the orange sunrise, please," Aella says, pleasing the baker even more.

Clapping her hands together, Marisol hurries behind the counter to pull out the croissant and pair it with a fresh batch of lemon hibiscus iced tea. Placing the croissant in a white box, she pulls out a piece of coffee cake and carefully sets it in the box as well for Michael before closing the lid.

Michael pays Marisol for the treats in what look like coins Aella has never seen before and promises to make a point to visit again soon, in which Marisol is happy to keep him to his promise.

Sitting at a small table outside of the cafe, Aella and Michael enjoy their pastries and tea. The croissant melts in her mouth, still warm from the oven, as she watches the people of Isethas stop and chat with one another in between their daily routines.

It is so different from what she was accustomed to. There is a sense of community here, with everyone knowing each other and seemingly content and happy, unrushed and nowhere to be, just enjoying the company they run into chatting away about anything and nothing.

"What have you been so focused on?" Michael asks with a curious interest as he takes the last bite of his coffee cake.

Brushing the crumbs from her hands, Aella takes a drink from her tea, washing down the last little bit in her mouth. "Just this place. The more I'm here, it's like I'm in a lovely dream. Everyone is so happy and full of life. The shops and this cafe, they're almost unreal. The children playing in the streets without any fear or worry that something might happen to them. I feel like I'm reading a really good heartfelt book, and I've fallen into the pages waiting for the plot twist." She says, looking at him. His features are warm and soft, not a sign of any of the sharp edges or stress she had seen lately. Telling him her thoughts and how she is feeling in this moment makes him happy, but she could also sense a sadness that is pushing its way in.

"Before the war, this is how all the realms were. We were all joined as one unit until..." Michael trails off in thought, bringing Aella back to the mountain where she and Cahtel sat off the edge looking out to the sea as he told her his story.

"After the war, we worked hard to maintain that joy for our people. It was a struggle in the beginning, especially with the loss our people had endured. Loved ones died defending and protecting these lands. Women lost their husbands and lovers. Children lost their fathers and mothers, becoming orphans, but we continued to fight and survive. Isethas only became what it is today after all that destruction, bloodshed, and pain because we came together as a community and refused to suffer. We refused to surrender to the loss and ruin, the rubble that no longer remains. This entire city was rebuilt by all of our bare hands so we can enjoy Marisol's pastries outside of her cafe at this moment." Michael's sadness drifts off, replaced by a sense of pride, not for himself but for his people. He was proud of what they did together and the work that went into rebuilding Isethas. The many years that it must have taken to rebuild was unfathomable, but it was also magical.

Aella understood more now than ever the real reason why Michael was so stressed and adamant about her controlling and suppressing her gift. It wasn't entirely because Michael didn't want Damien to have access to the portals; he feared a repeat of what had happened and didn't want Damien to be the cause of a relapse to the bandaid they all worked so hard to keep together.

"Family, you all became one big family, Michael. I keep my word impeccable. Damien will never be the cause of destruction to your realm or your family." Aella says, feeling a sense of pride for his people herself. Downing the rest of her tea, they continue to sit for a moment before moving on to shop for some clothing.

"Did Marisol's husband fight in the war?" Aella asks, changing the topic from Damien and also hoping that she didn't send Michael off into a dark place.

"He did. He was a good, hardworking man, but unfortunately, he did not make it. Marisol remained a widow for a long time until she met her second husband, John. They waited a while before having children, twin boys. They give her a run for her money, but they are respectful and well-mannered." Michael chuckles; even though Marisol, having lost her first husband in battle, is sad, she seems content and happy with her life now. With every wound that has healed, there is always a scar, leaving a reminder.

A QUAINT CLOTHING BOUTIQUE RESTS A FEW DOORS DOWN from Marisol's cafe, where a woman dressed in a bohemian jumpsuit approaches Michael and Aella as they enter. Her hair is a wild mess of dark curls in the best way, pinned back in a messy clip. The big round gold framed glasses she has on cover half of her face, and a bold red lip accentuates her plump mouth.

If Aella had to guess, the woman looks as though she is in

her late thirties, but given that Isethanians age differently, she could very well be in her early hundreds.

"Michael," the woman purrs in what sounds like a French accident. What a delicious surprise to see you." She grabs his face, kissing both cheeks. And you must be Aella!" Her green eyes light up with excitement, and she takes her in the same way by kissing both of Aella's cheeks as well.

"Hi, yes, nice to meet you..." Aella says, the subtle act of affection giving her pause.

"Please, call me Theo!" she insists. Michael smothers a laugh, watching the interaction as Aella is still getting used to such close contact with the people of this realm.

Clasping her hands together, Theo looks over Aella and purses her lips. "Aella, dear, do you always dress this way?"

Aella diverts from taking offense by the way Theo's tone is laced with judgment. She'd thrown on the only clean T-shirt she had and the pair of leggings with dirt smudges from the day before, but before she could answer, Michael cut in, "Aella is in need of some fresh clothes, nothing crazy, just the basics."

Right, just the basics. Looking down at her shoes, Aella begins picking at the skin around her nails, feeling slightly uncomfortable.

Theo scoffs, "*Incroyable*, just the basics," and rolls her eyes, "I am a firm believer that what you choose to wear externally reflects how you feel about yourself internally, but *Hélas*, just the basics it is." She sighs dramatically, and Michael is the one rolling his eyes now.

Taking in Aella's measurements, she writes everything down on a piece of paper.

"Feel free to browse while I get you *just the basics*." Theo says, quieting her voice, "If you see anything you like, snag it, and I'll see if I have the right size in the back." She winks and then scurries off to pull clothing from various racks and shelves.

Michael stands off somewhere in a corner of the boutique while Aella takes in all of Theo's creations, touching and feeling different materials made of the finest quality. Silks, cashmere, linen, and denim, all hand-sewn by Theo, which would cost a fortune in the real world.

A denim jumpsuit hanging from one of the racks catches her eye. It reminds her of something a French painter would wear while creating in their art studio. The jumpsuit has large pockets in the front to stuff brushes and pencils in.

Theo comes behind her with her arms full of clothes and urges Aella to take the jumpsuit off of the hanger. Glancing at the size, Theo lets out a sigh of relief, "*Destiné à être!* Meant to be, *mon cheri!*" Theo exclaims, urging her to set the jumpsuit on the pile in her arms and whispering that the jumpsuit is on the house.

Making their way to the counter, Theo places her new wardrobe in several paper bags and hands Michael the bill. Aella is curious to know how much her new clothes cost so that she can find a way to repay Michael.

Unfazed by the price, Michael reaches into his back pocket and pulls out a gold-plated credit card, handing it to Theo, who happily accepts it. Saying their goodbyes, Theo embraces Aella and asks her to revisit the shop whenever she wishes. If things were different, Aella would certainly take her up on that offer.

Michael and Aella walk around the city for a little while before going back to the palace so that she can do her work with Cahtel. Michael insists on carrying her bags so that she can take in the city fully without worrying about the weight of her new clothes.

In a normal situation, Aella and Michael could easily pass as an average couple just out for a late afternoon of shopping and leisure. But this isn't a normal situation, and Aella and Michael aren't an average couple, which reminds her to find a way to repay him for buying her more than enough clothes to get her through her stay.

"I want to thank you for today and for buying me clothes that I desperately needed. I would like to pay you back, of course. However, I know my form of currency isn't good here, and since I most certainly no longer have a job, I figured you might have a way for me to repay you." *Or an apartment, especially with the portal being a cluster fuck.* Aella would have to figure out a way to get that closed as soon as possible.

Michael smiles, intrigued by her request to pay him back, but he declines.

"That won't be necessary. I wanted to treat you today. Besides, you deserve a nice outing and some... clean clothes. I am honored that I could do it," He says sincerely, making Aella feel warm inside.

Nearing the end of a street, Aella admires the beauty of the fields and mountains. Michael doesn't speak for a few minutes, allowing her to enjoy the peaceful quiet.

"Whenever you are ready, we can go back to the palace. There is something I want to show you when we get back, and then we can meet with the others." Michael breaks the silence but matches the energy, speaking in a calm, soothing way.

Inhaling deeply through her nose, Aella takes in one last look at the city of Isethas and nods, letting him know that she is ready to get back.

When they teleport back, Aella doesn't feel quite as nauseous as the times before with Cahtel as she is starting to get used to it.

Landing in the gravel, Cahtel runs down the palace steps to greet them with a panicked look in his eyes.

"How was the city today, sir, Aella?" He asks, slightly on edge. Aella can tell that something is amiss by how his tail is moving at sharp angles.

"It was eventful. Any news?" Michael asks, picking up on his demeanor and his body language.

Cahtel contemplates for a moment on what to say, and if he didn't have fur covering his body, sweat would most definitely be beading at his temple.

"Hmm? Oh! Right, well, um, no... not entirely new. However, there is one little thing that I must inform you about, sir." Cahtel's voice shakes with dread, evident that whatever it is, he clearly doesn't want to tell Michael or Aella whatever information he has.

Michael shakes his head, moving up the steps to the palace, "I'm sure whatever it is can wait for when we are all together in the gathering room. Then you can tell me what has you so worked up."

Appearing even more on edge, Cahtel grimaces and nods. Aella doesn't like the feeling she got from it, especially since Cahtel must have waited all afternoon to tell Michael just to get dismissed and hold onto whatever it could be longer.

Right as Aella is about to protest, Cahtel takes off down the hall, disappearing, and Michael heads up the spiral staircase with Aella following him.

Thinking that Michael is just being polite, carrying her bags up to the room she is staying in, he stops and looks at her.

"Close your eyes," Michael commands softly, and when she does, he opens the door.

Feeling her heart kick up in speed, she can hear him set her bags down and then come up behind her, covering her eyes with his hands to ensure she isn't peeking.

Guiding her into the room, a breeze drifts over her arms.

"You may open your eyes," Michael says with seduction,

lacing every syllable.

Opening her eyes with hesitation, she faces the balcony. In the corner stands a beautiful mahogany easel with canvases stacked against it and a small table covered in unopened paints, brushes, and palettes.

Aella is in disbelief. After their conversation this morning, she had only dreamed of having a place to paint like this.

"How?" Aella gasps, not able to form a complete sentence.

"Before you came downstairs for breakfast, I pulled Ashlyn aside. She set this up for you while we were away in the city." Michael confesses, and the joy in his eyes is unmatched by how she feels. Her eyes begin to well with tears, and she realizes that Ashlyn had probably been acting cold toward her earlier because of this surprise and didn't want to blow their cover.

The clothes were one thing, but this was the best gift she'd ever received. Wiping her tears away, her brows furrow.

"Are you not pleased?" Michael asks concerned.

"No! This is incredible, Michael. I can't thank you enough for everything, especially this. I just don't know if I will have the time to paint. I mean, with training and everything going on." Aella says, remembering all of the issues at hand. Michael grazes his hand over her shoulder and nods in understanding.

"After training and lessons with Cahtel, you can paint as much as you want, Aella. There will be time to paint if creativity strikes. I know I made certain rules and guidelines, but seeing you this morning dreaming about a place to create that doesn't involve the stressors that grab at us made me want to do this for you. Art is therapy in its purest form." Michael says exuding confidence while encouraging her to do something she loves.

Aella couldn't help but want to thank him in other ways, with the sexual tension returning, causing her knees to shake with need.

Without too much time to think about her actions then, or really giving a shit, Aella grabs his face on impulse, kissing him deeply. A guttural growl forms deep in his throat as their lips move in tandem, even with teeth clashing.

Holding the back of her head, Michael loosens the bun her hair is tucked into, grabbing the tendrils taught with masculine force. The act alone makes her want to come for him as he pulls her in closer to where there isn't even a breath amount of space between them.

Pulling away to inhale oxygen into their lungs, Michael looks her deeply in the eyes, and liquid heat begins to pool inside her panties.

"If we continue down the path we are headed, I won't be able to stop or control myself," Michael warns in between his own pants, the challenge heightening Aella's arousal.

Teasing her fingers down his chest, she stops, then hovers over the button to his pants, feeling the agonizing throb and heat beneath the fabric.

Returning her eyes back up to meet his, she can feel her chest flush as she licks her swollen lips and moans, trailing her fingers down the seam to those now too-tight pants, intensifying both of their cravings for each other.

Swallowing thickly, Aella breathes, "I want this, I want you. Tomorrow isn't guaranteed. A week from now... everything could change. None of us have the answers, but what I know and am sure of is this, right now, in this moment. Two people coming together as one, and you are the person, Michael. You are everything I want and need right now."

Her body trembles from being so open and vulnerable. Her body trembles because the truth is she was unsure if he would reject her again, and her body trembles because she is being the most honest she has been with herself about the current situation at hand and because the feelings she has for Michael are more than lust and want. They are painful in the most pleasurable way.

A fraction of a second slips by then, and Michael scoops her into his arms, taking her to the bed. Lying her down, he hovers over her, kissing her passionately as she kicks her shoes off from beneath him, and he yanks her leggings down in one smooth motion.

Lifting her T-shirt up over her head, Michael kisses down her neck, savoring the taste of her skin, nipping at the sensitive flesh, then smoothing over the love bite with his tongue until he reaches the peeks of her breasts.

Closing his lips over the hard bud, he sucks and bites down gently, causing her hips to lift and move with need.

Chuckling under his breath, he hums with approval, "Patience, Aella, let me worship you." He says, deep and smoky. Looking primal and sexy, especially kneeling before her like she is a queen. Sitting back on his heels, he takes in every inch of her, then pulls her soaking panties off with his teeth, which is the hottest thing Aella has ever seen.

Moving his hands to her backside, Michael yanks her to where the bottom half of her body is hanging off the edge of the bed and drapes her legs over her shoulders.

Trailing featherlight kisses up her inner thighs, he teases and taunts her with his lips, taking his time while she writhes in his grasp.

His tongue glides over her center, tasting every fold and crease. Licking his lips, he gently kisses the bundle of nerves sucking on her, then pulls away with an audible pop.

"God's, you taste exactly how I pictured you would." He says approvingly, and before Aella can find the words to respond to his comment, Michael begins to feast as if it is his last meal on earth.

Aella gasps out, needing something to hold onto as she

reaches for his hair. She feels as if she is being resurrected from a long sleep.

Licking and sucking on the bundle of nerves, Michael moves one of his hands from where he's holding her, ensuring that her legs are firmly wrapped around his shoulders, and inserts two fingers, thrusting in and out and angling them to hit the spot that will be her undoing.

The pleasure borders on the line of pain becoming too much, but Michael doesn't ease up. Instead, he takes his fingers out and holds her hands while he continues to feast, drinking her arousal like he's parched and needs water.

Aella's vision goes black, seeing stars unable to muffle a scream as she comes. Her head falls back from the waves of orgasmic pleasure that take over, soaking Michael's face and the sheets beneath her from how much she is expelling.

Giving her a moment to return to her body, she props herself up on her elbows, unable to get over the smug look on Michael's face, who is clearly pleased with himself while he kisses her inner thighs again.

Aella sits up, pulling Michael to her, and kisses him, tasting herself on his lips, arousal dripping from her all over again.

Her hands move over his soaked shirt from her, undoing the buttons, and Michael tears his shirt off, not caring that it's ruined.

When she moves to unbutton his pants and finally have him inside of her, the door swings open, causing them both to startle.

Standing in the doorway is Ashlyn, who appears to be frantic and emotionally distressed.

"What happened?" Michael demands with a shout.

One hell of a cockblock.

"It's Christopher; something is very wrong."

Chapter Twenty-Four

Michael moves first, tossing Aella her clothes so that she can throw them back on. Ashlyn is still standing in the doorway, tense and unmoving. Once Aella is dressed, she runs to Ashlyn, noticing that the look in her eyes is etched with grief and sorrow.

Something happened to Christopher, but before jumping to the worst-case scenario, he very well could have gone through the portal alone back to Aella's apartment and got on the next flight back to the East Coast.

"Aella," Ashlyn begins and lets out a breath, "You need to brace yourself for what Cahtel and Torin are going to share."

Aella doesn't like the sound of that; she doesn't like it one bit.

Michael puts his hand on her shoulder then and says, "You do not have to come down right now if you need some time—"

Aella cuts him off, "No, I need to hear what happened or what Cahtel and Torin saw. There is a chance that Christopher went back through the portal, right? I mean, we can't jump to conclusions."

Michael agrees with her, but he looks as if what they are about to find out is farther from Christopher going back to the mortal realm to be with his current family.

Sitting in the lounge, Torin and Cahtel are quiet as Aella and Michael enter, with Ashlyn following them in.

Torin quirks a brow, eyeing them both, and smirks at Aella's shirt, which is not only inside out but backward.

Michael glares at him, and Torin chuckles, shaking his head, returning to his serious state. Aella sits down in one of the chairs, and Michael walks to the bar, pouring Aella a glass of wine to help aid her nerves. He takes a seat in his usual spot and then pats the space next to him for her to join.

"What happened?" Michael asks, looking at Cahtel after she sits down next to him.

"I tried to tell you when you returned to the palace, sir, but..." Cahtel begins to explain, and Aella places her hand on Michael's leg to keep him from lashing out due to the anger radiating off of his body.

"When I left this morning to check on the portal and the barrier, everything was fine with that. I mean, the portal is still a disaster, which we need to get figured out. Anyway, I went to the city. Everything was quiet and peaceful, nothing out of the ordinary, until I got to Christopher's home. The door was open, so I let myself in, checking on him, and everything was in shambles like a tornado had come through. It looked as though a robbery had taken place, and Christopher was gone. I teleported back here to get Torin to come back with me." Cahtel shares, then looks at Aella with dread and remorse.

Torin steps in, "We looked all over the townhouse for any sign of where Christopher may have gone. Our first thought was that maybe he had gone back through the portal and left the door open, but then that would mean one of our people had broken in and destroyed his place. When we checked his room, his luggage was still there, so we went to the tavern to see if he was drinking. The owner of the tavern told me he hadn't seen Christopher since he overstayed and went on his bender. Nobody has seen him since then."

Fear for Christopher's safety overpowers Aella. The need to go out and look for him right away anxiously claws at her, and not just for herself but for fear of his wife and child.

Aggressively picking at the skin around her thumbnail as she thinks of where to start the search, a sharp pain shoots up her hand as blood begins to drip onto the floor. Ashlyn had taken notice first before Aella even had time to process it herself by handing her a cloth to wrap around her oozing thumb.

"Where do we go from here? Should we go through the portal to my apartment first and see if he, in fact, did leave? Who would have done something like this?" The questions tumble out of Aella so fast, diverting attention from the spilled blood on the marble floor.

Torin speaks then, answering one of her questions, "We aren't sure who would have been capable of destroying his home here. The locals refrain from violent acts, especially since the war. I am going to ask the Messengers what they know in the Illusion Plane." He finishes, seemingly on edge by the task.

The Messengers. Aella remembers Michael mentioning something about them after the second time she had come to Isethas.

"I want to go with you."

Michael snaps, "No, Aella, it's too dangerous," but she wasn't asking for permission.

"Michael's right, Aella. Even I don't like going there when I have to; it feels like my skin is crawling each time." Torin expresses while grimacing, and Aella doesn't understand what the big deal is with her going. Christopher said so himself. She's basically up there with the Gods because of how powerful her gifts are.

The plus side is Torin will be with her, and he is all muscle.

Aella's stubborn and curious nature gets the best of her when she asks, "This Illusion Plane, is it like a realm? Wouldn't you need a portal to get there?"

"The Illusion Plane is neither a realm nor is it a physical place. It is like an in-between. It is dangerous because the Illusion Plane plays with your mind and can turn your worst fears into reality. Those who enter go to seek wisdom from the three Messengers; they are essentially like the Moirai. They are neither man nor woman, good nor evil. Unfortunately, there are those who have entered that have never returned." Cahtel explains, and a chill runs over Aella's body.

"So, the Illusion Plane, it's like a purgatory?"

Michael takes over from here and says, "It is worse than purgatory. Those who are unable to return become trapped, a ghost of themselves that wanders the plane, losing all sense of who they were before they entered. They feed from the emotions of newcomers who desire the same as they once did: answers to questions and a glimpse into the future, no matter how futile. Turning the weak-minded into nothing more than a shell."

Aella's throat dries at the image painted for her of the souls trapped in the Illusion Plane. But even with the information she has received from Michael and Cahtel about such a place, she needs to go. Aella has questions of her own that she wants answers to.

She nods with her decision firm and says, "I am going with you, Torin."

Flexing his jaw, Michael's eyes start to turn more white than blue. Seething through gritted teeth, he says, "I said no, Aella. This is non-negotiable."

"Then come with us!" She combats, and the room falls heavy. Her stubborn will is set on going, and no one can convince her otherwise. Aella is a glutton for punishment, and she knows this about herself.

"Watchers are prohibited from entering the Illusion Plane. Only guardians and the people of different realms may enter. Everything has a price, Aella. Even this." Cahtel warns, but he also knows that there is no talking her down from the ledge.

"Torin has gone and come back. If he can do it, then I can too, no offense." Aella justifies, and Torin rolls his eyes.

"That is because Torin is a guardian and doesn't go for his own personal gain. He has a mission when he enters to get information pertaining to the safety of Isethas and our people." Michael interjects, and Aella has to brush off the subtle jab.

Cahtel then says, "If I may, sir, I don't think it's a terrible idea that she goes. Perhaps the Messengers can give us insight on how to help her control her gifts better, which would benefit us by speeding this process up a little bit faster."

Ouch. Even though Cahtel has a point and a very good one. Even if his remark on speeding the process up makes Aella feel like a burden all over again.

"When do we leave, and how do we get there?" Aella asks, and Michael narrows his eyes on her, stands up, and storms out of the lounge.

"Now. The sooner we get on with this, the better." Torin states, grimacing again at the daunting task.

"There are a couple of things you need to know before going to the Illusion Plane. You are allowed three questions, one for each Messenger. Be very strategic with how you ask your questions and what you seek to know; when answering or giving away knowledge, they tend to respond in riddles, making it difficult to decipher." Cahtel scoffs at the end, he is obviously not a fan favorite of them.

"Why don't you come along with us?" Aella asks Cahtel, more curious as to why he didn't offer to tag along.

Torin answers for him, "The Messengers taunt Cahtel for what he is now, and the only person allowed to poke fun is me." Aella never doubted that the two rivals cared for each other, even if they grated on each other's nerves. It was strange to think that the Messengers would taunt Cahtel for what he had become, especially if Damien had found a way to curse him into the beast he appears to be now unless the Messengers knew something about it that no one else did.

"Okay, so three questions..." Aella says, thinking about what to ask them and how to ask, given that she would have to be very specific and word them appropriately.

"Don't overthink them too much. Simplifying them is crucial, as well as being specific." Cahtel advises while Aella thinks about the first question, the most important pertaining to where Christopher is or who took him.

"First question: what happened to Christopher the night his home was destroyed? I think that's good, right?" Aella says, but Cahtel shakes his head.

"Think differently; they could give you an answer of, I don't know, he was taken, and then that would leave you to your last two questions," Cahtel states, and Aella huffs out with frustration. This was going to be more complicated than she thought, *fuck*.

After a few seconds of pondering, Aella puts herself as a riddler and thinks of the best way to phrase her first question.

"On the night Christopher's home was destroyed, who took him? They will not only tell us who has him, but we will know where to find him with the name alone. If he did, in fact, leave of his own accord, then the Messengers would have to answer that nobody took him, and we have an answer that he just went up and left back through the portal like I initially suspected."

"Right, but then why would his home appear to be in peril?" Torin asks, considering whether the second theory is true. Perhaps he was looking for something valuable and destroyed his home himself.

"What else are you going to ask them, Aella?" Cahtel interrupts her spiraling thoughts, reeling her back.

"Well, we know Damien has an agenda, but we don't really know what his plan is, and I am sure we would all like to know what his plans are moving forward."

Torin and Cahtel nod in agreement, but Ashlyn sits quietly, avoiding any eye contact. Aella doesn't seem bothered by it, though; she is obviously in distress about Christopher's safety.

"Okay, third question: how do we control my gifts to prevent another war? I would say that is, along with the first question, equally important."

No one says a word. War is a promise, a reality that no one wants to face, but it also doesn't have to be, especially if Aella can control her gifts so that she can stop using them even if she can't suppress them entirely.

Aella feels a responsibility to prevent that from happening since she was born with not one but three gifts that very well could soon cause a more violent outbreak among the realms.

For all they knew, Damien could have an army ready for when shit goes down and is prepared to take over.

Michael breaks the silence by pushing off the door jam as he reenters the lounge after having had time to cool down. "As much as I hate to say this, that is a very important question, Aella. I hope, for our sake, you get the answers you seek."

Aella stands from her chair to turn and face him, wrapping her arms around him. "I will be alright; I'm strong, remember? We need these answers. This will help us."

"I never doubted you. I just worry," Michael whispers in her hair. Pulling away from him, Aella approaches Ashlyn, who is off to a faraway place, and she flinches when Aella touches her arm.

"We will find out what happened to Christopher, I promise." Aella gives her word, but she can't shake the unsettling feeling inside her. Ashlyn doesn't say anything back. Instead, she flicks her eyes to Aella, finally making eye contact. Aella knows then that she doesn't need to say anything because they are filled with nothing more than guilt and regret.

BECAUSE TORIN NEEDED TO GAUGE THE WEATHER BETTER before flying to the Illusion Plane, he flew Aella to the top of the mountain, where Cahtel had opened up to her a little about his past. That same spot on the mountain appears to be the best place for it.

Unable to shake the unsettling feeling in her stomach and the eeriness she felt from Ashlyn, Aella takes the opportunity to ask Torin if he knew anything.

"Is Ashlyn okay? I know that she and Christopher are close friends, but she seems really torn up."

Torin stiffens at the question, and Aella then realizes that there is something more between her father and friend.

Opening up his wings to test the wind off the ledge, Torin sighs, "It's complicated... She and Christopher used to be lovers. I try not to think about it since, you know, she and I are together. Before the war, they were inseparable, but he didn't love her back the way she loved him. It broke her heart when he decided to live in the mortal realm. I tried to pick up the pieces and show her that she was worthy of the love she gave him, but I don't think she ever got over him. I think she's still in love with

Christopher, and it breaks my heart even though I love her all the same." Torin explains.

Anger roots itself inside of Aella after learning the real history between who she knows to be her father now and Ashlyn. She thought that they had become friends and told each other everything. Why would she keep something like that from her?

"I'm sorry, Aella, I thought you knew. Ashlyn is kind and sweet, but she has her secrets. The night that the portal was created, Ashlyn came through it while they were asleep and lost her mind seeing Christopher in his bed with another woman, even though he had been in the mortal realm at this point for centuries. I think that's partly why your mother chose to leave. I don't blame her; I would have done the same. That would have freaked me out."

Aella thinks of when her mother was in her apartment and gave her the envelope with a way to contact Christopher. She'd told Aella about a woman who came through a portal while they were sleeping and, shortly after, found out she was pregnant with Aella, which confirms that she really did open a portal while she was in the womb.

A dark cloud forms above them from Torin breaking the news to her. He isn't the sharpest tool in the shed, and he realizes that he made a huge mistake by telling her all of that as he attempts to console her.

Aella was seeing red, her vision blurring on the verge of blacking out entirely. The waves below the cliffs and mountain start crashing against the rocks with ferocity as lightning ebbs and flows from the dark cloud, striking down around them.

Torin's pleas are snuffed out by the loud, thunderous bangs that bounce down the horizon. Chaos in the sea ensues as the creatures that live below try to escape until there is nothing but silence.

Aella falls down to her knees, screaming out in agony, "I trusted her! I told her everything, and this whole time, she lied to me. I told her about my mother, and she took that information for her own selfish pleasure!" Aella's rage and disgust for Ashlyn ailes her, causing her to vomit.

After expelling the sick feeling that swarmed within, she sits back, leaning against a boulder.

Torin stares at her, wide-eyed and pale from the event that took place and the massive storm she created, which was far more chaotic than the former.

"Holy shit. Aella, I am so sorry, I shouldn't have... are you alright? Do I need to take you back to the palace? Fuck, tell me what to do." He says, remorseful and stressed, but the cloud begins to dissipate, and the waves slow their crescendo. The wind around them dies down, and the air calms, almost too perfect for takeoff.

"I'm fine," She says, leaning her head back as she slows her breathing, "I'm glad you told me. No, I do not want to go back to the palace; we have shit to do. Let's go."

Standing up, she wipes her mouth off with her shirt that is still inside out and backward, unbothered by her disheveled state.

She didn't care about Ashlyn's thoughts or feelings now. Ashlyn fucked up by not telling her the truth, and now Aella has a new vendetta. It is one thing to have kept an old-aged secret from her in that Ashlyn and Christopher were once lovers; it is another thing entirely to have kept that she came through a portal that was never meant to be open and most likely threatened her mother because Ashlyn was eaten up with jealousy.

There is no coming back from something like this, and Aella wasnt going to let it go.

Chapter Twenty-Five

A ella and Torin didn't speak while he flew them just outside the Illusion Plane. If Aella had to calculate the time it took from the mountain to where they landed, it was about a thirty-minute commute, but the tense silence between them made it feel much longer.

Torin feels awful for telling her the truth about Christopher and Ashlyn, and Aella knows he will continue to do so for a while. But, despite the fact that the truth hurts, Aella needed to know.

After receiving the news, Ashlyn's behavior toward her made more sense, and Aella was glad to have an explanation, even if she hated how she felt about it all right now.

Thick fog coats the air around them as they approach the rust-wrought iron gate, deterring anyone from entering. The outskirts of the Illusion Plane look as though it could be a graveyard, and Aella secretly wishes that she had grabbed a light sweater before they left from the uncomfortable chill.

Torin opens the gate, and as they enter, the sounds of suffering moans and cries intensify, making Aella's head throb, the meltdown she had on the mountain aiding to the ache.

The further they walk, the more the crying becomes painful and almost too much until they reach a trail. Continuing down the path, there is nothing to be heard besides the echoing of their footsteps, *a small mercy.*

Aella takes in her surroundings of the strange place, almost exactly how she would picture purgatory. The trees are an unnatural shade of grey, and ripe red apples hang at awkward angles from their branches. The apples are so red that they almost look like the fake plastic ones someone's grandmother would place in a bowl as a table accent.

Torin and Aella continue walking down the path in complete silence as she tries to recite the questions she will soon ask the Messengers and which order.

Then, her mother's voice carries through the trees, causing Aella to stop even though Torin urges her to keep going.

"Did you hear that?" Aella asks louder than intended and flinches as her voice travels through the trees. Torin holds his finger up to his lips and scowls at her.

Lowering his voice, he leans down close to her ear and says, "You have to stay quiet. Whatever you heard is not real. Ignore it."

Goosebumps coat her exposed arms. Whatever that was, it sounded so much like her mother, and it crept her the fuck out.

"Aella, help! Help me, Aella!" The pleas and cries that come through now sound precisely like Tara's, and without making a rational decision, Aella begins to sprint toward where she hears her voice.

"Tara! I'm coming! Where are you?" She shouts, panicking and fearing for her friend as she charges through the trees for a rescue.

Branches hit her body as her feet carry her towards the

voice. But, to no avail, Tara isn't there, and Aella looks around to realize that Torin is also nowhere in sight.

Oh fuck. Fuck. Fuck. Fuck. Okay, Aella, think, retrace your steps...

Everything looks the same. The trees are the exact same height and color, and all of the branches are the same as their neighbor.

Aella fell for the trickery of the Illusion Plane within minutes because she was too vulnerable. She misses Tara and would take a bullet for her, and the Illusion Plane played on those emotions.

Feeling as if she is going to have another breakdown, Aella shuts her eyes tight and breathes, trying to ground herself instead of spiral, like she so desperately wants to do right now.

In through the nose, hold, out through the nose, hold.

Aella does this for three counts until she's ready to open her eyes and is confident she has a handle on her panic, allowing her survival instincts to take the wheel.

You got this, Aella! It's no different than camping, just in a really fucked up place that you may never leave. It's fine, you're fine.

Looking around once more, Aella picks a direction with her gut instinct, hoping for the best outcome.

As she begins walking through the trees, a shadow catches her eyes, moving along the branches, and stops when she does.

Swallowing too loud for comfort, Aella keeps her voice quiet despite the shouting she did only moments ago.

"H—hello? Torin, is that you?" She asks with a stutter. That confidence that she'd mustered is now a flickering flame ready to burn out once the thing casting a shadow makes itself known.

No response. Just deafening silence.

Shaking her head, she thinks she probably imagined it until

it moves as she does again, and Aella takes off into a sprint once more.

Turning her head to look behind her to see if the shadow is following her, she knocks into a wall of a man and flies backward, happy to see it's not just any wall of a man but Torin.

Scowling down at her with panic in his eyes, he reaches his hand down to help her up.

"What the fuck Aella? I told you to ignore it! You could have been lost forever!" Torin whisper shouts, holding her arm as he leads them back to the path like a child.

She didn't care, though. She was relieved that he had found her.

"How did you find me?" She asks quietly, still shaken from the woods and the shadow.

"I almost didn't. I chased after you the moment you took off running, but the trees shifted. You must have followed your gut or something because I was ready to return to the palace and get a search party going."

Aella pales and feels like she's going to be sick again, even though she has nothing left to expel from earlier.

"What do you mean the trees move?"

"It's all an illusion, Aella, hence the Illusion Plane. The only thing that doesn't shift or move is this pathway, which I encourage you to stay on no matter what you hear or think you see in those woods. Next time, you might not be so lucky." Torin warns and rubs his temples. Today has been a lot as far as emotional exhaustion is concerned, but they had to keep to their mission. Aella will not leave this path even if her life depends on it.

Ignoring the voices that beckon her into the trees is a lot easier said than done the farther down the path they get, but she presses forward, ignoring them as they all collide together, making it difficult to focus.

As they near the trail's end, three large onyx pillars stand in a line. Torin halts Aella from proceeding, pointing out the circle of salt rocks before the pillars she would have walked right through had he not.

"When you enter the circle, you must have your intentions set. Do you remember your questions?" Torin asks with hesitation.

Taking a moment, Aella nods.

"Good. Once you enter, say, *"I summon thee, for I, Aella Clarke, seek wisdom."* You will then disappear and enter a dark room on a platform before the three Messengers. After your questions are answered, they will send you back, and you will reappear in this circle. I will be right here waiting for you."

Aella begins to feel nervous, and her hands grow clammy as she enters the circle with more trepidation than she thought she would.

Bracing herself for whatever the outcome will be, she swallows and clears her throat, speaking the words Torin told her to say with set intentions.

Black smoke snakes up her body, making everything go dark like a black void, and in an instant, she is standing on a platform in a dark room. Looking down to see the circle that was made of salt is now a soft glowing ring, and the pillars before her are also lit with the same glow.

Sitting atop the pillars are grey-cloaked figures with the hoods pulled up, one per pillar. Squinting her eyes to better see their features, she sees that they are encased in shadows.

"Aella Rose Clarke. To what do we owe this pleasure?" Messenger One announces from their pillar, sounding amused.

"Yes, what a pleasant surprise. Intrigued truly." The Third Messenger states, snickering.

Reminding herself to remain calm, Aella holds her head high and says, "I have three questions."

The Second Messenger lets out a wail of laughter that bounces off the walls. The screeching sound of it makes her hands fly up to cover her ears, mimicking metal against metal.

"Well, straight to business, are we? Enlighten us, Aella! You have had quite the adventure as of late, and unfortunately, you have more than just three questions." The Second Messenger says with dark humor.

Aella struggles to hold onto her questions because she does have more. She has a lot of unanswered questions, and now she understands why it is so hard to get a straight answer from one of these things.

"The night Christopher's home was destroyed, who took him?" Aella asks, forcing the question out.

The Messengers adjust on their pillars as they lean into each other. A second passes and the First Messenger taps their elongated gloved fingers against the stone pillar he is perched on.

"Very well... Christopher, your father," the First Messenger drawls, "Oh, that is interesting, hmmm, let me see... The night his home was destroyed is a night like many. Hide and seek is a fun game to be played until what was once lost is found. An heirloom passed down for generations that holds secrets... Ah! Christopher is an unfair opponent, yes. He cheats his way to the finish line. Christopher plays for both teams. He is held captive where the sand once turned to gold and is nothing more but ruin."

Tucking the riddled answer into a filing cabinet in her memory, she feels pulled to decipher it.

"What is Damien's plan?" The second question tumbles out more manageable than the first, but she flinches, hoping that she worded it right. *Too late now.*

"Damien, who once was a bright star, burned out and fell to his despair..." The Second Messenger states, "What do loss and

321

love have in common? I'll give you a hint," it awaits her response, leaning back with their gloved fingers in a power position, but Aella isn't giving in to the satisfaction or their game.

"Oh, you're no fun! *Unpredictability*. Short and sweet."

Completely dumbfounded by the answer she received from the Second Messenger, Aella tucks it away with the first answer.

"Final question: how do I control my gifts to prevent another war?"

All three Messengers are still. Leaning into each other again, they whisper low enough to sound like mumbled nonsense.

The energy shifts in the room, making her feel uneasy, and then the Third Messenger throws their gloved hand up to silence the other two. The suspense from a simple hand gesture is a slow death by anticipation.

"A gift of power and destruction for a war that has yet to see its day..." the Third Messenger begins, and the other two sit silently, "Responsibility for such a gift comes naturally, although you have just begun the process of acceptance. You have yet to tap into what such a gift like yours entails, all three of them, to be exact. Why?"

Aella thinks about that; she hasn't really tried to tap into her gifts and explore them. She has only been working toward controlling them and learning that she was born with three gifts recently; the idea of mingling with them in that way kind of freaks her out.

"I don't know. I just recently learned that I had a gift that I always assumed was more of a diagnosed condition, let alone two additional gifts. It terrifies me not to know what I am capable of." Aella answers honestly because that is how she perceives them.

Despite the fact that her gifts are a part of her, they are still foreign and also border on the line of a chaotic disaster.

A portal that can lead you anywhere you imagine but can also have the ability to go rogue, like the one that is still open with diseased tentacles.

A manifestation of storms and natural disasters that mirror her emotions and could take out entire cities, if not realms. *Could they take out realms?*

The ability to move objects by a force of air as if they weigh nothing that could be used to throw at someone as a weapon.

Her gifts are deadly and dangerous, even if they contain beauty and a sliver of heroism.

"Hmmm, I see... that is troubling. I will answer your final question simply, Aella Clarke. The answer you need is not on how to control your gifts but if your gifts will end the war because war will come no matter how much control you think you may have over what you were born with. So, yes, your gifts will end the war. However, I cannot answer if such gifts will, in fact, end all existence, and that, my dear, is what should terrify you. Tap into your gifts and, at the very least, become acquainted with them. You will need them for what will unfold."

Smoke encompasses her after the Third Messenger finishes answering her final question.

When she reappears in the circle made of salt, Aella stumbles out, coughing uncontrollably to expel the smoke from her lungs.

Torin helps prop her up until she comes down from the coughing fit.

"Did you get answers?" He asks, evidently concerned that it was a waste of time.

Aella inhales the stale air, feeling her lungs rattle from the last little bit of smoke that threatened to suffocate her, and says, "Yes, I did get answers."

Torin nods, noting the look of worry in her eye from the information she now has stored in the filing cabinet of her brain, and doesn't push.

They walk down the path of the Illusion Plane in silence, aside from the cries and moans of agony that swim through the wood.

Aella found it much easier to ignore on their way out due to the heavy weight of the knowledge the Third Messenger gave her.

The day is far from over, and war is a promise.

Saddle up.

Chapter Twenty-Six

S itting together at the table in the gathering room, the energy that was once joyous and full of celebration is now filled with an uncomfortable ambiance.

With a piece of paper and pen, Aella jots down everything the Messengers had told her before the anger she harbors toward Ashlyn surfaces, and she forgets the details.

Michael could sense that Aella was angered when she and Torin arrived back at the palace and saw a twinge of guilt in Torin's features, but he would wait to ask Aella about it after the meeting.

Ashlyn sits at the table, unable to relax, as she, too, notices the change in them.

Aella stands from her chair now that everything is written verbatim and leads the meeting.

"Cahtel was right about the Messengers making it difficult to get a straightforward answer, but we have what I came for," she starts while reading over her notes, "First and foremost, I gained something very interesting about Christopher from the Messengers, amongst other interesting facts."

Aella looks directly at Ashlyn, which causes her to cower briefly. The subtle jab is prevalent, and everyone in the room takes notice, which, in turn, causes Michael to shift into his chair.

"But before I dive too far into that rabbit hole, I want to focus on Damien since he is one of our main concerns and targets at the moment. When I asked the Messengers about his plan, the Second responded with a question: *"What do love and loss have in common?"* The answer: *Unpredictability.* Do you have any thoughts as to what they may have meant?"

Cahtel and Michael exchange glances after Aella finishes, and Michael leans back in his chair, deciphering the vague answer that holds a lot of weight.

"Before the war and before my father got sick, Damien, like myself, loved our people and both of our parents. We both suffered a great loss with the death of our father and in return, we lost our beloved mother, the glue which held our realm together with her light. Perhaps the answer is simple, and his plan of action is that he really doesn't have one like we suspect. He has become unpredictable even when seeking the vengeance he believes he is owed. Damien is riddled with unhinged emotions." Michael says as he swipes at the table, removing crumbs that aren't really there. Aella doesn't like that, especially since he currently has Tara and Georgia kept somewhere.

If Damien really is as unhinged as Michael claims, then that is another problem all on its own and one that they really don't have the time to deal with.

"Damien isn't the only Watcher who seeks power and control, though, sir," Cahtel states, and Michael waves a dismissive hand as he leans forward in his chair, speaking as if this topic is more of an annoyance than an issue.

"You are not wrong; however, the other Watchers who seek

the same as Damien would need access to portals, which they do not since Aella is here with us. Damien has the accessibility to come between the mortal realm and Diatturus because Aella accidentally opened that portal, which we intend to take care of sooner rather than later. That being said, the others are not a concern of mine at the moment."

Ashlyn scoffs under her breath. The subtle sound triggers Aella, making her want nothing more than to punch her in the face and cause her to make a different sound entirely.

"That leads me back to Christopher," Aella says, making a point to look directly at Ashlyn before returning to her notes, "Christopher, like many, has his secrets. He has something worth of value that someone desperately wants, *"Hide and seek is a fun game to be played until what was once lost is found. An heirloom passed down for generations that holds secrets. Christopher is an unfair opponent. He cheats his way to the finish line. Christopher plays for both teams."* The First Messenger also mentioned something about him being held captive where the sand once turned to gold but is nothing more but ruin." Aella finishes, and Michael turns his body towards Ashlyn with his brow raised, staring at her to elaborate on whether she knows anything about the heirloom.

Confusion comes over Torin as he reaches for her across the table, but she moves her hand away, crossing it over her body, and scratches her other arm like she has an itch.

"Ashlyn, do you know what the Messengers may be referring to?" Torin asks, brushing off the way she dismissed his affection. It is clear that Torin is grasping at hope that she knows nothing, but that hope suddenly dies when tears fall from her eyes.

Ashlyn is caught with her hand in the cookie jar, only this is one giant cookie, and with enough pressure and force, the cookie is strong enough to break the jar altogether.

"Unfortunately, I do. I promised him I wouldn't tell a soul about the heirloom. I am sorry, I cannot say." Ashlyn responds, and the anger within Aella swirls beneath the surface.

"That is such bull shit, Ashlyn! How can you sit here and not say anything? Do you want the realms to end? Do you want to stand by and watch as your people, the people you supposedly care about, suffer a fate far worse than the one you are facing? Or are you so hung up on Christopher that you hold any kernel of hope you have left that he will one day love you back the way you do him?!" Aella shouts, and her nails begin to hurt from how hard she is digging them into the wood of the tabletop. Michael's brows reach his hairline as he pieces it together.

"What is she talking about?" He asks in a calm, even tone.

"She didn't tell you? Oh, that's rich. Nice work, Ashlyn." Aella spits, clapping her hands in applause, uncaring for the tears Ashlyn is shedding. Her face is red, and her eyes are swollen as she collapses into herself.

"I'm sorry. I am so sorry for everything. Please, Michael, forgive me." Ashlyn begs, becoming more fearful than remorseful for what Michael would do to her.

Michael sits there, confused as to why Ashlyn is so worked up, "Look, you and Christopher were once lovers, and I can understand why Aella is upset about that, but—"

Aella interrupts, crossing her arms over her chest, "She knew. Before Cahtel came through when I was fifteen and you first got wind of my gift, she knew."

"What?..." Michael's voice trails off, "What is she saying, Ashlyn?"

"When my mother was pregnant with me, before she even knew that she was pregnant, I opened a portal in the womb. Ashlyn came through while... while my mother and Christopher were sleeping. Ashlyn knew about Elissa's gift like you all did and that no one else had the ability to open portals at the time. She pieced it together, and she fucking knew, didn't you, Ashlyn? You knew that my mother was pregnant with me, Christopher's child, Elissa's grandchild, and you were so blinded by a jealous rage that you kept it to yourself before telling any of them about it. Didn't you?" Aella seethes, hurt, and anger, mixing and bubbling like oil and water.

"Please tell me this isn't true, Ashlyn," Michael says, equally hurt by such a betrayal. Ashlyn covers her face with her hands and shakes her head, "Yes, it's true. I've known this whole time."

Standing out of his chair, Michael looks down at her. His features are hard as stone, and his eyes begin to darken to something far more sinister than the white that Aella is used to when he becomes angry.

"I trusted you, and you betrayed me. You betrayed your people, and Christopher's life is in danger because of it." Michael says in an even tone that makes even Aella nervous.

"I— I'm sorry—"

"Leave! It is not I you should be asking forgiveness." Michael's voice booms in the gathering room. Ashlyn scurries out of her chair, glaring at Aella momentarily as she readies to flee.

Torin looks to be on the verge of protesting her stay until Ashlyn glances down at him and spits, turning on her heels, proving in this moment who she truly hid under the surface.

That sweet, generous mask she wears too proudly has cracked, and Aella got all the answers that she needed then.

Michael looks over to Torin as he wipes the spittle from his cheek and asks, "Did you know about that also? And do I need to ask you to leave?"

Fuck.

"I knew about her seeing Christopher and Aella's mother

but thought it was a coincidental portal that opened, but that was the extent. She didn't tell me anything else, and honestly, I forgot all about it until..." Torin trails off, thinking about whether or not he should tell Michael about the hurricane Aella almost caused on the top of the mountain.

"You idiot," Cahtel interjects, "portals aren't something that happens coincidentally. Well, Michael, there you have it. Torin is really as stupid as he makes himself out to be."

The comment adds more hurt to what Torin feels already, and Aella frowns at Cahtel, shaking her head. *Not the right time, Cahtel.*

"Alright, let's continue where we left off," Michael says, returning to the issue at hand despite the fact that he remains standing and is still angry with the news he has received, "What we know is Christopher has something that is far more valuable than a relic. Whatever this may be, it is something that not even I know about, which means it's dangerous. The who, where, and why is what we need to figure out. Aella, where did the Messengers say he was being held captive again?"

Clearing her throat, she looks at her notes again, "Somewhere where the sand once turned to gold and is nothing more but ruin."

"Cahtel, any thoughts on where they are referring to?" Michael asks, and Cahtel thinks through all of his knowledge of the realms.

"The only place that comes to mind isn't possible... they would have needed a portal to enter, but the sand that once turned to gold and is nothing more than ruin sounds a lot like Cleopparim," Cahtel says, scratching his head with his paw, and he is right. Cleopparim is another realm, and you need a portal to enter.

Christopher is an unfair opponent. He cheats his way to the finish line. Christopher plays for both teams. Aella thinks about what the Messenger told her, then what her father had said in the library,

"I think the reason why I never got blessed with such a gift is because I am not as good as they were. But you, Aella, you are good."

The library... wait, Aella remembers the book on dark magic, *Diablerie Memento Goety,* and what Ashlyn had told her while reading the tome: *"I'm honestly surprised that Michael has this tome in his library; you could manifest a portal with this spell"*

It hits her then like a ton of bricks: the book, a portal, Christopher, the heirloom, and Ashlyn.

"Go find Ashlyn, Now!" Aella shouts, and Torin jumps out of his chair and runs out of the palace to track down Ashlyn. If she had used the spell in that book to open a portal, then she would most likely be long gone now.

Michael and Cahtel stare at her with wide eyes on edge, waiting for her to speak.

"Diablerie Memento Goety, that tome you have or had in your library, Michael, there is a spell to manifest a portal, and Ashlyn knows how to read it."

Michael furrows his brows and pales, "Impossible, it was destroyed after the war..."

"Well, it wasn't, fuck, how did I not see it then? She was completely enamored by that book... wait," Aella goes through the memory of Ashlyn talking about what was needed for the manifestation to work, "Ashlyn said that in order for the spell to work, you would need a combination of herbs, but they were destroyed after the war and banned for recreation."

Michael swallows, appearing like he is going to be sick, and looks at Cahtel, "Why didn't you say anything about this? You were in there with them the whole time!"

Cahtel shrugs, appearing to be unbothered per usual, "I

was doing research on the elemental gifts; besides, I figured you knew you had the atrocity in your library, and then Christopher came in intoxicated. Let us not forget about the shitstorm of levitating books, by the way; there was a lot going on."

Huffing out in frustration, Michael asks Aella, "Did she mention what herbs were needed to complete the ritual?"

Michael is frantic. Stress and regret are an obvious combination that overwhelms him, and he is fearful of what the answer may be.

"No, she didn't. I thought you all said that Elissa was the only one before me who had the gift to open portals. How is it that there is even a spell to do such a thing?"

Cahtel speaks then and gives her the explanation for it, "There was only Elissa with the gift like you to open portals. However, the one who created *Diablerie Memento Goety* is of the purest evil to have ever walked the realms and wrote each passage entirely out of blood," Cahtel pauses for a moment. Chills encompass Aella's body as she thinks about the ink that was so different on the pages and how she gently grazed over them with her fingertips, "He is the Watcher of the realm that has long been sealed, even before our time, and forgotten about. In your world, he may be referred to as the boogeyman, the devil, or demon, the taker of souls. You see, dark magic comes with a price. Every time a spell is used from that book, there are consequences—a binding contract, in that you belong to him, *Ezra*. Once your time is near, he will collect. I never learned the language of that book because I didn't want to use it, especially since I am already enslaved to this body and life. Ashlyn will pay the price gravely from doing so."

The realm that has long been sealed, even before my time, and forgotten about. Michael had said that when referring to the succubi that came through during one of her episodes, then again during the first time she meditated with Ashlyn in the meditation room.

Michael slams his fist on the table, startling her from the nightmare, "I should have known, Fuck! Ashlyn asked me to grow Aconitum in conjunction with Solanum americanum. I had a few seeds for both stored away and hidden, she told me it would help alongside suppressing Aella's gift. I contributed to this mess..."

"What is Aconitum?" Aella asks with the sinking feeling that is now taking hold from the book's creation.

Michael sighs, rubbing his chin, "Wolf's bane, also known as devil's helmet. I need to go to the greenhouse and destroy those plants and any additional seeds they may have dropped. She didn't have a lot of dried herbs, so the portal creations are most likely limited. We need to get that book back and destroy it!"

Aella feels slightly relieved to know that she didn't have a large quantity of the herbs, even though she didn't know how much would be needed to create a portal. Finding Ashlyn and the book is going to add a wedge into things, especially now that she knows the devil himself made the book. If the realms are open entirely, they will be faced with a war of the undead as well, and that is the worst fucking thought to have ever crossed Aella's mind.

"So Damien isn't the only one we need to fear; I mean, in comparison to *Ezra* and whoever the Watcher of Cleopparim is, Damien looks like a saint right now." Aella attempts to add some humor, but she isn't wrong; in fact, they should consider using him as an ally at this point.

Michael flexes his fingers out across the table, tamping down his own emotions and spiraling thoughts when Torin runs back into the gathering room panting.

"I searched everywhere. I ran and flew overhead. Ashlyn is gone, Michael. She's not in Isethas."

There is an uncomfortable silence, a calm before a storm in which everyone braces themselves. Torin slowly steps back from out of the room, preparing to become a target with Michael's fury.

Time moves slowly as even Aella holds her breath for the unknown as to what will happen next.

Then, time picks up speed, and Michael snaps.

Picking up his chair, he throws it overhead at the wall. The contact splinters the wood as if it were nothing more than a toothpick. Pieces ricochet, and Aella ducks under the table so as not to get impaled by the sharp ends or, at the very least, hit, and she is grateful for the couple of training sessions she's had so far with Torin for the quick reflex.

He roars with rage so powerful it could take down the entire room. Michael breaks, shattering into himself with anger. Betrayal and hurt, fear and defeat. Defeat for a battle that hasn't yet surfaced. Defeat for trusting someone with his home and his people, but most of all, betrayal and that hurt trumps all that defeat, and Aella knows that feeling all too well.

When he comes down from his outburst, Aella comes out from under the table with hesitation. Torin remains standing in the doorway in case Michael decides to throw another chair on the off chance that he is the next target, while Cahtel moves his tail in idle circles.

Another moment passes by without a word from anyone as the wheels inside Aella's brain start to move, grinding and clanking away while she tries to think of a plan quickly but comes up with nowhere to start.

Cahtel clears his throat awkwardly then and says, "Mia, Mia of Cleopparim."

This is going to be a long ass night.

Chapter Twenty-Seven

Michael claims Ashlyn's now empty chair, and Torin sits down across from Aella. They must devise a plan to not only find Ashlyn but also get the book back before it falls into the wrong hands of someone else, like Mia.

Cahtel continues where he left off, "Mia of Cleopparim is not much different than Damien in that she too is sinister and hungry for power. We can theoretically assume that Christopher is, in fact, being held in Cleopparim, and Ashlyn may have been the one to create the portal to and from, with the book. The real question I am having a hard time understanding is whether or not he is being held against his will or if he is in this with Mia and Ashlyn. *He cheats his way to the finish line. Christopher plays for both teams.*"

"Could it be that Mia and Christopher were once lovers as well, and he and Ashlyn staged his home, taking the heirloom into Cleopparim like some fucked up trouple situation?" Aella asks, knowing that it probably wasn't the case, and turns her nose up at the gross images that filter in through her mind of her father, Ashlyn, and whoever this Mia chick is, having threesomes.

"As strange as that would be, it isn't completely unrealistic to think that, given what we know about the book and the herbs that Ashlyn had Michael grow," Cahtel states, and Michael shuts his eyes, taking on a huge responsibility for the part he had played in this.

Torin is quiet, his own hurt and confusion taking root not wanting to believe that Ashlyn is capable of such a betrayal to Isethas and their people but also to him. Torin loves Ashlyn with all of his being and finally opens his mouth.

"Ashlyn and Christopher were once lovers, and I fully believe that she still loves him, but above all, they have been the oldest of friends. Perhaps it is Christopher who asked her to create the portal after the book surfaced in the library, and she did so knowing the consequences but also because she would do anything for him. You all saw the guilt and remorse she carried. Maybe Ashlyn is truly an innocent participant in this."

Aella nods slowly, pressing her lips together. She would like to believe that Ashlyn wasn't capable of something so evil even though she lied to everyone for twenty-three years about what she knew. Every action has a reaction, though, and there are consequences no matter what.

"*Some of the most ruthless monsters walk in a falsified light.*" The last conversation Aella had with Damien filters through her thoughts then. Could it be that he was preparing her for this moment? The truth about whom she entrusted, like everyone else at the table, or was she trying to make sense of something that wasn't all that black and white?

The common thread between loss and love: "*Unpredictability.*"

Perhaps Ashlyn and Damien are more alike than not in that they act on impulse before thinking.

"What is it, Aella?" Michael asks, slightly perturbed by how she stares off into space, trying to make more sense of something that could theoretically not have an exact meaning or explanation.

Deciding to move on from what Ashlyn's true motives may entail, they will need to devise a plan on how to find her and get that book back regardless, which most likely means having to go into Cleopparim for the two, along with Christopher and the heirloom.

Aella already knows that Michael isn't going to like that idea, but they don't have another option, so instead, she directs the topic onto what the Third Messenger informed her about her gifts.

Another hard truth that Michael isn't going to like. *Better to get it out now than later.*

"My final question was on how I control my gifts to prevent another war. The answer isn't simple because war is to come," Aella pauses, looking around the room to Cahtel, then Torin, and finally landing firmly on Michael as she swallows back her hesitation before continuing, "The Third Messenger gave me a leg up I guess, for us all, in that no matter how much control I gain over my gifts, war is inevitable, but that does not mean that my gifts are not capable of ending the war... they do not know however, if my gifts will in turn end all of existence."

No matter how uncomfortable Aella is in this moment after telling them the truth about something they want to avoid by controlling her gifts, she continues to make eye contact with Michael, searching for some assurance.

A beat of silence skates by, and it is as though they are coming to accept such an unfortunate reality.

Michael then says what Aella has known to be true her whole life: the only rule she has lived by and applied every time she makes a choice, despite the possible outcome.

"Cause and effect, where every action has a reaction, and with those come consequences whether they be good or bad." Michael pauses for a moment, taking a breath, "War is coming, and many will die no matter how hard we fight. No matter how hard we survive, that is a consequence. Consequences I never wanted to experience again, and I hoped that we would avoid assuming all along that your primary gift could have been suppressed."

He leans back in his chair, and it is clear that Michael is exhausted both mentally and emotionally.

"So what do we do when war comes full circle again? I don't even know how my gifts would be capable of even ending a war, let alone all of existence." Aella says, pulling at the corners of her eyes with how exhausted she is feeling even though she knows she won't be able to rest, at least not fully with everything else now.

Acceptance. Gift. War. Ending of all existence.

"I suppose when we are in the thick of it, you will know. I cannot answer that. Perhaps the reason your grandparents didn't use their gifts in battle is that they knew what would happen," Michael says, leaning his head back against the chair's headrest as he closes his eyes.

Cahtel interjects, giving Aella a little bit of assurance she was looking for after not really getting anything from Michael. She understands, though, especially since this meeting has taken a completely different turn than what was expected and long.

"There is a natural order to things. There has always been and always will be. War is not a part of that process, and yet it happens time and time again. Your gifts, although they may not seem natural or what you refer to as *normal*, are, in a sense, because you were born with them."

Michael opens his eyes, shooting out of his chair in a huff,

"It has been a long day, and we need to eat before we continue. The first order of business is figuring out the heirloom and why it is so significant, along with how we will find Ashlyn and the book. I will have the cook prepare us a meal while Cahtel and Torin head to the library to start looking into any and all artifacts. We will reconvene there."

Everyone nods in agreement. Aella could use a minute to take a quick shower to wash away the Illusion Plane that still clings to her and refresh her mind. After being in the gathering room for as long as they had, she was more than happy to leave.

AFTER A MUCH-NEEDED HOT SHOWER, MICHAEL KNOCKS on the door with a cup of coffee.

"Thought you could use a little caffeine," he says, handing it over to Aella as she happily accepts.

"How are you feeling?" Michael then asks, and Aella quirks a brow, tamping down her sarcasm.

"I feel okay, all things considered. How are you feeling? This is a lot, Michael. We have a lot to figure out."

Michael sighs and sits on the sofa, "This is a mess," shaking his head, he rubs at his temples, something he has been doing a lot lately, "I don't know where to start. I wasnt expecting any of what happened... to be fair, I assumed that Christopher decided to go back to his wife and child after his drunk incident. I did not expect Ashlyn to have been involved, let alone have kept such a damning secret that could have—"

Aella interrupts where his thoughts are headed and says, "Don't do that to yourself. There are countless what-ifs, but they would have ended in the same result. Christopher obviously isn't who he claims to be. He did say he wasnt good, and as far as Ashlyn goes, we will find her and that book. As Cahtel mentioned, she will pay gravely for using it." Aella grimaces at the thought of what that means for her.

"Christopher has always been a bit of a poor sport. When he was younger, he was never any good at games or playing fair with others. He was uncoordinated and always found a way to cheat. I'm not surprised that those traits followed him as he got older." Michael says as Aella tries to imagine what Christopher was like as a child. He most likely didn't have many friends either, which is why he appears to be as charming as he is.

"What's going to happen to Ashlyn?" Aella asks, thinking back to the betrayal and the book. Despite being as angry as she is with her and not trusting her as far as she could throw her, she didn't want something catastrophic to happen to her either.

Aella likes to think that not all of the time spent together and the friendship that had blossomed was fake, *or was it?*

Ashlyn sold her soul to the devil, and not even the fates will have mercy on her.

"I am not sure Aella. Many years ago, a betrayal like the way she betrayed us would have ended in imprisonment or even death. Committing to *Diablerie Memento Goety*, well, that is a whole other imprisonment like Cahtel informed you."

Aella swallows her coffee down in an audible gulp. *Ashlyn is fucked.*

"An explanation from her would be nice. I want to understand why she kept what she knew about me this whole time, not that it will really make much of a difference now..." She sighs, with the warm cup of coffee cupped in her hands.

Michael sets his own cup down and pats the space next to him for her to sit for a moment.

"Shame is such an uncomfortable feeling. I can imagine how it must feel for you and mortals in general, but a mortal's life span is only so long, which is a gift," he says, peering into her eyes, but Aella isn't wholly mortal, and that is something else she will have to figure out. Would she age the same as a mortal does the older she gets? Or will the acceptance of her gifts and learning that she is half Isethanian slow the process down?

"Isethanians can carry shame for centuries if not dealt with and worked through. Perhaps Ashlyn kept what she knew because she was hurt to see Christopher and your mother together, and the answer isn't as malicious as we suspect, but more or less, she was embarrassed by her reaction to it and didn't want any of us to view her differently. That does not, however, excuse her behavior, nor does it justify her betrayal. She betrayed my trust and hurt Torin, whom I care for as much as he annoys me. Worst of all, she hurt you, which is unforgivable no matter how many apologies I may receive."

Aella reaches for him, pulling his lips to hers. Moving their lips together, Michael growls deep in his throat and pulls away momentarily to whisper gently, "If we don't stop this before we start, we will never leave this room."

Distractions, right. Aella chuckles and stands. Michael quirks a brow, need and longing for more of Aella as he regrets saying anything.

"The library awaits Michael." She teases, and he places a hand over his chest as if he's wounded.

Standing, Michael adjusts himself from the arousal that has taken hold. Aella glances down just below his waist and bites her lip from the reaction she got from him. Even if it isn't the best time for it, she is pleased with herself and confident in knowing that he still wants her just as much as she does.

When they enter the library, Torin and Cahtel are looking through books and various folders of papers and photos.

"Find anything?" Aella asks, taking a seat at one of the chairs.

Cahtel lifts his head up from his research and says, "I think so. We had to go through the archives of Christopher's family tree history. There wasn't any mention of a relic; however, looking at these old photographs, I see an item that stands out among several that I had never seen before." He motions for Aella to pick the pictures up. Michael comes over by her side to look them over as well.

"In these photos, there is what appears to be a glass sphere," Cahtel continues, " If my predictions are correct, which gods I hope they are not, then this sphere is actually a crystal ball. We haven't seen one in a very long time. They are used to seek visions into the future."

"Like what gypsies use to tell someone's fortune?" Aella says, thinking how ridiculous it is. People who claim to be psychics in Phoenix used crystal balls at craft fairs. It is all a scheme to get money. She couldn't help but laugh, although she was the only one in the library who found it comical.

Cahtel deadpans her, taking on a more serious tone, "These crystal balls are powerful, Aella. Should this be the heirloom that had been kept hidden, it will show anyone who has it not only our next move, especially in battle, but it will also show them exactly how to win. Not even the Messengers have that kind of knowledge."

Christopher is an unfair opponent. He cheats his way to the finish line. Fuck.

The severity behind Cahtel's statement sinks heavily inside of Aella. If what Cahtel says is true, then that means her father could have known about her before she was a forethought. Her chest feels tight from the thought. Christopher, her father, had the ability to see into the future. His whole family did, which begs another question: what did Elissa see in that crystal ball about the first war and using her gift along with her husbands?

Could it be that the crystal ball showed them what would have happened if they used their gifts on the battlefield?

There is a natural order to things. Or, perhaps, they were meant to die that day, and they accepted their fate.

Acceptance.

Aella knows what needs to be done to get the heirloom back, along with finding Ashlyn and the book, and Michael is going to have a bitch fit over it. She would need to open a portal into Cleopparim, but not having any idea of where it is or what it looks like, she would need some visual description.

"Do you have an old map of the realms? Before the war happened and the portals were sealed?" she asks suddenly, causing Michael to tense next to her.

Cahtel picks up on where her thoughts are headed then and stiffens equally, knowing that Michael isn't going to go for her plan.

"I do. Why?" Michael responds, unnerved.

"I need to go to Cleopparim and find Christopher and the heirloom before it's too late."

The library falls silent right as Louis enters with their dinner. He always has the most impeccable timing.

Chapter Twenty-Eight

"Absolutely not, Aella," Michael responds, and he is firm on this one. Unwilling to let her go due to how dangerous the realm is, the probability of something happening to her is likely. Aella, however, is set on going even if it becomes a fight.

She had assumed that Michael wouldn't go, but with Cahtel and Torin, she would be more than fine.

"I'll take Cahtel and Torin with me." She counters, but Torin shakes his head in objection.

"I'm sorry, Aella. I would rather go to Diatturus, and even then, it would take a lot of persuasion." Torin states, refusing her offer.

"Why? It can't be that bad... worse than the Illusion Plane?" Aella asks, taking a bite of chicken and raising her brow. *Nothing can be worse.*

"Cleopparim isn't what it used to be...what once was a beautiful realm full of lush tropical trees and plants, exotic buildings made of the finest marble and gold is now a desolate land of ruin. After the war, it has been said that Mia segregated her realm into two parts. The less fortunate dwell in the ruins of Cleopparim, while the wealthy live a lavish lifestyle inside the confined walls of her making. Should any of her people defy her, she has her guards execute them publicly by removing their heads while her people are made to watch and forced into disposing of what is left of the bodies. But before she allows them such kindness, a series of torture takes place, resulting in her victims begging and pleading for their deaths." After the little history lesson Cahtel gives, Aella feels a little less brave about entering the realm.

But despite how terrible the place sounds and how quickly they would need to enter to find the heirloom, book, Ashlyn, and Christopher, she knows there is no other option.

With Aella somewhat confident about opening and closing portals now, thanks to Ashlyn and her reflexes that are getting better with Torin's training, a solid plan and a night's sleep are all she needs once her adrenaline kicks in.

"Here is what I think; just hear me out," she says, glancing over at Michael, who wants nothing more to do with this idea, "Christopher and the heirloom are definitely in Cleopparim, and whether you agree to it or not, we need at least the heirloom if nothing else. We can also assume that Ashlyn is there with the book as well, which we also need, and I am confident in maintaining both. I can open and close portals, and Cahtel can teleport us once we are inside the realm. Tomorrow, we will get an earlier start on training. Torin can teach me more defense moves and, hopefully, move on to using a weapon should I need it. Cahtel and I go to Cleopparim, retrieve the heirloom and the book, and close the portal."

Everyone looks at Aella as if she's crazy or, at the least, grown a second head.

"That is a terrible idea, Aella, but you're right. There isn't another option. I'm in." Cahtel says in a flat, even tone, making Aella smile ear to ear.

Even though she was unsure her plan would work and was nervous, danger excited her. She would never tell them that, though.

Michael shakes his head and throws his hands up. "No! What part of no do you two not understand? You have defied my wishes several times now. There has to be another way."

But there isn't, and Michael knows there isn't another way, just like he knows Aella will go into Cleopparim despite his objection.

"This isn't like the Illusion Plane. This is far riskier, and they most likely know you are coming, thanks to the heirloom. This has trap written all over it." Michael says, and Aella thinks about that for a moment. *Well, shit.*

"Okay, yeah, probably. You're probably right, but what if they don't know? I mean, can anyone just use the heirloom, or is there like some secret code to it?"

Cahtel snaps to Torin and says, "Hand me the tome on heirlooms. Aella, you genius!"

Creasing her brows together, everyone grows quiet while Cahtel reads through the passages. After watching him shift his eyes over each line, Cahtel has an epiphany.

"It says here that with any heirloom, only the rightful owner or family member is subject to using them... Christopher, aside from you, Aella, and your relatives before, are the only ones that may see the future unfold in the crystal ball like a—"

Michael cuts him off then and snaps his fingers, "A seer."

"Yes, precisely." Cahtel nods in confirmation.

If that theory is true, then Christopher, at the moment, is the only one who can give Mia insight into what the crystal ball projects.

Aella would like to think that he would do anything and everything to protect her since she is his daughter and not tell Mia what the future holds, but he could very well betray her.

Christopher doesn't owe Aella anything, daughter or not. Entering Cleopparim is a risk, but Aella is willing to take it nonetheless, especially if it buys them more time in the event of the probable war that will soon take place.

"So, Cahtel, you're with me then?" She asks one more time, avoiding Michael, who is right next to her, feeling the anger that is radiating off of his body.

"Since there is no other way, yes, Aella, I am with you," Cahtel says grimly as he waits for Michael to lash out.

Aella, Cahtel, and Torin all wait for him to lash out, but when nothing happens, they all turn to look at him, shocked to see that there isn't another broken chair and his dinner plate remains intact.

"I am not happy about this and want a different solution, but Aella and Cahtel are right; there is no other way," Michael says and looks directly at Torin. "Tomorrow morning, you will train Aella for most of the day and teach her how to protect herself using a weapon of some kind should she need it."

Torin nods slowly, uncomfortable with the command since Aella is far from ready if placed in a situation where she needs to fight.

Even with the two training sessions together, there is still work to be done, and they will essentially be jumping a couple of chapters ahead.

Michael directs his attention to Cahtel, then, "You and Aella are there for two things: the heirloom and the book. Both are potentially in Mia's palace, and she will have her guards surrounding the confines at all times. When you arrive, I don't need to tell you both to be careful and alert. Make this a quick mission, and do not get caught."

After planning their departure for the following day, they collectively agreed on Aella and Cahtel leaving at nightfall as it would be easiest for them to move along the shadows undetected.

Since the eventful day, everyone retired to their rooms, with the exception of Michael, who went to the kitchen to make Aella the suppression tea.

As Aella crawls into bed, Michael enters the room with the tea and a solemn look.

"Thanks," she says as he hands it to her, "I know you do not like this plan, but—"

Michael interjects, moving to the edge of the bed, and Aella shifts over, propping herself up to give Michael room, "I do not like this plan. I abhor it. Everything about this screams at me that it is a terrible idea, Aella. My gut doesn't feel right, yet my heart tells me it has to be done. If anything happens to you..." he trails off.

"Hey, nothing is going to happen to me. You were so worried about me going to the Illusion Plane, and look! I came back in one piece." Aella says, trying to make light of a very intense journey she and Cahtel will embark on in less than twenty-four hours.

Michael narrows his eyes on her and huffs out through his mouth, "This is different, Aella, especially with Torin not going."

Scared little bitch.

"Yeah, really, I'm surprised you're letting him stay back anyway. That's okay, though. I don't need him to protect me; I'm practically a ninja now." She says, wiggling her brows on the last part.

Michael chuckles and shakes his head, "I hope for our sake

that is the case. You do have a gift that will get you back no matter what. Should things take a turn for the worse, Aella, promise me that you and Cahtel will leave even if you do not have the heirloom or the book. Open that portal and get back to us."

Aella takes a sip of the hot tea, burning her tongue with the quick action.

"Can I ask you something?" she deflects, not wanting to make a promise that she doesn't know if she can keep.

"You can ask me anything."

"Do you think that Christopher would work against you and Isethas? This is his birth home, and you are technically family in a way."

Michael furrows his brows thinking about that and says, "I would like to think not. You are his daughter; above all, it would be the most devastating to find out if he is working against you, his own flesh and blood. I suppose we will see the answer to that very soon, though."

Aella nods, sighing out through her nose as she thinks about Tara and her mother.

She knows Susan is still on vacation visiting with her friend Jan and is safe for now, but she isn't so sure about Tara.

"Do you honestly feel, without a shadow of a doubt, that Damien is still just as terrible as he once was?" Aella asks then and immediately wants to take the question back when Michael's features tense.

"I only ask because of what the Messenger told me and because of everything we learned about Ashlyn and the book and *the realm that has long been sealed, even before your time, and forgotten about.* I don't know Michael... something just seems different about Damien and what we assumed his intentions to be. I don't want you to think that I am backing out of my agreement to seal him away in Diatturus, but should things take a turn for the worse, his allegiance might be helpful."

Michael doesn't respond for a time, and Aella decides now is the best time to down the rest of the bitter tea.

"We aren't at that point yet, but should something happen, we will revisit it," Michael says and stands to leave.

Aella reaches for him on impulse, stopping him from walking away.

"Will you stay with me tonight? Just to sleep?" she asks, and his eyes soften. The complex, cold emotions swirling within them from her mention of Damien vanish swiftly.

"Of course, it would be my pleasure."

With that, Michael rounds the bed and slips beside her over the covers, pulling her body into his as she drifts off to rest.

***

THE FOLLOWING MORNING, AELLA AWAKES TO AN EMPTY bed, yet she is surprised to feel well-rested and ready to tackle training with Torin.

Unbothered to make up her bed, she pads off to the bathroom to change into leggings and a tank top, throws her hair back, and heads down to have breakfast with everyone.

When she enters the gathering room, Louis is setting the table with mugs and freshly brewed coffee.

"Good morning, Louis. It looks like I beat everyone down here," Aella says with a cheery voice and a chuckle.

Louis glances up from the table and gives her a warm smile. "Good morning to you, too, Miss Aella. Eggs Benedict is on the menu this morning, with a side of fresh fruit. I hope you're hungry!"

Aella's stomach growls, and her mouth begins to salivate.

She loves a good Eggs Benedict, and since Louis is making it, she could die later, happy knowing that was her last meal.

Taking a seat, she pours herself a cup of coffee and creamer and enjoys the quiet of the gathering room before everyone comes down for breakfast.

The broken chair from yesterday is gone, and no pieces are left behind. She wonders if Michael had cleaned it up or had one of the staff members do it, and she hopes it was him.

Cahtel comes in yawning, sleep still clinging to him, and Aella reaches over to fill his cup with coffee as he grumbles a *thanks,* perching in the chair next to her.

"You're up early," Cahtel states, noting how alert Aella is.

"We have a day ahead of us, Cahtel. It's kind of hard not to be awake with what we are about to do later," she says from behind her mug.

"Don't remind me," Cahtel drawls, licking out of his own mug, "Are you prepared for this?"

Stretching her arms over her head, Aella shakes her head, "Yes. If the worst case happens, we just portal back." She shrugs, and Cahtel rolls his eyes.

"Let's hope that if the worst case happens, you are able to even ground yourself and give over to your subconscious in the split second we would need."

Fuck. Didn't think about that, did you?

Aella waves her hand as if her doing so is just a walk in the park, "Ye' hath little faith, Cahtel. I've got this!"

Rolling his eyes, he mumbles under his breath, "We're doomed," and proceeds to lap up coffee from his mug.

Torin and Michael arrive then and take their seats at the table. They are both tense and quiet until Louis walks through with breakfast.

Aella inhales her food, eager to get to training, and Torin

stares at her in amazement at how much and how fast she finishes her plate.

"So, what are you showing me today?" She asks, diverting everyone's attention from how she just engorged herself.

Torin wipes his mouth with a linen napkin and leans to the side, eyeing her. "Have you ever used a dagger before?"

Her brows creep up her forehead, and her eyes go wide.

Let there be blood.

Chapter Twenty-Nine

Torin takes Aella to a gymnasium that is full of weights, targets, and dummies. Her jaw drops at the size of the room, and she folds her arms over her chest.

"Why are you just now taking me to an actual training center, Torin? I could have done so much by now!"

Torin laughs and says, "You weren't ready for this kind of training yet. The outdoors helps you connect internally and also exercises your mind with grounding. We are jumping ahead, which isn't a terrible thing, but before we begin, let's go through your stance and core work," Torin points to the mat and says, "Stretch out."

Unfolding her arms, Aella rolls her eyes and gets on the mats to stretch her limbs and is pleasantly surprised at how good it feels. She has become slightly more limber, and some desirable pops in her back and neck crack, almost bringing a smile to her face.

"You really don't want to go with Cahtel and me?" Aella asks when Torin joins her in the stretches.

"Nope." He says flatly.

"Why? What are you scared of? You're like a solid tank of muscle; besides, you kind of get off on that kind of shit, don't you?"

Torin shakes his head, twisting his body to stretch out his hamstrings, "I am not scared of anything. The reason for me not wanting to go is personal, and I would much rather keep it to myself."

Aella stops stretching and stares at him. With a sigh of frustration, he also stops stretching and faces her, "Aella, I don't want to talk about it. I am allowed to have my reasons. Just leave it alone."

Ashlyn.

"I think I know why you don't want to go, and I respect that. Torin, you deserve better—"

Holding up a hand to stop her from continuing, Torin says, "Don't. You don't know me, Aella. I love her. If I go, and my worst fears become the truth, I will lose it. Look, let's get to training; you and Cahtel will be fine, I know it. I mean hell, I thought for sure I lost you in the Illusion Plane, and you managed to figure a way out of the changing wood."

Aella cringes briefly at the memory. Referring to that area of the Illusion Plane as *wood* is a far cry from what it really is.

There was no sign of life as far as animals or insects go, except for the shadow that had been following her and mimicking her movements.

"And no, I did not tell Michael about you getting lost. I think that should remain our secret." Torin says, giving her a once-over.

"I think that is for the best, our secret." She nods in agreement. That's one less thing for Michael to flip a lid over.

Standing from the mat, Aella shakes her limbs out, getting into position.

Torin smirks as he says, "Straight to business. We have much to go over, especially when it comes to using a dagger."

"Wouldn't a firearm be more of use?" Aella counters, and Torin refrains from slapping a hand over his face.

"Unless you have a silencer on the thing, it will draw too much attention, and attention is not what you and Cahtel want or need if you are trying to get back unscathed. A dagger will be of aid, especially if someone is trying to tackle you. It gives close access in that one fatal jab to the jugular," Torin points at his neck, "Or the thigh, in this spot where there is a vital artery," he points to the area on his upper thigh, "they will bleed out within in minutes giving you enough time to flee. A firearm is best from a distance, not when you are being taken from behind by surprise."

"Won't the guards have firearms in Cleopparim?" Aella asks, concerned that a dagger wouldn't suffice for that kind of attack.

"They do, however, Mia likes to *interrogate* her prisoners. Guards are prohibited from using them unless her prisoners have escaped, in which case she has already started the interrogation process by means of torture. She likes to have fun with her *guests* first."

Aella wrinkles her nose at the mental images. This Mia chick sounds like a real piece of work and needs to be put on medication.

"Okay, let's review what you already know. Remember to use your core, duck, squat, and move."

Aella does as instructed, and they move through the training she is familiar with for the next few hours.

By the end of it, she is sore and exhausted, and they still have hours left to train.

Handing Aella a glass of water, she takes it greedily and drains the glass.

"Your muscle memory is impressive, which is a relief given that you will enter a beast of a realm. The only critique I have is remembering to engage your core."

Handing Torin the glass back, she stretches out once more, working out her already sore muscles.

She is thankful for the time to do such a task because when she glances over to where Torin is aligning the dummies, she takes notice of the roll of blades and daggers laid out on a table.

Torin picks a kong slender blade from the roll, tossing it into the air, and catches it by the handle when it lands.

Turning in one quick motion, he throws the dagger, and the sharp end hits one of the dummies in the chest with a soft thump, resulting in instant death should it have been a real person with how far the blade is driven through where the heart would be.

"Holy shit! I wanna do that." Aella shouts in disbelief, the aches and pains receding from the excitement of watching Torin throw the blades with effortless ease. Each dummy now has a blade in the center of its chest, a skill that had probably taken Torin a mortal lifetime to master.

"Play your cards right, and maybe I will teach you a trick on how to do it, but you have to promise me you and Cahtel will come back alive." Torin teases, though the weight behind his words is heavy.

Waving Aella over to where the dummies are, he hands her a dagger that is a lot heavier than she expects it to be.

After removing the daggers from the dummies, Torin demonstrates where the most lethal area is and motions for her to jab the blade there.

When Aella does this, the dagger doesn't seem to go through the thick foam of the dummy as she expects, and the thought of doing this to another person and what that would feel like turns her stomach.

Swallowing down the acid that begins to rise, Torin points to his core. It's a reminder that she isn't using it when stabbing the dummy.

"It's a lot harder than I expected," she says, feeling the dagger's blade only have made it a quarter of the way through.

"The material of the dummy is more dense than the neck of the living. You must get a feel for it and strike where it counts." Torin says while removing the dagger.

Walking back over to the roll of blades, he sets it down with respect.

"I'm going to show you how to get out of a situation should someone come behind you and attempt to grab you. This is where those reflexes of yours kick in. The idea would be, in this case, you have a sheathed dagger and can reach for it, turn, and strike once you are out of your opponent's grasp."

Raising a brow, Torin hands her a fake wooden dagger with a soft end. The weight of it is incredibly light in comparison to the other that she just used.

Picking up a garter strap and sheath, Torin motions for her leg and straps it around her upper thigh, tightening the straps, and takes the wooden dagger, sheathing it in.

"This clip over the hilt of the dagger unlatches like so," he demonstrates, unclipping it, "making it easy to access and pull it out when you need to in a hurry."

Aella nods and gives it a try herself a few times over to get a feel for when she would need to access it.

"Okay, let's get back into our stance. We will go through the previous training again head-on. Engage your core the whole time; duck, squat, and move. I will come up from behind you and wrap my arms around the front part of your body. You may feel a slight panic. I want to see how you would get out of this situation."

Aella gets into position, focusing on her footing by staying light and engaging her core. Her hand involuntarily hovers over the sheathed dagger at her upper thigh as she watches Torin, calculating his next move.

He kicks out, and Aella jumps back, avoiding a blow to her chest. He swipes right with his fist, and Aella ducks, missing a hit to her face. Then, without warning, Torin is behind her, wrapping around her shoulders and cutting circulation off from her arms.

That panic he warned her about takes hold as she squirms from his grasp, but there is no give.

"Think, Aella, use your core." He says, and Aella grounds herself even though she struggles to break free from his hold.

Utilizing her core as if it is her only saving grace, she lifts her right foot and kicks back. Torin falters slightly, loosening his grip enough for her to unsheath the wooden dagger.

Grabbing the dagger by the hilt in one solid movement, Aella jabs the dagger onto his upper thigh, spinning out of his grip and jabs it, pointing at his neck.

Torin steps back, clutching his throat as he coughs.

Aella drops the wooden dagger, cringing from her flight or fight instincts that took hold for that split second.

"That— was— good—," Torin manages to get out while inhaling air into his lungs.

"Fuck, sorry! Good thing it wasnt the real deal, right?"

Torin points to the water station, and Aella runs over to pour him a glass of water. Running back to him with water splashing out of the sides, she hands him the glass and begins picking at the skin around her thumb, worried that she may have caused some damage from the amount of force she used.

She didn't think she was that strong. However, put in a situation where you're trapped like that and need to fight for your life, an unmatched strength tends to kick in.

After he finishes downing the water, Torin lets out a

shallow breath, "That was really good, Aella. Even though I'm going to have a couple of nasty bruises."

"So you think I'm prepared?" she asks, and he laughs, getting back into position.

By the end of their training, Aella was drenched in sweat. Torin already had bright pink marks forming on his upper arms, neck, and chest from the fake dagger.

Even though this was the most challenging training so far, utilizing her body and mind as a weapon alongside a physical one, Aella is confident in her self-defense should she need to tap into that.

Before returning to the palace, Torin walks over to the roll of daggers and hands her a small blade with a handle made of silver and moonstone. It is heavier than the wooden practice dagger but lighter than the first she used on the dummy.

A beautiful weapon, yet the end is sharp enough that it threatens to gut her enemies with little effort.

"This was my mother's. She used to carry it everywhere; it was her good luck dagger. Before she passed, she asked me to gift it to someone worthy enough to use it."

"Torin, it's beautiful. I can't accept this. This was your mother's." Aella gasps, her heart squeezing at such a generous offering.

"It's yours now, you earned it. She would have wanted you to have it." Torin says with a soft smile.

Aella throws her arms around him, thanking him for the lethal gift and the training.

Securing the blade inside the sheath, Aella tightens the straps to her upper thigh and smiles at the added protection—a weight she can get used to now, making her feel like a badass.

Michael and Cahtel are in the library when Aella and Torin return to the palace.

Louis has just dropped off coffee and finger foods, which brings another smile to Aella's face.

After all that training, she was starving, and the caffeine, if anything, was necessary.

Michael sits up straight from being hunched over what appears to be a giant map of the realms before the first war took place.

"How was training?" He asks, sounding stressed. Torin smirks and shows him the red marks that will soon become bruises.

"I don't think we have to worry too much about Aella getting out of a situation," Torin teases.

Michael raises a brow and motions to Aella to sit next to him, then slightly regrets the invitation when he gets a whiff of her sweat.

Rolling her eyes, Aella scoffs, "Do I really smell that bad?"

The corners of Michael's lips tip up, "A shower wouldn't hurt."

Ass.

Pouring herself a cup of coffee from the side table, Aella pops a tiny finger sandwich in her mouth and peers down at the map splayed out before them in the center of the room.

She couldn't believe how many realms there are, or were, given that this was before the portals had been sealed, and she wasn't sure how many realms were still intact.

Looking closer, she notices different silver-like dots on the map.

"What are those?" She asks, pointing in between chewing the sandwich.

"Those are where the portals once stood before they were

sealed," Michael states as she looks at the one that used to be open in Isethas.

It is in the same spot where she created the portal, which has most likely taken over her entire apartment by now with its inky black tentacles.

Creasing her brow, Aella says, "That is where I opened the portal to Isethas from my apartment."

"Correct," Cahtel says, and Aella realizes something she couldn't figure out until now.

"I can essentially open a portal anywhere I am standing. Where that portal leads is where the portal once was open before they were sealed..." She trails off and remembers when she thought of Tara and her Mother.

"What is it, Aella? What are you thinking?" Michael asks with concern.

"Your mother makes the most excellent cup of hot matcha."

"I thought I could open a portal *anywhere,* like anywhere I wanted. My mother told me that she was going to stay with her friend Jan... this doesn't make sense."

Cahtel cuts in and says, "You have the ability to open a portal into any realm where there was once a portal before it had been sealed."

"I understand that now, Cahtel. Fuck."

Michael shakes his head, waiting for her to continue; then she explains, "When Ashlyn and I were in the fields, and she had me manifest a portal, all I could think about both times were my mother and Tara. If I can only open a portal into a realm that once had a portal that has been sealed, then that means my mother lied to me and isn't with her friend Jan. I think she and Tara are together in... Diatturus." She swallows thinking about that.

The last time she saw her, her mother was acting strangely. Then, she remembered the photo she had sent her wearing the floppy hat. *Where was the photo taken, though?* Aella didn't spend too much time focusing on the photo since she had just picked Christopher up from the airport.

Michael waves his hand and says, "We can't focus on that right now. Once we get the heirloom and book, we can tackle that—"

Aella cuts him off with frustration, "If Damien does anything to them, Michael, I will take the realms down myself. Mark my words."

Michael's eyes widen at the threat, and he holds his hands up in surrender, "Nothing is going to happen to them, Aella. Nothing."

Her eyes begin to well with tears, "How can you be so sure? Damnit," Aella covers her face with her free hand, "How could I be so fucking stupid."

Cahtel clears his throat nervously and says, "Michael is right, Aella. We have a mission right now to get the heirloom and the book. Can you handle this?"

Wiping her tears away, Aella replaces the frustration and worry with anger and determination.

"Point to me where this bitch Mia lives. When I return, I am going to get my mom and Tara. I'm done with this shit." Aella seethes, and no one is going to argue with her.

Michael points at the map, "Cleopparim is here and is roughly 1,000 kilometers larger than Isethas. The center of Cleopparim is where Mia lives, and here is where the portal will be opened. It would take several hours to reach the center on foot from where the portal will stand. Cahtel will teleport you both to the center and hopefully go unseen by her people." Making a point to emphasize the last part of going unnoticed. Suddenly, the anger Aella had felt a moment ago was replaced by nerves about what could unfold for her and Cahtel, a talking cat.

Aella nods her head now that she has a visual of where Cleopparim is on the map and where the portal will be open.

"Well, I suppose we should get going then. The sooner we can get this over with, the better," Cahtel announces, impatient with his own stress for the journey. Aella begins to tremble, feeling nauseous from the caffeine and the realization she had about where her mother and Tara most likely were being held. She brushes those thoughts away, focusing on the current task.

With nightfall now nearing, Aella downs the rest of her coffee in one gulp, preparing herself for what they would face when they enter Cleopparim.

This isn't like when Cahtel entered her room the first time they spoke in her apartment or when she came to Isethas, nor was this like when she and Torin went to the Illusion Plane to gather information from the Messengers.

What Aella and Cahtel are about to do is terrifying because they are both in the same boat, entering uncharted waters and a territory they are not welcomed into.

Aella and Cahtel will soon become uninvited guests, much like how she had viewed him from the start.

The difference is that they are the prey, waltzing into a cage that contains no bars.

Aella gets to her feet and looks over to Michael, then Torin, and Cahtel, letting out a breath before closing her eyes and grounding herself, feeling the dagger at her thigh for added weight and comfort as she hands over the wheel to her subconscious opening the portal.

Chapter Thirty

Cleopparim is not what Aella had in mind when they exit onto the other side, as she closes the portal so that not a soul can enter.

The air is dry and hot, much like the summer evenings in Phoenix. The desert landscape is desolate, with not a lot to hide behind.

Cahtel and Aella walk a little bit toward a building that is now a crumbled heap of ruin. Looking at the broken pile, Aella imagines what the building may have looked like before the war.

Crouching behind the pillar, Cahtel listens for any signs of life that may be lurking in the shadows. Once he ensures the coast is clear, Cahtel leans into Aella's ear to speak quietly.

"You see those lights off into the distance? That is the center. After we teleport, we must move fast along the walls of the buildings. I will aim at teleporting us in one of the alleyways."

"Wait! Why not just teleport us to the palace?" Aella asks, worried about being seen or caught before getting to the palace.

"Mia will have the parameters guarded. The worst-case scenario would be to teleport and pop up in front of one of them. As long as we move amongst the shadows in the alleyways, we will be fine. Once we know where her guards are located, we teleport into the palace."

Aella nods and then asks, curious about one thing, "How will we know where Christopher is?"

Cahtel waves his paw towards his nose in response.

"Right, okay, I'm ready." Aella swallows down the bile creeping up her throat, hoping that she doesn't get sick from the teleporting.

Wrapping her arms around Cahtel, she shuts her eyes, focusing on her breathing.

When she opens them, she's relieved that she doesn't feel the need to retch and that they are on solid ground.

Pushing their backs against the wall of a building in the alleyway, Aella covers her mouth so as not to make any noises.

Cahtel listens intently for footsteps before they start walking towards the direction of the palace.

When the coast is clear, they continue on as Aella concentrates on softening her own footsteps while they move along the walls and shadows, only stopping when Cahtel hears something.

A small rat jumps out of one of the trash bins, startling Aella, and a gasp flies out of her mouth.

Cahtel quickly turns around and scowls at her from the involuntary noise.

"*Sorry,*" she mouths with a grimace.

Rolling his eyes, they keep going until they reach the end of the alleyway. Cahtel stops abruptly, peering out from the shadows down the street, and quickly backs up a few paces, motioning Aella to mold herself against the wall.

A figure walks by the alleyway then, his footsteps loud and

hard against the gravel. Right as he passes, Aella and Cahtel think the coast is clear until they hear them coming back again.

The figure stops just outside of the entrance and shines his light down the alleyway. Aella's heart begins beating so fast and loud that she thinks whoever is shining the light can hear it.

Pressing the back of her body to the wall with her arms outstretched, she can't get close enough, and the need to become the actual wall is daunting.

Another figure approaches then, and the light clicks off.

"You see anything?" Comes the voice of a man.

"Nah, probably just one of them rats again." The one shining the light says, as he tucks it away, and then says, "Mia informed me that she is having a meeting with Lawrence about what to do with her newest pet. Poor bastard, that's what ya get for trustin' a blonde bitch."

Fuck, these men must be a couple of her guards.

Cahtel turns slightly to look at Aella with wide eyes from what they are overhearing.

"What was the blonde's name again? Ah, right, Ashlyn," the second guard says, scratching at the back of his neck.

"I want nothin' to do with any of that mess. That book she carries is terrible business, I tell ya. I ain't no superstitious, but somethin' 'bout it just don't sit right with me, mate. None of it sits right with me, the book and that crystal ball."

Bingo.

"Oi, what have you then? Another lap and a swift stop at the tavern for a pint?" The second guard asks, and they continue walking on, doing their rounds as their voices and conversation grow quiet.

Cahtel is the first to move back down to peer around the corner to make sure the guards have indeed left, and he waves at Aella to follow.

When they cut across to another alley, Cahtel says, "There

are only a few more streets to climb, and we should be just outside of her palace."

"Did you hear what those guards said, Cahtel? What if..." Aella begins and trails off.

"Yes, I heard. We will be fine. Let's just complete our mission and get back to Isethas." Cahtel says, assuring Aella while assuring himself.

Waiting a few more moments before moving, Aella feels a tickle in her throat from the dry heat that is starting to get to her as they climb further up, weaving in between buildings and alleyways.

Forcing herself not to have the coughing fit that she wants to let out from the heat exhaustion, she thinks about the extremes she would go to for even just a sip of water at this point.

When they near the end of their journey, Cahtel sprints behind a large shrub that is about twenty feet from the front of the palace. Aella does the same and rolls onto her belly to stay hidden.

At least five guards are handling the front, watching for anything that could be deemed suspicious.

Cahtel signals Aella to follow him. She crawls on her hands and knees, keeping low to the ground as they slowly move towards the back of the palace.

Splinters and rocks embed themselves into the palms of her hands and knees, causing her to hiss through her teeth.

Cahtel glances back at her, making a face to stay quiet no matter how much pain she is in.

Once they reach the back, they hide behind a large palm as Aella begins to pull the debris out of her hands. Warm blood coats her palms, and Cahtel looks down to inspect them in the dark.

Not having anything to wrap them in, Cahtel starts licking at her open wounds.

Pulling her hands back in disgust and fear of infection, Aella scowls at him for doing such a thing, especially out in the desert.

"It will stop the bleeding." He says quickly, not having enough time to argue about it.

She hesitantly lays her palms out for Cahtel to finish licking at the wounds. His tongue is rough, making her wounds feel like they are going to be much worse.

After he stops licking, Aella looks down to see they have stopped bleeding in the moonlight.

Cahtel looks around again and says in a low, quiet voice, "Okay, there aren't any guards on the back end yet. They must be on some rotation. It looks like where that window is up top, there is an empty room, or someone is asleep because there aren't any lights on. Either way, we will still need to be quiet."

Cahtel and Aella are both nervous. This is it. They are about to enter one of their enemies' domains, and their only plan is to find the book and heirloom.

Aella looks over to Cahtel and nods her head, ready. Placing his paws on her shoulders, they both take a deep breath as he teleports them inside one of the rooms to Mia's palace.

TO THEIR RELIEF, THE ROOM IS EMPTY AND APPEARS AS though nobody has stayed in it for quite some time due to the layering of dust and cobwebs that decorate the furniture and the fixture hanging overhead.

Taking in the space, Aella discovers that it isn't just any ordinary bedroom but a nursery.

The only furniture that seems to be covered in plastic, preserving its finish, is a crib.

Cahtel gives Aella a stern look that tells her he doesn't want to be in this room any longer from the eeriness of it all as he senses that it is a tomb haunted by someone's dead infant.

Although Aella is equally creeped out, there is a heavy sadness that lingers in the space.

Cahtel presses his ear to the door, listening to make sure no one is walking the hallway on the other side.

Motioning for Aella to open the door quietly, the handle is locked from the inside with no key in sight. That creepy feeling now turns into something much more sinister and dark.

The room they are in is undoubtedly haunted, but not in the way stories are told around a campfire in the middle of the woods. No, this room has been left and forgotten, hiding a dark secret from someone's malicious doing.

At that moment, Aella feels compelled to walk over to the crib. Cahtel attempts to stop her, but she has to see what is underneath the plastic. For all they knew, a copy of the key could be inside the crib, along with whatever else they would soon find.

Carefully pulling the plastic over so that the crinkling doesn't alert anyone, Aella covers her mouth from the horror that is kept inside.

A small tight bundle of blankets and an infant frozen in time lay preserved in a glass casket inside of the crib.

Cahtel's suspicion about what this space may be is correct. Assuming this is more of a tomb than some forgotten room, but whose child was this? And what happened to her?

Seeing such a sight makes Aella's eyes well up with tears for the heartbreak and devastation endured by losing something so precious and innocent. Wiping her tears away, Aella looks around the crib and suddenly spots the key right on top of the casket.

Picking it up, she carefully pulls the plastic back over the crib, cringing from the slightest crinkle.

Aella slides the key into the door's lock, and with the best of luck, it clicks into place. Aella and Cahtel share the same emotion of being more than happy to get out of the room.

Moving quickly like water but remaining light on their toes down the empty hallway, much like they did in the alleyways, they hide behind turns and corners as they wait for guards to pass.

The adrenaline that kicks in for Aella now that they could be subject to a cat-and-mouse game is unmatched by anything else. Remembering that their only objective is for two items, she clears away the images of the frozen infant in the room that will be the cause of many nightmares to come.

Cahtel uses his impeccable sense of smell to follow Christopher's scent. Sniffing the air, he raises his head to point down a massive flight of stairs made of stone.

There would be no creaking, and Aella is happy about that, although should she take a tumble, it would not only hurt but result in some broken bones that neither of them can afford.

By the time they reach the bottom, there is what appears to be a cellar door. Aella gives Cahtel a look that says *something isn't right about this*, and Cahtel agrees, nodding his head for her to open the door anyway.

Pushing the door open quietly, they enter the cellar and are greeted with the stench of damp mold and darkness. The air is thick with despair, a warning to turn back.

As they move on through the darkness with trepidation, Cahtel spots an entryway to a dimly lit hallway. The hallway has sconces that look like something out of medieval times, with cobwebs and damp stone walls from perspiration. Their footsteps echo, a telling sign that they are the only ones down here.

At the end of the hallway stands a heavy door made of iron that is slightly ajar and has light seeping through the cracks from the other side. Halting in their steps, Cahtel peeks through the gap to glimpse as to what is on the other side. A sudden cry for help is unleashed, and Aella and Cahtel realize whoever is being held captive is in the room alone. Pushing the door open, they sneak in hastily.

The room isn't just any ordinary dungeon or cell. This room is a torture chamber.

Aella immediately notes the various surgical tables and trays covered in rusty tools that look as though they have never been sterilized. A choke pear catches her eye, along with various other torture devices she'd learned about in History. In fact, all of the torture devices on display and in the cell alone were commonly used during the Spanish Inquisition, aside from the cabinets that contain modern-day medicine, which turns her stomach at the thought of anyone enduring this kind of pain.

Looking around the space some more, Aella and Cahtel freeze. Chained against the wall, Christopher sits unnaturally, bruised and bloodied.

Chapter Thirty-One

Instinct takes over as Aella runs to Christopher, tugging on the heavy chains his hands are shackled in, embedded in the stone wall. Cahtel urges her to keep it down for fear of being caught, but she is fuming.

Christopher squints through swollen eyes, giving her a soft smile caked in dry blood, "Aella, is that you?" He forces through a thick, dry throat and coughs uncontrollably.

Aella then searches the space for a glass of water, but to her dismay, there isn't one.

Why would someone here show that kind of mercy?

"Yes," Aella responds quietly despite her shaking voice, "We are getting you out of her now," unsure of how they will be able to unchain him.

"Y—you shouldn't be here! She will kill you, Aella. You and Cahtel need to go back to Isethas right now." Christopher demands, fear clawing its way into him. Cahtel also searches the space for some key or utensil that Aella can use to unshackle him.

"What happened to you?" She asks, confusion taking root. She thought he and Ashlyn were in this together.

Christopher shakes his head in defeat and sighs deeply before answering.

"When Torin took me home after the day in the library, I was attacked. There were at least two others when I entered, but they were cloaked in black and their faces hidden. I was knocked out, and when I awoke, I found myself chained in this room. They took something significant that has belonged to our family for generations. The only person who knew about it was Ashlyn. Mia has been torturing me in hopes that I will tell her what I see in the crystal ball, but I have refused to. I could never betray Isethas or you, for that matter. How they gained access to Isethas is a mystery... you need to get back. If Mia gets her hands on you... please go." Christopher struggles to get out what little information he has from the torture he's received from being held captive. They had assumed Christopher was behind this, but the truth is he was just an unfortunate fool used as a pawn to get what Mia wanted.

Fucking Ashlyn, that conniving bitch. Ashlyn better hope that Aella doesn't get her hands on her because she is going to do some damage.

"Hey, I need you to stay with me, okay? We aren't leaving with you. Do you know where they might have the heirloom and the book?"

Christopher is in and out of consciousness from being so brutally tortured and beaten. Shaking him slightly to keep him present, he grunts from the aches and pains the subtle movement causes him.

Furrowing his brows, he says, "The heirloom is being held in Mia's chambers. It is guarded at all times. You won't be able to get in unnoticed. I don't know anything about a book, though."

Aella glances at Cahtel, who shakes his head at her request. It is far too risky, but they didn't have much of a choice.

"Ashlyn used a spell from a book to create a portal from Isethas to Cleopparim. She set all of us up. Do you know where she is?"

Christopher sighs and throws his head back, pushing out a dry laugh, "Of course she did. Ashlyn has always been calculated in her own way. I should have known never to trust her with such a secret. I haven't seen her since we were all in the library."

Beautiful.

"Where are Mia's chambers located?" Aella asks, the heirloom being at the top of her priority list.

"Second floor, third door on the left..." Christopher trails off as his eyes lull shut.

"Cahtel and I will be right back. I promise we are going to get you out of here." Aella assures him while getting to her feet from being crouched down. Cahtel hesitates and paces for a moment.

"Cahtel, we can do this. We have to do this." She says, tamping down her own stress and feelings of defeat.

"If we get caught—"

Aella cuts him off, holding her hand up, "We will not get caught. You're my *Vanilla Ice*, remember? We are a team, and we will get in, find the heirloom, save Christopher, and get home. We won't have time to process how smoothly this will go down."

A sparkle shines in Cahtel's eye, and he says, "Okay. We are in this together, second floor, third door on the left. I think I can teleport us in,"

"Atta boy! Besides, Torin taught me how to go for the jugular. We got this!" Aella adds with some nervous humor. Cahtel places his paw on her arm, and she inhales, hoping that they will get the heirloom unscathed.

Aella and Cahtel appear in what looks like Mia's chambers, and they both let out a sigh of relief because the chamber is empty. Unlike the rooms in Michael's home, the chamber is completely outdated, and it is clear that Mia's taste is extreme.

Everything is covered in gold, giving her space an over-whelming sense of maximalist tackiness, much like the rest of her palace aside from the nursery and the cell in which Christopher currently resides.

Both Cahtel and Aella begin searching the chamber but come up empty. Wherever the heirloom is being kept, it has to be under lock and key and not all that easy to discover.

A chest sits next to the bed. However, when Aella pulls the door to open its contents, it is locked. A frustrated huff leaves her, and the thought of breaking the chest open is short-lived, considering the guards just outside would be alerted.

Everything in this palace worth of value that they need seems to be locked, and she remembers the key in her pocket from the nursery. Knowing it may be a coincidence, it doesn't hurt to try.

When she slides the key into the latch, it gets stuck, and panic takes hold as she tries to pull it out. Doing so knocks a small glass ornament off and shatters it as it hits the stone floor.

Sweat beads at her temple, and Cahtel looks at her franti-cally. They hear the guards just outside shuffle about, and a jangle of keys makes a noise as one slides into the door handle.

Quickly, Cahtel and Aella run to hide in the closet just before them as she quietly pulls the door ajar.

A guard steps in, looking around the space as Aella covers her mouth and nose with her hand. He notices the small class ornament now shattered on the floor and breathes out, "Shit," as he bends down, picking up the broken pieces.

Another guard steps in and asks, "What is it?"

The one picking up the broken pieces responds, "This trinket fell off the chest. Mia is going to be enraged."

"Didn't her mother give her that as a child?" the guard who stepped in after the former asks.

"Yeah, I believe so. Hurry, help me get this mess cleaned up before she gets back. I believe she will be up any minute now."

Both guards clean up the rest of the broken pieces as one hisses out from getting cut.

As they leave the chamber, the key slides into the handle, locking it in place.

Cahtel whispers to Aella, "If Mia is on her way back inside the chamber, she must have the key on her."

"Yeah, Cahtel, that's great and all, but how are we going to not only get the key from her and leave to get Christopher—"

Aella stops whispering as they hear Mia's voice echo just outside. The jangle of keys clanks together again, a telling sign that Mia is about to enter her chambers.

"Thank you, Nolan, that will be all for now," Mia says, sounding sweet and innocent.

Aella peers through the crack of the ajar door in the closet, taking in as much of Mia as she can see. Her long black hair is tied back in a thick braid, and she is dripping with gold from her ears down to her feet. There is so much gold that it could blind someone, a tacky illusion in that she appears to be covered in riches and wealth, unlike the ruins just outside of the center of her city.

Cahtel shoves at Aella so that he can get a look, too, given that his eyesight is a lot sharper.

Pushing down on his shoulders so that they both get a view of what Mia is doing in her chambers, she sighs, sitting on the edge of her bed, rubbing at her delicate wrist and turning her head from side to side as if she is loosening up some tension from the meeting she had prior with whomever Lawrence is.

Her eyesight trails down to the stone floor, and she bends over to pick up a piece of broken glass from the trinket that had been sitting atop the chest next to her bed.

Aella holds her breath as Mia inspects it, holding it up, and glances over to the chest, realizing what had been knocked over and broken.

Shooting up from her bed, tears threaten to break from her eyes as she stomps off over to the door and bangs on it for one of the guards to unlock it.

Clutching the piece of glass in her palm, blood begins to trickle down, dripping onto the floor, but Mia seems utterly unfazed by the self-inflicted pain.

When the door is open, one of the guards glances down, noting the blood that drips from her fist, "Your majesty, is everything alright?" He asks while his tone is nothing more than nerves.

"Nolan," Mia purrs in a sweet, innocent tone, "Can you explain to me why the glass hummingbird my mother gave me is no longer on the chest by my bed?"

Nolan swallows, and sweat forms at his temple, "Apologies, your Majesty. I heard a crash and came in as soon as it happened. I cleaned up everything I could. I didn't want to upset you."

Mia reaches up her bloodied hand and cups his face, the act causing a subtle flinch from Nolan as she smears crimson across his jawline.

"There, there," Mia coos, making Aella and Cahtel equally tense and uncomfortable, hiding in her closet still, "Unfortunately, Nolan, I am upset. You see, that hummingbird was the only thing my mother gave me. The only shred of kindness she ever bothered to bestow on me is now broken. Where are the remains?"

He hesitates momentarily, voice trembling for what will

come of him next, "They are in a box. I did not discard of them yet. I was going to piece it back together."

Mia hands him the small piece of glass that is coated in her blood and says, "Nolan, it will be pieced back together as if it never broke in the first place. Should you fail... well, you will not. Your life depends on it."

"Yes, Your Majesty," Nolan responds, taking the piece of glass from her cut palm.

"Before you leave, I would like to take a bath. I have had a headache of a day," Mia sighs, turning back into her chambers.

"Of course. Would you like lavender added to your bath, your majesty?" Nolan asks as he follows after her.

"Yes, and if you would be so kind as to find my lover, I could use her company," Mia says as she approaches the chest.

Aella and Cahtel remain still, watching Mia remove a long chain with a key attached around her neck. She sets the chain on top of the chest, the key they need to unlock the chest in which the heirloom resides.

Slipping out of her gold satin gown, she discards the fabric as if it is nothing more than one of Aella's ratty old T-shirts. Standing completely exposed and nude, a vulnerable position that would have Aella covering herself for fear of any threat. However, Mia is the threat, and everyone who abides by her rules and follows her orders fears what she is capable of.

Nolan returns from the bathroom, unfazed by her being in the nude. He doesn't so much acknowledge that she is standing before him, her body every man's dream with her voluptuous backside and tiny waist that curves up to the swells of her breasts. Her skin is the color of rich caramel, with not a single imperfection marring her body.

"Is that all your majesty?" Nolan asks, looking straight ahead like a robot as if one look into Mia's dark brown eyes will turn him into stone.

"Yes," Mia drawls, "if you happen to find my lover, tell her that the bath and I are waiting. I want the bird pieced back to perfection by the time I retire for bed."

Nolan gives a curt nod and heads out the door, locking it as it shuts. Mia sighs and heads into the bathroom. Aella and Cahtel wait until they hear the splashing of water to know that she is secure in the tub.

Mia begins to hum a tune to herself while she soaks, giving Aella the perfect opportunity to quietly cut across the room from where the closet is to open the chest and retrieve the heirloom.

Cahtel places a paw on her shoulder to draw her attention to him. He looks at her with a sense of urgency but also worries that they will be caught.

Aella presses her lips together and then moves, adrenaline taking hold.

Quiet as a mouse, she opens the door enough to slide her body through and peers through the bathroom's archway. Aella can make out Mia's long, slender legs, bent inside the tub, as she tiptoes across to the chest.

Holding her breath, she carefully picks the key up and listens to ensure Mia is still humming her tune in the bathtub.

Gently pushing the key into the lock, she waits before turning it, fearing the subtle click will alert Mia. Suddenly, it appears as though Mia holds her breath and dunks her head under the water, and Aella takes that quick moment to turn the key entirely and open the chest.

Inside, wrapped in purple silk, is the heirloom. With unsteady hands, Aella carefully picks the heirloom up securing the silk around it, and cradles it to her body. She can hear Mia coming up for air, the water splashing outside of the bathtub.

Cahtel peers through the ajar door and gives Aella a look of warning to halt before cutting across back inside of the closet. Then, he nods, telling her it's now or never.

With the wrapped heirloom and the key in hand, Aella moves again, tip-toeing back into the closet, bracing herself for the teleportation back into the cell.

They have to be quick, especially when Mia gets out of the bath and realizes the chest is empty.

When Aella and Cahtel are back inside the cell with Christopher, they are relieved to note that no one else is in the cell with them, but that would be short-lived. Setting the heirloom down, Aella runs to Christopher, but her epiphany of making it this far dwindles due to the shackles and the lack of a way of unlocking them.

Frantically looking around again, she wonders if the key that unlocked the chest could possibly fit inside the shackles.

Reaching down for the chain, a shrill scream is the only warning they need to know that Mia has discovered the heirloom is missing. Loud footsteps echo through the upper levels of the palace, much like a stampede.

Aella rushes to slide the key into the locks with unsteady hands, and to her disbelief, it works. Those loud, rushing footsteps sound like they are getting closer to them, flying down the palace's steps, and Cahtel gives Aella a solemn look. They won't make it back to Isethas, not all of them anyway.

Aella senses that Cahtel is forming a plan of his own, and she shakes her head, "No, Cahtel. I won't do this without you. We are all going back. I just need a second to ground myself—"

"We don't have a second, Aella; they are coming. I will run out there and create a distraction so that you and Christopher can get back safely with the heirloom."

Panic overrides her, the shouting growing increasingly louder. This isn't supposed to happen. They were supposed to get the heirloom and the book, which was the plan. Plans change, though, and not everything goes accordingly.

"Cahtel, please. Just shut up, let me think, let me ground myself. I can do this. I can open the portal, and we can get back." Aella feels her emotions taking hold of the adrenaline, fear, panic, and frustration that they are in this situation.

"It's too late. Let me do this. I'm your *Vanilla Ice*, remember? This is the only way you and Christopher can get back to Isethas safely. I will hold the guards off long enough for you to open the portal back to Isethas and close it, but we have to do it now."

Tears start falling down Aella's cheeks. She can't live with herself if something terrible happens to Cahtel, even though he is about to sacrifice himself for her and Christopher.

"One last thing," Cahtel says before running through the flames, "You never cease to amaze me, Aella. Should this be the last time we see each other again, I want to thank you. Thank you for seeing me and being a friend. Thank you for showing me that Television show you love so much, even if I didn't get the opportunity to finish it. You are brave, Aella Clarke, and I have never been more proud of the strong warrior you have become. I don't do well with goodbyes. Do not cry for me; I will be fine. The battle has just begun."

In an instant, Cahtel runs through the cell door through the cellar, diverting the guards from coming through as they chase after him in a cat-and-mouse game.

Aella forces her mind to turn off, which is the hardest thing she has done yet, especially with Cahtel using himself as personal bait. Shutting out the chaos and noise from above, she grounds herself envisioning her orchid, granting access so that her subconscious mind can take over.

Time slows down. The shouting above becomes nothing

more than a buzzing, and the silver swirling wall of a portal is now before Aella and Christopher.

Helping Christopher to his feet, he is too weak and disoriented.

"Come on, Dad, we have to go." She says, urging him. *Dad...* She had never once called him that, but it was enough to get him moving.

Hobbling down the hallway of the portal, they reach the other side into Isethas while Aella carefully carries the heirloom. Torin is standing just outside of the portal with a concerned look on his face when he notices Christopher.

Helping keep Christopher upright, Aella closes the portal, sealing it off the same way she had opened it.

The field in which they are standing in, is the same field where the portal from her apartment remains open. Aella collapses in the grass, panting and sweating from all the adrenaline and stress.

She hates that Cahtel sacrificed himself so that she and Christopher could return without being caught, even if it were the only way. She will come back for her friend and kill anyone who gets in her way; that is a promise.

What Cahtel did was selfless and honorable. He did what he did because he cares about Aella, but most importantly, he did it because he cares for the safety of everyone involved.

Once he gets Christopher settled on the grass, Torin approaches Aella and looks around for Cahtel, noting that he isn't with them.

"Aella? Where is..." Torin trails off, and the tears begin to form in her eyes again, falling down though she has no care to stop them this time. She doesn't have the strength to answer him, but the look she gives him, along with the inaudible tears, is enough.

Rubbing his face, Torin blows out his response, "That fuck. Why did he do it?"

"It was the only way Christopher and I could make it back with the heirloom," Aella responds solemnly.

"And what about him?" Torin gestures to Christopher, who is a battered mess.

"He had nothing to do with this. We need to get him back to the palace and well-rested before the questioning begins. Where is Michael?"

Gentling his tone, Torin says, "He is on his way. I will wait with you before I take Christopher back to the palace."

Aella nods only once, already thinking of a way to rescue Cahtel from the torture he is most likely to be subjected to by now. She is and will get Cahtel back, just like she is, and she will save her mother and Tara and get the stupid book one way or another.

"Is he... Alive?" Torin asks, bracing himself mentally for the answer.

Aella smirks slightly, "You know our Cahtel, he is alive. I am going to get him back, Torin. One way or another, he is coming home, and we will deal with whatever trauma comes with it."

Michael shows up and runs over to Aella, completely missing Christopher. He takes note of the heirloom and looks around the field, finally spotting Christopher on the grass but no Cahtel.

Furrowing his brows, Michael leans down to inspect Aella after seeing the state Christopher is in.

"Are you alright?" He asks, unnerved.

Aella shakes her head because the truth is she isn't alright and won't be alright for a while. But she will be. At some point, Aella will be alright.

Normal.

Chapter Thirty-Two

For a split second after returning to the palace and into her room, Aella felt safe. That feeling recedes and turns into guilt while her friend is a prisoner trapped in a nightmare far worse than what she has experienced, having had sleep paralysis.

Aella knows that Mia won't outright kill him. Torturing him, however, is a given. Mia will use Cahtel as leverage, and knowing that makes Aella sick.

Michael had drawn Aella a hot bath, adding salts and oils to help soothe her nerves and sore muscles, even if it was just for a momentary release.

She hadn't spoken to him since they'd returned to the palace. Aella didn't really know where to start; everything happened so fast that by the time they got there, she was trying to process it all herself.

Helping her out of her clothes, Michael lifts her and sets her gently into the water, tenderly working out the tension in her shoulders. She is in such a haze, mentally fried, and overcome by a new kind of grief that Michael taking care of her in this way doesn't faze her.

"I'll be right back," Michael assures her as he leaves the room. Sitting with her thoughts, another sob breaks through, but this time it's different. The tears she has shed since being here and the outbreaks she has had, though emotionally driven and catastrophic depending on the circumstance, were different.

The sob that leaves her body is a soul-wracking, heart-clenching, you just lost a family pet, kind of sob.

The kind of sob that brings you to your knees as though your heart is slowly dying. The kind of sob that overtakes you, and your lips turn blue because you can't take in any air, and you're completely and utterly helpless.

It's the kind of sob that squeezes you internally, one that no matter how much anyone tries to console you and show any ounce of sympathy for what you are feeling, they simply can't.

Aella feels as though she doesn't deserve this hot bath with the salts and oils or Michael's tender care. Cahtel is in a literal hell, surrounded by pain and suffering. Aella can't imagine what will happen to him now that he is trapped there.

She had endured her own kind of trauma from the time she and Cahtel entered Mia's fortress of masochistic enjoyment to the time she left with her broken father.

The lifeless babe who looked like she was sleeping in a glass casket is something that she will never forget and will most likely keep her up at night, another monster that will haunt her dreams from now until forever.

The torture chamber with the blood-rusted tools used to sever, cut, and do god knows what that were strewn across trays. Or the stench of mold and rotting flesh that she could still smell clinging to her body, forever burned inside of her nostrils, that will never go away.

Everything that she witnessed and experienced in the short trip to Cleopparim and back came crashing down on her. There is nothing that could save her from this trauma. It doesn't matter how many therapy sessions she receives when she has a *normal* life.

The worst part is that she doesn't know how she will be able to mentally face a war that is soon approaching. Cahtel had warned her that there is evil in the world books didn't dare write about, and Mia is just a minor cliff note.

Michael reenters the room with a bottle of wine and two glasses. Noticing Aella's red face and tears, he swiftly removes his own clothes and gets into the water, pulling her body towards him and holding her as he strokes her head while rocking to calm her.

"Talk to me," Michael says, soothing her. Taking a deep breath, Aella pulls away to face him. Michael takes the opportunity to pour her a glass of wine, which she happily accepts, swallowing two gulps before starting.

"That place is horrific, Michael and Cahtel..." She holds back another sob, "He sacrificed himself so that Christopher and I could have a chance to get out."

Aella's bottom lip trembles as she relives those final moments with him. The last look in his eyes, before he ran out into the stampede of guards, carried a sense of longing yet *acceptance.*

"Cahtel is strong. He has endured so much in his life, Aella. We will get him back." Michael consoles her, understanding the fear she feels for Cahtel.

"Christopher wasnt a part of this as we expected. They had him shackled in Mia's torture chamber... the little information he gave me was that someone attacked him, and he blacked out and woke up there." Aella says, proving Christopher's innocence in all of this.

Michael's brows crease, "What of the book?"

Aella shakes her head, "He didn't know about the book, nor had he seen Ashlyn since the day in the library."

Aella wracks her brain, recalling the minor details of the journey.

The first is when the two guards almost caught Cahtel and Aella in the alleyway:

"Poor bastard, that's what ya get for trustin' a blonde bitch."

"None of this sits right with me, the book and that crystal ball."

The second is when Mia is speaking with her guard, Nolan:

"Yes, and if you would be so kind as to find my lover, I could use her company,"

Aella then whispers, *"Some of the most ruthless monsters walk in a falsified light."*

Her eyes shift around, piecing everything together more fully.

"Mia and Ashlyn are lovers," Aella announces, meeting Michael's eyes.

"What?"

"It all makes sense now, first with the guards, then Mia and Nolan. Some of the most ruthless monsters walk in a falsified light! Holy shit, Damien knew something that no one else did. Ashlyn has been planning this for a long time, Michael."

Michael shakes his head, not wanting to believe any of it, but Aella figured it out. Ashlyn has been plotting and planning this since the war and when she learned about Aella's gift. She wanted Aella to suppress her gift as much as everyone else did because it would have caused a hindrance in her plans, but she needed Aella to get Christopher here so that she could get the heirloom and, in doing so, have Michael grow the plants so that, she could use the herbs in conjunction with the book.

The question is, why? Why go through all of that trouble for the items?

Perhaps Ashlyn really didn't want something horrible to happen to Christopher and hoped he would comply. But what is so important that they know what the future holds in the crystal ball?

Michael stands out of the tub abruptly, pulling Aella from cabinets that are open in her mind that are also throwing questions at her like shit at a wall.

"Where are you going?" she asks, not wanting to get out of the warm water just yet, her glass of wine still half full.

"*We* are going to find Torin and see if Christopher is lucid enough to give us more information." He responds, reaching his hand out to help Aella to her feet.

BY THE TIME THEY DRY OFF AND GET DRESSED, THE SKY IS lightening. They hadn't slept a single hour since her return, and it was going to be yet another long ass day. While Louis brings them coffee, Torin meets with Michael and Aella in the gathering room.

It feels much larger and more empty without Cahtel's presence, making Aella mourn even more. Despite being tired and in desperate need of rest, Aella knows there will be plenty more restless nights ahead.

"How is he?" Aella asks Torin after they both take a drink of their coffee.

"In pain but awake. Now is the time to ask questions before the healer comes," Torin responds, waiting for the coffee to set in.

He seems on edge. They all are, but something is different with his demeanor.

"Good. Have you seen anything indicating if Ashlyn is still here in Isethas?" Michael asks, raising a brow. Torin lowers his head, his cheeks taking on a pink hue as he sips his coffee, contemplating how to answer, which makes Aella and Michael equally unnerved.

Torin answers nonchalantly as if it isn't the biggest deal in the world, "I may have run into her after I returned with Christopher."

Michael tenses and grits through his teeth, a small vein in his neck bulging, "What do you mean ran into her?"

Due to Michael's response and sudden shift in the room, Torin clears his throat, finding a common ground in the predicament. "She came by to see if everything was okay. She feels terrible for what happened in the gathering room and wants to apologize."

Aella feels the room darken around her, and she realizes Torin has no idea about the latest news involving Ashlyn. He is still wrapped around her little lying, betraying finger, believing that there is good in her and that all of what happened with the book, heirloom, and Christopher is just one big misunderstanding.

"Where is she?" Aella pushes out with adrenaline as she gets to her feet on shaky legs, her heart sinking into the pit of her stomach with anxiety taking hold.

Torin gives Aella a confused look and says, "What is going on? She's with Christopher. She wanted to stay with him until you—"

Aella screams, taking off into a run out of the gathering room, "NO!"

Michael and Torin take off after her then, but Aella moves fast without thinking. Her heart is racing, beating in her eardrums. The room where Christopher is staying seems too far away.

When Aella reaches the door, she hesitates, entering for what she may find. Her gut warns her, cautioning her to prepare for the worst. Forcing herself to overcome what she will discover, she pushes open the doors, seeing Christopher's lifeless body on the bed.

Running to him, she grabs him by the shoulders, shaking him, but there is no pulse. Her ears begin to ring, and her vision goes fuzzy, blackening around the edges. She doesn't notice Torin and Michael are in the room with her as she collapses onto the floor.

Michael swoops her up as she kicks and writhes in his grip. The walls begin to shake from her agonizing screams, causing the lights overhead to flicker before bursting from the energy that has been expelled from her.

Torin remains standing a few feet away from the bed, unmoving and pale, overtaken by shock. Christopher was alive and lucid less than an hour ago.

Michael spots an empty syringe on the marble floor. Crouching down while still cradling Aella in his arms, he picks it up with one hand and smells the little bit of liquid beading from the needle's tip. The lingering scent of Solanum americanum burns his nostrils.

"You stupid, stupid fool! Do you know what you have done?" Michael shouts at Torin, who remains frozen.

"I don't understand... he was fine a few minutes ago," Torin says on a shaky breath. Flinching as Michael tosses the syringe at him. He catches it but nearly drops it from how badly his hands tremble. Aside from the shock and the disbelief of seeing Christopher dead, Torin is hurt. He loves Ashlyn and doesn't want to think she would do something like this, especially to one of their own.

"The syringe was full of black nightshade. Ashlyn is working with Mia, Torin."

Torin shakes his head, not wanting to believe the accusation.

"No. That's not possible. She would never... she loves Christopher." Torin says, trying to rationalize the absurdity.

"She is Torin. I didn't want to believe it either, but Ashlyn is a betrayal to you, me, and all of Isethas. You should have come to me the moment you saw her. Damnit!"

Looking around the room, Michael notices that the heirloom is missing.

"Where is it?" Michael snaps, searching around for it.

"Where is what?" Torin snaps back, still not wanting to believe any of what Michael told him.

"The heirloom."

Torin purses his lips together, pointing to the empty table at the end. Michael slowly looks over at him, the promise of death and destruction swirling in his eyes.

"All that work Aella did was for nothing. Cahtel sacrificed himself for nothing. You will find her, and you will bring her to me now." Michael spits, carrying Aella out of the room with him.

Aella was in and out of consciousness during the encounter, but when Michael gently laid her on her bed, she found the strength to lift her head up.

Her eyes are swollen and red, a throbbing headache forms behind her left temple, and her voice is hoarse from all the screaming.

Curling into the fetal position as defeat makes its way over her, Michael strokes her shoulder in light waves.

"We will find her, Aella. She will not get away with this." He says, assuring her that there will be a price to pay for murdering her father.

"I don't understand. Torin is right. She did love Christopher... how could she do something like this?" Aella's eyes fill

Samantha Hardy

with tears again, stinging her swollen lids as they escape. She is exhausted. So much grief in the last several days would be considered a lifetime for any *normal* person.

Grief has always been complicated for her, as it is for anyone, but she had gotten so good at making herself numb to most things that should cause her such heartache in life. That was before, however, and this is now.

"She couldn't have gotten far. My guess is that she went to the greenhouse to retrieve more of the plants for herbs. When we have her, I am going to kill her for this," Michael promises. Aella sits up fully then and dries her face.

"No. I want to be the one that ends her life with my hands, but first, we need answers from her, and I know exactly how we will get them."

AFTER GETTING UP FROM THE POSITION SHE HAD BEEN ON the bed for some time, Aella went to the bathroom to splash cold water on her face and used a cold compress over her swollen eyes. The headache that had started to form is now a full-blown migraine, and she desperately needs one of those magic pain relievers to mediate it.

Michael left the room shortly after taking Aella back and went down to the lounge to take the edge off. Torin hadn't returned yet, and Aella was beginning to feel less optimistic about him finding and capturing Ashlyn before she made it back to Cleopparim.

Deciding to leave the confines of her bedroom, Aella heads down the staircase to join Michael in the lounge while they await for Torin.

As she makes her way down, Torin busts through the doors with Ashlyn in his arms, unconscious, the look of guilt etching

392

his features. Quickening her pace but still mindful of not taking a tumble, Aella meets Torin at the end, with Michael rushing over to him from the lounge.

Aella is more amazed that he managed to catch Ashlyn before she went back to Cleopparim, even though it is evident she put up a fight. His timing couldn't have been better despite the fact that he has a busted lip and scratches on his arms. The superficial wounds don't seem to bother him as much as the wounds that he mars internally now.

Torin didn't just love and care for Ashlyn; she was the love of his life, and now she is nothing more than a stranger. The sad reality that he has to live with is knowing that what they had and shared together for many years wasn't real.

Devastation is an agonizing constant that will hold him from now until, well, possibly forever. The trust he bestowed on Ashlyn is gone, much like his heart.

Torin probably wishes Ashlyn had gotten away so that he didn't have to knock her out to face the wrath of the fate she will face within the confines of Michael's palace.

"She won't tell me where she put the heirloom. It wasn't with her when I found her," Torin says as Aella approaches.

"I want to speak with her when she is conscious," Aella states, and Michael snaps his eyes at her but hesitantly nods.

Michael ushers Torin to follow him and glances at Aella, "Wait for us in the lounge."

Aella watches them as they walk away down the hallway until they turn a corner, and she can't get a clear view of them.

Doing as he instructed, Aella carries herself to the lounge, which increasingly makes her migraine throb with every step. When she walks through the doors, she sits down on the chaise, leaning her head back, and pinches the bridge of her nose.

What is taking them so long?

They really haven't been gone all that long, but with the

migraine and impatience to interrogate Ashlyn, Aella needed something to dull the pain quickly. Standing up, she rounds the bar and begins looking through drawers and cabinets, trying to picture what the bottle of pills looked like that Ashlyn had given her.

To her luck, she finds a bottle with no label and hopes that it is the same bottle as the time before. Popping two in her mouth for safe measure, she swallows them dry and decides to pour herself a glass of wine since she is already there. *It's five o'clock somewhere.*

Michael and Torin finally enter then, and the energy in the room is heavy and charged with bitter hatred, primarily oozing from Michael. Torin just looks more like a sad puppy who just got scolded for urinating on the carpet.

"Helping yourself now?" Michael asks in an attempt to lighten the air even though there is nothing light about it.

Aella shrugs, taking a sip, her migraine turning into a more tolerable dull ache.

"I had a headache. Thankfully, I found your pain relievers." She says, coming around the bar to sit back on the chaise.

"Pain relievers?" Michael asks with a frown.

"The bottle in the drawer behind the bar. Ashlyn had given me the same thing the last time I had a headache, and it went away." Aella responds, cringing at the mention of her name, especially with Torin in the room.

Michael sighs and says, "Don't take anything else unless you ask me first."

Aella understands his point and mentally agrees. At this rate, Ashlyn could have easily poisoned her.

"Is she awake?" Aella changes the subject. The sooner she can get this over with, the better.

Michael sits across from her in one of the chairs, "She is, and she is not happy. She is locked in one of my cells in the basement, which is warded against magic of any kind. There is no escaping for her."

Aella focuses on Torin, who is standing in the doorway, still staring off into space. He is tormented and torturing himself even though he has done nothing wrong, and Aella hates this for him.

Ashlyn doesn't deserve the slightest kindness of being locked in a cell. She is in the safest place she can be, and that grates on Aella's nerves more than anything.

Aella drinks the rest of her wine and sets the glass on the bar.

"Take me to her."

Chapter Thirty-Three

L eading Aella down the hall past the library, Michael turns a corner, and before them is a heavy iron door. Unlocking the latch with a key, he pulls it open, and an assortment of stairs cascades into darkness.

Walking down the narrow stairs using the walls on either side as a guide, Michael stops in front of yet another locked door. The accuracy of keeping something or someone locked away is unmatched.

Once inside, a row of locked cells sits empty, except for the one with Ashlyn at the very end. Before Aella approaches that cell, Michael halts her from continuing.

"I will be right outside this door. She cannot harm you or get out of the bars." He says in a low, quiet voice.

Aella isn't scared of Ashlyn; in fact, she isn't really scared of much right now. This encounter is peanuts compared to the trip she and Cahtel took to Isethas and what is to come.

Aella gives Michael a tight-lipped smile, and she heads down the rows of cells. Looking over her shoulder, Michael is on the other side, closing the door with a light click so she can have her moment alone with Ashlyn.

When she gets to her cell, Ashlyn is sitting at the very back on a cement bench, staring through the bars at Aella. Ashlyn's expression is blank, but her eyes are sinister.

Aella has to remind herself that she not only trusted Ashlyn but befriended this murderous traitor. Now that Michael is out of the space, the air suddenly becomes thick and hard to breathe. Sensing Aella's discomfort, Ashlyn smirks, tilting her head to the side in a serpentine way, appearing less human and more sadistic.

"Oh, Aella," Ashlyn purrs, then clucks her tongue, eyeing her up and down, "You have caused quite the commotion with your little visit to Cleopparim. Mia is not pleased and completely distraught to find that her little toy has gone missing. I was so hoping that I would have been able to give her the good news that it was taken care of, but here I am."

Ashlyn twirls her golden strands between her fingers, taunting Aella with the intentional jab of killing Christopher, but Aella doesn't so much as tick.

"You know," Ashlyn continues, "Christopher could be such an idiot. You should be grateful that he's gone since he never knew you existed. Actually, you should be thanking me, really."

Anger consumes Aella, making it hard for her to tamp down her emotions. This is what Ashlyn wants; she finds amusement in Aella's hurt and feels empowered for taking someone away from her.

Aella's blood boils, but she will not give in to the reaction that Ashlyn seeks from her.

Collecting herself, Aella stares through the bars at Ashlyn, void of emotion.

"Why did you do this?"

Ashlyn stands up and walks around the square she is being

held inside, gliding her delicate fingers over the bars without bothering to answer.

"Hmmm, that is an excellent question, Aella, one that I have many answers to," Ashlyn starts, then sighs, "But you see, the thing is, I'm not really feeling like answering any questions right now. Maybe come back later?" She giggles, continuing her slow walk around the enclosed space.

At that moment, Aella reaches in through the bars, grabs the back of Ashlyn's head, and pulls her hair tight through the bars. The force behind her grip causes a yelp to escape, and her eyes water from the chunks that are ripped out. Ashlyn claws at Aella's arm, breaking skin, but Aella won't let go.

Ashlyn screams, panicked as golden waves fall to the floor, "You stupid bitch! I'm going to—"

Aella cuts in, gritting through her teeth, "Going to what, *Ash*? Kill me? As far as I'm concerned, you're already dead. So, I suggest you answer my question. Otherwise, it will be a *very* long, torturous ending for you." *Liar.* Aella swallows down the bluff despite how calm and sure of herself she sounded. The truth is she didn't know how to torture anyone, nor did she think she had it in her to so much as cut off a toe.

Releasing her grip, Aella drops the clumps of hair that are spotted in blood, and the acidic taste of bile stings her throat. She is surprised at how hard she pulled Ashlyn's hair out, along with the look of horror on Ashlyn's face as she backs away to the far corner of the cell, her eyes wide from the threat.

Aella maintains her steely, cold exterior, staring Ashlyn down, hiding her disgust over what she did just by pulling her hair out.

"What do you want to know?" Ashlyn asks, shaking as she clutches at the bald spots on the back of her head. The queasiness washes away from Aella, turning into satisfaction from the distress Ashlyn appears to be in now, especially since she looks like the Cynthia doll from *Rugrats*.

"Perhaps I didn't make myself clear the first time I asked," Aella states, "That's okay. I'll repeat the question: Why. Did. You. Do. This? Was that simple enough for you?"

Ashlyn glares at Aella and folds her arms across her chest.

"I did love Christopher," she begins, looking down at her feet, "That much is true. Killing him, however, was necessary to guarantee my role. He was dead weight. Mia and I had a thing when Christopher and I were together. We had an... open engagement so long as we returned to each other. After the war, Christopher decided to end things with me. I didn't take that lightly for obvious reasons; rejection is still rejection. When the realms were sealed, that was it. No more Christopher and no more Mia."

Ashlyn pauses, thinking back to that time, and a tear falls down her face, but she quickly swipes it away.

Ashlyn smirks and says, "Mia had a lover too, with whom you are quite familiar with. It's funny how things come full circle. Anyway, she got pregnant with his child. Unfortunately, the father kept that a secret because he did not love her or want anything to do with their child. When Mia gave birth to her daughter Cleo, she was heartbroken, and well, postpartum is a bitch. She couldn't handle the cries of her daughter, so she did what any *loving* mother would do and tried to get her to stop crying. When she realized what she had done, she had her preserved in a glass casket so baby Cleo could sleep forever. Frankly, I don't care much for the corpse, but keeping her safe and sound locked away makes Mia happy. Everyone grieves, Aella. You are not the only one, my dear."

Aella feels sick. Ashlyn is sick and demented, and Aella would be lying if she admitted that she wasnt curious to know who the father of Mia's child was or her former lover. But she also knows that Ashlyn is diverting the topic, leaving little breadcrumbs without giving her solid answers.

Ashlyn quirks a brow, noticing the subtle crack in Aella's expressionless exterior from the way Aella's brows crease together momentarily while she tries to piece everything together.

"Ah, right, you don't know..." Ashlyn pouts, batting her eyelashes, "Well, it doesn't really matter now; that was long ago. Anywho, nothing is ever really as it seems, *sweet*, Aella. That poor excuse of a man couldn't face the consequences of his actions then and still can't. Besides, we were in the middle of a war when it all happened, and things got... messy—complicated, really. I suppose the only thing you and I have in common is going for those who are *emotionally* unavailable."

Aella has had enough of Ashlyn's taunts and games despite her now wanting to figure out who the father is and how they could ever sleep with Mia. Aside from her irresistible exterior, she is a textbook psychopath.

"Why do any of this? Why betray Michael and Torin? They cared for you; I cared for you and trusted you. You had a family, Ashlyn, a damn good one." Aella says, unable to make sense of any of this. For someone to throw away all of this over petty rejection is unimaginable.

Ashlyn throws her head back and laughs, mocking Aella, "You know nothing, girl, absolutely *nothing*. The question you should be asking yourself is why Michael didn't come with you and Cahtel into Cleopparim. I'm sure he was steadfast in not wanting you to go, but did he even offer to go along, or did he stay back like the coward he is?"

Fuck, she has a point. Why didn't he come? Aella's face goes slack thinking about that.

"And there it is. Food for thought," Ashlyn says, adjusting her shoulders. "The why is simple, Aella: Power just tastes so much sweeter than love and admiration. Torin was easy, and pleasure is still pleasure no matter who you receive it from. I had my fun, and soon, we will all get what we deserve."

Aella shakes her head, "You're disgusting, you know that? I can't wait to watch the light go out from your eyes for what you have done. Where is the book and the heirloom, Ashlyn?"

Ashlyn chuckles at the threat, knowing it is another lie, and shrugs her shoulders. "One is hidden, and the other, a gift." She yawns, bored by the conversation.

Aella balls her hands into fists at her sides. Frustration is an understatement. She wants to rip her own hair out because of Ashlyn's inability to give a straight answer. Ashlyn has nothing to lose, but then again, she has nothing to gain. Her soul is already marked from using *Diablerie Memento Goety,* and then something occurs to Aella.

"Aside from your betrayal, you could have very easily convinced me to open a portal to Cleopparim; why go through all the trouble to have Michael grow the plants you needed to create herbs in conjunction with using the manifestation spell from *Diablerie Memento Goety?*"

Ashlyn leans back, eying Aella, and a slow, serpentine smile forms on her lips, "You honestly believe I went through all of that trouble just to get into Cleopparim? Oh Aella... you see, the thing that not even Mia is aware of is he, the one and only, has awoken, and soon the realm that has long been sealed and forgotten will fully open, all thanks to you."

Aella unclenches her fists, "What are you talking about?"

"I had been searching for that book a *very,* very long time. You can only imagine my pleasant surprise when it just so happened to have fallen into your lap. A part of me envies you for it. *Diablerie Memento Goety,* written and created by evil incarnate from his very own blood. Everyone thought it was destroyed during the war, but the book is indestructible. I could not find it because it didn't want me, but you, it very much wanted you, like a *magnet*."

An uncomfortable chill falls over Aella, goosebumps rising on her arms.

"What do you mean it wanted me?"

"The war that is to come will be unlike any other. There is already a crack in the seal, and soon, his army of the undead will filter through, raining hellfire and destroying the realms to where there is nothing but ash consuming the souls of every living creature to have walked..."

Ashlyn trails off, enjoying this moment, "It was my lucky day when I had the book in my hands and was able to give myself to him, an agreement so that when all is forgotten and time is recycled, I will be unstoppable. Finally, I am getting to become what I have always dreamed of, what I have always wanted: a God. My sweet Mia thinks that the book and the heirloom are a pair; she seeks power as much as any of the other Watchers, including Michael, in his own cynical way. I needed a place where I could communicate and perform rituals with the book that would, in turn, get me closer to *Ezra*, but then you and Cahtel had to ruin it. I will admit that perhaps my ending Christopher's life was a bit impulsive, but I was frustrated. Oh well, now neither of us can access the book, and the heirloom is gone forever."

Aella's brows rise slightly. Ashlyn just revealed which of the two items is hidden, even though she doesn't want to use the book herself.

"Michael so desperately wanted to suppress your gift in opening portals because he wanted to prevent another war. Little does he know, the other Watchers are the least of his concerns when *Ezra* comes through to take over. That little portal of yours that remains open is just a tiny glimpse. He wants you, and he will do everything in his power to take you with him."

Aella knows she is turning white from Ashlyn's confession, "Why me?"

We are fucked, we are all fucked.

"Because you are the key, the only one who will unlock the door and help end all of existence."

"Your gifts will end the war. However, I cannot answer if such gifts will, in fact, end all existence..."

Mother Fuck.

AELLA LEFT THE WOLF IN SHEEP'S CLOTHING AFTER SHE had received the newest piece of information and didn't tell Michael anything about it as they climbed up the stairs.

Torin had waited for them at the top of the steps and appeared anxious about what Ashlyn had shared with Aella, even though the same look of sadness and hurt at the truth of what she had proved herself to be was still there.

There were so many things tugging and pulling inside Aella's brain now. The war to come isn't just between the other realms and Watchers; no, it will be catastrophic. Aella swallows down her panic, thinking about how she could have cracked the seal to the realm that had been closed forever.

"Tap into your gifts, at the very least, become acquainted with them. You will need them for what will unfold." The Messenger's suggestion filters out of one of the open filing cabinets. They were warning her in preparation for the real battle ahead.

Then, she thinks about when one of those things crawled over her body, speaking to her in some otherwordly language. Was that when she cracked the seal? While she was having an episode of sleep paralysis, the very one that sent her to the hospital to be *cured?*

And the portal that remains open from Isethas to her apartment that has decaying tentacles suffocating it.

"That little portal of yours that remains open is just a tiny glimpse."

Is that what everything will look like when the realm that has been sealed and forgotten about is fully open? A black void of death and decay, with demonic beings feeding off of the souls of every living being to walk from Isethas to the mortal realm and the realms in between?

Aella realizes that Torin and Michael are staring at her to tell them what she gathered from Ashlyn. She can't help but pity Torin. All he was was a toy for Ashlyn, and she used him for her own selfish pleasure. But when he hears what Aella just learned in the basement, hopefully, he will have a different perspective.

"Ashlyn and Mia are lovers," *there, rip it off like a bandaid.* Aella looks at Torin, catching the subtle flinch from her words, then looks to Michael, "That's not all... The war to come will not be between the other Watchers, and I don't think Ashlyn is lying about it either since she has nothing to lose," Aella takes a deep breath, her hands shaking from the terror that will be unleashed the more the crack in the seal fissures.

Michael and Torin both stare with unease, and so she continues, "*Ezra* has awoken, and there is a crack in the seal to the realm that has long been sealed since before your time and forgotten about."

Michael shakes his head and begins pacing, "This can't be true. How would Ashlyn know about Thazian becoming unsealed?"

So that's the realm that has been sealed and forgotten about.

Aella cuts in, "Because it was me. I left a crack open in the seal at some point when I was having what I thought was an episode when one of the succubi came through into my room. This war that is to come is more significant than any of us. This won't be like the one you all experienced prior. Ashlyn read from *Diablerie Memento Goety* primarily so that she could make a deal with *Ezra*. She wants unmatched power and to be a God."

Michael stops mid-pace, and his features go slack. "Why would she do that? She knows what will come of her..."

Aella shrugs, "Ashlyn is a monster, perhaps—"

Torin hits the wall behind him with a fist and shouts, "Don't call her that! I love her! There has to be some explanation. How could she?"

His bottom lip quivers, the heartache too much for him to bear, thinking about how the one he loves could be so selfish in not only putting other lives at risk but her own.

Watching him cry is heartbreaking. You can feel the desperation and sadness, like hands grasping at thin air to keep him from falling off the edge of a cliff.

Aella softens her tone and says, "I'm sorry, Torin. If you need closure, now is the time to do it—"

"No. I don't want to see her again. Just kill her and get it over with." Torin sniffles and walks away, leaving Michael and Aella. He needed space and time to clear his mind, and neither Aella nor Michael would keep him from doing so.

Ashlyn's death is definite, whether it be at the hands of Aella or someone else, but her soul belongs to *Ezra* now. Either way, Aella will enjoy every second of her ending, with Torin's emotions adding fuel to the fire.

Chapter Thirty-Four

By the time Aella and Michael have Louis prepare some food for them, nightfall is nearing. They end up back in the library to do some research on the realm that had been sealed before Michael's time, Thazian. Aella finally learns the name for it, and it isn't *Hell*, which makes it sound less daunting despite having seen one of the demonic creatures firsthand.

With the bit of new knowledge about the war they will be facing, having allies is going to be a necessity, and the first person that comes to mind is one that Aella already knows Michael doesn't want to entertain, even if blood does run thicker than water.

She hasn't forgotten that Damien still has her best friend and mother, but something tells her that maybe Damien really isn't the one they should have feared all along. Ashlyn had her own agenda. She used everyone who was closest to her in order to get what she wanted.

They will also need to formulate a rescue mission for Cahtel, and fast. Mia, being an ally, is out of the question, along with her people. She's just as batshit crazy as her current lover, Ashlyn, and is probably doing the most unthinkable things to Cahtel over her not being in Cleopparim.

Who could Ashlyn have given the heirloom to? Where is the book? How do I close that damn portal? Who is Cleo's father? Is it Michael? No... no fucking way he would have impregnated her. Or did he? He didn't offer to go to Cleopparim with Cahtel and me. Is Cahtel being fed? How do I become friends with my gifts? Thanks a lot, Messengers. You really helped us out here, bastards.

Question after question overrides Aella's brain, jumping around from one thing to the next until Michael pulls out a dusty old text about Thazian.

Of course, it's in a language that Aella doesn't understand, written in different symbols, so she just sits back, giving herself a self-inflicted headache from everything. She's surprisingly calm after the conversation with Ashlyn, if you would even call it that, and she is realizing that her shot at having a *normal* life will most likely never happen, given the probable end to all existence.

"Did you know that Mia had a lover before Ashlyn?" Aella asks Michael, who is fully invested in the text. He stalls for a moment, glancing up from the pages and readjusts, clearing his throat.

"I was unaware, but that doesn't surprise me. Many beings from different realms have other lovers just like mortals do."

Aella notes the quick change in his tone, and her earlier assumption makes her blood run cold.

She swallows loudly, thinking about whether or not she should tell him about the child. If he is the father, then her moral view of Michael will change forever. Would it really matter at this point, though? Especially with more significant issues at large?

Fuck it.

"Whomever her former lover was, impregnated her with a daughter. Cahtel and I had the unfortunate introduction when we entered the palace."

Michael's expression turns grim, but his eyes remain on the text reading along.

"A daughter? What did she say to you? If that's the case, she has to be around your age in mortal years." He says in a calm, even tone.

Interesting... Aella never mentioned when Mia would have been impregnated. Michael has secrets of his own, and this one is one he doesn't want to divulge.

Aella's body language changes, but her tone remains flat and even, pretending that she hasn't just figured it out.

"No, she didn't say anything. We snuck in while she was asleep, thankfully, and made our way out." Aella lies. For some reason, she feels as if Michael doesn't need to know the horrors they witnessed, and a part of her feels as if he doesn't deserve to know either.

Aella also changes her objective by changing the subject. What is done is done, and moving forward, they will all need to work together to gain allies. Mia and his past lovers don't have any bearing on this, *or do they?*

"So, I think we need to plan our next move on forming allies," Aella states, noting that his shoulders relax slightly as he reads.

"I agree with that. What about the heirloom and the book? You didn't mention those two after you spoke to Ashlyn."

"Oh right, the heirloom was given away, I guess, and the book is hidden. Honestly, it's probably best that it stays that way for now, right?" Aella says, biting the hangnail off of her thumb.

Michael looks up from the text and sighs, "What do you mean *given* away? We need to find that heirloom!"

Aella straightens her back, dropping her hand from her face, "I understand that, Michael; trust me, I do. But we have a lot of new shit on our plates now. If you can pry it out of her, be my guest. No one can use it that isn't a part of my lineage anyway, so unless you know of any others I may be related to, that heirloom is nothing more than a decoration in somebody's home."

Closing his eyes, Michael pinches the bridge of his nose. The shitstorm that is anything and everything now is almost comical.

"I think we need to contact and work with Damien. We can go through the portal back to my apartment, and I can call him. We need allies, Michael. And whether you want to accept it, he is still your brother. You thought Damien was the threat, and maybe he still is one, but if—"

Michael interrupts her, clenching his jaw, "No. You and I have a deal, remember?"

Aella rolls her eyes and refrains from clenching her own jaw, "The *deal* won't matter when *Ezra* and his army of the undead break through Michael! There will be no more Isethas or Cleopparim. There will be no more mortal realm or fuck, my shot to having that *normal* life I dreamed of. Everything you have worked for since the first war and rebuilt, along with everything we have worked on since I came here, will be for nothing if we cannot play nice with each other and prepare for this battle. I'm supposed to be figuring out my gifts and how to end the war without contributing to *Ezra's* plan of wiping out all of existence! We need to get Cahtel back, and I would, at least for the sake of knowing I was able to, one last time if shit goes bad like it's projected to, hug my mom and my best friend. I just lost my father at the hands of someone you knew longer than I have been alive. So, yeah, Damien isn't looking too bad as an ally right now."

Michael sits tense and still across from her. As much as he wants to object, he can't argue with any of what she's said. Michael hadn't seen or spoken to his brother in centuries since the first war and didn't want their first reunion to be under these circumstances. However, they didn't have a lot of options or really any other at this point.

Michael takes a couple of deep breaths, contemplating her proposal before giving his final answer.

"I don't love this idea, and the history between you two still makes me angry," he states. Aella shifts a little with discomfort, given he has no right or reason to, especially with the theory she has formed in her mind about him being Mia's ex-lover and the father to her unalive child. "But, you are right. We need allies, and he is my brother. The Messengers didn't give a direct answer as to what his plans are, so it's safe to say he doesn't really have any concrete plans. This doesn't change our deal in the end should we win this next war."

"So, we are in agreement, then? We contact Damien and work together," Aella asks, making sure she is hearing Michael correctly.

"We are for now. This is not a vacation for him, nor is it a homecoming. We still need to be cautious. Damien can flip a switch just as easily as tying a shoelace." Michael warns.

The apple doesn't fall too far from the tree.

Chills take over Aella as she thinks about going back through the portal of decay. It seems like so long ago, with every event that has transpired since Aella was last in her apartment with Cahtel before she picked Christopher up from the airport.

Shit. Fucking shit fuck fuck.

"Christopher's wife and child... I completely forgot about

them." Aella says in a whisper. Her heart sinks a little in the pit of her stomach.

Everyone in the mortal realm is just going about their daily lives, completely unaware that there are other realms and that the gates of hell will soon open, raining fire on everything in their path.

Aella knew that Christopher would eventually leave as Cindy aged and their son got older, but the guilt she feels about this is heavy. She has probably been calling and texting him nonstop since he left, leaving her in the dark about his *business* trip.

Christopher will not return home, and Cindy will be left alone as a single mother and confused about what happened to her husband. Perhaps it is better that it happened now than later.

Michael's eyes soften as he takes in Aella's internal conflict, "People leave Aella. Your whole life, you believed your father left and wanted nothing to do with you. Christopher's wife will be hurt and angry for a long time, but she will find another. Perhaps this is what was meant to happen. The pain of losing someone you love by them being taken from you and dying is sometimes worse than thinking they chose to leave. I know that sounds harsh, but letting her believe that he abandoned them, as selfish as that may be, is a mercy."

A mercy.

Aella presses her lips together and nods solemnly. Michael knows both well, considering he has lost the ones he loved on the one hand and, on the other, has chosen to leave.

Michael and Aella decide to call it a night, and he agrees to go with her through the portal to her apartment to contact Damien as long as he is in the mortal realm in the morning.

Even though they are both exhausted, Michael doesn't forget to make her the suppression tea and sends it up with her to her room, letting her know that he will be up in a while after he finishes his reading on Thazian.

When she gets into bed, she drinks the tea without a single gag and passes out within seconds, her mind and body shutting off entirely to nothing.

Morning comes too soon. Every ache from her head down to her toes is inflamed. Her feet are swollen from insufficient water, and Aella feels a kink in her neck from sleeping on it wrong.

She is groggy and grumpy and needs three of those pain relievers on top of a triple shot of espresso.

Grumbling as she gets out of bed, Aella trudges into the bathroom to take a quick shower in hopes it will wake her up. Feeling the way she does is the first time she has felt since before she came to stay in Isethas.

What the fuck?

Even with the training she had done with Torin and the prior events, she never felt this bad in the morning. Chalking it up to lack of sleep since she returned from Cleopparim, Aella tries not to give it any more attention than she needs to right now.

When she is dressed and ready to go to the portal with Michael, Aella heads down to the gathering room. The smell of roasted beans eases some of the tension in her neck.

Michael is sitting at the table with a cup of coffee when she enters, engulfed in the same text from the night before.

"Did you even sleep?" She asks, sliding into one of the chairs.

Michael grumbles his response, and Aella considers that to be enough of an answer.

Busting into the room, Torin stumbles as he claims a chair reeking of a brothel. His appearance is evident in that he did what most men would do to get over someone: he got under several.

"For fuck's sake Torin. Pull yourself together; you reek of the seven seas." Michael scowls with disgust. Aella holds back a laugh that quickly dies when Torin glares at Michael in response.

"Yeah? Well, good. I feel much better, thank you very much." Torin responds, reaching for a cup to pour coffee from the French press.

Michael huffs out and rolls his eyes. Everyone is in a foul mood this morning.

Aella leans back, rubbing at her neck to work out the kink that lingers, and sips her coffee.

"Have you learned anything about Thazian?" Aella asks Michael. Michael appears flustered, flipping through pages as he searches for some sort of answer that isn't there.

"Not yet," he snips his aggressive page-turning sounds as if he is going to tear one of them at any moment. "Torin, after you shower, you are to escort Aella to the portal and go with her to her apartment. I have far too much work to do."

Troin scoffs at the order, "Maybe I, too, have some work to do, *Michael.*"

Michael looks up from the pages, his eyes bloodshot, another confirmation that he did not get so much as an hour's worth of sleep and most likely drank alcohol into the early morning.

"I was not asking, *Torin*," Michael grits out, "This is an order, and you will do as I say."

Torin leans back in his chair, staring Michael down, thinking of a way to combat him.

Aella looks between the two of them, sensing a brawl that

could take place at any moment, and says, "I will just go by myself. It's not a big deal; I can handle it—"

Michael cuts in, "No. You will not go alone. Torin is going with you, and he is *delighted* to be doing so, aren't you?"

Torin stands out of his chair abruptly and gives Michael a tight-lipped smile, not saying anything as he storms out of the gathering room to wash off last night's rendezvous.

Aella's stomach growls loudly in the now silent space. Her cheeks flush from embarrassment, but Michael doesn't seem to notice. He didn't mention anything about Louis bringing in breakfast, and all she could smell was the coffee, an indication that he would not be cooking this morning.

"Is Louis making breakfast?" Aella asks timidly. She's starving, and with her and Torin going in through the portal, food is necessary.

"I gave him the morning off. Help yourself to the kitchen." Michael responds in between reading a passage.

Scooting out of the chair, Aella heads into the kitchen to scrounge something to eat since there isn't enough time to cook some eggs.

After rummaging through the cupboards and refrigerator, she settles for a banana and granola, just enough to hold her over.

Torin is back in the gathering room, waiting for her return with an unhappy look on his face.

She's not excited to be entering the portal of rot and decay herself, but having a curmudgeon tag along with her doesn't improve the situation.

"Ready?" Torin asks in an irate tone.

"Yep! Oh wait, let me go grab my cell phone so I can call Damien. I'll be down in two seconds," Aella says, rushing out of the gathering room and back up the stairs.

Torin halts her and scowls at Michael, "What the fuck does she mean *call* Damien?"

Michael glances up from the book once more, annoyed to be interrupted by his research, "Had you not gone on an all-night bender with the ladies of the night, you would know. Aella can catch you up to speed."

"Nope. This is bull shit Michael. You cannot be serious!"

Michael slams his fists on the table and stands, narrowing his eyes at Torin, clenching his jaw to the point of cracking a tooth, "I don't like this any more than you do. We need allies, and Damien is a start. Soon, Thazian will be open, and *Ezra*, along with his army of death, will rain down. This is far worse than what we could have ever imagined. You will stop with your self-pity now and focus!"

Torin stays planted, and Aella isn't sure if she should continue up the stairs to get her phone or step in between them during a fight that is undoubtedly about to happen.

But, to her surprise, Torin turns and mumbles that he will wait for her outside, so she continues up the stairs in a hurry in case he changes his mind and goes on another bender.

When they land just outside of the portal of death and decay from Torin flying them over, Aella attempts to halt Torin from entering.

"Hey! I get it, you're hurting, and this situation is shit on top of shit, but Michael is right, Torin. You think that I am enjoying any of this, too? I trusted Ashlyn, and despite whether or not you want to believe that she is innocent, she's not," Aella says as she tries to keep up with his pace, but he keeps going until she yells, "She killed my father! She killed him, Torin. Is that not enough for you to see?"

Torin turns to face her, tears filling his eyes again, "I don't understand..."

Aella begins to get emotional then and runs to Torin, embracing him in her arms as they mourn together.

"I don't either, but we are a team. We are a family, and we are going to figure this shit out together, okay?"

Torin nods and wipes his own tears away.

"Now, we both need to soldier up. This portal is a fucking disaster," Aella states with a laugh that escapes from her.

THE PORTAL IS A BLACK HOLE. AFTER THEY WALKED through the opening, Torin had halted Aella from pressing forward. There is no hallway, nor is there any indication that there were any wall sconces that had once cast a soft glow.

Aella pulls her phone out and turns the flashlight feature on, realizing her battery life is at ten percent.

As they continue on, Torin says in a low voice, "What the fuck is that smell?"

Aella smothers a gag. The smell of rotting eggs and sulfur washes over them the farther down they get from what used to be the hallway to the portal she'd manifested.

Aella then feels something slither over her foot and shrieks, "Something just crawled across my foot, Torin!"

"What do you—"

Torin's question gets cut off as he gets pulled away down the hallway, and a loud grunt comes out of him.

Fuck!

"Torin? Torin! Where are you?" Aella shines the light from her phone as her hands shake, but she can't determine where he is. Nothing but a black void and sticky tar is to be seen.

Aella takes off in a run the best way she can with whatever is clinging to the souls of her shoes, frantically searching for Torin, and then she hears something.

There is a gargling sound that isn't human or animal. Hot breath fans across the back of her neck, and inky black tentacles come into focus, grabbing her arm and causing her to drop her phone.

She panics as she feels whatever this thing is latching onto her to take her away somewhere inside of this portal.

Think Aella!

She reaches down her leg and unlatches the dagger that Torin had given her as she swipes at the tentacle that's latched onto her.

A shrill scream comes from it as it loosens its grip. Aella takes off again in a run, her shoes growing heavier with the tar, hoping that the direction she's headed is away from whatever that thing was despite that she doesn't have her phone.

She can hear the slithering of snakes and a whisper as the thing calls out to her, *"Aella, we are waiting for you, Aella."*

"Torin! Yell out to me if you're alive, please!" She shouts frantically, but there is nothing other than her and the sounds of the monster.

Panting, she takes a second to calm herself even though nothing is calm or rational about this. She feels a tentacle wrap around her ankle, and without hesitation, she swipes at it, accidentally stabbing herself in the process.

Aella cries out in pain and terror from the monster that is trying to take her along with the self-inflicted wound.

Aella takes off running again, screaming and shouting down the black void of a hallway, listening to the slithering echo of the tentacles chasing after her. She needs to find Torin but doesn't know if he is still in there with her or if he made it through to the other side.

She continues to pump her legs, pushing herself to the max with her oozing wound and potential infection that she will have to deal with once she gets through to her apartment.

Wiggle your big toe! Wiggle your big toe!

I accept my gift. I am in control.

She hears the monster getting closer, laughing and mocking her. Its tentacles slip and slide across the tar-like substance it secretes as it splashes onto her back.

"Do not be afraid, Aella. You are almost there. Keep pushing!" Elissa's voice echoes through her thoughts as she almost succumbs to the terror that is chasing her—the horror that snatched Torin, who is nowhere to be heard in the black void of nothing.

Her heart is thumping inside her chest. The tentacles are mere inches from her again, and the heat from the monster is like standing too close to the open flames of a fire.

Wiggle your big fucking toe!

Suddenly, she is pulled through to the other side and is in her apartment. Falling onto her backside, she scoots her body away, facing where the portal stands, and holds the dagger out in case those tentacles come through. But when she looks at where the opening to the portal once was, there is nothing but a solid wall.

"What the fuck?" Aella breathes, gets to her feet, and runs up to it, patting the wall with her hands.

"No... No! No, no, no, no! Torin!" Aella shouts, hitting the wall with her fists. Her leg is oozing blood and throbbing from the stab wound, but that pain will only be temporary. Frantically trying to think of what to do while adrenaline courses through her body, she is startled by an unexpected voice behind her.

"That gash looks pretty painful, Ell," Damien says. She quickly turns and points the dagger at him, but Damien is not alone.

Aella collapses onto her knees when she sees who is next to him.

Tara looks down at her with soft eyes and says, "Hey girl, I missed you."

Meanwhile, Aella's mother is in the kitchen heating water in a kettle to boil.

What the actual fuck?!

Chapter Thirty-Five

Cahtel

I hate this god's forsaken place with every fiber of my being. What has it been now? A day? A week? I have nearly lost count with every lashing I have received since being caught and held captive.

I would do it again for her, though. I would do it all over again if it meant that she would be safe. The girl, Aella. A constant need to repeat her name on a never-ending loop for fear that I may forget from the abuse. *Aella*

Thinking about her and that name brings me a calm I never knew I needed. I love her. I know that I love her because only someone who loves another would sacrifice themselves the way I did.

I am a fool. She doesn't love me back, for I am a *monster*; how could she? A reminder for when they come down to have their fun. Poking and prodding at me as if I am a *beast* locked in a cage at a freak show.

Lawrence, the man who partakes in my abuse, while Mia watches with sick satisfaction. She doesn't like to get her hands dirty, no. But she does enjoy the verbal torment before the physical aspects take place.

Her long nails that skate along my spine, digging into my fur as if I truly am the *beast* they portray me as.

Ugly. Grotesque. Monster.

They think that with enough torture, with enough abuse and torment, I will break, and in a way, I have. Living in this hellish nightmare, but so long as I am the *good little pet* that Mia envisions, my beatings are reduced to a *minimum*.

My meals consist of very little when I am offered such a luxury. It's laughable, really, when they serve me *rat* on a silver platter, raw and decaying.

I'm ashamed to admit that while hungry enough, I eat what I can without retching. Swallowing down the dead rodent while its bones splinter and organs combust with every chew, forcing a smile on my face while I do so, *good little pet.*

Occasionally, if Mia is feeling generous enough after eating everything from the platter, she graciously offers me a moldy piece of bread and a glass of milk to wash down the blood and guts, *a mercy.*

I have been through worse conditions, though, and that is what aids in what little sanity I have left.

She will come for me, I know she will, *Aella.* When she does, I just hope I am still me, Cahtel, her *Vanilla Ice.*

Aella. Cahtel. Vanilla Ice.

The door creaks open now, and in walks Lawrence with a shit-eating grin on his face.

Playtime.

"Well, look who's up and alert. What a good little pet!" Lawrence says in his sick, twisted voice, sending shrill shivers down my spine.

"There will be no playtime today, I am afraid. Mia is expecting you to accompany her in the ballroom. Her people,

I'm afraid, are starving. You should feel honored to be given the delicacies we have offered you. Such a spoiled *little pet* you are." Lawrence drawls and chuckles.

Just kill me.

He approaches me, and I trail him with my eyes, calculating his every move. The shackle I have been placed inside of is a collar chained to the stone wall. He unlatches the chain but holds it taut, tugging my aching body with him.

The pads of my paws are still healing from the latest endeavor, and I hope that Aella's hands are fully healed and that no scar remains from when they were cut and marred by the debris.

Perhaps, knowing that she is safe and unscathed, is all I need while I suffer for whatever time I have left in this life.

Good little pet.

Acknowledgments

I want to thank my mother, who has always believed in me with everything I have put my heart and soul into. I would also like to thank my partner for pushing me to do hard things no matter how uncomfortable. Thank you to my friends and family for supporting me in my endeavor and pushing me to create something so vulnerable, much like the paintings I spew on a canvas, despite being my own worst critic.

Thank you to my editor and cover design team for making my dream come true and helping me bring an innovative idea I had come to fruition. My gratitude for the amount of love and support, along with the many hours spent on the sofa with my two dogs, Bodhi and Jude, typing away.

Lastly, I want to thank you, the reader.

About the Author

Samantha Hardy is an artist and emerging author of Fiction and fantasy. This is Samantha's first book in the *Loss and Ruin* series, and the second will be published within the following year.

Like most of her art, Samantha has taken an interest in writing based on dreams she has by turning them into literary works of art for the reader to paint their own picture.

Samantha has additional works in progress that will be announced soon.

Stay tuned.

"Time is a ticking clock. Eventually, there will be no metronome."